ANGELS LOST

THE Z-TECH CHRONICLES

BOOK TWO

RYAN SOUTHWICK

Published by Water Dragon Publishing
waterdragonpublishing.com

ISBN 978-1-953469-18-2 (Trade Paperback)

10 9 8 7 6 5 4 3 2 1

FIRST EDITION

For Robert and Ray,
without whom these characters would not exist.

ACKNOWLEDGEMENTS

T HE JOURNEY TO PUBLISHING this second book of the series — with a novella and novelette in between — was almost as long and full of twists as the first, and required nearly as much support to finish.

Thanks first and foremost to my mother, who is my alpha reader and confidant. Her wonderful input gave me the confidence to produce the second volume.

To Ray, whose invaluable comments and attention to detail improved the quality of this book ten-fold, and without whom Mark would not exist. This book (and the next) are exciting mostly because of you. I can never thank you enough.

To Robert, whose incredible imagination brought these characters to life. I miss you.

To Keri, whose countless hours delving into the series and chatting with me about this and that were not only inspiring, but tightened the level of realism to a level I couldn't have achieved alone.

To Jo, for the amazing support and professional feedback that brought depth and feeling into these chapters. Your ability to bring worlds to life is unmatched. Thank you for sharing a small part of your talent with me.

To all my other friends and family who volunteered as beta readers and offered your frank advice, I treasure the time you invested and your courage for giving me your honest opinions. I took each to heart, and, as some of you may notice in this final version, your voices were heard.

To my first editor, Anna, whose criticisms were hard to take, but, without which, the protagonist would have paled. Thank you for your wisdom, and for telling me what I needed to hear, not what I wanted to hear.

To my current editor, Steven, whose continued support and guidance led to this much shorter and more focused novel. Splitting the original manuscript into two separate books — *Angels Lost* and *Angels Fall* — put a few more gray hairs on my head, but the effort was worth it. Thank you.

To Richard Desmarais, for the wonderful cover art, which I fell in love with immediately.

To Niki, for the wonderful cover design that brought Richard's artwork to life.

To Jiné, for all your help with absolutely everything along the way. I treasure your friendship, your partnership, and hope they continue through the series and beyond.

And for my wife, Louise, who finally got her vacation, but probably needs another one.

1

CALUM

C ALUM MACLEAN REACHED FOR HIS GUN at the sound of his name. A large man in jeans and a collared shirt pushed his way through the bustle of the terminal at San Francisco International Airport with an uneasy look. Calum forced himself to relax. It was the middle of the day in a large crowd, and the sun shone brightly outside. He had little to fear until evening.

"Glad you made it," the large stranger said. His smile was genuine, but dull. Overhead lights glared from his shaved head. He extended a meaty hand. "I'm Don."

Calum glanced at his teeth. Don's coffee-stained canines were blunt. That eased Calum's immediate fear, but did nothing to improve his mood. If Don wasn't a vampire, then he was from the local Chapter — and Calum wasn't happy with the local Chapter. Not happy at all.

"I'm glad I made it, too," Calum said, ignoring the proffered hand. "Though I'm sorry I wasn't here sooner."

Don looked confused, which wasn't surprising. Although Calum had been away from his native Scotland for decades, at fifty-eight years old, he still had a strong accent, which was difficult for most Americans to understand. The noisy airport didn't help, either.

Calum gestured with a black-gloved hand for Don to lead them outside. "It seems my invitation was lost in the mail," Calum said.

Don led them toward the short-term parking lot. He cleared his throat, eyes darting everywhere except at Calum. "Mr. MacLean, w-we called you as soon as —"

"As soon as what? Protocol dictates quite clearly that you were supposed to escalate the moment you discovered the vampire. But, for God knows what reason, you decided to wait until it became a genuine epidemic!"

"We thought we had it contained!" The sweat on Don's forehead glistened under the flickering fluorescent lights of the multi-level garage. "He was only out of his casket for a few minutes before we caught him." He pushed the elevator call button.

"Contained? Have you actually read the local police reports?"

Don tugged his collar and nodded. Police reports were the first thing Calum had requested after he'd received the call he'd hoped he never would. Incidents of missing persons had risen over the last three months — and sharply over this last month. Divorce rates in San Francisco had also risen, as was expected when vampire victims leave their families and become slaves to their sires. Reports abounded of people wandering the streets with no recollection of how they arrived, or why, dazed from a vampire's memory-inhibiting venom.

The signs were all there, and they painted a grim picture.

Calum tensed when they exited the elevator into the dark underground parking level. Down here, where the sun never shone, a vampire could live indefinitely, so he stayed vigilant until they were safely in the car — a black sedan with tinted windows. The stereotype made Calum cringe. Too often, Chapter members mistook their stations in the organization for privilege, purchasing cars or clothing they believed distinguished them, instead of allowing them to blend with the rest of the populace.

Pride, he thought disdainfully. *Focused on their image instead of their duty.*

They weren't solely to blame, however. Only two Chapters had faced vampire breakouts since the Society's formation over a century ago. Calum's Chapter, nestled in the highlands of Scotland, had been one of them. There were dozens of Chapters around the world, which meant that few Chapters, and fewer members still, had any practical experience fighting vampires.

Which, if the rumors of a vampire outbreak are true, doesn't bode well for our chances of success.

Calum mulled on that while the lavish black sedan sped from the airport.

•   •   •

It was a short ride to their destination. Don pulled into a gravel lot and parked next to *another* expensive black sedan. Calum ground his teeth.

It figures.

Don led them along a rusted railroad track into a concrete tunnel in the side of a hill.

So cliché, Calum thought. America had few castles, so the Chapter had chosen a creepy lair instead. *I'll bet a tenner they have garlic hanging inside.*

He was right, unfortunately. The short, dark tunnel ended in a large pile of rubble. Don escorted him through a steel door off to the side, revealing a dimly-lit concrete stairway leading down. Tasty but otherwise useless garlic hung in strands along the walls to either side. Don looked at them proudly, but his smirk disappeared under Calum's hard stare.

"He's down this way," Don mumbled, then continued his descent.

Six stories below the surface, the stairs leveled into a long concrete tunnel, with offshoots to either side as far as Calum could see. Solitary incandescent bulbs hanging from black wires provided scant illumination. It had the feel of an old bomb shelter, from when the Cuban Missile Crisis was at its peak. The underground complex was large enough to house an entire community, which seemed excessive for the three residents of the San Francisco Chapter. Still, he couldn't criticize them too harshly. Their headquarters was inconspicuous and, with a few modifications, would be easy to defend.

Perhaps there's hope for them yet.

Don stopped before a metal door. Four large, recently installed bolts were another point in the Chapter's favor, showing they had not underestimated the strength of their captive.

Especially if their captive is who he claims to be.

Don reached for one of the bolts, but Calum caught his arm in a firm grip.

"Is the prisoner secured?" Calum said quietly, forcing himself to be calm.

"We chained him up as soon as we put him in there," Don said with a touch of annoyance. "He hasn't been out of those shackles since."

"And how do you know he's still in them?"

Don shrugged. "He hasn't escaped yet, and he hasn't been fed since he got here, so he's weak. I don't see how he could escape."

Calum bit his tongue to keep from snapping at the dolt. "I can think of a few ways. Let's assume he did escape his shackles, just for a moment."

"H-he's so weak ... What would it matter? Either one of us could —"

"I once saw a vampire who had been buried for decades break a man's arm like it was tinder," Calum said in a strained voice, his considerable patience nearing its end.

Calm, he told himself, taking a deep breath. *Anger is the enemy of the skilled warrior. He who embraces calm and deliberation wins the day.*

But his words had the desired effect. Don hustled down a side tunnel, then returned a minute later with a semi-automatic pistol. He stood several feet back and aimed with practiced skill at the door, just to the side of where Calum stood.

Calum gave the barest of nods.

There's hope for this one. He just needs some discipline and experience to harden him.

He didn't relish the idea of anyone living through what he himself had, but some things could only be learned the hard way.

With any luck, it won't come to that.

Calum slid the bolts back, his hands trembling from an apprehension he just couldn't shake, then he drew his own pistol and pushed. The door swung inward, squealing on rusted hinges. He stepped back and raised his gun, giving them both a clear shot inside.

A middle-aged man in fifties-era clothing hung from shackles against the far wall of the large room. The prisoner squinted at the wan light from the hallway. A thick mustache stood out against the encroaching stubble on his pale face. His unusually large, black eyes eventually adjusted to the light. He regarded Calum with amusement.

"What's he grinning about?" Calum said over his shoulder.

"Don't know," Don said. "He hasn't spoken much, despite some mild, um … encouragement."

Calum grunted. "What's your name?"

The man — *or creature,* Calum corrected himself — flashed a quirky half-smile. "Have your boy fetch me a drink," he said in a scratchy voice. "Then I'll tell you."

Calum couldn't place his accent. It sounded Eastern European, but could just as easily have been Middle Eastern or West Asian.

"That's not going to happen," Calum said.

The prisoner chuckled. "I only meant a glass of water."

Calum nodded to Don. The big man looked surprised, but scurried off. He returned shortly with a paper cup, which he handed to Calum before resuming his position. The shackles prevented the vampire's hands from reaching his mouth, so Calum cautiously approached and raised the cup to his lips.

"If you bite me, it'll be your last meal."

"I shall not bite the hand that quenches my thirst." The vampire drank the contents with a few swallows and sighed. "My thanks," he said softly, his voice smoother than before.

"You could thank me by throwing yourself and the rest of your clan on a raging bonfire to rid the world of your plague. But let's start with your name, as we agreed."

The prisoner smiled. Calum fought a wave of panic when he saw his sharp fangs. The last time he'd seen teeth like that, he and his Chapter had been fighting for their lives. The last of his friends had died in that attack …

He relaxed his finger, which he'd unconsciously tightened on the trigger.

"Very well," the prisoner said. "My name is Almos, born in the ninth century, once Sacred Ruler of the Hungarians, descendant of the great Attila of the Huns. And if you share my desire to avoid a catastrophe such as the world has never seen, you will listen very, very carefully."

2

NEW BEGINNINGS

A NNE PERRIN TOOK A DEEP BREATH. "Okay, let's do this!" She opened the employee room door, but Doris slammed it shut.

"Wait! There's a thin spot on your cheek. I'll fix it, hang on ..." Doris turned Anne toward her and applied a few more strokes with her makeup brush. "That should do. Just try not to rub your face."

"Thanks. All right, final check. How do I look?"

Doris studied her. Cappa and Doris had worked diligently for two hours back at the Z-Tech factory to give Anne a less corpse-like complexion, and their combined skill had produced amazing results. When Anne had finally been allowed to look in the mirror, the pallid, venous-skinned ghoul was gone. In her place was the healthy thirty-six-year-old woman she had been just three weeks prior. Colored contact lenses made her unusually large, black pupils appear smaller and closer to their natural brown hue. Her long auburn hair fell in lazy ringlets, just as it always had. A generous bust and curvy hips still rounded her hourglass figure, despite a liquid-plasma diet.

Even her canines had been disguised to look like regular teeth. After weeks of living with the razor-sharp points in her mouth, the blunt porcelain caps Charlie had made for her felt odd against her tongue. Holes near the tips, where venom flowed when she fed, were the only evidence that they were anything but normal.

Anne instinctively reached for her heart-shaped pendant. Its squishy surface was pleasantly warm in her cold hands and pulsed gently between her fingers — unlike her own heartbeat, which had fallen still. She lamented the loss of Mark's amber pendant, given to her to help protect from William's sire influence, but William's presence in her mind had remained dormant since their last encounter. It was no surprise, considering the headache he would receive from the defensive program Zima had added to the computer implant above Anne's right breast.

Unfortunately, the presences of the other vampires had disappeared as well, leaving her blind to their locations and numbers.

William could have transformed half the city into vampires by now, and I'd never know it.

"I think that does it," Doris said with a final nod. She scratched her coppery hair, ruffling her immaculate beehive hairdo. "You sure you want to do this, hon? You have a billionaire for a boyfriend. The addition of your meager waitress salary ain't gonna make a difference."

"I know, it's just ... being at the factory with everyone is great, but I need purpose in my life. I want to be a productive member of society, not just a plague on it, which means I need to discover if I can work among the populace without eating them. What better way to ease into it than doing a job I'm familiar with in a place where I'm comfortable?"

"Yeah, but what if you get hungry in the middle of your shift? You tapped my veins this morning, so I'm out. Would you be able to control yourself until you got back to Z-Tech?"

"I think so," Anne said. "Besides, Dela let me snack on her before I left the factory, and ..." Anne unzipped her purse, which hung from a hook on the wall, and withdrew a large thermos. "Mark gave me a care package for the road, just in case."

"Is that his bl…" Doris wrinkled her nose. "Dear Lord! I may never drink coffee from one of those again. All right, if there's no talking you out of it, then let's do this before Hal has a conniption. Ready to face the world, kiddo?"

With trembling hands, Anne bound her amber hair into a ponytail, smoothed her dress uniform, then took a breath, which she realized she hadn't done in minutes. "Ready!"

Doris led the way out of the employee lounge. Bright kitchen lights stabbed Anne's eyes, but the photo-reactive layer Mark had added to her contact lenses quickly darkened, giving her sensitive eyes time to adjust.

Smells from the grill filled her acute nose: Hector was cooking ham, blackened catfish, herbed salmon, and hamburgers. One burger was so overcooked that she pitied the patron for whom it was destined.

He might as well serve it with a side of Tums.

The dining area was half-empty, which was normal for a Monday night. Dozens of voices hit her at once and threatened to overwhelm her senses. Even whispered conversations from across the diner were as clear as if the person speaking stood right beside her. Anne gripped her skirt to keep from covering her ears.

I'll need to get used to this eventually.

She steeled herself and headed onto the floor.

The aroma of the food did nothing for her appetite, but the customers themselves were another matter. One whiff made her salivate; it was like walking into a gourmet potluck, where each person was a unique, but equally flavorful dish.

All but one person, of course, whose scent was earthy and irresistible, but in a very different way. Anne smiled at Zima, who sat at the counter, cradling her untouched coffee. Her ice-blue eyes habitually scanned the surrounding area. Perfectly cut platinum-blonde hair swayed when she gave Anne and Doris a quick glance, then her expressionless gaze returned to the crowd.

Anne brought over a pot of coffee.

"So tell me," Anne said, adding a splash to Zima's already full cup, "what's a beautiful girl like you doing in a place like this?"

Zima brow-knit — an infinitesimal movement of her eyebrows that indicated she was puzzling something new, and one of the very few facial expressions in her repertoire — before turning her gorgeous eyes to Anne. "I am here to ensure all goes well on your first night back at the diner, as we discussed. Have you forgotten?"

"I was just being cute," Anne said with a grin.

"Oh."

Anne leaned over the counter and planted a firm kiss on Zima's lips, drawing looks from nearby customers.

Let 'em stare.

She caught her workmate Julie's eyes, who was looking at them with a big grin. The waitress in the collared shirt and tie gave Anne a double thumbs-up before loading her next round of orders.

Zima noticed the exchange and cocked her head slightly to one side, indicating she wanted more information.

"Julie gave me some really great advice the night before … before I was kidnapped," Anne said. "She's happy to see that I listened."

"She advised you to kiss me? Whatever her reasons, I shall be sure to thank her later."

"No, silly! She said I shouldn't be ashamed of what I feel, or of who I am. You're my girl, Zima, and the whole world's going to know it."

Zima looked at the kitchen. "Hal does not appear pleased with your proclamation."

Sure enough, the grizzled restaurant owner stood with his hairy arms crossed, scowling in their direction.

"I shall be right here." Zima turned back to the crowd.

Anne grimaced. "I think that's my cue. Off to work. I don't want to make a bad impression on my first day back. I'll visit later, if I can."

Anne ran her fingers through Zima's perfectly bobbed hair, then began her rounds.

Work had never been so easy. Although her heightened metabolism — which had been artificially raised by her computer implant — was a pain because of the large amount of blood she needed to consume to survive, it also gave her plenty of energy. She whizzed from table to table, deftly balancing heavy orders in one hand while sliding between chairs and maneuvering around staff. Her keen sense of smell saved two customers the trouble of returning their undercooked hamburgers, allowing her to subtly suggest that Hector return them to the grill before they'd left the window. She also prevented a few stomachaches by sniffing out a jar of expired mayonnaise and two eggs that had started to turn.

Best of all, Anne enjoyed laughing with her customers again. For all her years in the trade, she never tired of seeing a smile when she cracked a joke — especially when it helped turn someone's mood around. Some nights were challenging, when her legs ached and her energy was low, but she had no such impediments tonight.

Or perhaps ever again.

She was in great spirits when she approached a pair of gentlemen who had just been seated.

Anne flashed her porcelain smile. "Welcome to Hal's! Can I start you off with something to drink?"

"Aye, a lemonade for me," the older man said in a thick Scottish accent. His wavy gray hair was gelled back to cover the nape of his neck. A thick goatee and severe expression gave him a sinister air, but his voice was soft and pleasant.

Books and covers, Anne thought, trying not to judge.

She turned to his companion, a larger, portly man with a shiny bald head. "And for you?"

"I'll have a whiskey on the —" He cleared his throat at a stern look from the older man. "Just a Coke, please."

"Gotcha. Two very non-alcoholic drinks coming right up." Anne gave the larger man a sympathetic look. "I know how you feel. A stiff drink sounds good to me, too, but duty calls."

Plus I don't think my stomach can handle anything except blood ...

"You could learn from the lass, Don," the older man said, his scowl deepening. "She takes her job seriously."

Don clenched his jaw, but lowered his eyes to the table. "Yes, Mr. MacLean."

Anne felt as if she'd walked into a movie, where an experienced cop was paired with a rookie who had to prove himself.

Poor Don, she thought. *MacLean looks like one hard-to-please mentor.*

"I'll be right back with those," Anne said, then hurried to the kitchen.

Zima caught her arm along the way.

"Be aware," Zima said quietly. "They both carry concealed firearms in their jackets."

"Yeah, I smelled the gun oil." Anne glanced back at the pair. "I think they're cops."

"Unlikely. American police prefer domestic sidearms. Theirs are military-grade pistols of Middle-Eastern origin."

"So ... are you saying I should ask them to leave?"

"No. Just exercise caution, and minimize contact, if possible. I shall monitor them closely until they depart."

Feeling less bouncy, Anne went to the kitchen window. A loud "pssst" caught her attention before she loaded her next tray. Hal was gesturing her over from the door of his office. Anne set her tray down and joined him, wondering what she'd done wrong.

"That was quite a performance out there, kid," Hal said in his gruff voice once they were inside.

"Oh, sorry. If kissing Zima was too inappropriate, I'll save it for after —"

"Nah, that don't bother me, though it is unprofessional. Not 'cause you're both women," Hal said hastily, "just kissing in general. It makes customers uncomfortable." He shook his head. "No, I mean the whole night. You're working so damn fast, it's like there's two of you out there."

Anne fidgeted with a button on her work dress. She'd been so caught up that she hadn't stopped to think how her enthusiasm would appear to others.

Chalk it up as a learning experience.

Unsure where Hal was going with the conversation, Anne kept silent and stared at the desk.

Hal twiddled his sausage-like thumbs. "I just wanna make sure you're not overdoing it, that's all. You got nothing to prove here, so don't kill yourself trying to outshine the other girls. You just got back from medical leave, and I ain't gonna fire you if you take an extra breather every now and then. Know what I mean?"

"I ... I do." Anne fell silent and looked at him with gratitude. She was touched by his unexpected concern, even though he'd completely misread the situation.

Medical leave is putting it very *mildly.*

"Thanks, Hal."

He grunted. "Don't mention it." His eyes strayed around the room.

The silence stretched. Anne was about to excuse herself when he cleared his throat.

"So, is, ah … is Charlie gonna stop by tonight? You know, now that you're back on the clock and all …?"

Anne grinned. *I guess his motives weren't altruistic after all. Oh well …*

"Yes, he and Cappa said they'd stop by for a late dinner. They should be here soon."

The relief on Hal's face was comical. "Ah, good. That's … that's good. It'll be nice to see them. Hasn't been the same around here without him. Or you," he said quickly. "Now, if you'll excuse me, I got a few calls to make."

He'd already forgotten about Anne by the time she closed the door, which was just as well.

She went to the bar to fill the drink order.

Minutes later, Anne returned to the odd duo's table, carrying their drinks on a small tray.

"… spread so thin, I don't know what more you want us to do," Don said, waving his hands.

"The lot of you are lazy and undisciplined," MacLean said coolly. "You've had weeks to find —" He quieted at Anne's approach, glancing at her with the side of his eye.

Don hadn't noticed her, however. Veins pulsed on his rapidly reddening head. "*W-weeks?* This isn't some Podunk town in backwater Mississippi, Calum. It's San Francisco, for crissake!"

In a sweeping gesture, Don knocked the tray from Anne's hand just as she was lowering it to the table.

Anne snatched both drinks from the air with ease and righted them before they spilled, caught the tray on her knee, then set the drinks on it.

"Whew!" Anne shook a drop of lemonade from her hand. "That was a close one. All right, big guy, let's try this again, but without the karate moves this time."

MacLean stared at her, wide-eyed. "That was amazing, lass."

Anne grinned at the compliment, but her conversation with Hal came back to her like a splash of cold water.

I have to appear normal.

Trying to maintain her composure, she set the drinks on the table and casually folded the tray under her arm. "It was nothing. Happens all the time. Waitress reflexes, that's all. Any of the girls could have done the same."

"That I'd like to see." MacLean's smile didn't quite reach his eyes.

Anne mentally kicked herself. *Next time I'll just let the damn drinks fall.*

"Well, I can go tip one of their trays to prove it," Anne said. "But I'm pretty sure they'll charge extra for the show. Assuming they don't take it out on my hide."

"No need," MacLean said with a genuine laugh. "That was fine enough entertainment for the evening."

"On to my next trick, then," Anne said, relieved to move off the subject. "Are you ready to order?"

•   •   •

Calum MacLean watched their nimble server hustle back to the kitchen.

"She's good," Don said. "I thought sure those drinks were goners."

Is he really that dense? Only once in his life had Calum seen someone move that fast — and it wasn't a happy memory.

Blood on the walls, the screams of my mates from the cellar while vampires fed on them like animals ...

"Yes," Calum said quietly into his cup. "She's very talented."

"And easy on the eyes."

Calum ground his teeth. "Perhaps you should ask her out."

If she is a vampire, she'd be doing the world a favor by ridding it of your stupidity.

"Hmm, maybe." Don looked thoughtfully in her direction, then shook himself. "Anyway, like I was saying, we've exhausted our network looking for signs of those —"

"We'll talk business later," Calum said. *Vampires have keen hearing. She may have already heard too much.* "Tell me about this wondrous city of yours."

Don looked confused, but eventually shrugged and regaled Calum with his knowledge of San Francisco. Only half listening, Calum kept an eye on their waitress, who moved from table to table with the grace of a great hunting cat weaving through the reeds. He also watched the stoic platinum blonde with the porcelain skin at the bar to whom she often spoke, and who was also glancing at them.

Calum sipped his lemonade, but it had lost its flavor. He set it down and pretended his stomach wasn't tied in knots.

He'd found a vampire, all right. The question was, what next?

3

TIM

TIMOTHY CHEN HELD HIS BREATH, then carefully moved the fine solder wire to its target. The wire, less than a millimeter thick, looked enormous under the large magnifying glass. It shook with his every heartbeat, causing him to repeatedly miss his mark on the tightly packed circuit board. He eventually set the soldering iron back onto his workbench and sighed, wishing he could quiet his pulse for just a few minutes so he could finish the last piece of his latest invention.

He stood and stretched, restoring circulation to muscles that had been hunched over his desk for several hours. A glance at his watch showed he had missed dinner yet again.

Not that it mattered much. His parents were traditional Chinese, which meant his mother cooked every night regardless of who was there to eat. There would be plenty of leftovers — unless his younger sister brought her boyfriend, in which case there would be slim pickings.

Probably just rice and the vegetables no one else wanted, he thought ruefully.

He paced around his workshop — a moderate space he and several others were renting from his alma mater, San Francisco State University, bargain-priced for recent graduates who were still looking for work.

Tim certainly fit that description. A year earlier, when he'd finished his post-graduate degree in Computer Science with a minor in Electronics Engineering, he'd been full of grand ideas for inventions that would change the world. He'd been sure that one, if not all of them, would be eagerly snatched up by some large corporation keen to capitalize on his revolutionary new technologies, and that by now he would be sipping *mai tais* from his remote office in Hawaii while his products took the market by storm.

Reality hadn't cooperated with his plan. Stacked in one corner of his shop were the results of a year's work, his amazing ideas come to life — which, apparently, no one cared about. He'd sent queries to company after company. Each had responded with a similar message: "Thank you for your submission, but we do not feel there is enough market interest at this time to justify investment in your product." When that had failed, Tim had tried approaching companies personally, with the hope that actually seeing the product would change their minds. Most hadn't returned his calls, let alone granted him an appointment, so he was trying a new tactic.

His cell phone rang as if on cue. The name on the screen was Jody, one of the other post-graduates who also rented this workspace. He grabbed it from the table — it was the latest Z-Tech model, a graduation present from his parents — and put it to his ear. "Hey Jo, what's up?"

"Tim! Conway just got a call from his uncle. You know, the guy who owns Hal's Diner in the City? Anyway, you'll never guess who's going to be there tonight!"

Tim nearly dropped the phone. He knew exactly who she meant. He'd heard rumor that Charlie Z, president and CEO of one of the largest tech manufacturers in the world, had become a regular at the diner. Attempts to schedule an appointment with Charlie had failed, so Tim had been begging Conway to ask his uncle to call him the next time Charlie was going to make an appearance. "That ... that's great! Tell Conway I totally owe him."

"Trust me, he knows you do."

Tim hung up, grabbed his backpack, and stuffed his gadgets inside it. With one last check that he had everything, he pulled on his hoodie, and ran for the door, hoping he wouldn't have to wait too long for the bus.

If he couldn't make an appointment with Charlie through regular channels, then Tim would simply make his own.

And what better place to meet than a restaurant?

After all, everyone had to eat.

4

TIRED

"**C**AT GOT YOUR TONGUE?"

Charlie stirred at Cappa's voice, aware that he'd been staring blankly at the dashboard while she drove them through the night to Hal's Diner. "Mm. Darn cat seems to be doing that a lot lately."

Cappa's worried look tugged at his artificial heart. "It's getting worse?"

He wanted to lie and say it was getting better. But it wasn't, and he was done with lying — to Cappa, to Anne ...

... and to myself.

"Yes," Charlie said softly. "I'm always tired, and it's becoming harder to concentrate."

Thick fog dappled mist on the windshield. He watched the wipers smear the tiny droplets, blurring the sea of taillights before them into a sheet of red.

Cappa nodded slowly, then brushed back a strand of dark brown hair that had fallen over her round face. Another quick swipe also caught a tear rolling down her cheek.

"I just ran a diagnostic on your systems. Everything seems normal." She pulled up several reports for him, which hovered before his artificial eyes. "I thought of a few more things we can check as well, just in case —"

"They won't find anything, Cappa." Charlie waved a hand, causing the reports to vanish.

"You never know ..." She sniffed and dabbed a tissue at her nose. "When ... when are you going to tell the others?"

Good question.

He remained silent, however, cursing his own cowardice. Cappa had taken his decline in health pretty hard. That Charlie still hadn't told any of the others only made things worse for her because she had no one to talk to about it. Since she'd learned that his life energy — his *chi* — was dwindling, her outlet had been to dote on him virtually every second he wasn't with Anne, and sometimes even then.

Cappa's doting had good and bad points. Often it meant subjecting him to a barrage of tests in a desperate, but futile, attempt to find a scientific explanation for his fatigue. As an android, Cappa didn't have a spirit of her own and couldn't relate — a fact she frequently bemoaned — so she focused her energy on what she did understand, and that was technology.

On the good side, they had spent more quality time together in the last week than during all the previous few months combined. Although she was always with him as a co-pilot in his cyborg body, where she played a crucial role regulating his system functions, they rarely talked unless Cappa was physically present in her own body, as she was now. She had begun to ask probing questions about his past: where he was born, his childhood home, what his parents were like, middle school, girlfriends, and everything in between. Things she had never seemed interested in before, she now clung to, hungry for details, including ...

"I called *Sensei* yesterday," Cappa said casually. "He asked how you were doing. I lied and told him you were fine."

Charlie nodded. *Here it comes ...*

"Among other things, he mentioned that Master Wung is still at the same monastery where you trained." She glanced at him. "Just in case you were wondering, or wanted to pay him a visit or something."

"I doubt Master Wung would be happy to see me. Not after I broke my promise and walked out on him."

"That was a long time ago, Charlie. You know what they say about time healing all wounds."

"Enough time, perhaps, but Master Wung is old and has a long memory. Maybe in another decade or so."

Cappa tapped her immaculately painted fingernails on the steering wheel. "What about projecting your spirit back into your biological body? Have you given that any more thought?"

He clamped his mouth shut and stared at the dash.

"Charlie, I know you're scared it won't work, but you promised me you'd try after Anne stabilized. Given that she's back at work, I'd say she's stable enough."

Charlie sighed and rubbed his eyes. "I did promise, didn't I?"

"Yes you did." Cappa gently squeezed his hand. "But you don't have to do it alone. You'll have a whole cheering squad behind you. I'll even buy pom poms, if it will help."

"It probably won't, but seeing Mark in a cheerleader outfit would be entertaining."

She laughed, and Charlie was happy to see a hint of Cappa's old, cheerful self. Melancholy had taken the usual bounce from her step, and he hadn't realized how much he depended on her to lift his spirits until his crutch had disappeared.

Cappa glanced at him. "So you'll give it a try?"

Charlie ran a hand through his thick brown hair. The neon lights of Hal's Diner were just coming into view, a swath of colors through the mist-smeared windshield. The thought of projecting his dwindling spirit back into his biological body was frightening. Where he had once done it ten times a day — when his *chi* was strong — he now feared that pushing his diminished energy into the body he was born to would be like trying to fill a swimming pool with an eyedropper.

But it's either that or fade into nothing.

"I will. Let's talk to Mark when we return to the factory."

Her obvious relief made him realize just how worried she'd been. He suddenly felt guilty that he hadn't agreed to do it sooner.

She pulled the car into a nearby parking garage and eventually found a spot on the third level. On their walk to the exit, Cappa stopped at the stairwell entrance and surprised him with a hug.

"Thank you," she said softly.

Charlie kissed the top of her head. "Sorry for being such a pain. We'll fix this, just like we fix everything."

Cappa pulled away, face lit with her trademark smile that he'd missed so much. Charlie followed her down the cement stairs, fighting a bout of panic.

He hoped he was right.

•　　　•　　　•

Anne spotted them as soon as they walked into the restaurant. Charlie forgot all about his fatigue when her face lit up. If Cappa's smile was the torch that led him through the darkness, then Anne's was the sun that banished the night and heralded the new day. She hurriedly finished with her customer and headed over.

Hal beat her there. The portly restaurant owner spread his arms as if welcoming old friends into his home. "Why, if it isn't Charlie Z and his lovely assistant, Cappa!"

"Partner," Charlie said.

Hal's outstretched arms drooped. His eyebrows lifted.

"Cappa's not an assistant," Charlie said. "She's a full partner at Z-Tech. You got the 'lovely' part right, though." He smiled to take some of the sting from his words.

"F-forgive me," Hal said. "I meant no offense."

Charlie glanced at Cappa, who stared back incredulously.

"What?" Charlie said. "It's true."

"Yes, but you've never introduced me like that."

"What do you mean? I've always said you're lovely."

Cappa elbowed him playfully. "You know what I mean!"

She glanced at Hal, who was watching the exchange with the same trepidation as one watched two dogs growl at each other.

"We'll talk about it later," Cappa said. Her bedazzling smile reappeared, and she turned back to their host. "It's good to see you too, Hal. It's been far too long, and we've missed the wonderful meals of your fine establishment."

Hal puffed up like a hairy peacock and looked meaningfully at the surrounding patrons. His voice projected as if he were performing on stage. "Then please, let me show you to your special table."

Charlie and Cappa followed him to a high-backed booth embossed with chrome trim, like the table, bar stools, and other pieces of the 50's-style diner. Once they were seated, Hal personally took their drink orders, as he usually did, then delivered their order to the bar.

No sooner had Hal left than Anne fell in beside Charlie. Before he could say a word, her mouth covered his in a tender kiss. His ears burned at the public display, but he soon forgot his embarrassment and simply enjoyed her soft lips — even if they were cold.

"I've missed you," Anne eventually whispered.

Charlie laughed. "It's only been a few hours."

"Yeah, well, I've been spoiled lately."

"Apparently." He donned a serious expression. "Ms. Perrin, I'm going to have to ask you to keep a professional distance."

"Or what, exactly?"

He hooked her waist and pulled her close. "Or I might do something inappropriate to you in a very public place, and I wouldn't want to tarnish your angelic reputation."

She laughed and ran her fingers through his hair. "That's not much of a threat, Mr. Z. I happen to like it when you tarnish me." Despite her teasing, she stepped out of his embrace and put on her waitress face. "I'll go check on your drinks. Hal will be back shortly to take your order. Assuming he remembers to bring the menus, that is."

Charlie tried not to stare at her gorgeous figure while she walked to the bar. "She's certainly coming out of her shell, isn't she?"

Cappa grinned back at him. "She's not the only one. I haven't seen you do anything like that in public since ... well, ever!"

"Mm. Speaking of which ..." Charlie scratched his head, hesitant to ask his next question. "Do you think you might ever ... find someone special?"

"Oh, I don't know," Cappa said casually, straightening her silverware. "There are so many special people in my life already ... I don't know if I can handle any more."

"I'm serious, Cappa. I worry about your happiness. It's possible that I ... well, I won't be around forever, and I just want to make sure —"

Don't you dare talk like that, she sent to him through their communication link, the words scrolling across his vision. Cappa's message was laden with feelings of hurt and sorrow, though her face betrayed little beyond a slight furrow of her brow while she stared at her place setting. It's like you've already resigned yourself to oblivion, and I won't accept that. She turned her eyes to him. You've helped so many people — all of us, at one time or another — and we never doubted things would work out because we believed in you. But now you're the one who needs saving. Please, have a little faith in us, and believe that we can save you, too.

"Because we will," Cappa said aloud, her voice breaking. She covered her mouth and looked away.

"I … I'll try." Charlie smiled to lighten the mood. "Regardless, you didn't answer my question."

"You're right, I didn't."

A waitress with short, spiky blonde hair stood between them and derailed his train of thought. "Hi, my name's Julie, and apparently I'll be your menu server tonight."

"Why thank you, Julie," Cappa said, her despair replaced with a smile. "I didn't know there was such a thing as a menu server."

"There wasn't until just now. Hal disappeared into his office again, and I figured he just forgot. Sorry about that."

"Are you kidding? We were seated by the owner and have a dedicated menu server. What's there to apologize for?"

"Glad to hear you say that." She tugged her necktie and smoothed her black slacks, which seemed a stark contrast to Anne's work dress. Face flushed, Julie leaned close to Cappa and lowered her voice. "And let me know if you'd like anything else, like …" She set a torn piece of paper in front of Cappa with a phone number scribbled on it. "Maybe coffee sometime?"

To Charlie's surprise, Cappa's face filled with genuine delight. "I'd like that, Julie. How about tomorrow?"

Julie blinked in stunned silence. "G-great! I'm off tomorrow, so call me anytime and" — she stumbled into a chair and swore. "J-just call me." She hastily retreated to the kitchen.

"Well I guess that answers that," Charlie said with a wry grin. "So you're seriously going out with her?"

"Why not? She seems like a nice person." Cappa quickly scanned the menu, then put it back on the table. "The entrees have changed! I think I'll try the new blackened catfish —"

"That's not what I meant," Charlie said.

"I know. And before you say it: no, I won't lead her on. I'm not looking for anything beyond friendship. I don't have hormones to fuel any sort of lust, and I don't intend to add it to my programming anytime soon. I'll set her expectations straight on our first meeting, then let her decide if she wants to keep seeing me."

"But that sounds ... lonely."

"Why? Plenty of normal people go through life with only friends for companionship. The way I see it, I'm lucky. I have some really amazing friends who I would do anything for, and I know they would do the same for me. How many people can say that?"

"Not many." Charlie grabbed a menu and sighed. He made a pretense of reading, but he was just going to order the special. It made Hal happy, and it didn't matter to him because, like Cappa and Zima, he couldn't taste anything anyway.

"You don't sound convinced," Cappa said.

Charlie tapped his menu while considering his response. "Friendship isn't the same as being in a relationship. When you find that someone special — your soulmate, so to speak — it's different from normal friendship. Deeper, more fulfilling."

"I have a soul sister," Cappa said to Anne, who was just approaching with their drinks. "Isn't that close enough?"

"Hardly," Anne said.

"Cheeky! Were you listening this whole time?"

"The hard part is *not* listening. I can hear every conversation in the restaurant no matter where I stand, and it's really distracting." She brushed a stray lock of auburn hair behind her ear. "Anyway, it's not the same, Cappa. I love you dearly, but not the same way I love Charlie and Zima. It's not that I love you any less — I can't imagine my life without you in it — but you and I have a different sort of connection."

Cappa laughed. "This is starting to sound like an intervention." She looked over at Zima, who sat with her back to the counter, eyes scanning the crowd. ANYTHING TO ADD? Cappa sent the message to Zima, accompanied with feelings of sarcasm, but included Charlie in the broadcast.

No, although I am learning much from this conversation.

"It's not an intervention, just something to think about," Anne said. "Imagine being with someone who makes you feel whole, who you truly can't live without."

"I already have someone like that," Cappa said softly. Her pleading eyes met Charlie's. And I don't want to lose him. This time, her message was sent only to him.

A short, uncomfortable silence settled over them, broken by Anne gently clearing her throat.

"Incoming," she said in a low voice. "I think Hal finally remembered that he forgot your menus."

She stepped away, clearing a path for Hal, who rushed toward them with two menus in hand.

"Sorry, I got distracted by a phone call in the back. Here … Oh, I see someone already brought your menus. Good." He tossed the extra menus on an empty table. "So, the special tonight is, eh … it's …" He counted on his fingers, mouthing the days of the week, then closed his eyes and grunted. "Anne, could you please tell our guests what the special is?"

Anne stifled a laugh. "Certainly, Mr. Caterino."

Once their orders were in, it wasn't long before the salads came. Cappa made a great show of enjoying hers. Charlie stabbed a few leaves with his fork.

His hand suddenly felt like lead; the plate cracked under the force of his blow. Pretending like nothing had happened, he raised the fork to his mouth.

Moving his arm was like operating a crane while blindfolded. He tried three times to get the food to his mouth before finally giving up. The fork dropped with a clatter.

"Are you okay?" Cappa said, her face a picture of concern.

"I'm, uh … I feel …"

Charlie didn't finish the sentence, because the world went black.

•　　　•　　　•

Anne saw Charlie's head dip from the corner of her eye, but, when she looked over, he seemed fine. Cappa's expression was dire, as it often had been of late, although Anne wasn't sure why. Cappa gestured for Anne to come over. She couldn't hide her disappointment when Cappa and Charlie rose from the table.

"Leaving so soon?" Anne said.

"Yes, s-sorry," Cappa said, wringing her hands. "Mark just called. We need to be on an early call with a company in Lisbon, which starts in about twenty minutes, so we have to high-tail it back to the office."

"Oh, I see. Well, thanks for dropping by." Anne wrapped her arms around Charlie and smiled. "I'll see you later, Mr. Z." She tried to kiss him, but he turned his head at the last second and squeezed her in a tight hug.

"You bet." He awkwardly patted her back. "It was good to see you, honey. I can't wait to get you in the sack later."

Get me in the sack?

Anne looked to see if anyone else was listening, glad that she could no longer blush.

And since when did he start calling me "honey"?

"Um, o-okay ... I guess I'll see you later. In the s-s ... what you said." She reluctantly turned away, and yelped when he swatted her rear. She rubbed her backside and shot him a look.

What the hell is wrong with him tonight?

Feeling decidedly less perky, Anne stalked off to finish her rounds.

5

MISSED IT BY THAT MUCH

T IM LEAPT FROM THE BUS and glanced at his watch.
Seventeen minutes from Ocean Street to downtown. That has to be a new record.

He sprinted the two blocks from the bus stop to Hal's Diner. Unless Z-Tech's CEO had one of the shortest meals in history, he should still be there, but Tim wasn't going to take any chances.

This is my big break. I can feel it!

He paused at the door of the diner to catch his breath and smooth his terminally spiky hair. Steeling his nerves, he walked inside, exuding the confidence of someone who couldn't fail.

Not tonight.

"Excuse me, miss?" Tim said to an attractive auburn-haired waitress.

"Be there in one sec."

"Ah, actually ..." Tim read her nametag. "*Anne*, I was just wondering if Charlie Z is dining here tonight?"

Her shoulders sagged. "Sorry, you just missed him."

"Missed him? Um ... do you know if he'll be back?"

"I doubt it. Why, do you need to talk to him?"

"Yes! I …" Tim forced himself to be calm. "I have an invention he might find interesting. I was hoping to show it to him."

"Ah. Well, it's probably best you missed him. He wasn't himself tonight."

Tim balled his fists, but kept his voice calm and polite.

It's not her fault, after all.

"Do you know what day and time he normally dines here? Or how to contact him?"

Anne smiled, warm and friendly. "I might. Give me your contact information and I'll pass it along the next time I see him."

"You will? Great!" Tim frantically looked around for something to write on.

Anne produced a pen and pad from her work dress. Tim scribbled his information down, then handed it back.

"You want a table?" Anne said.

"Sure, though it's just me, so I'm happy to sit at the counter."

"Anywhere you like. Someone will be right with you."

The restaurant was mostly empty, which wasn't surprising for that time of night. Tim sat heavily on a cushioned stool two seats down from the only other patron at the counter — a platinum blonde woman in baggy gray clothes who sat facing the dining area. Her ice-blue eyes sized him up when he plonked his backpack down on the stool between them, but she quickly lost interest and turned back toward the dining room.

Tim craned his neck to see what she was looking at, but nothing seemed unusual. "Are you looking for someone, miss?"

"No," she said evenly. Her eyes continued to dart from table to table.

I can take a hint.

Tim turned back to the counter with a sigh and grabbed a menu jammed between the condiments. It was typical diner food, but that suited him just fine. While it didn't hold a candle to his mother's traditional Chinese cooking, every now and then he craved a nice, greasy cheeseburger.

"Welcome to Hal's, hon," an older waitress said with a Southern drawl. "I'm Doris. Can I start you out with something to drink?" She grabbed a pen from the depths of her sculpted copper hairdo and took an old-fashioned carbon notepad from the pocket of her uniform.

"A Coke, please."

"You got it. Need more time with the menu?"

"Nope. Bacon cheeseburger, please."

Doris flashed a big-toothed smile. "A man who knows what he wants. I like it. Back in a jiffy with your drink."

The blonde had ignored their interaction.

No shock there.

Jody would have been quick to point out that a porcelain beauty like her was way out of his league, which was probably true. Rather than stare at the counter and dwell on his unfortunate miss with fate, he dug into his backpack and pulled out the invention he had intended to dazzle Charlie with.

Jody often said he was a born engineer. She meant it as a dig at his penchant for function over form, and this was no exception. The device looked like a cell phone strapped to a circuit board tethered to a small, squat radar dish with a gray ribbon cable. He carefully lined up the pieces on the counter.

Might as well give it a test run.

"What is that?"

Tim was surprised to see the platinum blonde staring at his contraption. "Something I've been working on for the last few months."

"You do not appear to have made much progress," she said evenly.

Her neutral expression made it difficult for Tim to tell if she was making fun of him.

I bet she cleans house at the poker tables.

She tilted her head slightly. "What is its function?"

"Put your cell phone on the counter and I'll show you."

"I would prefer to know its function first."

"That takes all the fun out of it," he said with a grin.

Ice-blue eyes continued to stare at him.

"Look, I won't damage it, I promise, but it really is more impressive as a demonstration."

She was so still that he thought she may have fallen sleep with her eyes open, but she soon took her phone from her jacket and set it on the counter.

"A Z-Tech phone, perfect. That's the model I've been practicing on. Can you please put it in airplane mode?"

She complied with a few taps, then looked at him expectantly.

"Okay. Now, what does airplane mode do?"

Her brow knitted just a fraction of an inch — the first facial expression he'd seen her make. "I assumed you knew when you instructed me to enable it."

"Sorry, I was just being dramatic. Airplane mode disables all radio connections to the device, right?"

"Yes."

"So there's no way to access the data inside without plugging into it directly?"

"Correct."

Tim smiled and powered up his device. He pointed the radar dish at her phone and, with a few taps, locked onto it and ran the program. "Tell me, then, how I know that you have ..." He frowned. "This can't be right. You only have one contact on your phone?"

"That is correct."

"By the name of Anne Perrin?"

"Yes."

"Who you've called ... *zero* times?" Tim scratched his head. "Is this a new phone or something?"

"No, but that is irrelevant," the blonde said. "I believe your demonstration was successful, and you were correct to say it would be impressive. I am familiar with theories on remote access to connectionless systems, but to my knowledge, there has never been a reliable prototype."

"Um, thanks." Tim was tempted to look around for the camera, sure that someone was playing a joke on him.

Hot girls like this aren't into tech. Are they?

"You have demonstrated that it can read information. Is it also capable of transmitting data to the remote device?"

"Almost. Sending is trickier than I thought it would be. I've had to factory reset my phone dozens of times because I accidentally flipped the wrong bit and corrupted the data, but I think I'm close."

"That would be quite an accomplishment. What do you intend to do with your design? Such a tool would be of interest to many organizations."

Tim turned off his device. "Yeah, that's what I'm afraid of. I —"

"Here you go, hon," Doris said. She stumbled and nearly spilled his drink on the counter. "Whew, that was close! Almost ruined your ... huh, it looks like you raided the dumpster of an electronics store."

Tim rubbed his neck. "It's a little rough, I know. But it's really a —"

"Don't waste your breath on me, darlin'. That stuff goes right over my ..." Doris trailed off when she noticed the blonde staring at him. A sly grin touched her lips. "Oh, I'm sorry, did I interrupt? Daddy would have skinned me alive! Where are my manners? Your burger will be right out, hon. I'll let you two get back to your little chat."

Doris quickly retreated, but the blonde's ice-blue eyes remained fixed on him, which made his ears burn.

"Anyway," Tim said, "I was hoping Z-Tech would be interested, which is why I came. I heard from a friend that the CEO would be here tonight."

"I am sure he will be interested. If he is not ..." The blonde slid her phone over to him. "Please enter your contact information. I shall then call you so you have mine as well."

"You ... you want my number?" Tim tugged his collar. The restaurant was suddenly warm. "I don't get it ..."

"If Z-Tech will not purchase your design, then I will. Call me, and I shall promise a fair and equitable arrangement."

"But ..." After a year of dead ends with his other inventions, the sudden interest caught him off-guard. While he was eager to make his fortune, he was well aware of the dangers his invention may pose in the wrong hands. "Who do you work for, anyway?"

"No one."

Right.

"I, ah ... I appreciate the offer, but I'm not looking to offload my design to the first bidder — or even the highest. If you're just going to turn around and sell it to some corrupt government halfway around the world ..."

"I would not. My interest is personal, and the design would stay with me."

He looked at her, trying to gauge if she was being genuine. But, as before, her poker face was absolute. In the end, he took her phone and entered his contact information.

What the hell. If nothing else, I'll be the first call on a hot chick's phone.

He handed it back to her. True to her word, she dialed his number. He pulled his own phone out and was disappointed to see the caller ID was blocked. "Okay, I got your number. What's your name?"

"That is unimportant unless we do business. Also, unless you are adept at negotiating with foreign organizations, I suggest you limit advertisement of your invention to Mr. Z and myself."

"Why? So you won't have to worry about competition?"

"I refer to your safety. Charlie and I will both treat you fairly, but there are many who would not hesitate to kill or kidnap you — or those you care about — to acquire that prototype should they discover its existence. The choice is yours, however. Do as you will."

With that, she turned her back to the counter, her eyes darting between the other patrons as before.

Hands shaking, he packed away his invention and waited for his meal in silence.

Tim knew when he'd been dismissed.

●　　　●　　　●

Calum stroked his thick goatee under the neon glow of Hal's retro sign. The San Francisco night was cool. A low fog hung overhead, reminding him of his home in Scotland when he was a child.

When I still had a family.

Don patted his expansive stomach. "I'm stuffed! I'm rarely at a restaurant long enough to order two meals, though I'm hardly complaining."

"Glad you enjoyed it," Calum said on their walk to the parking garage. "That may be our last relaxing meal for a while."

That got Don's attention. "W-what do you mean?"

Calum glanced back at the diner, satisfied they were far enough away to not be overheard. "Our guest back at headquarters confessed he'd converted one other into a vampire: a man by the name of William. The woman who served us was also a vampire, which means they're multiplying, just as he said they would. I'm willing to bet the pale lass at the counter was a vampire as well, but it's hard to say because she never left her seat."

"Wait, you mean Anne? No, she can't be. She's so sweet!"

"She has lightning reflexes, and her hands were pasty white where the makeup wore thin. Trust me, lad, she's one of them."

"But ... why pose as a waitress?"

"Aye, that's one of the things that doesn't add up. The blonde was still and observant, as I'd expect a vampire to behave, but the waitress was active and fidgety. I've not known a vamp to keep up that level of activity for long, yet she never stopped."

"We should get the others down here and —"

"Let's not be hasty. She seems established. We'll set up a stakeout and see if we can identify any others. Two vampires will be risky enough for the four of us to take on. More vampires would be suicide. We need more information if we're to come out of this alive."

"Looks like she's well-connected, too."

"What do you mean?"

"The guy she was kissing? He's the head of a big company in town."

Calum paled. "How big?"

"Real big. It's one of the largest computer manufacturers in the world, and their factory's not far from here."

Och, if the vampires already have their hooks in a major corporation ...

Over the years, Calum had imagined dozens of doomsday scenarios. Most of them began like this. "So, this guy ..."

"Charlie Z."

"Does he get out much?"

Don shook his head. "Rumor has it that, until recently, he hadn't been out of his factory for years. He even sleeps there."

Calum frowned.

Years ...

The timeline didn't fit. Their captive claimed to be the top of the vampire chain, and had been asleep for decades prior to his disturbance a few months ago. *Unless he was lying ...*

Don wrung his hands, regarding the diner as if it were a viper's nest.

Calum, however, was much more worried about the factory. "Come on," he said, resuming their walk at a brisk pace. "You drive. I need to make some calls."

"Eh?"

"I have a feeling we're going to need more than just reinforcements." Calum gripped the pistol in his coat. It suddenly felt like small comfort. He didn't like the idea of seeking their benefactor's help. The mysterious organization made him uneasy, but they had the manpower — and, more importantly, the firepower — he needed to keep this vampire problem from escalating into full-scale Armageddon.

Given the options, calling his creepy benefactor was a no-brainer.

Calum grabbed his phone, said a silent prayer, and dialed.

6

RICH FRIENDS

D ORIS LOCKED THE RESTAURANT DOOR AFTER ANNE and Zima had shuffled outside. "Well, that could have gone worse."

"It sure could have," Anne said. "I didn't even have to drink my snack."

Doris shuddered. "You're washing your own thermos tonight, kiddo. Hanging around you is enough to make even a staunch carnivore go vegetarian."

"Sorry." Anne knew Doris was joking, but the comment still stung — mostly because it was true. The wonderful support from all her friends made it easy for her to forget that beneath her makeup hid a creature designed to hunt and feed on human beings.

If that isn't the very definition of a monster, I don't know what is.

Zima took point, as usual, and led them down the sidewalk toward Z-Tech. Cars passed in a steady stream, swirling the low-hanging fog in their wake. Once upon a time, Anne would have loved to be inside one of them with the heater on, but her pulseless body no longer minded the cold and, even after a full night of work, her feet weren't remotely tired. Walking just seemed the natural choice.

Doris wrapped an arm around Anne's shoulders. "I was just teasing you, kiddo. Believe it or not, I'm almost used to the sight of blood now."

"You shouldn't have to be."

"Neither should you. But it's where we are, and there's no sense moaning about what we can't change."

That was also true, unfortunately. Charlie and Mark had worked diligently since her transformation to find a cure, but the virus had mutated every cell in her body so dramatically that they weren't even sure where to begin. It didn't give her much hope for the future, which was why she was so thankful to have an upbeat friend like Doris.

Anne smiled and gave her a gentle hug. "What would I do without you?"

"Let's not find out, shall we?"

Zima fell in beside Anne and held her other hand.

"Oh, that reminds me," Anne said. "Who was that boy you were talking with at the counter, Zima?"

"Timothy Chen."

Anne shook her head at the short answer. *I should know better by now.*

"And what did Mr. Timothy do to deserve the honor of your attention?"

"He had a curious invention."

"It sounded like you were more than just curious," Anne said. "Since when did you start buying technical designs?"

Zima met her eyes briefly before resuming her visual scan of the surrounding neighborhood, mostly comprised of restaurants and shops that were closed for the evening.

"You were listening," Zima said. "Very well. I suspected what the device was when he placed it on the counter, although I did not expect it to work. I do not believe he understands its true worth, or the danger he will be in should his invention become known. For his sake, I hope he heeds my advice and keeps the knowledge close until Charlie or I are able to acquire it."

"Which brings me to another question: Why did you say you're separate from Z-Tech? Why not just tell him you represent Z-Tech and save him a step?"

"Because I do not. I owe much to Mark and Charlie, but I am neither a partner nor an employee of the company. Therefore, I have no right to negotiate on their behalf."

"That's a technicality," Anne said. "You're like family. I doubt they would mind, especially if you were doing it to protect some kid."

"Be that as it may, me acting as a separate interest also gives Tim the illusion of choice. Hopefully he will not feel the need to seek additional offers."

Doris popped her gum. "And here I thought you two were just having a friendly chat, when really you were trying to talk him off a ledge he didn't know he was on. How much do you think that pile of scrap is worth, anyway?"

"I estimate four hundred million US dollars on the international market."

"Holy jumping Jehoshaphat," Doris said, covering her mouth. "I almost spilled a Coke on it!"

Anne looked at Zima skeptically. "And, knowing that, you offered to buy it? Isn't that a little dishonest?"

Zima brow-knit. "What do you mean?"

"Well, four hundred million dollars ... You said you'd treat him fairly."

"Yes. It was not a lie."

Anne laughed. "But you don't have four hundred million dollars lying around, do you?"

Zima just stared at her.

"You're kidding! H-how do I not know this?"

"You have never inquired about my finances, so I assumed you were uninterested. It was not my intention to deceive you."

Doris cackled loudly and squeezed Anne's arm. "So let me get this straight, sweetcakes. You have a billionaire for a boyfriend and a millionaire for a girlfriend?"

Zima's stare made Doris choke on her gum. Red-faced, she coughed it out on the sidewalk.

"You're a billionaire, too?"

Zima nodded.

Doris shook a fist at the fog-shrouded heavens. "Lord! Why does Anne get all the good ones?"

•   •   •

The fortress-like Z-Tech factory was a welcome sight to Anne — its towering concrete walls a symbol of safety and solace.

The trio walked through the open gate to the guest parking lot and entered the modest reception area. Anne spared a glance for the unused coffee maker, idly wondering why Charlie and Mark kept the thing around when she had yet to see anyone visit the factory who didn't already live there.

They pushed through the door marked "Employees Only", and made their way down the long, white hallway.

Doris' feet dragged along the smooth concrete floor. "Home at last. Mr. Jacuzzi, here I come! You two joining me?"

"I think I'll pass," Anne said. "Zima, are you up for some you-know-what?" She waggled her eyebrows.

Doris rolled her eyes. "Have fun, you two. I'm going to soak these weary bones in a nice hot tub and let the jets work their magic on my back. Don't stay up too late!" She waved and disappeared down the hall.

Anne gathered Zima in her arms and smiled. "So, what do you say? Shall we hit the gym for a little sparring practice?"

"Yes, if that is your wish."

"Definitely. I need to blow off some of this energy."

Zima kissed her tenderly. "There is a more pleasurable way to achieve your goal."

"You're incorrigible," Anne said, laughing. "Who says we can't do both? Can we start with the gym, though?"

"Of course."

"Great! I'll go change and meet you there."

She bid Zima a quick farewell at her bedroom door, then went to her own room and spent the next ten minutes, and half a bottle of makeup remover, undoing Cappa and Doris' masterpiece. Having never worn contact lenses before, it took Anne a few tries to get them out, and she squirmed at the uncomfortable sensation when her fingers touched her eye.

That's definitely going to take some getting used to.

When she finally finished, Anne looked in the mirror and sighed at the creature staring back at her. Her complexion was ghostly white with a scattered web of blue venous lines. Without the contacts, her eyes appeared unnaturally large. Combined with dilated pupils, she looked more like a space alien than a person. A single tear rolled down her cheek in memory of the normal girl she had just erased.

Anne turned away with a sniffle and changed out of her work uniform into loose-fitting pants, a sports bra, and a long-sleeved shirt, then left her room in darkness, just as it had been the entire time.

She considered a detour to see Charlie on her way to the gym. She wanted to talk to him about his strange behavior earlier, but that could become a long conversation, and Zima was waiting for her.

The sound of crying stopped her just outside the gym. Curious, Anne followed it down the hall to Cappa's bedroom door. She started to knock, then hesitated. In the two months she'd lived at Z-Tech, she had never heard her soul sister cry, nor been invited into her room.

Anne clenched her jaw.

She couldn't leave Cappa crying. Not if there was something she could do to help.

"Cappa? Are you all right in there?"

The crying stopped, followed by shuffling on the bed. "Yes," Cappa sniffed. "Yes, I'm fine. I was just taking a nap."

"Come on, I heard you crying. Can I come in, please?"

Silence, then more shuffling.

"Cappa, if you're upset, please talk to me. I just want to help."

A foot tapped, followed by a few shuddering sobs, then silence. "All right," Cappa said in a strained voice. "Come in."

Cappa's room was just as Anne imagined it would be: windowless, like her own, but larger; a queen-sized canopy bed with a country floral print occupied the center; a matching set of antique white dressers stood to one side, topped with jewelry boxes and necklace stands. To the other side was a large, mirrored vanity station full of beauty products, where Cappa sat cleaning tear-streaks of mascara from her cheeks.

Anne put her hands on Cappa's shoulders. "Hey," she said warmly to Cappa's reflection.

Cappa managed to mouth the word "Hey" before her composure broke. She buried her face in Anne's shoulder and heaved in big, uncontrollable sobs. Anne hugged her close, stroked her hair, and whispered softly to try and calm her down.

"What's wrong?" Anne said once Cappa's sobs had quieted to a soft whimpering.

Cappa swiped a tissue from the desk. "Sorry, I think I ruined your shirt."

"That's alright. You owe me a few, after all the outfits of yours I've ruined."

That brought a smile. "True, and I didn't smear yours with blood."

"Or burn a hole through it with a plasma gun."

Cappa rubbed her chest and laughed, though fresh tears spilled down her cheeks. "Right. Tell me again why we're still friends?" She dabbed the tears away, and her expression sobered. "It ... it's Charlie."

"Oh, did he upset you, too? He was acting so strange at the diner. I never thought I'd hear him say —"

"That was *me*," Cappa said, her lip quivering. "Charlie was unconscious."

"He ... *what?*"

"Passed out! Right in the middle of dinner. I had to take control of his body to keep him from face planting in his salad. Scared the hell out of me! That's the real reason we left in a hurry."

"But ..." Anne's head was spinning. "Is he okay? Where is he?"

"Yes, he snapped out of it after a few minutes. He's resting in his room right now, but ..." She covered her mouth, shoulders shaking with fresh sobs.

"What is it?" Anne didn't like where this was going one bit.

"He's so weak! Not physically, but mentally. He walks around like he's in a daze."

"I ... I hadn't noticed."

"That's because he puts on a good show for you. But when you're not around ... I swear, sometimes he'll stare at the wall for an hour, and it's getting worse."

The dam burst again and Cappa collapsed into her shoulder.

"Anne, I'm so scared! Charlie is everything to me — my mentor, my partner, my friend ... I can't lose him. I can't!"

Feeling numb, Anne held her tight while trying to wrap her head around what she'd just heard. "Does Mark know?"

"As of a few hours ago, yes. He's in the bio lab right now, preparing the body."

Preparing the ...

Anne's eyes flew wide. She grabbed Cappa by the shoulders. "You're kidding! After all this time, Charlie's finally going to make the jump? B-but why are you in here? Why aren't you helping Mark with the —"

"Because I'm a *wreck!*" Cappa collapsed to her knees, crying.

Feeling guilty for her foolish question, Anne followed her to the floor and gathered her close. Cappa's normally playful air and cool confidence made it easy to forget she had begun her existence as a program to aid Charlie with his research. Unlike Zima, she had evolved into something so human-like that Anne often forgot she wasn't.

And, like most people, Cappa needed support, too.

"I tried to help Mark," Cappa said, clinging to her arm. "But I just kept messing things up, so he suggested I take some time to pull myself together." She looked at Anne with uncharacteristic anger. "My mind exists in three — count them, three! — different systems, synchronized in real time, but capable of running independently. You'd think one of them would be able to pull themselves together to be of use when Charlie needs me the most. But no! We all share the same data, so the other two are just as rattled as I am!" She covered her face with her hands and shook her head. "You don't want to know what the manufacturing floor looks like. It's going to take me weeks to clean up that mess."

"You're allowed to be upset."

"I don't want to be upset; I want to help! But the more I think about it, the more upset I become, which makes me even more incompetent ..." She gripped Anne's arm painfully tight, reminding her just how strong Cappa really was. "I'm going crazy! I want to turn my emotions off and be like Zima, just for a little bit, but I can't."

"I do too, sometimes. But, speaking from experience, ignoring your problems in the hopes they'll magically go away seldom works."

Cappa snuggled into her and stared at the floor. "What do I do, Anne?"

"Exactly what you are doing."

Cappa raised her eyebrows.

Anne smiled down at her. "Leaning on your friends. You're not alone, and neither is Charlie. We'll pull together. We'll save him. Just like everyone pulled together to save me."

"B-but we didn't save you! You're still a vam ..." Cappa bit her lip and looked away.

"A vampire, yes, but one who still has her own free will, which is more than any of William's other vampires can say." She turned Cappa back toward her and kissed her forehead. "Pulling that off was nothing short of a miracle, but that's what we do. We'll get through this, I promise. Just hang in there. Okay?"

Cappa nodded into her shirt. Anne gently rocked her and stroked her hair. She hoped she'd given her soul sister the confidence she needed to face the future, which Anne herself was still trying to muster.

7

THE JUMP

CHARLIE WATCHED THE OTHERS scuttle about Z-Tech's biological laboratory with a strange sense of detachment. This was *his* lab. Every flask and syringe in the glass cabinets along the wall had its place. Scalpels, forceps, and other medical tools lay in sterile drawers, grouped by function, and perfectly spaced for easy access. Chemicals of every variety lined a large, sealed, reinforced cabinet on the far side of the spacious white room. *Charlie* usually manned the computer workstations, oversaw preparations, and ensured everything was in order. It was someone else's job to be in distress, to need healing or some miracle cure.

Tonight was different. He glanced at the body lying next to him — his real body, a biological doppelgänger of the mechanical construction his soul currently inhabited.

Except the body he had been born into wore a mask attached to an artificial ventilator to keep it breathing, an intravenous drip for nourishment, and electric wires leading into its chest to keep its heart pumping. It felt like a horror movie, where the victim died and watched as a disembodied spirit while others did their best to save him.

Those rarely end well for the victim, Charlie thought. He pried his eyes from his corpse — *body*, he reminded himself. *I'm not dead!*

Not yet.

That in itself was a miracle.

He should be dead. He'd accidentally poured his entire soul into this mechanical contraption, and his real body had just stopped working. They'd managed to get artificial ventilation and circulation going, and it had been on life support ever since, kept in working order with a regular routine of cleaning, stretching, haircuts, and electric stimulation to prevent his muscles from atrophying.

And now here they were, nearly six years later, ready to see if his body would accept his spirit back.

The moment I've been dreading.

Charlie's luck had finally run out. His mechanical body was strong, but it couldn't sustain his spirit. It was time to go back.

Or try.

"How's it looking, Mark?" Anne said. "Are we ready?"

Her usual Zima shadow bustled under Mark's direction, assisting with the preparations. Holding Anne's hand instead was Cappa, who, in contrast to her normally collected self, looked so flustered he feared she may actually fall apart.

His best friend, Mark, typed away at a nearby computer that displayed colorful graphs. Attached to Mark's muscular arm was his girlfriend, Dela. The busty redhead had focused her feisty energy on helping Mark and Zima. Amazingly, she hadn't argued with Cappa once the entire evening.

"I think so," Mark said. "His vitals look stable. Brain activity is ... is zero, but the cells are definitely still alive."

Charlie half expected Anne to break down at the news, but she just squared her shoulders and nodded.

"All right, let's get this show on the road!" Anne turned her oddly large, black eyes to him and smiled, fangs glistening in the fluorescent light.

She's still gorgeous, he thought with a sigh.

"Ready to do this thing, Charlie?" Anne said.

Her enthusiasm had him grinning with the others. "Ready as I'll ever be, Captain."

Cappa didn't share their mirth. If anything, she looked even more worried than before. She sat next to him and ran her fingers through his thick brown hair. "Just … be careful, okay? Don't do anything crazy. I'd rather have you in this body and weak than stranded in the ether. Or wherever it is your spirit goes when you project."

"If I ever figure that out, you'll be the first to know, I promise."

Charlie took a deep breath.

This was it.

After all these years, all the worrying, I'll know once and for all if I'm trapped in this body forever.

The thought did nothing to calm his nerves. Charlie clenched his jaw and looked to the ceiling. "I'm ready," he lied.

"Everything's going to be fine," Anne said. She stood next to Cappa and squeezed Charlie's hand. "We're all here, and we're rooting for you."

Charlie had a feeling the reassuring words were meant more for Cappa than himself.

"Every step of the way," Mark said, sliding his chair closer. "I'll have whatever you want to eat here so fast it may still have the cook attached."

"And I'll be waiting at the finish line." With a mischievous grin, Dela nestled the top of his biological body's head between her ample breasts. "Come on, Charlie! Boob heaven is waiting right over here, but you've got to work for it!"

Charlie couldn't help laughing. "Great, I'll be able to enjoy it for all of three seconds before Mark beats me to a pulp."

"Yeah," Dela said, "but I promise those three seconds will be worth it."

Anne bent over and gave him a lingering kiss. When she finally straightened — far too soon for his liking — her cheeks were tear-streaked. She hastily wiped them and smiled.

"And I promise that if you make it through this, my reward to you will leave Dela's so far behind that you'll have trouble remembering who she is or why you cared in the first place."

"Now that's a problem I look forward to."

"Then get going, and ..." Anne's voice softened. "Either way, just come back safely. Okay?"

Charlie smiled, but couldn't bring himself to make a promise he may not be able to keep.

•   •   •

Anne said a silent prayer once Charlie's eyes had closed. Cappa collapsed into her. Anne held her close and comforted her soul sister as best she could.

Minutes passed. Anne didn't know what she'd expected — a floating apparition? A flash of light? A glowing nimbus? But what she saw was ... nothing.

Is it working?

The question danced on her tongue, but the only other time she'd witnessed Charlie project his spirit, he had requested silence, so she swallowed her curiosity and remained patient.

It was hard, and the others didn't seem to have it any easier. Cappa chewed a fingernail and kept glancing between Charlie's bodies. Mark worked a hand exerciser so hard she thought it was going to snap. Dela leaned over the top of Charlie's real body, head resting on his chest, her eyes opened wide and staring. Doris stood behind Anne, kneading her shoulders with stress-induced brute force.

Good thing I don't bruise anymore, Anne thought.

Zima stood off to the side, watching everyone in turn. Anne longed to go to her for comfort, but Cappa clung to Anne with a death grip. This was where she needed to be.

Anne couldn't have said how long they all stayed like that before Charlie finally stirred again.

A giant fist crushed her unbeating heart. Cappa heaved a sharp sob. Even Dela whimpered.

Charlie's eyes had opened on the wrong body.

"What happened?" Cappa said in a thin whine.

"I ... I can't do it." Charlie's voice was faint, a bare whisper on the wind. "I couldn't even project this time. There's just not enough of me left."

Cappa leapt to her feet. "Don't say that! Of course there is. Y-you just have to try again, that's all. Come on, close your eyes and —"

Charlie silenced her with a gentle hand to her cheek. "It's not going to work. I tried, Cappa. I used every trick I knew, but ..."

Tears streamed down her cheeks. He pulled Cappa into a hug, but she brushed him away and straightened, wiping her face with her sleeves.

"You know what this means," Cappa said.

Charlie rubbed his eyes. "I already told you: I don't think Master Wung will help."

"Master who?" Dela said.

"The person who taught him how to project his spirit," Cappa said, not taking her eyes from Charlie. "They had a falling out when Charlie cut his training short to resume his cyborg experiment from where it stalled."

"And you think this dude can help?" Dela said.

"Probably. The question is whether he will." Cappa's lips trembled. "But for some reason, Charlie would rather die than ask forgiveness!"

"Well that's an easy one." Dela pulled out her phone. "What's his number?"

"He doesn't have one. I know," Charlie said at her incredulous look, "it's hard to imagine in this day and age."

"Then what are we waiting for?" Anne said. "Let's pay him a visit. I'm sure we can make a convincing case, especially in person."

All eyes turned to Charlie.

"All right, but ... you'll have to stay here, Anne. It's a long drive."

"How long? The car is sun-proof, so I'm sure I'd be fine for —"

"China."

Anne's heart sank. "I ... I don't suppose you have a private jet that's sun-proof, too?"

"Actually we do," Mark said.

Dela whacked him in the arm, eliciting a yelp.

"You have your own jet? Why the hell didn't you say so! And here we've been sticking to the local scene when we could have gone some place exotic like ..." She noticed the others staring and cleared her throat. "Sorry, I got a little excited. So, China ..."

Charlie took Anne's hand. "Even if you survived the plane ride, it's several days drive through remote countryside. I doubt we could find a suitably shielded car, let alone sun-proof accommodations. Then there's the question of what to do with you once we arrived at the monastery, how we'd feed you —"

"Okay, I get it! Taking me would be a pain." Anne flopped beside Charlie and wrapped an arm around him. "Take Zima instead," she said softly.

Zima head-cocked.

Anne nestled into him. "If I can't be there, it'd be nice to know my better half — or third … whatever — was there to support you."

"That's a nice thought, but the situation with Master Wung is … sensitive. It's going to be hard enough explaining myself as it is without having to cover for Zima, too." Charlie gave Zima a weak smile. "No offense."

Zima shrugged.

Doris put a hand on Cappa's shoulder. "Ain't y'all forgetting someone? Like the most organized gal this side of the Mississippi?"

"I thought Cappa going with him was a given," Dela said. "She already lives in his head."

"Won't help none if he needs an extra pair of hands, and I'd wager lurking in his head don't hold a candle to being by his side when he needs a hug. Ain't that right, sugar?"

Cappa nodded.

Dela wrung her hands and swallowed. "But she runs this place, right? You sure it won't crumble to dust if she leaves? Sorry, Mark, but I've seen your room …" She shuddered.

"Cappa will still be here," Charlie said. "You can't get rid of her that easily. And besides, I like the idea of bringing her along."

Cappa brightened. "Well, if that's the case, then —"

"Hang on," Dela said. "What do you mean she'll still be here?"

"There's another copy of her running in the basement," Mark said, and suffered another blow to the arm from Dela.

"There's a basement? What's down there? Wait, let me guess, that's where you keep the Olympic-sized swimming pool and Ferris wheel! Jeez, I can't believe you. What else are you holding out on, a private island? Your own themed amusement park?"

"We sold the island after the last typhoon," Mark said. "And the amusement park was a bust. No one wanted to ride a computer-themed rollercoaster or bob for circuit boards, apparently."

"When we get back to that disaster area you call a bedroom, you're so dead."

Mark rubbed his arm. "I'm halfway there already."

"The only other things down there are miscellaneous supplies," Charlie said. "Don't ask about the attic, though."

Dela started to snap again, but deflated at his cheeky grin. "Now I see where Mark gets it from."

Doris clapped her hands. "So it's settled? Cappa is Charlie's designated travel buddy?"

"I hope so," Cappa said. "I just booked two non-refundable tickets for eight o'clock tomorrow morning from SFO."

Anne glanced at her phone and sighed.

Five hours from now.

She snuggled closer to Charlie and tried not to imagine what Z-Tech was going to be like without him. Hopefully it wouldn't be for long.

8

SECURITY ROUNDS

Anne quietly closed Charlie's bedroom door behind her to join Zima and Cappa in the hall. Charlie was sound asleep. While Anne was disappointed they couldn't spend more time together before his trip, she understood the ordeal from earlier had taken its toll, and she couldn't begrudge him his rest.

"I am going to make my security rounds," Zima said.

Anne nodded and started toward her bedroom. Security was something Zima did alone.

Zima caught her hand before she'd taken a step. "Will you join me?"

"Well ... sure, but I don't know how much help I'll be. The only thing I know about security is that I hate passwords."

"Do not worry, I shall perform the work. I only wish for your company."

Anne looked at Cappa, who was dabbing her eyes with a laced handkerchief.

"Go on," Cappa said with a wave. "I'll be fine. I've never packed for a trip before, so I have a lot of work to do." She frowned. "I don't even own a suitcase! We have to be at the airport in a few hours, and the malls are closed."

"Mark owns several suitcases," Zima said. "I am sure he will lend you what you need."

"I should have thought of that. I'm such a mess. Thanks, Zima, I'll ask him." Cappa twirled the hanky around her finger. "Not that there's any problem with it, but why the sudden interest in taking Anne on your security rounds? If you're just looking for some private time, I can think of better places to romance a girl."

"It is difficult to explain ..." Zima brow-knit before continuing. "So many of my routine simulations have been adjusted to include Anne, they now outnumber those that do not. Functioning has become more efficient when she is with me."

"So ... what you're saying is that you feel more comfortable with Anne around?"

"Yes, that is an accurate interpretation."

Anne melted. "Well, when you put it that way, how can I refuse?" She took Zima's arm. "Lead on, you smooth talker. Keep saying stuff like that and I might let you have your wicked way with me when we get back."

Zima head-cocked. "I would never harm you, Anne. I do not understand —"

Anne hushed her with a kiss. "It's an expression. It means I'll let you ravage me to your heart's content."

"But I have no wish to destroy or mutilate you in any —"

She pressed her lips to Zima's again, then whispered in her ear, "Another expression, darling. It means I want you to run your Desire program."

"Oh."

Cappa laughed and stuffed the hanky into her dress pocket. "You two are as entertaining as it gets. I'm tempted to tag along on your security rounds so I don't miss the rest of the show."

"You are welcome to join us," Zima said.

"No thanks, I'll give you some privacy in case your program accidentally runs before you get back."

"As you wish. We shall meet you in the garage before you depart."

"And let us know if you need anything," Anne called as Zima pulled her down the hall.

•   •   •

Security rounds turned out to be an educational, yet frightening, experience. In addition to the mundane things Anne had expected, like checking doors and alarm connections, for the first time she saw what really protected the factory.

Hidden within its ordinary concrete walls was an arsenal of fully automated turrets sporting a variety of weapons, including machine guns, high-velocity gauss rifles, and even missiles.

"The turrets are capable of tracking and destroying all known missiles and aircraft, as well as ground targets," Zima said while they walked. "The structure itself is one of only two buildings in San Francisco rated to withstand a nuclear attack. The governor has requested several times to store emergency provisions here, but Mark was able to defer his requests to the other site."

"Would that have been so bad, though? It sounds like a great opportunity to help the community."

"Allowing storage of emergency supplies would also invite others inside the factory, which both Charlie and Mark are opposed to, but Z-Tech does much for the welfare of the city simply by being within its limits. Taxes are unfavorable for manufacturers compared to other states, yet Charlie insisted the company remain in California. Given Z-Tech's annual gross income, its taxes represent a sizable percentage of the city's revenue."

Anne was still digesting that when Zima showed her another surprise.

"Why ... why are there explosives in the wall?" Anne said, taking a healthy step back.

"They serve two purposes."

Anne took another step back when Zima inspected the wires with probing fingers.

"In the event of a breach, they may be detonated individually to deter invaders or, if the situation merits, they may be detonated as one for complete destruction of the facility."

Anne gulped. "You're telling me Z-Tech can self-destruct?"

Of course it can. No super-secret lair would be complete without it. I just never thought I'd be living in a place designed to mushroom cloud if something goes wrong.

"Correct. Mark and Charlie are adamant about keeping their technology from the wrong hands. The charges are placed such that all of the critical technology — the manufacturing floor, weapons lab, and bio lab — will be completely incinerated."

Cappa once quipped that the boys were paranoid.

Anne had thought it a joke, but tonight proved it was anything but. "Not ... not that I really want to know, but how is it triggered? I don't see any big 'Do Not Press' buttons anywhere."

"Mark, Charlie, Cappa, and I each have an encryption key. Any one of us may trigger individual charges with a signed wireless data transmission, but complete destruction requires election of three or more of us as a safety precaution in case one becomes compromised."

Anne was shaking by the time they reached the last charge. Even in the movies, she had never seen so many explosives in one place.

"Are you well?" Zima said. "You are more pallid than usual."

"Better than I would have thought after seeing enough ordnance for two whole armies."

"Good, we are almost done."

There's more? You've got to be kidding, Anne thought, but dutifully followed.

Zima led them up a flight of stairs Anne hadn't known existed, where they emerged onto the roof. The sky was just starting to lighten, the barest hint of purple on the horizon, but that wasn't what caught Anne's attention. Although the factory was only a few stories high, the view from the top of Z-Tech was still breathtaking. Lights from across the bay twinkled on the water like dancing fairies. Skyscrapers to her left towered to the heavens — stolid sentinels of the night lit with every color imaginable.

Anne felt humbled, a tiny cog in an enormous machine. She was still staring when a tug on her hand brought her around, and she noticed for the first time that a small den of privacy screens had been erected near the water. Zima led her inside, and Anne gasped at what she saw. Right out of a romance movie, a comfortable blanket covered the ground. Two dinner candles in beautiful crystal holders stood to either side of lush red roses, and ...

"Pillows?" Anne grinned. "You little minx! I —"

Zima pulled her into a kiss — not the casual peck from earlier, but a full-bodied embrace seething with passion. It wasn't hard to tell that Zima had activated her Desire routine.

Anne responded in kind, and they slowly sank to the waiting blankets, the unlit candles forgotten under the open sky.

9

FAREWELLS

S O FAR, THE EVENING HAD GONE BETTER than Zima had anticipated. Anne was reacting favorably to the romantic preparations. Zima could not have predicted Charlie's condition, but even after thousands of simulations, bringing Anne to the roof had still had a sixty-four percent chance of success.

Everything was going according to plan until she noticed that Anne's hands had stopped their sensual exploration. Zima compensated by stroking Anne's inner thigh — a particularly erogenous area she had discovered early in their physical relationship.

That's when Anne started to cry.

Zima terminated the Desire routine.

Another pathway immediately started it back up, so she terminated the routine again.

A third pathway turned it back on. Zima killed it.

A light brush across her breast made a fourth pathway fire it back up. Then it was the tickle of Anne's hair on her neck, a shift of posture where Anne nestled between her legs. Zima continued to terminate the routine until all pathways had been exhausted, then scheduled a reminder for later to create a more effective kill process.

With her Desire routine finally terminated, her breathing stilled, her nipples flattened, her groin stopped throbbing, her facial expression returned to neutral, and her body no longer demanded to be touched everywhere at once.

Zima missed the pleasant sensations, but she put her wants aside and turned her attention to Anne's distress. She first played back every moment since they had arrived on the roof, analyzing them for something she may have done to upset Anne. The search revealed nothing, so Zima rewound further and further until she reached the beginning of the day. When that also yielded nothing, she submitted the day's events for detailed analysis.

The result was simple: Anne was upset about Charlie.

Anne's sobs intensified. Her shoulders shook uncontrollably, arms wrapped around Zima with enough pressure to break a normal person's ribs. It was well within Zima's structural tolerance, however, so she searched for an appropriate solution to console her girlfriend.

The search was difficult — not because she couldn't find something appropriate, but because it was hard to choose from the vast library of simulations she had built over the last few months specifically for Anne. She sifted through forty-seven thousand eight hundred and twelve simulations, ranging from shooting practice to reciting Shakespeare, discarding one after another due to low confidence scores.

In the end, the highest-rated simulation was also one of the simplest. Zima gently pulled Anne's head to her bare chest and stroked her hair until her wailing dwindled to sporadic hiccupping sobs. By that time, the stars had disappeared, and the sky was turning pink. Privacy screens would be insufficient to shield Anne from the morning sun, so Zima retrieved the robes she had stashed under the blankets. She dressed Anne before dressing herself, as a proper guardian angel should, then ushered her to the stairway just as the rays of the sun touched the clouds overhead.

•　　　•　　　•

Zima and Anne were wearing fresh outfits by the time they met everyone else in the garage. Anne's earlier distress was gone, but Zima estimated an eighty-four percent chance she was still upset and was simply feigning confidence for Charlie and Cappa's sake. Zima squeezed her hand in what she hoped was a reassuring gesture, and was rewarded with a grateful smile.

"Nice that you both changed to see us off," Cappa said with a wink.

Charlie ran a hand through his hair, which Zima knew indicated he was uncomfortable, although she could see no apparent cause. Zima ran another data analysis.

The results returned faster than the last. Charlie was leaving soon. He wished to say farewell to Anne, most likely with a hug and kiss, and Zima was obstructing his path.

Zima reluctantly released Anne's hand and stepped away. The space between her fingers felt empty. Lonely. Anne was focused on Charlie, however, and did not appear to notice.

A guardian angel does not feel jealousy, Zima thought.

She repeated it to herself when Anne fell into his arms, then seven hundred and fifty-three more times over their lingering kiss.

"I'll try to hurry back," Charlie said. "I feel terrible leaving when you're in the middle of all this."

"Don't worry about me," Anne said, resting her head on his chest. "I've got a pretty good support crew. You just focus on getting better."

"I will." Charlie kissed her again, triggering another two hundred and twenty-one anti-jealousy recitals in Zima, then he moved on to Doris.

"Don't take 'no' for an answer," Doris said, wrapping him in a hug. "If that shriveled old geezer gives you any lip, you just point him my way. He'll be begging to take you when I'm done with him."

"I don't doubt it," Charlie said, laughing.

"Safe travels, you two," Mark said, embracing them each in turn. "And, like Anne said, don't hurry back on our account. You've taken care of everyone else, now take care of yourself for a change."

Cappa hooked Mark and Charlie's arms and smiled.

"Don't worry," Cappa said. "He's not leaving mainland China until I'm convinced he's better."

Charlie's smile faltered, and she jostled him.

"What, do you think I'm coming along just for the sights? These fine folks have entrusted your care to me, and I'll be damned if I let them down by bringing you back one second before you're ready."

Then all eyes were on Zima. She stepped toward the departing couple and loaded her farewell solution, but stopped short of pushing it into execution.

Something was wrong with it. She reviewed the solution closely, looking for what it was that bothered her, but all the elements were there: a friendly gesture, a kind farewell to each of them, and an offer to help with the luggage. It was simple, and fulfilled all the requirements she had requested.

The requirements.

That was the problem. When she had chosen this solution, she had been focused on the quality time she and Anne would be able to spend together, but had not considered the other effects of Charlie and Cappa's absence. While the others watched, Zima ran thousands of simulations modeling life at the factory without them, pushing her processors to their limits.

The results were distressing. She had not realized how much she depended on them each and every day. It was true that Zima would still be in communication with the version of Cappa who would remain at the factory, for which she was grateful, but Charlie ...

Zima discarded the short farewell simulation and assembled a new simulation request, this one with a larger requirement list covering the additional sentiments she wished to convey. Dela arched an eyebrow while Zima's processors churned. She rejected solution after solution due to low confidence scores. When Anne's expression turned to worry, Zima stopped processing and chose the highest rated solution so far — still much lower than desired — and pushed it for execution.

"I do not pretend to understand what ails you," Zima said to Charlie, "but I know that many lives, including my own, would be very different without you, and not for the better." The next part of the solution — a small kiss on his cheek — drew a mix of gasps and chuckles. "I do not want to imagine a future without my mentor and friend. I wish you a safe journey and swift recovery, and shall do my best to keep Anne safe and happy in your absence." To Cappa she said, "I shall miss your physical presence, but since you will technically still be here, saying goodbye seems unnecessary."

Anne gave Zima a big hug. "That was very sweet. Thank you."

Zima increased the confidence rating on that solution to one hundred percent and flagged it for later analysis.

"Time to go," Cappa said. "Thanks again for the loaner suitcase, Mark, and —"

"Hang on," Dela said. "Aren't you forgetting someone? Like Charlie's comatose twin?"

"Shipping a body on life support to China would be difficult to explain to customs," Charlie said. "Not to mention the logistics of carting it across the backroads of China to a place with no electricity. I'll feel better knowing it's here under Mark's care unless I absolutely need it."

"Let me know if you do," Mark said. "I'll get it to you somehow."

"Thanks." Charlie took a last look around before getting in the car.

Soon their vehicle disappeared around the block.

Zima laced her fingers with Anne's. Her hand felt whole once again, and the chaos within her settled.

"Does their departure sadden you?" Zima said.

"Of course, but it's better than the alternative." Anne shook herself, then smiled. "Come with me, Zima. I have a surprise for you in the gym."

"What is it?"

"Wouldn't be a surprise if I told you, now, would it?"

Intrigued, Zima let herself be led from the garage.

•　　　•　　　•

When they arrived at the gym, instead of heading for the mats, as Zima had anticipated, Anne went straight for the jacuzzi. Zima looked around the small, tiled room, but saw nothing that did not already belong.

Unless ...

Zima peered into the swirling waters. The bubbles made it difficult to see to the bottom, so she applied stop motion filters, then reconstructed the clear sections from each into a single image that allowed her to see a virtual picture of the bottom.

Nothing.

"Anne, I do not see —"

Anne's body pressed against her back. Two hands slipped around to cup her breasts. Soft lips brushed her ear, then her neck. Zima reached back and was surprised to find Anne's clothes were already absent.

Seven independent pathways triggered her Desire routine at once. Zima made no attempt to stop them. The familiar heat returned to her groin, causing her to moan softly.

"Sorry I spoiled your romantic rooftop plans," Anne said. Her hands wandered down Zima's stomach, sending a torrent of pleasure signals through her body that made her shudder. "Can I make it up to you?"

Zima nodded, but Anne was already unbuttoning her shirt. Zima let her, savoring the touch of her fingers that lingered on each catch, slowly pulled down the zipper of her pants, then rid her of the obstructions.

Anne scooped her up and lowered them both into the tub. Zima clung tightly and kissed her on their way down. Her body's need to be touched returned in force. She straddled Anne on her aquatic seat and pinned her to the wall. Her pleasure sensors were on overload. She pressed her breasts to Anne's, desperate to stimulate every possible centimeter of her skin.

"I'll take that as a yes," Anne said with a laugh.

That was the last intelligible thing said by either of them for the next seventy-seven minutes. At minute seventy-eight, Zima could see Anne was fatigued, and reluctantly deactivated the Desire routine. The aching desire fled as quickly as it had come.

Or it should have. Even with her Desire routine disabled, her body remained in a state of arousal, longing for Anne's touch.

That had never happened before.

"How are you feeling?" Anne said, snuggling close.

Three more pathways triggered the Desire routine. Zima turned it off each time, but the aching need blossomed within her own programming, flaring heat in her groin. She had to make a conscious effort to keep her hands from straying back to Anne's erogenous zones. "I am ... finding it difficult to control myself."

"What do you mean?"

Zima couldn't help kissing her. Anne was smiling when she finally pulled away. "I wish to pleasure you again."

Anne laughed. "Well I'm a quart low right now — no thanks to you, naughty girl — but a quick trip to the fridge can fix that. Turn off your Desire routine and I'll be right back."

"That is the problem. I have already deactivated it, but the feelings persist. I cannot make them stop."

"Wait, does that mean ..." Anne threw her arms around Zima, showering her with kisses.

The need became insistent. Zima wrapped her legs around Anne, undulating against her, and kissed her neck.

"Does that mean it's finally integrating, like we'd hoped?"

"I believe so," Zima said, panting.

Anne sagged. "You don't sound happy about it."

Zima cocked her head. It was true, but she was unable to determine what outward sign she had given to clue Anne in.

"I can just tell," Anne said. "What's wrong?"

With great difficulty, Zima made herself stop kissing Anne long enough to answer. "The last time the Desire routine was used to alter my behavior, many years ago, the experience was similar."

Anne sobered, and Zima knew her point had been made. The Desire program had originally been used to transform Zima from a pacifistic network security program into a weapon of mass destruction who derived pleasure from killing. By the time she had met Anne, most of the Desire program's damage had been undone, but Anne knew how difficult the healing process had been for Zima — as well as Charlie, Mark, and Cappa.

"Anne, we both wish for my feelings to be more natural, but I am now concerned about unexpected escalations."

"You're worried about losing control."

"Yes." As if to illustrate the point, her hips began rocking on their own, grinding against Anne. "These feelings may strike at an inopportune time," she said, breathing heavily. "As pleasant as they are, I ... I ..."

Waves of pleasure rippled through Zima, causing her entire body to shake with explosive release. She cried in ecstasy, shuddering in Anne's embrace. Anne held her tight until it had passed and Zima was able to speak again.

"I ... am not sure they are worth compromising your safety."

"I'm confused," Anne said. "Are you talking about your ability to protect me during combat, or protecting me from yourself?"

"Both. I cannot predict where the intensity of my feelings will end. In a critical moment, instead of generating combat simulations, I may be planning our next intimate encounter. And if these desires become intense enough ..." Zima turned away, unable to meet her eyes. "You have suffered enough from the assault in your bedroom as a teenager. I could never forgive myself if I forced myself upon you and re-triggered your PTSD."

"You're unbelievably sweet." Anne stroked her cheek. "First, don't ever, ever, ever compare yourself to those jerks who attacked me in my bedroom. Second, for it to be considered forced, it has to be unwelcome." Anne kissed her tenderly. "Which it never will be. Third, I'm not the helpless girl I was when we first met. I'm more than capable of handling myself in a fight now. I want you to be happy, Zima, and to explore all the wonderful things these new feelings have to offer. Please don't sacrifice your happiness just to protect me. It's an angelic sentiment, but I couldn't live with the guilt."

"But that is my role. I am a protector. I am your guardian angel, am I not?"

"Oh, Zima ..." Anne smiled. "Angels come in many forms. They're not always fiery juggernauts who smite evil with a giant sword. A guardian angel can be someone who gives you a hug when you're feeling down. Who says the right thing at the right time to put a smile on your face, or provides wisdom in times of need."

Zima rested her head against Anne's generous breast, soft and pleasant on her cheek. "Then I have been grievously mistaken."

"How so?"

She kissed Anne's neck and hugged her close. "I was never the guardian angel. It has been you all along."

"We've been guardians for each other, Zima, which is nice. It's too much responsibility for one person to bear, don't you think?"

Zima thought back to her hours of training, of vigilance, of trying to be the best guardian she could possibly be — time she could have spent with Anne instead. "Yes, it is too much."

"Good. Now that we've put that to rest ..."

Anne nibbled Zima's ear, sending a pleasant tingle down her spine.

"Cross your legs for a minute and let me run to the fridge for some fuel. We're just starting to make progress on integrating the Desire routine into your core, and there's no way I'm going to leave you wanting."

"How will crossing my legs help? If anything, the stimulation will —"

"It was just an expression. Think of something else to take your mind off, like combat maneuvers or dirty socks. That's how most people do it."

"Very well, I shall try."

Zima was just preparing a queue of de-stimulating simulation requests when she heard footsteps from outside.

"I believe Mark and Dela are approaching," Zima said.

"Maybe they're here to use the gym?"

"Perhaps, but it sounds as if they are coming this —"

The door opened. Mark and Dela's playful chatter ceased when they spotted Zima and Anne naked in the jacuzzi.

Judging by their lack of clothes, they had come with similar intent.

"Oh! Sorry guys," Dela said, making no attempt to cover herself. "We, ah ... didn't expect to find you here."

Anne covered her breasts. "That's okay, help yourself. We'll continue in the bedroom."

Zima was first out, followed by Anne, but they both turned at a loud *smack.* A red handprint stood out on Mark's arm, and Dela was glaring at him.

"Oaf! Look away when a lady exits the tub," Dela said.

Mark shrugged. "I was only looking at Zima. I helped make her, after all, and you can't blame an artist for admiring his own work. Besides, I'm not the one who was blatantly ogling."

"It's not the same! I'm a woman, plus I've only seen pictures of Zima until now. And I have to say, they hardly do her justice."

Please tell me you'll share this video later, Cappa sent over their link. You're making me sorry I sent my eyes to China.

Yes, Zima replied, if I am able to obtain everyone's permission.

Cappa responded with a sob.

Dela went straight for the tub. Freckles covered her otherwise fair skin from head to toe. Her breasts were twenty-three percent larger than Anne's — which were two hundred and thirty-six percent larger than Zima's own — but the rest of Dela's body measurements, including her hips, stomach, and thighs, were smaller, closer to Zima's than Anne's. Where Anne's top and bottom were well-proportioned, giving her an accentuated hourglass figure, Dela's otherwise trim figure made her breasts seem comparatively enormous. Dela sank to her neck in the warm water with a smile and a sigh, then gestured Mark over.

The difference between male and female bodies still puzzled Zima. Where she, Anne, and Dela appeared soft and round, the lines around Mark's muscles made his body appear to be chiseled from stone. He was six percent taller than an average male, his shoulders fourteen percent broader, and, Zima knew from the readings of his implant, that his percentage body fat was six-point-two. His skin was hairless, as Zima had observed professional body builders to be. With his short, sandy-blond hair, hazel eyes, and prominent jaw, he resembled many of the male models featured on magazines she had seen during her occasional trips to the store.

Mark slid in next to Dela and smiled, relaxing against the jacuzzi wall.

"Now that's what I'm talking about," Mark said. "You guys want to join us for a bit?"

"Thanks," Anne said, "but my girl needs some loving, and I intend to deliver."

His smile widened. "I never thought I'd see the day Zima needed anyone, let alone in bed, but I'm glad it's here. Have fun you two."

"We should hang out sometime, Z," Dela said. "Let's pick a night and go do something."

"What activity do you propose?"

"Maybe we can go clubbing. I'd love to watch you drink some bozos under the table. Then we can smack them around if they get fresh, maybe start a bar fight. It'll be fun!"

"The last time Zima fought in a bar, it ended badly," Mark said.

Dela bounced in her seat, splashing water over the side. "Do tell, do tell!"

"Think 'trained killing machine meets barroom creep' and you'll get the idea. If Charlie hadn't been so quick to react, it would have gone much, much worse."

"Fine! A night club, then," Dela said. "Or skeet shooting. We can catch a mixed martial arts match. I don't know, we'll think of something. What do you say, Z?"

"I do not object, as long as we are home before dawn so Anne does not —"

"I meant just the two of us. No offense, Anne, but I miss my pal."

"None taken," Anne said, covering herself with a towel. "I think it's a great idea. I've monopolized her lately. Spending time with someone else will be good for her social growth."

Zima ran three hundred and forty-seven simulations of the suggested activities, then compared the results to her time spent with Anne. They were overwhelmingly in Anne's favor.

But she had learned to trust Anne's judgment. If Anne believed it best for her to spend time with someone else ... "Very well, I agree."

"Great! How about Saturday? That'll give me a few days to plan things out."

"If that is your wish."

"All right, it's a date! You won't be disappointed, Z. I promise."

"A date?" Zima replayed the conversation, but could find no point where she had agreed to a romantic relationship with Dela. "I apologize, I think you misunderstood my —"

Dela splashed water at her feet and grinned. "I don't mean a *date* date, just a play date. Friends go on dates, too. It doesn't mean we have to sleep with each other."

"Oh."

"Speaking of which ..." Anne gave Zima a towel, which she wrapped around her torso, then took her hand and pulled her toward the door. "Come on, lover. Let's get you sorted."

Zima's core program unexpectedly stirred her loins again. She followed Anne to the kitchen and crossed her legs while Anne drank her meal. As predicted, the stimulating pressure only increased her longing. No sooner had Anne thrown the blood bag away than Zima scooped her up and carried her to the bedroom, where they spent the rest of the day happily exploring the extent of Zima's newfound passion.

10

IF AT FIRST YOU DON'T SUCCEED

TIM CHECKED HIS BACKPACK AGAIN to make sure his invention was safe and secure, made one last pass at taming his unruly hair, then turned to his waiting audience. "Well? How do I look?"

"Like a geek in a suit," Conway said without looking up. A thin trail of smoke drifted from his soldering iron held steady against a circuit board. Tim always marveled how someone as big as Conway — tall, broad shoulders, muscled arms — could work with such precision.

"You look handsome," Jody said, which got Conway's attention. She flipped her long black hair at Conway with an impish grin, then returned her scrutiny to Tim. "The sleeves are a little short, but passable." At barely five feet tall, Jody had to reach up to straighten his tie.

"Thanks. All right, I'm off for Take Two."

Tim made for the door, but was surprised when they grabbed their things and crowded behind him.

"Y-you're both coming?"

"You kidding?" Conway clapped him on the shoulder. "I wouldn't miss this show for anything. Besides, I haven't seen Uncle Hal in a while."

Jody batted Conway's arm, then clung to it. "Fess up, meathead, you're just going because your uncle gives you free food."

"I cannot tell a lie ..."

"You cannot pass up a cheeseburger!" Jody tapped a sandaled foot. "Are we going or what?"

Tim hesitated. Conway wore slacks and a fashionable, form-fitting shirt that showed off his powerful physique, but Jody's short shorts and midriff tank top, while pleasant on the eyes, were hardly appropriate for a business meeting.

"Don't worry," Conway said. "We'll stay out of the way and let you do the talking. You won't even know we're there."

"Unless you start to flounder with the Z-man," Jody said. "Then we'll swoop in to save the day."

Tim rolled his eyes. "Like you did the last time I let you come on a sales pitch?"

"That guy was a jerk! You'd think someone had welded his eyes to my chest. He got off easy with a drink in the face, man." Her tiny brandished fist was about as threatening as bunny slippers.

"That's a point," Conway said. "Maybe you should let Jody make the pitch. There's a reason female salespeople have higher closing rates in the tech market than males."

"Gross!" Jody actually stuck her finger down her throat and made a gagging noise.

Yeah, not so much.

"Okay, you can come," Tim said. "But we sit at separate tables, and you don't know me. Deal?"

"Fine by me," Conway said. "More room for my dinner plates."

•   •   •

The sun was just setting when they stepped off the bus and made the short walk to the diner. True to their word, Conway and Jody let Tim enter first, where he was seated by the older waitress, Doris, who had served him with such enthusiasm last time. The others followed shortly after and, thankfully, got a table on the other side of the restaurant. Charlie Z was nowhere to be found, but Tim hadn't expected him to be there yet. Casual inquiries had revealed he typically dined later in the evening, and usually on Saturdays.

Well it was Saturday, it was early, and Tim was damned if he would miss his big chance again. He glanced at the counter, and was disappointed the strange pale-skinned blonde was absent.

It would have been something to have them both here on the same night.

Her surprise offer from a few days ago had sparked his imagination. He daydreamed of watching them bid over his invention, higher and higher, until the figure was so large that he couldn't imagine how he'd spend it all in one lifetime.

That wouldn't happen, of course. The blonde had made it clear she'd give Z-Tech first pick, which meant no bidding, and he'd likely have to take whatever was offered. Tim thanked Doris for the Coke, then nestled the backpack containing his invention securely between his feet.

He really hoped Charlie's first offer would be a big one.

11

GOODBYE

ANNE SET HER BOOK ON THE TABLE OF Z-TECH'S LOUNGE and sighed. "For the last time, Zima, I'll be fine. Have a great time, and tell me all about the concert when you get back."

"No. It is not safe for you to travel to the diner alone." Zima turned to her waiting date. "I am sorry, Dela. Perhaps we can reschedule."

Dela waved a pair of tickets in the air. "Z, do you have any idea how many favors I had to cash to get these? This is the concert of the year!"

"Then you should take Mark so they are not wasted."

"Or I can ask Mark to take me to work instead," Anne said. "If getting me safely to and from the diner is the only thing holding you back, I'm sure I can sweet talk him into a ride." When Zima hesitated, Anne took her by the hand and lowered her voice. "Are you worried about your needs flaring when I'm not around?"

"No. They may flare, but I can endure the discomfort for a few hours, if necessary."

Anne sighed in relief. The five days since Zima's Desire program had become part of her core had been nothing short of a sexual endurance trial and, while there were signs that her impulses were coming under control, they still had a long way to go. They would get through it, Anne had no doubt. She would support Zima in any way necessary and, although Zima clearly needed her, Anne suspected a little separation may be necessary to help her move forward.

"Look, I know you're worried about me," Anne said, "but even guardian angels need a night off every now and then. You've definitely earned this one. Plus, I'm much more capable of defending myself than the last time that bastard William kidnapped me."

That much was true. Not only had Mark replaced the plasma pistol William had broken, they had modified the metabolic hack Zima had used during Anne's fight with William. The modified metabolic hack used keywords to activate and deactivate, *kaninchen* and *schildkröte*, which were the German words for rabbit and turtle, respectively. Speaking *kaninchen* increased Anne's strength and reaction times enough that even Zima had a hard time keeping up with her, though it burned through her body's energy reserves faster than a hummingbird in a tempest. Saying *schildkröte* brought her metabolism back down to normal — where Anne was usually tired enough to want to sleep for a week.

Dela threw an arm around Zima's shoulders. "Besides, your best friend — me! — will be absolutely crushed if you don't go."

Zima brow-knit, then reluctantly nodded.

"Good choice, Z! These guys put on an unbelievable show, and ..." Dela pulled a fancy gold key from her pocket. "Guess which car Mark's letting us take?"

"Speaking of," Anne said, "I'll text him right now to make sure he's okay with —"

"I have already communicated with Mark," Zima said. "He has agreed to escort you to work, and shall pick you up when you are ready."

"You leave nothing to chance," Anne said with a laugh.

"I wish that were the case."

Zima kissed Anne lightly, which thankfully didn't smear Doris' makeup job, then turned to Dela. "Come, I shall drive us to the stadium."

"But … he said I could drive!"

"I have seen your driving. We have a fifty-eight percent greater chance of reaching the event without a traffic incident if I drive." Zima held out her hand expectantly.

Dela slapped the key into her palm. "Only because we're running late. But we *will* talk about this again!"

Anne listened to them banter about each other's driving skills until they reached the garage, then the door closed, and their words became too muffled to make out.

Her phone rang, and Anne wasn't surprised to see Cappa's name on the screen.

"It must be hard letting Zima go," Cappa said through the speakers in Anne's techno glasses. Her ghostly image appeared a few feet away, laced with sympathy.

"Yeah. I miss her already, especially with Charlie gone, but I meant what I said about it being a good experience. I really hope they have a good time."

"I can see it going either way."

Cappa sat her virtual bottom on the couch and smoothed her ethereal sundress. Not for the first time, Anne marveled at the effort Cappa put into making her virtual self seem realistic.

"Zima hates crowds and has never been a music fan, but it just goes to show how far she's come," Cappa said. "There are a lot of things she wouldn't do before she met you, and the only other person I know who can bring that girl out of her shell is Dela."

Anne sat down next to her. "Wow, that almost sounded like a compliment."

"Dela and I have our differences, but she makes Mark happy, and keeps Zima company when you're with Charlie."

"Have … have you heard from him?"

"No, sorry, but you'll be the first to know when I do."

Anne sighed.

Charlie had left for China almost a week ago. Cappa had lost contact with her other selves two days after they left, which had apparently been expected given their mountainous destination.

Yet with all the technical marvels she'd seen, Anne still had a hard time believing they were completely unreachable.

No one would be happier if they could be reached than Cappa, however. She had practically begged Anne to leave her techno glasses on, and struck up conversation at every opportunity. Anne sometimes gave them to Doris just to give Cappa some variety, but the android's stranded consciousness didn't seem to care who wore them, so long as she had someone to talk to.

Anne heard the padding of Mark's loafers in the hall long before he poked his head into the lounge. Although they were only going to the diner, he wore a pressed shirt, slacks, and sport jacket suitable for any of the fanciest clubs in town.

"Ready, Anne?"

"You tell me." She stood to give him a clear view of her makeup.

"Doris should get an Oscar. It's miracle work, as usual. Bringing your new toy?"

"Yep." Anne patted the plasma pistol in her purse. "Never hurts to be prepared."

Mark faked a teary sniffle. "You make me so proud."

•　　•　　•

Traffic was terrible. Anne suspected walking would be faster — and had said as much in the garage, but Mark wouldn't hear of it. One thing she'd learned about him early on was that he was happiest behind the wheel, even when traffic was at a standstill, so she'd dropped the subject and climbed into the car he'd picked as the flavor-of-the-week.

"You up for *jiu-jitsu* lessons tomorrow?" Mark said at a stop light.

"Why? Don't I already know all your moves?"

"Your implant knows them, yes, but there's a big difference between reflex and knowing how to consciously employ them."

"I thought reflex was the better of the two. Isn't that why people practice the same stuff over and over?"

Mark grinned. "Yes, but most people don't cheat by stealing someone else's hard work. They spend years learning which moves to use in what situation. You skipped that part."

"It's worked out pretty well so far."

"True, but it may be a different story against vampires who actually know how to handle themselves."

"What, like ninja-vampires? Just what the world needs."

"We don't know what William's up to. Maybe a super ninja army is his end-game strategy."

"The words 'William' and 'strategy' don't belong in the same sentence."

Mark stared at her, hazel eyes reflecting the red taillights ahead.

"Fine," Anne said. "Tomorrow it is. I don't have to call you *sensei*, do I?"

"No," Mark said, laughing. "I'll just be happy if you show up. Ah, here we are …"

Anne stepped out beneath the neon lights of Hal's Diner and waved back to him in thanks.

"Pick you up at closing," Mark said from inside the car. "I'm around, so if you need a ride sooner, do me a favor and call me. Zima will kill me if I let you walk home by yourself."

"Aren't you being a touch dramatic?"

"No, that was almost verbatim."

"Liar."

Mark gave a wry grin, waved, and was soon back in gridlocked traffic. Anne hurried inside.

"Hey, hon," Doris said at the door. "Need help getting ready?"

"Why?" Anne dropped her voice to a whisper. "Did I smudge something?"

"Not a spec. You look great."

"Whew! Okay, back in a few."

Changing into her uniform didn't take long, especially not with her vampire grace and hypermetabolism. Anne wasn't surprised to see the odd duo, Calum and Don, sitting at one of her tables. At first, she thought Zima's warning about them had been just paranoia — a common trait among Z-Tech residents, apparently — but not only had the pair returned every night since then, they arrived early and stayed almost until closing.

The younger bald one, Don, had calmed considerably from the brash, confident person who had accidentally knocked the drink tray from her hands on his first visit. Now he stammered and shook whenever she approached, and rarely made eye contact. Anne couldn't figure out if he was trying to work up the nerve to ask her out, or genuinely afraid. She really hoped he was shy, because the only reason he'd be afraid of a friendly waitress like herself was if he knew what she really was — and the ramifications of that were frightening.

"Hey, Anne," Julie said around the large tray on her shoulder. "Guess who asked for you again tonight?"

Anne glanced back at the duo who, as usual, were just picking at their meals. "Wonderful."

"Are they bothering you? I can tell them they're stuck with me."

"No, I'll take care of them. Thanks, though."

"You bet, but let me know if you need a rescue. That's my specialty." Julie grinned and went to the kitchen.

Might as well get this over with.

Anne checked her porcelain canine caps with her tongue and approached the duo with her best waitress smile. "Hey guys, I hear you want me all to yourselves again tonight. What have I done to deserve such an honor?"

Don gave a strained laugh, as if she'd just told him a joke at gunpoint. The older one, Calum, maintained his cool air, but even he seemed jumpier than when they'd first met.

"It's your sense of humor, lass," Calum said. "Where I'm from, the service is so terrible, you're lucky if the food stays on your plate when they toss it in front of you."

"Really?"

"Aye. And the servers growl if they have to come to your table more than once. One actually bit me when I flagged her down for more water."

"Get out!"

"No, see here ..." Calum pulled back his sleeve. Sure enough, a horseshoe of teeth mark scars shone bright on his forearm. "They had to pry her mouth open with a wooden spoon to get her off. She was worse than my ex-wife." He looked thoughtful for a moment. "Come to think of it, she was my ex-wife."

Despite her discomfort around them, it was hard not to laugh at his easy humor. "So where exactly are you from? Just so I know never to visit there."

"The fair Highlands of Scotland. And before you ask, no, I don't miss it one bit. It's lush and green, aye, but right miserable in the colder seasons, which is most of the year."

"W-where's your girlfriend tonight?" Don said, glancing briefly at her before returning his eyes to his untouched meal.

The question caught Anne off guard. She had been open about her affection for Zima, but this was the first time a customer had called attention to it. "She, um, went out with a friend. Without me, if you can believe it. Supposedly, it's the concert of the year." Anne cleared her throat and resisted an urge to wring her hands, wary of her protective makeup. "So … can I get you anything else? Seems like you guys are still working on your meals."

"We're good for now, lass," Calum said. "Sorry you're stuck here with us louts while your bird is off having fun, but we'll entertain you, if we can."

"You're doing a good job so far. Keep it up and I might be paying *you* at the end of the evening."

Don's chuckle was so tight that Anne thought he was choking. Once she was sure he was breathing okay, she excused herself to make the rest of her rounds.

Strange guy …

Odd couple aside, the night went smoothly, but the constant noise of the restaurant bothered her more than it had the previous few nights. Anne was glad when her break finally came. Instead of hiding in the employee room with a book, as she normally did, Anne went to the cool, quiet rear service alley. The smell from the dumpsters was terrible, but it was better than the deafening street noise out front. She walked a few paces upwind and sniffed. Putrid odors still carried from neighboring business' trash.

Anne looked skyward, where fresher air waited on the roof overhead. Her skirt made climbing prohibitive, however, so she huffed against the wall, plugged her nose, and tried to enjoy the chill night.

The breeze carried a distant word that snapped her to attention.

"… vampire."

Anne darted behind a foul-smelling dumpster and hid. Mention of vampires wasn't uncommon in the City, even before she had discovered they were real. Vampire pop culture was alive and well, especially among the Goth subculture. If she hid every time she heard the word, she'd never make it out the front door. But she was alone this time and, though it was well lit, the alley was deserted, and her guardian angel was nowhere near.

The next words brought goosebumps to her already cold skin.

"... Z-Tech ... Charlie."

"... Zima."

The last turned her fear to anger. Was it one of William's crew? Or worse, had someone discovered Z-Tech was somehow tied to the vampire problem? Were there new players in the game? She desperately hoped not.

But there's only one way to find out.

The words had come from farther up the alley, and the speakers were hidden from sight. Anne looked to the roof again, then at her constricting skirt. A quick pull tore the seam on one side, and a similar pull freed the other side, exposing her pale thighs almost up to her waist.

Praying no one else from Hal's chose that moment to take an outside break, Anne scrambled up the wall like a squirrel to the roof. She leaped from building to building, soaring with ease across the wide gaps, until she was directly above the source of the voices. Two men in street clothes — human, by their look and smell — leaned against a classic black town car. Anne settled down to listen, but unfortunately their talk had turned to sports. She waited patiently through a deep discussion on internet memes, followed by a new video game one of them was stuck in, and how the boss levels were so unbalanced that he was going to ask for a refund. She ground her teeth, sure that her break was almost over, but the topic she hoped for didn't come up again.

One of their phones buzzed. He pulled it from his pocket and read the screen. "Huh. Boss man says the blonde's at some concert in the South Bay with someone. Wants us to go check it out."

"Concert? As in the one I've been trying to get tickets to for months?"

The other flashed his screen in confirmation.

"Gee, that won't be hard. There will only be like a gazillion people to sift through."

Do they mean Zima? How the hell could they have known … Her jaw clenched so tight she nearly broke her porcelain canine caps.

Calum. That son-of-a-bitch wasn't being friendly; he was fishing for info.

And, like an idiot, I gave it to him.

They headed for the car, parked just below her. Anne knew she had only seconds to act, but she hesitated. Her plasma gun was in her purse back at the restaurant, which was less of a concern since she wasn't facing vampires. In her shoes, Charlie would have played it safe and captured their cell signals to learn their identities, she had no doubt. Mark would have some gadget he could put on their car to track them, and Zima …

Well, Zima would jump down and beat the information out of them.

What the hell, it works for her.

Anne vaulted the lip of the building, exhilarated by the four-story free fall, and landed easily on her feet next to the surprised driver.

"Evening, boys," she said with a toothy smile. "Let's chat about those orders of yours."

• • •

Tim swirled his soda straw and sighed.

Charlie hadn't showed. Again. He had known it was a risk before he'd come, but it was hard not to be disappointed.

Jody patted his arm. "Cheer up, there'll be other opportunities."

"Thanks." He'd switched tables after a few hours, tired of sitting by himself, and his friends' company helped. A little.

Conway emerged from Hal's employee area with a big smile. "Aren't you glad you brought me along?"

Jody whacked his arm. "Depends on what you found out, meathead. Spill it."

"You know that big-knockered waitress who's been serving us tonight? Her name is Anne Perrin, and Uncle Hal says she just happens to be Charlie's girlfriend!"

"Heck! She'd know his schedule inside and out," Jody said.

"More than that," Tim said, daring to believe his luck. "She could arrange for a more formal meeting." He frantically scanned the restaurant, but couldn't see the auburn-haired waitress anywhere.

"I asked one of the staff in the kitchen," Conway said. "Anne's on break out back. You can chat with her alone and plead your case. It's perfect."

"In a creepy, stalker-ish way." Jody shuddered.

But Tim was already in motion, heading for the back with his invention in tow.

This is it, he thought, emerging into the service alley. *Finally, my big break.*

Anne was nowhere to be seen, however. He paced up and down to see if she was hiding behind a dumpster, but there was no trace of their server anywhere.

A woman's voice farther up the alley spurred him into a run.

Something big is going to happen tonight, all right. I can feel it!

• • •

Even though Anne had expected the men in the alley to pull guns, it was still a shock when they did. She'd never been threatened with a firearm before. For all her shooting and sparring practice with Zima, she had never practiced disarming an opponent, and her magic bag of Mark's *jiu-jitsu* tricks came up empty.

In other words, Anne was scared.

But only for a moment — and in cyber-mutant-vampire terms, that wasn't very long at all. The men were incredibly slow compared to her amped-up reflexes, and she had landed so close that it was an easy thing to snatch their pistols out of their hands before they'd even cleared the holsters.

I wonder if this is how it feels to be Zima.

She spun the pistols around and had one trained on each by the time their jaws finished dropping.

"Now, now," Anne said with a ruthless smile. "I said chat, not shoot. But since you decided to bring firearms to the table ..." She cocked the hammers dramatically, just like the movies. "Let's skip the pleasantries and cut to the part where you tell me who you are and why the fuck you're tailing my girlfriend?"

A trickle down one of their legs dampened her tough-girl mood.

It was effective, but eewww ...

"Anne!" a male voice called from the direction of Hal's. A tall Chinese boy in a suit jogged around a dumpster and smiled when he saw her. "Thank goodness, I thought I'd never catch you."

Anne hid the semi-automatic pistols she'd captured behind her back and faced him. The boy looked familiar, and it took a second for her to place him.

The kid with the billion-dollar invention.

"Oh, hi, ah ... Tim, is it? Look, this isn't a good time —"

Anne felt the pain in her back before she heard the shot. White-hot agony ripped through her chest, exiting in a spray of blood between her two captives, spattering Tim's face and suit. A second shot caught her shoulder before she could turn, and a third her stomach. Not waiting to see if there would be a fourth, she dived behind the black mafia car, screaming with every painful movement. Tim took off running the way he'd come, feet kicking like a madman.

Good boy.

That Anne was still alert and functioning was a miracle. Her former captives stared down the alley, apparently just as surprised as she was at the hail of gunfire. Anne peeked under the car. Although she couldn't see above the knees, there was only one set of them, covered in jeans with a new pair of men's sneakers.

All that from one guy?

She'd only seen two people shoot that fast, or that accurately, and neither Mark nor Zima likely wanted her dead.

It was only a matter of time before William's goons started carrying weapons, I guess.

Anne chanced a few shots over the car. One hit, but it didn't seem to slow him down, which confirmed her vampire theory. His return shot, thankfully, only grazed her temple before she ducked back down.

I need my plasma gun.

Running as Tim had was out of the question. Even with her super reflexes, she'd been shot three times in under a second. Bulletproof or not, Anne would be dog meat by the time she reached the next dumpster.

Unless ...

Anne stuffed the pistols in her skirt pockets, slid her arms under the car, and heaved upward with an agonizing scream. She'd never tried to lift a vehicle before — especially not after being shot full of holes — and was almost as surprised as the two lackeys when the tires lifted from the ground, and the car came to rest on its side. With another painful scream, she spun it sideways to block the entire width of the alley. The shooter was still pretty far away. Even with his vampire speed — he *had* to be a vampire — the impromptu blockade should buy her enough time to make it back to the diner.

Then it would be Anne's turn.

Gritting her teeth against the pain of her injuries, she sprinted with everything she had for the next safe zone.

Except it wasn't very safe. A dozen yards from Hal's stood Calum and Don, pistols in hand. She reached for her confiscated guns, but Calum already had her in his sights. His trained shot caught her before she could draw.

Pain exploded in her leg, a thousand times worse than the wounds in her chest. Anne crumpled in a shrieking, writhing mass, clutching her leg as if it might fall off.

And then she wasn't writhing. Her leg still burned like a super nova, but her muscles wouldn't respond. When Calum stood over her, his earlier mirth was gone. He was cold fury staring down the barrel of a gun. For a moment, Anne was sure he would finish the job with a cap to her head, but a question from Don snapped him out of it.

"Is one bullet enough to keep her subdued?"

In response, Calum shot her in the arm.

More nova-like pain blinded her, except Anne couldn't move a muscle, not even to scream.

"Best to not take chances," Calum said. "Call the lads. Have them meet us at the end of the street. After all that racket, the police will be here soon."

That was the last thing Anne heard before the world went black.

12

MY MOUTH WAS OPEN

T IM WAS STILL SHAKING when he emerged from the police station, and was relieved to find Jody and Conway waiting outside.

"Jesus," Conway said, looking him up and down. Tim had washed most of the gore from his face, but his jacket and shirt were still a mess.

Jody surprised him with a hug. "I-is any of that blood yours? You sure you weren't hurt?"

"No, not ... not like that poor waitress." Every time Tim closed his eyes, Anne's chest exploded in a fountain of red. He wiped his mouth, which still tingled with the coppery taste of her blood.

Part of him wondered why he had run — what had prompted him to duck into the furniture store and hide like a child avoiding punishment.

If there was something I could have done ...

But there wasn't. Tim had no idea how she'd managed to jump a car with three gaping gunshot wounds, but he was pretty sure it had been Anne's last action on this earth. Sticking around would only have added another dead body to the count. His.

And Charlie ...

Once the Z-Tech executive found out about his involvement, Tim may very well get the audience he was looking for, but what would he say? *"Yes, Mr. Z, I saw your girlfriend get mowed down, just before I ran for my life. Oh, by the way, check out this neat invention ..."*

He dropped his backpack and gave it a swift kick.

It all seemed so pointless. He never would have been in that alley in the first place if he hadn't been chasing her down for his own gains. It wouldn't have changed her fate, but it certainly would have changed his. Even if he made a fortune from his invention, he suspected this horrific night would haunt him for the rest of his life.

Conway grabbed his bag and nodded across the street. "Come on, I brought my parents' car so you wouldn't have to bus home."

"Thanks, man." Tim looked at his friends, both concerned in their own way, who had been his lifeline of support for the last several years while he pulled himself together.

A waking nightmare of blood erupting from their chests made him gasp. Jody clung tight; Conway readied to catch him, but Tim waved them away.

"Sorry, I'm okay. Let's ..." Tim rubbed his stomach. "Let's just go. I'm not feeling so well."

"Maybe your mom's awesome cooking will help."

Tim doubted it. Although his stomach hurt, he was hungry, and, for some reason, even a home-cooked meal didn't sound very appetizing.

13

BAD NEWS

MARK PACED THE FRONT OF HAL'S DINER. Police cars lined the street, fewer than he expected for a homicide, but it was just as well because he didn't want them getting too close.

At least Doris grabbed Anne's purse before they arrived.

Her phone and plasma gun were still inside her bag, and Mark hadn't relished the idea of explaining the space-age pistol to the investigators.

What he really wanted was access to the crime scene so he could perform his own forensics, but the closest he had come was the second-hand report of an eyewitness — some unlucky kid caught in the crossfire. The wounds he described would certainly have been fatal for a normal person. But Anne was far from normal, even for a vampire, and the fact that there were no bodies at the scene meant she may very well be alive.

And if she was taken by whom I think she was … He didn't want to imagine what William would do to her after his failed revenge at the Revelation Hotel. *All the more reason I need access to that crime scene right goddamn now …*

Doris pushed through the diner entrance, shaking her fists. "You *think* they'd make an exception for the closest thing Anne has to family in this town, but being her best friend don't get me any privileges. I tried shouting a spell, but that just got me the boot."

"Oh my God. Her family …" Mark buried his face in his hands. "The police are going to contact her parents."

"You bet they are, but don't worry. I got her brother Doug's number, and I'll keep them out of it for as long as I can. Anyways, it ain't like they found a body …" Doris choked on the last word and covered her mouth, tears brimming. "Have … have you told Zima?"

"No, the concert isn't over for another two hours. I sent Dela a message asking her to let me know when they're on their way back."

"Won't Zima be pissed we didn't call her sooner?"

"I'm more worried about the people she'd hurt barreling through a crowded stadium to rush back, when there isn't much she could do anyway."

Doris touched his arm. "I know you got good intentions, hon. You and Charlie have taken care of Zima like no one else could. But put yourself in her shoes for a sec, and have a little faith in all the good work you done so far. From what I know, Zima ain't the same person she used to be. She might surprise you."

Oh, Doris, if you only knew …

But she did know. Not firsthand, of course, but enough to appreciate Zima's violent side. And she was right about how Zima had changed. Mark hardly recognized the clingy android who followed Anne around like a puppy, yet it was that same attachment that made him worry. Zima had never been in love before. Her relationship with Anne had just started to bud when William had kidnapped her the first time, and it was obvious to anyone that her feelings had multiplied since then.

She killed an entire den of vampires in the blink of an eye, not knowing for sure if Anne was even there. What will she do this time?

It didn't matter. Zima would find out. The only question was how upset she'd be at Mark for not telling her sooner. "You're right," he said to Doris.

"Want me to make the call? You got enough on your mind. The least I can do is offload the soft stuff from you."

"No. I appreciate the offer, but it wouldn't feel right. Zima and I have our own history. She'd expect me to tell her."

But there's someone else I need to prep first.

He pulled up Dela's number and hit the call button.

It rang a dozen times before she picked up, drowned out by a wall of rock music.

"Hey, Dela. Is Zima near you?"

"No," she yelled, "I had to run clear over to the restrooms to even have a chance of hearing you. What's up?"

Mark briefed her on what they knew.

"*Shit!* Z's going to fucking freak! What do I tell her?"

"Don't. Text me when you're back by her side and I'll send her all the details. Keep her calm if you can, but get out of her way if things look dangerous."

Dela swore a few more times before signing off, leaving Mark to compose his message to Zima while anxiously awaiting the signal to send it.

"Was that really necessary?" Doris said.

"Yes. I just hope it was enough."

Dela's message came a minute later. Mark took a deep breath, said a silent prayer, and sent his message to Zima. Several tense minutes passed before he received a response.

I CANNOT CONNECT TO HER IMPLANT, Zima sent through their link.

I KNOW, Mark replied. THAT WAS THE FIRST THING WE TRIED.

WILLIAM IS THE LIKELY CULPRIT, Zima sent. ONE OF HIS VAMPIRES HAS A REGULAR HUNTING LOCATION, WHERE I SHALL ARRIVE IN APPROXIMATELY TWENTY-SEVEN MINUTES TO EXTRACT INFORMATION FROM HIM.

IS DELA GOING WITH YOU?

YES. SHE INSISTED.

Mark rubbed his face. CAN YOU TELL HER I'D REALLY PREFER THAT SHE DIDN'T?

"You look troubled, hon," Doris said.

"Zima's paying one of William's lackeys a visit, mafia-style. And Dela wants to tag along."

"Jesus Lord … That girl's going to get herself killed!"

"Tell me about it."

DELA HAS ACKNOWLEDGED YOUR WISHES, Zima sent.

For a second, Mark thought the night may not be a complete disaster, until he read the message again. YOU SAID "ACKNOWLEDGED", NOT "AGREED". SHE'S GOING ANYWAY?

YES.

Of course she is.

I HOPE THIS GOES WITHOUT SAYING, BUT PLEASE KEEP HER SAFE, Mark sent.

I HAVE NO INTENTION OF LOSING ANOTHER LOVED ONE TONIGHT. MY TARGET TYPICALLY HUNTS ALONE, SO THE THREAT SHOULD BE MINIMAL. DELA SHALL BE SAFE WITH ME.

I hope to God you know what you're doing, Zima.

"So what next?" Doris said. "Wait for Zima to break a few fingers and find out where they're keeping Anne?"

Mark shook his head. "From what Anne said, William's hold on his lackeys is absolute. If he doesn't want her found, I doubt Zima will be able to make her target say anything William doesn't already want us to know. We need more info, like a description of who took her, so we can ask around to see if they were spotted anywhere else in the city. If we can identify them, we may also get an idea of where they might have taken her."

"That's a lot of *ifs*," Doris said in a small voice.

"So let's start whittling them down." Mark looked up the street. "Where does that back street exit?"

"Both ends."

"Flip a coin, then, and let's go."

They walked the short distance in silence, until Doris said softly, "What are we going to tell Charlie?"

Mark rubbed his chin and sighed. "We're not."

"Now hold on, cowboy. I thought we just went through this with Zima."

"Zima's different. She won't die if she drops everything to help."

"Ain't that Charlie's choice?"

"Charlie needs to get better. If he finds out about Anne, you know as well as I do that he'll swim the Pacific if that's the fastest way to get back here."

"And you really think Cappa's going to go along with not telling him?"

"It was her idea. In fact, she's so adamant that she won't even tell herself."

"I can't even pretend to understand that one," Doris said.

"Normally, Cappa synchronizes data in real-time with all three of her minds. What one knows, they all know. Her two other selves are in a data dead zone right now, which means they have no idea what's going on here. But if they do get a data signal, they'll try to sync up. Cappa's going to prevent that from happening, so even she isn't tempted to bring Charlie back before he's ready."

"I think you just made my headache worse. So she's basically going to lie to herself? Don't that require some sort of therapy afterward?"

"You're not far off," Mark said. "The separation will probably cause personality divergence, which Cappa's never had to deal with. And the longer they're apart, the worse it's going to get. She's still not sure what she'll say when her other selves request a data sync and she has to refuse. I mean, how do you tell yourself a convincing lie?"

"You don't. You trust yourself." Doris pulled her phone out, gave a few taps, and put it to her ear. "Hey, Cappa. Mark said you got a little internal conundrum if your better halves call. I'll put you on speaker so we're all on the same page." She tapped her phone and held it out between her and Mark. "Look, if I was you, I wouldn't come up with some crafty lie that'll get you all upset. Just say you can't sync up, you got a good reason for it, and that you just got to trust yourself. You being you should understand that you wouldn't say such a thing unless it was important, right?"

"But that's the problem," Cappa said through the tinny speaker. "Something so important that I wouldn't tell myself would have me chewing my fingernails down to the metal, then I'd chew Charlie's fingernails ..."

"Worse than trying to puzzle something you're bound to figure for a lie?"

"I guess it depends on the lie."

"Just my two cents, hon, but honesty's always worked for me. You got your own demons, but know I'm here if you need to talk. We'll catch up more later."

"Wait! Can ... can you keep me on the line? And maybe turn the camera on, so I can see?"

"Of course, you poor thing. I'd give you a hug, too, but I don't think my phone has cuddle sensors."

At the mouth of the alley, the upturned black car was visible even from the fringes of the yellow police tape, bumpers wedged between the buildings on either side.

If only I could see the license plate …

Most disturbing was the splash of red on the concrete, and the huddle of investigators around it.

At least they're wearing gloves.

Mark hoped there would be enough blood left when they were done to get a sample to see if it was Anne's — or, if it wasn't, hopefully it would hold a clue to its owner.

Something shiny caught his eye near Doris' foot. As casually as a six-foot-three bodybuilder could, Mark stooped to pick it up.

Brass casing. And not just any casing …

Mark had been in the weapons business long enough to recognize military-grade ammunition when he saw it. He slipped it into a pocket. The firing pin and ejection marks could probably tell him which gun had fired the shot, but he'd need to return to his shop to figure that out.

"Ain't taking evidence from a crime scene illegal?" Doris whispered.

"Only if I get caught."

Apart from the shell, there wasn't much to see, since the car blocked their view of the rest of the alley, so they walked around to the other side.

A few crimson drops trailed under the police tape to the curb.

"Hey, Doris," Mark said. "Got a hanky?"

"No, but …" She ripped a square of fabric from her apron. "Here you go."

Mark turned his back to the officers on the other side of the tape, pulled his pocketknife, and scraped some flecks of the dried blood onto the scrap of apron, then turned his attention to the street. The trail stopped right at the curb, which meant they had probably loaded the wounded person into a vehicle. It was a busy street, unfortunately. Tire tracks would be hard to pin down, and any witnesses to the crime were likely transients who were long-gone by now.

Or were they?

His eyes drifted to the closed businesses across the street, then to the windows above them. Most people didn't think twice about what occupied the innocuous floors above their favorite stores. Often they were leased as business space, but sometimes they were apartments.

Businesses would have been closed at that hour, but residences ...

Several windows had a clear view of not only the street, but the alley beyond as well.

And many had lights on.

"Doris, when does your shift end?"

"I'd say it ended roughly when I found out my Anne was missing."

"Good. I could use some of your Southern charm."

Doris followed his gaze to the windows and smiled. She popped a mint into her mouth, straightened her hair, and nodded. "One silver tongue, ready for action, hon."

Mark led the way across the street to a side entrance, dialed a random apartment number into the security pad, and waited.

With any luck, someone would let them in so he didn't have to crack the box open and do it himself.

14

INTERROGATION

D ELA HELD ON FOR DEAR LIFE while Zima tore around another turn. The back end of their insanely powerful sports car drifted out, but Zima kept it under tight control — just as she had every other time Dela thought they were about to spin off the road.

"How much farther?" Dela said, her knuckles white on the oh-shit handle over the window.

"One-point-four miles."

Still plenty of time to wrap ourselves around a tree, Dela thought, but kept it to herself.

"When did Anne last feed from you?"

"Just before we left," Dela said. "Why?"

"It will improve the odds of your survival should you become involved in a physical altercation, which will also provide me with a greater range of strategic options."

Dela mulled on that while Zima parked beneath a freeway overpass. Parked cars lined the street, yet no pedestrians walked the sidewalks. When Dela looked up the street, she saw why. Auto body shops lined both sides for several blocks, all of them dark.

Except one.

"That is our destination," Zima said, pointing to the lighted shop. "The proprietor is a vampire named Michael Torag. He changed his hours three weeks ago and is now the only twenty-four-hour auto body shop in the area. From what I have observed, he feeds on late-night customers, keeping them until the memory-inhibiting venom wears off. Patrons leave believing they had opted to wait for the work to be completed and had simply fallen asleep."

Dela snickered, drawing a head-cock from Zima.

"Sorry," Dela said. "It just gives 'body shop' a whole new meaning. Please, go on."

"I shall enter first. If there are any humans present, I would like you to keep them in their places while I interrogate Michael. Otherwise, please ensure the blinds are closed."

"Aw, I don't get to break any bones?"

"Perhaps. We shall see how resistant he is and re-evaluate as necessary."

"I-I was kidding."

"Oh."

Dela gulped. It was probably just her imagination that Zima sounded disappointed.

"Do not speak on the walk over," Zima said. "I do not wish to give away our presence or identities until the last possible moment. And allow me to conduct the negotiations once we are inside."

"Ah, okay, um … what should I expect?"

"No matter the outcome, it shall be over quickly so that we are not overwhelmed by reinforcements. It would take far too long to review all four hundred and eighty-three scenarios I have prepared with you, so it is best if you stay near the entrance and assist as the situation demands."

"A polite way of saying 'Stay out of the way and follow my lead.'" Dela cracked her knuckles. "All right, let's do this!"

Torag's was one of the nicer shops on the street, in Dela's estimation. A cement path led past the bright neon "Open" sign to a glass lobby. Zima pushed her way inside, with Dela a few steps behind.

The guy sitting behind the counter, a portly Filipino with a thin mustache, smiled when the door opened, but his eyes flew wide when he laid eyes on Zima. His hand blurred beneath the tabletop, emerging a fraction of a second later with a revolver big enough to give Dirty Harry penis envy.

No sooner had it crested the table than a flash of orange light turned it — and his hand — into glowing slag.

His scream snapped Dela from her shock. She quickly closed the door and fumbled with the blinds.

"Michael Torag," Zima said, training her plasma pistol on his chest. "Do you know who I am?"

He bit back a cry and nodded. "The D-Dark Angel."

Zima head-cocked, but said nothing.

Uh oh, the Dark Angel comment must have caught her off-guard.

"Th-that's right, you piece of shit," Dela said, crossing her arms. "The Dark Angel has come to take your soul back to Hell if you don't cooperate!" She waited, but Zima remained silent.

Crap! I forgot that she doesn't handle metaphor very well. I'm just making things worse.

"Tell us where William is keeping Anne," Dela said, "or DA here is going to blow the fingers off your remaining hand, segment by segment, until you wish she'd started with your head. *Comprende?*"

Zima seemed to finally catch up. She moved forward and aimed for the hand cradling his charred stump.

Michael retreated until his rolling chair bumped the wall. "Wait! Y-you mean the waitress? I-I-I don't know what you're talking about! We didn't —"

Zima grabbed his good hand and fired so quickly that Dela rubbed her eyes to make sure it had actually happened. Michael's scream, and the charred hole in the desk, told her it had.

Jesus Christ, Zima! It was just a threat …

But again, Dela should have known better.

Zima doesn't threaten.

The problem was that his denial looked sincere.

"Z—, er, Dark Angel, I think he's telling the truth."

Another flash. Another scream. Another smoking hole. Dela did her best to hide her shudder.

"I don't know what you're talking about!" Michael blubbered. "W-William didn't mention any plan to kidnap her, I swear!"

Dela paced menacingly behind Zima. "Sure, and he tells you *everything*, right?"

"N-no, but ..."

Zima aimed for his next finger segment.

"Wait! He wouldn't tell me, b-but if he'd captured her, we all would have felt it. His stronger emotions always filter down, even to us Seconds, b-but I haven't felt anything in weeks."

Zima head-cocked. "Why do you refer to yourself as a Second?"

"It's what they call his indirect descendants, people sired by vampires that *he* sired. I was sired by —"

Michael screamed again, this time grabbing his head.

"Guess his sire doesn't want to be named," Dela said. "That also means they know we're here."

"As anticipated." Zima tightened her grip on his hand.

Michael screamed. The sound of bones cracking made Dela's stomach turn.

"Michael Torag," Zima said, "do your brethren approach?"

"Yes," he grated, spittle dangling from his lip.

"Then deliver them a message from the Dark Angel: I have been lax in hunting lately, because I have been enjoying my time with Anne. If she has been murdered, or I cannot find her, or I discover a single falsehood in your statements, destroying your clan shall become my sole reason for existence. I will start with you. Your sire may influence your answers, but believe me when I say that you shall tell me what I wish to know before you beg for death, including the identities of your sire and brethren. Your clan will follow your fate, one by one, until your sire is too afraid of their own shadow to set foot outside of their hiding place." Zima leaned closer. "Do you believe me, Michael Torag?"

He nodded, jaw quivering.

"Good, for the opposite is also true. If you learn of her whereabouts — or anything at all — it will benefit you to tell me as soon as possible. I shall give favor to those who facilitate Anne's safe return, which would give your clan a survival advantage over the others.

"To reiterate, your clan has two paths from which to choose: favoritism, or extinction. Are we clear?"

Michael nodded again, cringing into his chair.

"Very well. You may also tell your brethren to halt their advance, unless they wish to hasten their own demise, for I will not hesitate to kill any who approach this night." Zima grabbed a pen and scribbled on a pamphlet. "You may reach me at this number. Any attempt to contact me in person, however well intentioned, shall be met with lethal force. Goodbye, Michael Torag."

Dela open the door for her, heart pounding like thunder, and kept her mouth clamped shut until they were in the car and well away from the neighborhood.

"That ... that was something, Z. Do you practice that badass routine in the mirror?"

"I owe much to you. Thank you for the assistance when I faltered." Zima glanced at her, brows knitted. "Are you well? Your heart rate and blood pressure are dangerously high."

"Damn right! I've never been so scared in my life."

"You were never in danger. Even if he had fired his weapon, I stood between —"

"No, I mean scared of *you!* Holy cow, 'favoritism or extinction' ..." Dela shook her head. "And the deadpan way you delivered it. Wow! I've never seen anything as terrifying as you were when talking down that vamp-dweeb tonight. I believed every word. The mutilation was a little much, but —"

"Was there reason to doubt my sincerity?"

"About what?"

"The ultimatum."

"No! That's my point. It was a hell of a performance."

"'Performance' implies entertainment or insincerity. I was not performing."

"You ... seriously meant all that stuff about torturing and killing his entire clan? If things don't, ah, go well with the investigation?"

"Yes, and that is only the beginning. I will tear this city apart brick by brick to find Anne if I must." Zima flexed her right hand, something Dela had seen her do several times that night, then glanced over again. "Your vital signs are still abnormally high. Are you sure you are well?"

"I ... I'm fine," she said, thankful when Zima didn't call her out on the lie.

Zima doesn't threaten ...

"Z, we're buds, right?"

"If you refer to friendship, yes. I enjoy our time together, and hope you feel the same. Why do you ask?"

"Don't take this the wrong way, but it's hard to tell sometimes. At the concert, you watched the musicians on stage with the same deadpan look you had when you blew Michael's fingers off."

"I see." Zima brow-knit, then turned to her. "Are you concerned that I would intentionally cause you harm?"

"Not concerned so much, but seeing you in action tonight got me thinking, and I just want to make sure I'm not on your shit list for any reason."

Zima head-cocked, which made Dela smile.

"That I'm not one of the people you'd hurt, like Michael."

"I am sorry if my lack of emotional expression has given you doubt. Cappa has cautioned me that over eighty percent of human communication is non-verbal, but until recently I have had little interaction outside of Z-Tech, so it has not been an issue. I consider you a close friend, Dela, and would not knowingly cause you harm. I hope you believe me."

Dela considered that while the streetlights zipped by.

Zima doesn't threaten.

And she doesn't lie.

"I do, Z. Sorry for bringing it up."

She amiably chucked Zima's arm, and nearly jumped out of her seat when a set of pearly whites greeted her.

"My God! Is that fright show supposed to be a smile?"

Zima's lips quickly resumed their neutral positions. "It was. How did I do?"

"Perfect, if you were going for 'insane ax murderer.' Do that the next time we question someone and you won't need to shoot their fingers off to get them to talk."

"'We'? You would accompany me again?"

"Hell yes. Anne's still out there, and I'll be damned if I sit on my hands while everyone else does the work. Besides, you're a superhero now — the Dark Angel! — and every hero needs a sidekick. I think we make a good team, don't you?"

"You are certainly more adept at navigating conversation than I. Perhaps we are a good balance."

Thoughts of the two of them skulking the streets in costumes made Dela grin, but her smile faltered when she saw Zima flexing her right hand again.

"You okay, Z?"

"No," Zima said softly.

"What's wrong? Something with your hand?"

"Only that it is empty. This is the hand Anne normally holds when we are together. Her touch brings me peace, and ..." Zima squirmed in her seat. Her breathing quickened.

Just like it had in the hot tub.

"And relief," Dela said.

"Yes."

"Can't you, ah ... relieve yourself, so to speak?"

"No." Her squirming intensified. She gave a short, frustrated gasp. "Although the Desire routine was designed to respond to any stimulus, as a normal human body would, my exposure has been solely to Anne. My core pathways do not copy the Desire routine's behavior; they form from experience."

"And Anne has been your only experience so far."

"Yes." Zima was breathing hard now. Her knees clamped together. Dela had never seen her in the throes of passion and was surprised to see an expression of longing on her face. Zima was horny, plain and simple, but was powerless to do anything about it.

Yikes.

Like most people, Dela had been in situations where she really wanted sex, or to be touched, but the feeling either passed, or was remedied as soon as she found some private time or a willing partner, both of which were easy to come by.

I can't believe I'm going to say this ...

"Would ... would you like me to try and ... relieve you?"

Zima glanced at her. For an uncomfortable second, Dela thought she was going to take her up on the offer, but Zima shook her head.

"It will not work, but I appreciate the gesture," Zima said. "Your discomfort is evident, which makes your offer yet another testament to the level of our friendship."

Thank God.

"Will it pass?"

"I do not know. These feelings are new to my core, and Anne has always been there to provide relief when my needs have flared. Without her ..." Zima crossed her legs, rocking in her seat, face twisted with agonized longing. She didn't finish the sentence.

Nor did she have to. Dela knew what that intense need felt like, and how frustrating it was to have that need go unfulfilled.

It wasn't cute. It wasn't romantic. It was torture, and it wasn't to be taken lightly.

Dela hugged herself, hurting for her friend and reeling over the implications. Zima didn't just miss Anne, she needed her on a basic level.

And without her, Dela realized with growing unease, *the deadliest warrior the world has ever known may slowly go insane.*

15

REGROUP

M ARK WAS HAPPY TO FIND Zima and Dela waiting in the garage when he and Doris finally returned to Z-Tech. His girlfriend stood wide-eyed and shell-shocked, which Mark had been expecting. Dela idolized Zima, but she had never seen her in action before tonight, and her ashen face said it all.

At least she's still in one piece.

"What did you discover?" Zima said as soon as he stepped out of the car.

"That San Francisco residents really don't like opening their doors to strangers," Mark said.

Doris grinned. "He's just sore because I got more info than he did."

"Let's debrief in the lounge," Mark said. "My feet are killing me."

Once they had settled in, he was surprised when Dela sat next to Zima instead of himself. The display of bonding was encouraging, until he noticed the worried glances Dela kept casting her way.

That's not good.

Mark looked at Dela and Zima. "Why don't you two go first?"

"As you wish," Zima said.

She recounted their visit to the vampire, describing each brutal detail with trademark ambivalence, occasionally interrupted by colorful elaborations from Dela that, despite the gory topic, made Mark smile.

"My lie-detecting algorithms are not optimized for vampires," Zima said in closing, "so it is difficult to know if Michael Torag was telling the truth. But Dela believed his sincerity when he claimed William was not involved."

"That backs our findings," Mark said. He filled them in on what they had discovered in the alley, including the license plate number he managed to get while the car was being towed away.

"After that, we knocked on every apartment with a view of the alley," Doris said. "It weren't many, but a few had peeked out their windows when they heard gunshots. They said some girl with brown hair flipped a car on its side and took off running in a bloody mess. The guy who shot her hopped the car like a kangaroo and left a good-sized dent in the door where he landed, which is odd because they said he weren't a big fella."

Zima brow-knit. "Vampires are hunters, adept at leaving no trace of their passage. That description does not match their known behavior."

"And it sounds like he was abnormally dense," Cappa said from Doris' pocket. With a start, Doris fished her phone out and put it on the coffee table.

"What, like a cyborg?" Dela said.

Mark shrugged. "As we know, Z-Tech isn't the only player in that game, and if it was sent by the same organization that made Zima ..." He swallowed. "Let's hope they were targeting the vampires, and not Anne specifically."

Dela's eyebrows shot up. "You mean there might be another Zima out there? Like her archnemesis?"

"It is a disturbing thought, yet conceivable," Zima said.

Mark leaned forward. "Imagine Zima without the warm fuzzies."

Dela's shudder said she understood.

"Cappa, I know it's a stretch," Mark said, "but can you check for any word in the underground about cybernetic operatives?"

"On it," the phone said.

"Thanks. A resident near the other side of the alley also heard gunshots, and when they looked, they saw several men carrying a woman's body pile into a black sedan."

"Sounds like we'll find her when we see a parking lot full of black cars," Dela said.

"Which could be any taxi or limousine service," Mark said, "but it can't hurt to keep an eye out. Next, the police had an eyewitness. Any idea who it was?"

"Julie saw several guys head out the back door about the time Anne disappeared," Doris said. "One of them was that kid who wanted to sell his doodad to Charlie."

"Wait ... *several* guys? Who else went out?"

Would be nice if she'd mentioned this earlier ...

"Two goons who been asking for her the last few days. You'd think ..." The color drained from Doris' face. "I got to be the dumbest sleuth in the west."

"I know to whom she refers," Zima said. "The large one's name is Don; the older one is Calum MacLean."

"I doubt they'll show their faces at the diner again," Mark said. "But if they do ..."

"I'll ask the staff to call us if one of them shows," Doris said. "They'll know right who I'm talking about."

Mark clapped his hands and paced the coffee table. "Great. Zima, you —"

"I am searching local, Federal, and INTERPOL law enforcement databases for name or facial recognition matches, and shall extend the search to foreign governments as necessary."

"And what was the kid's name?"

"Timothy Chen," Zima said. "I will send you his contact information, unless you would like me to interrogate him."

"No, I'll do it. Just get as much info on Don and Calum as you can. Hopefully it'll give us a clue where they would have taken her. All right, everyone have their marching orders?"

There was a chorus of nods, and an "Aye, aye" from Cappa.

"Good. It's late, but bug who you need to, and apologize later for waking them up. I'll call Timothy, and will stop by his house if he doesn't answer."

Dela looked at Zima with a worried expression. "Are you okay now?"

"Yes, it has subsided for the moment. Thank you for the concern."

Dela nodded, then latched onto Mark's arm. "I'll go with you, since I can't help the Dark Angel hack police networks."

"You really like the superhero thing, don't you?"

She stood on her toes and gave him a quick kiss. "I thought that was obvious, muscle man."

"As a warning, I don't do spandex. Period."

"Never say never." Dela purred, trailing a finger down his chest. "I can be very persuasive. Especially if you let me pick your hero name."

"I already have a name I'm quite fond of, thanks."

Her grin had "rascal" written all over it. "We'll see. I have a knack for catchy nicknames, and for making them stick."

Mark sighed. Unfortunately, he didn't doubt her one bit. While Mark pulled out his phone to call Timothy, Dela led him from the lounge to their bedroom, where she closed the door.

He set his phone on the bed when he saw her worried look. "What is it?"

"Zima," Dela said softly.

"Look, I know her techniques can be brutal and a little unorthodox, but —"

"I can handle the brutality. It's her sanity that worries me."

Mark listened to her story of Zima's unfulfilled needs with a mixture of fear and wonder.

"It's no joke," Dela said in closing. "I've never seen Zima betray even a hint of emotion, but tonight she was suffering. Big time. I'm worried, Mark, and not just because I care about her."

"You should be." Mark wiped his trembling hands over his face. "If Zima loses it, she may very well destroy the city to find Anne."

"So ... you really think she'd do it?"

"Absolutely. She doesn't eat. She doesn't tire. She can punch through a cinder block wall. And she's *very* focused. There's no building she can't enter, and no one who can stop her from trying — including us. And that isn't what worries me the most."

"What? You think she'd hurt people?"

"I know she would. Not indiscriminately, but, as you witnessed tonight, Zima's primary interrogation technique is torture. If she suspects someone knows something about Anne and they're not being forthcoming, she won't hesitate to torture the information out of them."

Dela clamped her hands between her knees and shivered. "So what do we do?"

"As soon as we're done with Timothy, I'll talk to Cappa to see if there's anything we can do to ease Zima's suffering, but apart from that ..." Mark picked up his phone and punched Timothy's number in. "We keep looking for Anne. We find leads, give Zima hope, and support her if she needs help coping, just like a real family should."

Dela nodded, though her eyes were haunted. She rested her head on Mark's shoulder.

Mark called the number, hoping now more than ever that Timothy Chen would answer.

16

A PRISON BY ANY OTHER NAME

*P*AIN. *THRASHING. YELLING. PAIN. BLACKNESS.*

Pain. Hunger. Snarling. Blood! Feasting. Rapture. Blackness.

Anne gradually came to, unable to distinguish whether the feral flashes had been real or just remnants of a terrible dream.

Smells of earth, stone, iron, gunpowder, mold, and people filled her nose. The air was damp, still, and quiet, leaving Anne with the uneasy impression that she had been sealed in a cave somewhere, far underground.

Her eyes snapped open.

While not quite a cave, the dark, windowless cell was a close second. Thick shackles bound her spread-eagle to a concrete wall, fastened with enough industrial-sized bolts to secure a raging rhino. A wooden bench was the only other feature in the spacious square room. Faint light came from a narrow gap beneath a riveted metal door, which was thick enough to knock that same rhino senseless should he try to ram it down.

Someone really didn't want her to leave without saying goodbye first.

At least I'm not gagged, like the last time I was kidnapped.

The scene from the alley came back in a rush. Anne looked down at her chest, expecting a bloody mess, and was surprised to see a clean sweatshirt and pants where her tattered work dress should have been.

They changed my clothes. What courteous gunmen.

Her torso tingled where her wounds should have been — or may still be, for she couldn't see through her clothes, and her hands were fastened tight against the wall.

Her leg and arm wounds still hurt, though nowhere near as much as they had. Anne gave her leg a tentative flex. A stabbing pain made her yelp.

I won't be running a marathon anytime soon. What the hell did Calum shoot me with?

Anne's cry must have attracted attention, for she heard several sets of feet take position on the other side of the door, followed by the cocks of pistol hammers. Bolt after bolt screeched back, so many that Anne imagined the entire side of the door lined with them, then it finally opened.

Standing in the doorway, flanked by two men in fashionably dark clothing with pistols at the ready, was none other than her mystery shooter. Although she hadn't seen his face, his sneakers were the same ones she'd glimpsed under the car in the alley. Gelled sandy-blond hair, hazel eyes, tanned skin, a pleasant round face ...

Swap his dress shirt and jeans for swim trunks and he'd be the natural star of any beach movie, ever.

His heavy-footed approach gave her pause. Only Zima, Charlie, and Cappa sounded as if each of their steps might crack the floor. Her mouth fell open when she heard the electric hum of high-powered circuitry emanating from his chest.

Is he a cyborg? An android?

Without ceremony, he jabbed a fat syringe into her shoulder. Anne winced, watching her tainted blood slowly fill the vacuum tube. He carefully tucked it into his jacket. His lips parted into what was surely meant to be a smile, but came off as a puppeteer tugging the corners of his mouth with invisible strings.

"Greetings," he said cheerfully. "It is good that you are awake, because I have many questions. Answer them promptly and there will be no need for further discomfort."

An android. Definitely.

Anne clamped her mouth shut, her head reeling. Her exposure to Mark and Charlie's colorful history was minimal, but only one organization she knew of besides Z-Tech were capable of such technology: the bastards who had turned her beloved Zima into a murder-craving monster, then sent her to kill Mark and Charlie. Anne didn't even know the organization's name. It was only ever discussed in hushed tones, and the one time she'd asked, Cappa had said it was best if she didn't know. As the creepy, hazel-eyed machine looked her up and down, Anne suddenly disagreed.

"Please list the names and residences of all individuals who have been afflicted with the vampiric disease," the sandy-haired android said. "You may begin with your own residence, the Z-Tech factory, and confirm the infection status of known residents Charles Z, Mark Suther, and Cappa Z."

He doesn't know about Zima? But Calum must have seen us together ...

It didn't matter. They were her family, and she'd be damned if she gave these pricks one lick of information that could be used to hurt her loved ones.

Anne stared back at him, her jaw set. They stayed quiet for several minutes — him waiting patiently, as only a machine could, and her with nothing better to do than hang around.

"You have chosen not to cooperate." His face fell, as if his puppet strings had been cut. "Very well. Anne Perrin, I am authorized to offer you a sizable fortune for the information I require, transferable to the bank account of your choice. The exact amount will depend on the quality and quantity of the information, and may be up to, but not exceed, one hundred million US dollars."

"You're ... trying to bribe me?"

"Correct. Are the terms acceptable?"

Anne thought about it. The more she considered, the more absurd the offer sounded.

Even if it was genuine, no one would be crazy enough to let someone like me go, and there's no guarantee they wouldn't just kill me anyway. He's baiting me, and doing a terrible job at it.

She continued staring at him.

"I take your silence as refusal. Very well, we shall commence with the next phase."

The android struck the side of Anne's face with the force of a gorilla swinging a lead pipe.

Bone cracked. Pain exploded under her eye. The room spun madly, and Anne was glad for the shackles anchoring her to the planet.

Her vision cleared of splotchy colors just in time to catch a blow from the other side. She screamed, barely clinging to consciousness and the sparse contents of her stomach.

When the room came back into focus, Calum was yelling at her interrogator. His words were a jumble to her addled mind. He gestured sharply out of the room, and soon she was blessedly alone again in her dark concrete-and-steel prison.

She couldn't have said how much time had passed before Calum returned, but it was long enough for her face to stop throbbing, and for feeling to return to her lips. Instead of the abuse bot, this time Calum's bald buddy Don flanked him, gun at the ready, as if Anne were some sort of monster.

Oh, right …

What surprised her was the vampire who walked in behind them. His suit, like most of Cappa's wardrobe, was vintage. Dark, oiled hair capped eyes black as midnight. While shorter by a head than either of the humans, he carried himself with undeniable confidence that made him seem ten feet tall.

The vampire winced when he saw her face. He raised a thick eyebrow at Calum.

"Zane acted without orders," Calum said, balling a fist. "He's forbidden from seeing her again without first talking to me."

"And you think he'll obey?" The vampire's accent was hard to place, but his voice was smooth and confident.

"I have no reason to believe otherwise."

"I don't trust him," Don said. "When he smiles, it's like … well, he's scarier than a clown!"

Calum turned with a frown. "Are you really that daft, lad? There's an honest-to-goodness vampire standing right next to you, but it's circus clowns you're afraid of?"

"That's different." Don scratched his head. "I can tell what Almos is thinking just by looking at him. But clowns ... they got those freaky smiles no matter if they're happy, sad, or trying to cut your heart out with a chainsaw. Zane's worse because he shows you the face he thinks you want to see, but it's got nothing to do with how he's feeling. Me and Joe were talking about that yest–"

"Can we save this discussion for later, when I'm not here?" Calum gestured to Anne. "It's your turn, Almos, but she stays in irons. Clear?"

"Perfectly." Pools of black focused on her. "Hello, my dear. Anne, is it?"

She nodded.

"Almos," he said, laying a hand on his chest. "A pleasure. Let's start simply, Anne. Who sired you?"

She pressed her lips into a thin line. If these people belonged to the organization she believed they did, any information she surrendered would somehow be used for their private gain — and most likely sold to the highest bidder.

William is the top of the vampire chain. If they get control of him somehow ...

Him having an army of bloodsuckers under his so-called leadership was bad enough already. Given purpose and competent direction, they would be a frightening force.

Anne had no intention of being the catalyst for the vampocalypse.

"I-I don't know," she lied. "One day I woke up in a dumpster in the Mission District with no idea how I got there. The next day, I bit my best friend. Almost killed her. And then ... then I became this." The heroine in her favorite novels, Jayne Madison, always said the best lies were mostly true.

That was about half true. Hopefully it's enough.

Almos flashed a toothy, but sympathetic, smile. "My dear, if you fear repercussion from your sire for betraying him or her, you need not worry. We are a half-dozen stories underground. The earth shields your mind, so you may speak freely."

"It does?"

"You tell me. Can you sense your sire?"

Anne checked the tiny spot in the back of her mind where William's presence, once a great elephant, now skulked as harmlessly as a solitary mouse in a vast field.

Even the mouse was gone.

This would have been nice to know a few weeks ago …

But then, if they had known, they might have just squirreled her away underground. Zima might never have hacked Anne's implant to provide enough biofeedback to give William, or any of his goons, a splitting headache whenever he tried to reach her. Zima's hack was better than hiding, in her opinion, because it not only gave her freedom, but inflicted pain on the son-of-a-bitch if he got cocky.

A total win-win.

"Now," Almos said, "will you tell me who sired you?"

"Like I said … I don't know."

Calum stood beside Almos and sighed. "You're a terrible liar, lass. I called that bluff from across the room."

Crap.

"I'm sorry to have to do this, but we have to be sure," Almos said. "Just relax."

Someone touched her mind, and Anne knew without a doubt it was Almos. Unlike William's dominating presence — a sergeant shouting in her ear — Almos' was soft, more like a friend hailing from across the street.

Before Anne could puzzle the implications of that, her implant's defensive program kicked in, causing that section of her brain to go berserk. A wave of mild nausea hit her, as she expected it would.

Almos, however, grabbed his head and fell to the ground screaming — also as she expected. She almost felt bad for him. Almos was polite with a fatherly air, which was the polar opposite of William, for whom her mental trap was designed. But Almos had brought this on himself by not warning her of his intentions.

Guilt turned into terror when three guns trained on her.

"What are you doing to him?" Calum yelled, his face contorted in rage. "Stop it! *Now!*"

"I can't! He needs to sever his link with me. I-I wouldn't know where to begin, or if I even can."

Under normal circumstances, Anne's lightning reflexes would have saved her from Calum's shot. She saw the moment he decided to pull the trigger: his tendons flexed under his skin, arm tensed, giving her plenty of warning. She could just as easily have dodged as snatched the gun away and turned it on him.

But, chained to the wall as she was, Anne could only watch the horror unfold.

Calum squeezed the trigger in slow motion. She heard the catch release, saw the hammer drive home, and the fiery explosion of gas from the chamber. Anne swore she could even see the shiny bullet pushing headlong through the muzzle flash on a collision course with her abdomen.

And there wasn't a damn thing she could do except close her eyes and wait.

As with the shots to her leg and arm, agony exploded in her abdomen, burning as if someone had poured molten lava inside of her. Anne's scream drowned Almos' tenfold, until the paralysis froze her vocal cords, and all she could do was cling to sanity like a child in a hurricane.

Then the storm swallowed her.

•   •   •

Anne woke to her worst nightmare: in the middle of surgery with some guy digging around in her gut.

She cried out, struggling with all her might to break free of her restraints, but she was still weak and managed only a pitiful squirm, which Almos ignored and continued digging around. Someone offered their arm, which Anne bit down on without a second thought. She drank deeply and let the delicious flavor take her mind from the unthinkable activity below.

"Got it!" Almos stood with a shiny bullet pinched between a set of bloody forceps.

It was then she noticed the arm she was sucking belonged to Calum, the dreamy look on his sour face as out of place as candy on a plate of Brussels sprouts. After another minute of drinking,

Almos suggested she relinquish. Anne took a few extra revenge slurps before releasing her meal, then hung her head, gritting her teeth against the lingering pain.

"In all my years," Almos said softly, "I've not seen human or vampire take the punishment you have this night and live."

"Is that supposed to be a fucking compliment?" Anne grunted when a spasm sent fire through her abdomen.

His voice dropped to a whisper. "Silver is poison to us, a fast-acting paralytic that attacks the nervous system. A single silver bullet has ended many a vampire's life. None have survived two, let alone three, as you have. What's more, you awoke with a silver bullet still inside of you, which should be impossible. You're quite a curiosity, Anne Perrin."

"G-glad my misery has piqued your interest," Anne said, panting. Pain stabbed her with every breath. "Anything else I can do while you're here? Cough up a lung? My spleen? Kidneys will cost you extra."

"Forgive me. I'll herd your happy thrall and the others away so you may rest."

Only after their footsteps had faded did Anne allow herself to cry.

17

CHICKEN SOUP

TIM PUT HIS PHONE ON HIS BEDROOM DRESSER. Z-Tech's Vice President, Mark Suther, had reached out to him personally regarding the waitress' murder. Tim had answered his questions, describing everything with as much detail as he could remember, given the few seconds he'd been on scene before he'd turned tail and run.

A shiver made him pull the covers up tight. The ceiling register was blasting hot air into his bedroom, but no matter what he did, he couldn't seem to stay warm.

Guess it's no surprise that I caught something after all that stress. His stomach growled — usually his body's demand for Mom's home cooking, but even the thought of swallowing food made him gag. *Gotta love the flu.*

He curled into a ball, and was grateful when sleep claimed him.

Morning, if anything, was worse. Tim awoke to uncontrollable shivering. He grabbed a few blankets from the closet, tossed them on the bed, and climbed into his bed fortress, as he had when he was a child.

It helped, but not much.

The phone startled him awake. He reached a trembling hand and swiped it from the dresser. Jody's face lit the screen. He didn't feel like talking, but if he didn't answer, she'd just come over anyway. She was the mother hen of their small group and, for some reason, fussed over Tim the most.

"Hey J-Jody."

"Tim, you sound terrible! Where are you?"

"Home. I think I caught something. G-going to take the day off and rest."

"Is your mom at work?"

"Think so."

He could almost hear her frowning over the phone. "I'm coming over."

"Jo, you don't —"

"Just for a few minutes, okay? I'll bring soup or something."

His stomach rumbled at the offer, but thoughts of Jody — not the soup — made him salivate. "O-okay."

It felt as if he'd just closed his eyes when the doorbell rang. Too exhausted to make the trip downstairs, he texted her to come in. Jody entered with a large black thermos, and brushed the socks off his dresser to make room.

She unscrewed the cap. "Hungry? It's just the canned stuff, but this was a staple in my house when my brothers and I were sick."

One whiff of the chicken broth turned his stomach.

She came all this way, though ...

"Sure, I'll try some."

Jody sat her small frame next to him, spoon at the ready. Tim managed to keep the first bite down, but the next made him gag.

"Sorry," Jody said, setting the cup-lid aside. "Maybe it's a stomach flu?"

"Could be, I've been shiv —"

Another smell stopped him cold. It was sweet, fragrant, and promised to quell his aching hunger.

And it came from Jody.

Tim shook his head to clear the nonsensical notion, but couldn't take his eyes from her smooth, olive skin.

Jody noticed him staring and smiled. "Someone perked up in a hurry. Want another bite?"

A bite ...

"No, I want ..."

He took her tiny hand in his. Jody glanced down but didn't pull away.

"I want ..."

He brushed her hair back, and was surprised when she closed her eyes and nuzzled his fingers.

This is crazy! She's Conway's girl. I-I couldn't ... I shouldn't!

He leaned in. Jody's lips eagerly met his. Fingers clawed over his shoulders, down his back. She tasted wonderful, more amazing than he remembered from his last relationship several years past. He kissed her deeply, savoring everything she was, then moved to her cheek, her neck, her shoulder, lapping the delightful taste of her skin.

She whipped her shirt off with a flourish, unfastened her bra, and drew him back to her heaving chest. Minutes later, they were a sweaty tangle of limbs. Stronger than he would have guessed for her size, Jody pushed him over, rolled on top of him ...

... and fell right off the bed. She was up in no time, however, and crawled back on top of him with a predatory grin.

"Jo! Your arm is bleeding."

She glanced at the gash below her shoulder and shrugged. "I hit the table on the way down. It doesn't hurt, though, so let's worry about it later. For now ..."

She kissed him again, running her hands down his chest. Tim yanked her under him, smearing blood on the pillow.

That's when the incredible smell hit him. It was everything he wanted, everything he needed to feel better. To be whole. His lips trailed down her neck and over her shoulder to the open wound. A dab of his tongue to the line of red erased all doubt, sending a shiver through him that dwarfed his kindled desire. He closed his mouth over the gash and began to suckle, savoring every tiny swallow.

"Tim, what are you —"

Tim unceremoniously slipped his hand between her legs. Her question died with a moan, allowing him to drink his fill until her passion peaked, turning her into a happy, quivering mound.

He felt invigorated, his earlier fatigue a faded memory. Tim kissed her with renewed passion, then gave Jody the attention she'd deserved the first time around.

Sometime later, both of them spent and relaxed, Jody nestled against him and sighed.

"Guess I should talk to Conway today," she said.

His heart lurched. "And ... tell him what?"

"The truth." Beautiful brown eyes met his. "That I'm in love with someone else, and I have been for a while."

Tim mulled on that while he enjoyed her warmth, which warded off his shivers. The three of them had met in the same college engineering class. He'd always considered Jody to be attractive, but his lanky build and unruly hair seemed like poor competition next to Conway's muscles and keen fashion sense. Like the stunning platinum blonde at Hal's, Tim had simply written Jody off as out of his league. Beyond that, however, she was every geek's dream: She had a great figure, liked to wear skimpy clothing, and was into all the same techie stuff he loved.

She's almost too good to be true.

Yet here she was, naked in his arms — and in his parent's house, no less. It didn't make sense. Not only was Conway better looking, his family was also rich, while Tim could barely scrounge bus money most days. He bit his tongue at the inevitable question, but curiosity won out.

"Why me?"

Jody ran a hand over his chest. "Conway's nice. Talented, even, but aimless. He doesn't have any ambition beyond his next workout. With his trust account, he probably won't need to work a day in his life. I ... I tried to imagine our future the other day, and all I could see was me hanging on his arm, going from party to party, eating fancy food ..."

"That doesn't sound so bad."

"I didn't work my butt off for an engineering degree just to be some guy's trophy girlfriend. You have plans. You want to be somebody in the engineering world, and ... and I'd like to be part of that. I think we'd make a good team."

"So you slept with me to get on the ground floor of my future empire."

He yelped when she pinched his arm.

"Don't be a jerk! I meant what I said about … really liking you."

"I, ah, think you used a different word before."

Jody hugged his arm. It may have been his imagination, but he swore he could hear her heart racing.

"I did. But it's okay if you don't feel the same," Jody said, though her tone suggested it wasn't.

Tim hugged her close, and chose his next words carefully. "I'd be lying if I said I loved you."

Her heartbeat slowed to a crawl.

"But I really like you," Tim said, pulling her tight. "You're funny, smart, and we have a lot in common. I think the only missing ingredient is time."

Her pulse quickened, chest pounding like a jackhammer against his wrist. "R-really?"

"Really."

At least, I hope so.

He kissed the top of her head, drinking her scent once again. Her wound had stopped bleeding, but it was still slick, and the smell was delectable, which bothered him even more than cheating on Conway.

No, not cheating, he thought. Jody and Conway weren't exclusive, to his knowledge, so he hadn't breached any social contracts.

It was a technicality, but it still made him feel better.

Jody patted his arm. "I'd better dress this cut and go change."

"You're … leaving?"

"Yeah. Unfortunately, there's a family dinner tonight I can't miss. My aunt and uncle flew in from Boston. Mom would kill me if I skipped out."

"That's too bad. My family's at the Hu's tonight, so we'd have the place to ourselves."

"Don't make me feel worse than I already do." Her tender kiss told him exactly where she'd rather be. "Besides, you need to rest. I'd feel guilty if I put you in the hospital just to satisfy my own selfish needs."

"I can think of worse ways to go."

Her brilliant smile sent a pleasant chill through him. "There will be time for that when you're better."

Watching her dress was painful, like stealing beauty from the room one garment at a time.

"Take care of yourself," Tim said while she gathered her soup thermos. "Chances are you caught whatever bug I have."

"I know." She gave him a long, luscious kiss that tempted him to pull her back into bed. "It was worth it. I'll call you later."

The chills returned shortly after Jody left, and Tim guiltily found himself missing her body heat more than her embrace.

Sleep was long in coming. When it did, fevered dreams featuring Conway made him toss and turn. Conway was first sad, then he began yelling, and eventually came to blows with Tim for stealing his girl. He became more and more enraged, cutting him with knives, breaking bones, punching out his teeth.

Tim woke screaming. Conway was nowhere to be seen, but the pain persisted, effusing his entire body with an agony he'd never imagined. He reached for his phone to call emergency services, sure that he was dying. A spasm caused him to knock it from the dresser, where it clattered to the other side of the room.

Tim curled into a ball. He couldn't have said how long he spent writhing, screaming, wishing for an end to the unbearable suffering — hours? Days?

Finally, it faded.

Tim crawled to retrieve his cell phone and hit the power button.

The bright screen was like staring into the sun. He shielded his eyes and fumbled to turn it back off.

Not good. I've got to get to a hospital.

Tim scrambled out of his pajamas to dress.

That's when he caught his reflection in the dresser mirror. Pale, venous skin made him look like the walking dead.

No, no, no … Don't tell me I'm a freakin' zombie!

He rushed to get a closer look. Large black eyes, and —

"Ow!" His tongue pricked on something sharp. Tim pulled his lip up, and nearly fell over when he saw his own sharp canines.

Not … not a zombie, then. This can't be happening!

But it was hard to deny what was right in front of him. Being a vampire would also explain his earlier thirst for blood.

Oh God … Jody!

Tim hit the power button on his phone again, squinting in anticipation, and was happy to be able to read the screen this time. He punched her number and said a silent prayer.

Please, please, please tell me I didn't turn her into a vampire, too ...

"Can't get enough of me now that you've had a taste, huh?" Jody's tone was pleasant and teasing.

That's so not funny, Tim thought, recalling his rapture while suckling her wound.

"Hey Jo, sorry to interrupt your dinner. How ... how are you feeling?"

"My legs are a little sore," she said with a quiet laugh. "But other than that, I'm fine. Is that why you called?"

"Ah ... sort of. Look, I really need to talk to you. In person. Tonight."

"Tim, I told you, Mom will kill me if —"

"I know, Jo. Believe me, I wouldn't ask if it wasn't urgent. Blame me. Tell her your annoying friend is having a nervous breakdown or something."

It won't be far from the truth.

Silence fell, followed by a sigh. "This had better be *Apocalypse* important, because if it turns out to be a booty call, you're a dead man."

Dead man ...

He winced at the irony. "Let's meet at the workshop. And ... bring Conway."

"Tim! I told you, I'll handle him. Tomorrow."

"No, it's not that. It's ..." *Much, much worse.* "Just bring him along, okay? You'll see why when you get there."

"You're starting to freak me out."

"Me too. See you soon?"

"Yeah, I'll borrow the car and ... and pick up Conway on the way over."

The phone went dead. Tim stared at it for a minute, then finished dressing. He topped off his outfit with a large hoodie he'd received last Christmas. It was gaudy, but the oversized hood obscured his face, and it had big pockets in which to hide his pasty hands.

It would have to do. He pulled his hood up and hurried out of the house.

•   •   •

Tim arrived at the workshop well ahead of the others. He was a pacing, nervous wreck by the time they arrived.

"Jo!" he said from the depths of his hood. "Are you still feeling all right?"

"Fine." Jody cast a furtive glance at Conway. "Now, are you going to tell us why the hell you dragged us out here?"

Conway didn't seem to notice her discomfort. "Yeah, there's a juicy steak waiting for me at home. It's never as good reheated."

"Yeah, I'm sorry, guys. It's ... probably easier to show you." Tim pulled his hood back and bared his teeth.

They gasped, eyes wide.

Conway was the first to recover. "Good one," he said, breaking into a smile. "You had me going there for a second. That's one hell of a makeup job. Did your sister help —"

"It's real, and that's not even the worst part." Tim grabbed their hands and put them to his still chest.

Jody swallowed, looking nearly as pale as he did. "Th-there's nothing. And you're so cold!"

"Like you just walked out of the refrigerator," Conway said, his expression unreadable.

"Yeah, and I'm ... hungry. Really hungry. And the problem is, I know exactly what I want to eat."

Conway winced. "Brains?"

"Blood," Jody said softly. "That's why you were sucking on my cut earlier. I thought you were just being kinky —" She clamped a hand over her mouth, cheeks burning red.

That got Conway's attention. He looked between them, frowning. Tim could see the wheels turning in his head.

"Wait ... Jody, are you the vampire who turned him?" Conway put a hand to her cheek. He peeled her lips and examined her teeth. "You look normal. Feel normal. I don't get it."

They both stared, mouths open, until Tim recovered enough to stammer, "No, Conway, we, uh ..."

"I slept with Tim," Jody said. "This afternoon. I'm sorry, i-it shouldn't have happened this way, but we were in his room, and things just sort of ... escalated."

Conway flopped onto the couch, rubbed his face, and sighed. "Guess I shouldn't be surprised."

"What are you talking about?" Tim said. "Aren't you angry?"

"A little. A heads-up would have been nice, but ... let's face it, you guys make a better couple than she and I did. I figured it was just a matter of time."

Jody sat delicately on the other end of the couch. "You're being awfully understanding about this."

"I'd say we have bigger problems right now." Conway looked at them with the most serious expression Tim can remember seeing on the big man. "First, if Jody didn't turn Tim" — she shook her head emphatically — "then who was it? Did anyone with especially sharp teeth bite you lately?"

"No."

"Positive?"

Tim threw a wadded piece of paper at him. "I'm pretty sure I'd remember some ghoul sinking their fangs into me!"

"I don't know," Conway said, looking pensive. "Dracula had some sort of mind control power, didn't he? Maybe they bit you and made you forget."

"Why would they do that?" Jody said. "No, most vampire fiction agrees that you have to drink a vampire's blood to become one."

Tim rubbed his mouth, eyes distant. "How much?"

"Depends. Some claim one drink is enough, others say you have to die with a vampire's blood in your veins."

"The waitress," Tim said.

They looked at him quizzically.

"I was splattered all over when they shot her, and some of it got in my mouth."

"That makes perfect sense!" Conway jumped off the couch, pacing excitedly. "Uncle Hal said she was out for a few weeks on medical leave — some blood disease she was being treated for, but get this: When she returned, she was a total powerhouse, doing the work of three waitresses without breaking a sweat."

"And she wore those funky sunglasses when she walked into the restaurant," Jody said, "even though it was dark out."

"I can see why," Tim said. "Even the streetlights make me squint."

"I didn't notice any pointy teeth on her, but then, I wasn't really looking," Conway said. "All-in-all, I'd say we have a pretty good idea who turned you."

"Only problem is she's dead!" Tim plopped into a rolling chair and spun around in circles.

"I don't see an issue," Conway said with a shrug.

Jody whacked his arm. "What are you talking about, meathead? How's he supposed to learn the ropes?"

"What's there to know?" Conway counted on his fingers. "Drink blood. No sunlight. Don't eat garlic. Keep away from holy water. Easy!"

"But what if I don't want to be a bloodsucker! You guys smell so good … I almost bit four people on the bus ride. I had to get off a few stops early so I didn't go crazy."

"Then I'd say you haven't thought it through, pal."

Jody crossed her arms. "Do I have to say 'meathead' again?"

"Vampires are supposed to be super-strong and lightning-quick, like Uncle Hal said Anne was when she returned. Have you tried lifting a car or anything?"

"No," Tim said. "I've been too busy trying not to eat everyone!"

Conway walked over to the desk and gathered a few of Tim's recent projects.

"What are you —"

"Catch!"

Conway threw five components up at the same time, four of which had taken Tim weeks to get right. Tim jumped from his chair and snatched every one of them out of the air.

"Are you crazy? Those took me …" His words died when he saw Jody staring wide-eyed.

Conway smiled like the happiest salesman in the world. "And Tim is hungry right now. Imagine what he'll be able to do once he's eaten."

"Speaking of …" Jody took a tentative step forward. "D-do you need to eat?" She pulled her collar down with trembling fingers, exposing her luscious neck.

As had happened several times on the way over, Tim's canines extended of their own accord. A tart taste filled his mouth.

Next thing he knew, his fangs were buried deep in her tender flesh.

The most delicious flavor he had ever dreamed of flowed down his throat, filling the aching void in his stomach. Tim drank in large gulps, relishing every swallow.

It felt like he'd only just begun when strong hands gripped his shoulders.

"Tim, don't forget. She's small."

Tim growled in warning, but a trickle of sanity filtered through his ravenous hunger, and he knew Conway was right. With a tremendous effort of will, he unlatched from her neck. Jody fell to the couch with a dreamy smile.

A terrible thought hit Tim like a truck. "Oh God, what if … what if she turns into a vampire, too? We still don't know for sure how this thing spreads."

"Like I said, I can think of worse fates." Conway rolled up his sleeve and tapped the veins on his wrist. "Still hungry, pal?"

This is insane …

They knew next to nothing about what had actually happened to Tim. The vampire theory could be romanticizing an *actual* plague, with repercussions far beyond …

Conway's veins derailed his thinking. Feeling as if he were in a trance, Tim raised the big man's arm to his mouth and drank, putting Conway in the same stupor as Jody.

An hour later, the effects of his bite appeared to be wearing off. Talking to his friends during that time had been amusing, as if they were stoned out of their minds, but they both seemed healthy.

More than healthy, in fact. Jody's bandage had fallen off, and Tim was amazed to see only a faint pink line where the deep gash had been just hours before. The bite marks were but a memory.

Jody held her head with a groan. "I … I need water."

Tim grabbed bottles from the mini fridge and handed one to each, which they quickly drank.

"Tim, we need to talk to someone at Z-Tech," Jody said. "Anne was the CEO's girlfriend, right? They must be involved somehow."

"No way," Conway said. He ambled to the fridge and grabbed another bottle. "We'd be asking for trouble, trust me."

"But what if they can reverse it? If they have a cure, that'd be nice to know."

Tim nodded. "A few details would help as well."

"No." Conway stretched dramatically. "Let's say they're involved, or responsible, even. Maybe it's a top-secret experiment they've invested billions into. What are they going to do when they find out their cash-cow is in the hands of some kid?"

"'Experiment' implies that it's unstable," Jody said. "All the more reason we should get their help."

"You think they'd let that waitress work in a crowded public place if she wasn't in top condition? No, they let her out because it's working. She was cleared to live and interact with normal people, or I'll eat my shorts. But that doesn't mean they'd let Tim run free. Maybe Anne is a prototype."

"Which means they might use me as the guinea pig," Tim said.

They were in conspiracy theory territory, Tim knew, but Conway had made a disturbing point. Tim had left the gory details out of his conversation with Mark Suther, concerned that a graphic description of Anne's chest erupting in a fountain of blood would be more upsetting than helpful, so there was a good chance they didn't know Tim had been contaminated. To Jody's point, Z-Tech may have a lot to offer, but if not … once he came out, there would be no going back.

Several childhood comics went through his head, each starring a hero on the run from the government organization who created them — organizations who would stop at nothing to recover their valuable asset.

It didn't sound like a fun way to live.

Jody appeared to be thinking the same. She nodded grimly. "So, what do we do then? Keep Tim locked up in here? Let him feed off us while we keep hydrated?" Her scowl said what she thought of that. "I mean, what do we tell his family?"

"Tim's a big boy," Conway said, clapping him on the shoulder. "It's high time he flew the nest and moved in with his two best friends. Like tomorrow."

Tim shrugged him off. "I can't afford an apartment, genius. That's why I live with my parents."

"And what's this 'we' business?" Jody propped herself on an elbow. "I'm in the same boat as Tim, plus I have no desire to live with two guys who don't clean up after themselves."

"I'm a tidy roommate who not only cooks but also does laundry," Conway said. "As for housing … I have the perfect place. And don't worry about rent, because I already own it."

Jody chucked a pillow at him. "What the hell are you talking about? Last I checked, you live with your parents, too."

"My folks bought me a house in the City as a graduation present, but I haven't moved into it because living with them is easier."

Head reeling, Tim paced their small space. "So I say goodbye to my family, move in with you guys, then … what?"

Conway smiled. "That, my dear friends, is where things get *really* interesting."

The intense gleam in Conway's eye was so contrary to the laid-back person Tim knew that he wasn't sure if he should celebrate the spark of ambition Jody claimed he'd been lacking, or run in terror from what may be a complete disaster.

He had an uneasy feeling they were headed for both.

18

THE MASTER VAMPIRE

ANNE HAD READ BOOKS where characters were completely isolated for long periods. The side effects were harrowing enough in print, but it was quite another thing to experience them first-hand. Every noise in the distance and every shadow under the door held significance — a reminder that life existed outside her cell. She had no measure for the passage of time, not even a heartbeat to count the seconds, giving her new appreciation for the saying that silence is deafening.

Chained spread-eagle to the wall as she was, Anne couldn't move beyond a limited flexing of muscles and turning her head, all of which she did constantly to release her restless energy.

To occupy her mind, Anne first tried using her implant. Unlike herself, Mark could operate his without keywords, but she hadn't asked him for lessons yet — a fact she now regretted. She concentrated in every way she could imagine to get the implant to respond, with the hope of composing a message to her friends. If the implant heard her, it kept the information to itself. A monster headache eventually made her give up.

She hummed for a while, then sang until her throat dried out. Even her dry coughs were a comfort of sorts. She counted the echoes from the concrete walls until her sensitive ears could hear no more, then coughed louder to see if she could up the count.

Eventually, she ran out of sensory games, so her mind drifted back to her friends. Were they looking for her? Had they heard from Charlie? Was *he* looking for her? How was Zima holding up? Was Doris driving everyone crazy? Had Mark invented a new sensor that would find her, even this far underground?

Her imagination played these questions out as short films with happy endings: Yes, they had called the Army, Navy, Air Force, and Marines to find her. Charlie was not only fine, but leading the search, kicking down doors and turning over every rock. Zima was worried but stalwart; she had located their secret headquarters, disabled their operatives in four-point-six seconds, and was interrogating them now for information that would soon lead to Anne's rescue. Doris had started a public campaign rallying the citizens of San Francisco together in a tireless door-to-door search to find her best friend. Mark had stowed a new invention on NASA's latest rocket. It was hurling through the atmosphere, destined for a geosynchronous orbit. Any minute, it would start collecting data from around the world that would allow them to pinpoint her location.

In truth, Anne had no idea what geosynchronous meant, but it sounded science-y.

She nearly cried in joy when the door squealed open. She didn't care who it was, so long as they would talk to her. It turned out that Calum, Don, and Almos were the lucky winners.

Almos was first in. Calum and Don hung back with their weapons ready, as before.

"How are your wounds, my dear Anne?" Almos said.

Anne flexed her silver-injured areas. "A little sore, but I think I'm okay. Almos, please tell me … How many days has it been?"

His bemused smile irked her. "It's been twelve whole hours, and you have lived to tell the tale."

"W-what? No! It feels like a week at least!"

"I would show you, if my pocket watch still worked, but I have no reason to deceive you."

"That's crazy. And they lock prisoners in solitary confinement for days at a time?"

"Longer. Now, imagine lying in a tomb, many stories below the earth, for decades on end."

Her eyes grew wide. "You did that?"

"On several occasions throughout history, and will do so again if we are successful here."

"Who are you?"

Aside from a perfect fashion match for Cappa …

"The reason for your predicament, and this city's, I'm afraid," Almos said. "I am the highest living order of our kind. I was woken prematurely" — he glared at Don — "and before I could reach another underground sanctuary, I was forced to sire another. The authorities intervened, however, and I sent him away before I learned his identity, intent on meeting him later. It would have worked, but thankfully these fine folks captured me before we met up."

"Sorry, I-I'm still confused. Who forced you? Who are these guys? Why'd they wake you up? Why haven't they chained you up like me? And why are you glad to be a captive?"

Calum stepped closer, his sympathetic eyes a sharp contrast to the pistol trained on her chest. "We can't answer all your questions, lass, I'm sorry. If you escape, your sire will make you tell all, and that would put my boys at risk."

His boys …

Calum's concern for his people made him a poor fit for the head of an evil espionage operation, but then, Anne didn't have a lot of experience beyond her Jayne Madison novels.

And I'm pretty sure the author, Georgette Parker, didn't, either.

"I will answer the first and last," Almos said. "If anything will make you more cooperative, it is likely those. I was compelled to sire another by something I refer to as the Entity, for it has no name of its own that I am aware of, and neither do I believe it human, even relative to you or me. It has but one intention, and that is to grow the number of our kind."

"Like world domination? That doesn't make sense. I mean, if everyone's a vampire, then who would they feed on?" The logistics of vampires running the world were unimaginable, especially given their sensitivity to light. Anne pictured a world of human cattle ranches and shuddered.

"Not everyone," Calum said. "Almos says this Entity has a specific number of vampires in mind."

"Only once did I come close to achieving that number," Almos said. "It was sometime in the thirteenth century, and that was when I glimpsed pieces of its larger goal. They were imaginations of our world, yet not our world. A cold place of endless night where strange creatures roamed amidst alien foliage, with not a single human to be found."

Anne could only stare.

Calum scowled. "You get what he's saying, lass? If this thing has its way, there may not be a place for any of us *anywhere,* vampire or no."

"But ... how do you know this thing isn't just dreaming? Or that you're crazy? How is it going to accomplish all that? Last I checked, there are still a lot of people on this planet, and I doubt they'll give it, or themselves, over willingly."

I know four people in particular who'll have a thing or two to say before they let some mystery being destroy civilization as we know it.

"Excellent points," Almos said, "and that is where my case falls short. I have neither seen nor met this Entity, nor do I have any inclinations of how it will accomplish its dream. It exists in my head, just as a normal vampire sire would, but its thoughts are unlike any vampire's mind I have ever touched. It communicates by image and intention, though there is something very foreign in the way it thinks. Whatever it is, it is almost certainly not like you or me."

"Am I interrupting?"

Everyone turned at Zane's voice from the doorway.

"I didn't call for you," Calum said with a growl.

Zane's puppet-smile snapped into place. "My employer — and ultimately *yours* — would like to be kept in the conversation, and has asked me to be the information conduit. Therefore, I shall remain here until the interrogation concludes."

Ultimately yours?

"Zane doesn't work for you?" Anne said to Calum.

"None of your business, lass," Calum said, but his hard stare at the android — Zane had to be an android! — told her she was right. All traces of compassion vanished when Calum turned back to her. "Almos' story has a few holes, but I'm not willing to bet the world that he's wrong. We've had scant luck tracking the bloodsuckers, let alone capturing one before you. So as of now, you're our only key into their network. If we let Almos go topside to sniff them out, that Entity will snatch him up in no time."

"With my knowledge of this organization and their defenses," Almos said, "I would be forced to bring a sizable vampire army down on their heads. The denizens of this place wouldn't survive the night."

Calum moved to Almos' side. Anne was struck by the likeness between the two.

It faded when Calum's pistol pointed once again at her chest. "So I'll ask the same question as yesterday, and hope there's more sense in that pretty head of yours this time. Who sired you?"

Anne was still wary of their intent, but in truth, she didn't have much information on William anyway. If he'd eluded her resourceful friends at Z-Tech for this long, Anne doubted her captors would get much further. "His name is William Taplin. And before you ask, I have no idea where he is, nor how to find him."

"Tall fellow?" Almos said. "Gray eyes, sandy hair, muscular build? Bit of a chip on his shoulder?"

"If by that you mean 'major asshole,' then yes, that describes him."

Almos scratched his chin with a puzzled look, but it was quickly replaced with his quirky smile. "That is the gentleman I sired."

"'Asshole,'" Anne said. "Say it with me ..."

"You have no clue where your sire might be?" Calum said. "You're bonded to him, so you must at least know his vicinity."

Anne shook her head. "We don't get along very well, if you hadn't guessed. He shut me out a while ago, and, apart from the occasional fantasy of breaking his neck, I try not to think of him, either."

Calum looked to Almos, who nodded. "What she says is possible, but ..."

"Can you at least tell us their numbers?" Calum said to Anne.

"I wish. When he shut me out, their presences vanished as well."

Calum's gun was suddenly at her temple, cold steel biting with every shake of his trembling hand. "You're only alive because we thought you'd be useful! Consider that before you answer the next question. How many vampires live in that factory of yours?"

"N-none."

He ground the barrel into her skull. "Liar! That blonde tart you're always fawning over —"

Anne snapped her fangs at him and growled with such ferocity that everyone in the room jumped back.

"*Leave her the fuck alone!*"

"Can't do that," Calum said, regaining some of his composure. "There are two ways this story can end, lass. Either the vampires win, and the world ends in darkness, or we cull the threat now by reducing their numbers back down to one. Perhaps not even that." He gave Almos a guilty glance, but the master vampire simply nodded.

Anne gulped. Understandably, their culling plan didn't include leaving any vampires alive. Even her.

It wasn't the first time Anne had considered the necessity of her own death to end the vampire plague. As long as even one vampire lived, the threat to humanity would never truly be over. Although Charlie and Zima would never admit it, Anne knew she had been living on borrowed time from the moment William had made her drink his blood. However, it was one thing to contemplate her fate in the comfort of her loved ones at Z-Tech, and quite another when chained to the wall, facing her soon-to-be executioners. The good news, if she could call it that, was the likelihood of Calum's success in the foreseeable future was slim, which meant Anne may yet live to see her loved ones again.

"My girlfriend is not a vampire," Anne said with measured calm. "Nor is anyone else at the factory, so leave them out of this."

"You must think me daft to —"

"Did you feel her skin? Her warmth?"

Calum's silent scowl indicated he hadn't tried.

"You've caught the wrong bloodsucker, Calum, because not only do I know squat about William or his operations, I'm just as concerned about the vampire threat as you are. We're actively fighting them — and, by the sound of it, doing a much better job than you. The best thing you can do for the cause, and for yourselves, is to find a vampire William hasn't ostracized and let me go before my friends figure out where I am."

"Is that a threat?"

"A warning. The last time someone kidnapped and tortured me — that's right, you're not the first — was when William turned me into a vampire. My friends went through hell to find me, and believe me when I say it didn't end well for my kidnappers."

"Sounds like bluster, lass. I think you know I can't risk you walking out that door without more to go on."

One glance at Zane steeled her. Anne would never align Z-Tech with the monsters who'd enslaved Zima, or hand them any information that might give them an advantage.

Or allow them to discover Zima's true identity.

Anne would let the world end first.

The best she could do for now was hold her peace and wait for a rescue. She imagined Zima barreling down the halls, guns blazing in a glorious rescue that left not a single one of her captors alive.

She shuddered. Her gory daydream wouldn't be far from reality, if Zima had her way. Surprisingly, the thought of seeing Calum dead left a sour taste. He'd shot her three times now, and even despite that, she sensed no malice behind his ever-present frown, only the desire to do the right thing for the world.

If only we'd met under different circumstances …

But they hadn't. She was a prisoner, him her captor, and his organization posed a threat to those she held dearest.

Meeting Calum's gaze, Anne pressed her lips firmly, and kept them that way.

"That's a shame." Calum holstered his weapon. "We could have helped each other, but I guess it doesn't matter. We may not need you anyway."

"W-what do you mean?" Anne said when he turned to leave.

So much for my vow of silence.

"For weeks we'd been trying to catch a vampire, with nothing to show for it," Calum said. "Then Zane steps off the plane. Less than three hours later, we have you, and that was before we crafted silver bullets for his odd machine pistols. Now that he's properly armed, I can only imagine what a whole night roaming the streets will yield."

Calum's tone hinted he wasn't as excited about the idea of Zane running loose as he let on.

He nodded to Don. For an uncomfortable second, Anne thought it was the signal to finish her off, but instead they filed out and bolted the door, leaving her in relative darkness to think about their strange conversation.

On a whim, Anne began counting her foot taps on the concrete. It was difficult to say how close each tap was to a second, given her lack of heartbeat for rhythm, but she had hit nine thousand four hundred and eighty-one when the door opened again, this time admitting a lone figure who quietly closed the door behind him.

"Good evening," Almos said softly.

"Almos! I, ah, don't suppose you brought any of the delicious red stuff with you?"

His puzzled look from earlier returned. "I didn't think you would be hungry, since you fed earlier this morning and have been chained to a wall."

"Yeah ... I need to eat more frequently than other vampires."

"I should say so. I, or any of our kind, could survive for years immobile as you are. Most of your human hosts are out for the evening, but I'll ask the remaining guard if they will open their veins for you."

"Sorry to be a pest. If that makes me a rude houseguest, I'll happily pack up and go."

"Would that it was in my power, Anne Perrin. You don't seem the threat Calum presumes you to be."

Anne sighed. "I can't really blame him. I wouldn't let me go, either. And *please* don't tell him I said that."

"You may safely confide in me. That is, in fact, why I have gone through great pains to visit you alone, against Calum's orders."

"I see. Trying to pump me for information, good-cop, bad-cop style?"

"It would appear so," Almos said with a chuckle, "though perhaps not for the reasons you suspect."

"All right, good cop, give me your spiel."

"Very well. To begin with, everything about you is wrong."

"Flattery will get you everywhere, smooth talker. Are you going to compliment the vivid blue of my varicose veins next?"

"I meant it in the best possible way. What I said earlier is true: vampires are natural, patient predators, able to make a statue seem restless by comparison, which is also how we conserve energy when food is scarce. Yet you squirm in your restraints as though pure sugar flows in your veins."

"So I'm out of the Bloodsuckers Club because I fidget? You guys are strict."

"Your energy," Almos said. "Your tolerance for silver. You heal faster than most, which is saying something. Your mannerisms. The disdain you show toward your sire. I spoke with Calum after you fed from him. He remembered everything that transpired, which he should not have, and he smiled more in that hour than in the weeks I've known him combined. Even the effects of your bite are different, and … if it is not too forward, did I hear correctly that you are in a relationship?"

Anne pursed her lips, but decided there was no point in lying, since anyone who had spent any time in the diner would know who her love interests were. "Two, in fact."

"You meant what you said about them not being vampires?"

"Yes! I'm the only monster among them. Lucky me."

Where the hell is he going with this?

"And you truly love them?"

Anne ground her teeth, willing back her tears. "With all of my unbeating heart."

Almos smiled, his black eyes gleaming. "That is both curious and wonderful."

"They are pretty great, I've got to —"

"You misunderstand me. A vampire's first and only loyalty is to their sire. Always. The need eclipses family, friends, children, and humanity itself. New vampires will leave their loved ones without looking back, feed from them if necessary, and live only to serve the whims of their new master."

Anne fell silent while that disturbing thought sank in. William had compelled her, certainly, but she felt not one iota of loyalty to the son-of-a-bitch.

It must be my implant.

Troublesome as it was, she was convinced now more than ever that implanting that computer before she turned into a vampire was the best decision her friends could have made. A sudden thought drew her eyes back to him. "So, what does that mean for you?"

"As the saying goes: it is lonely at the top. I spent many centuries fawning over something I couldn't see, touch, or talk to in any meaningful sense. There was satisfaction in dealing with my direct sirelings, but feelings of adoration move upward with our kind. Even so-called siblings — those who share a common sire — are often more competitive than cooperative, constantly vying for the favor of their master."

"That sounds terrible," Anne said softly.

"It is the worst form of slavery to be bound to a master with the illusion that you have given yourself freely. Fortunately, the long centuries have given me time to reflect, and, in a sense, regain some of my humanity. Unlike William and his line, I care what happens to this planet, and everyone on it."

"Don't take this the wrong way, but if that's true, you were the only vampire on Earth for several decades at least. Why didn't you just, I mean ..."

"Kill myself?" Almos chuckled mirthlessly. "A dozen times over the centuries I set out to do that very thing, but two issues have always held me back. First, we vampires are instilled with instincts not present during our humanity, such as the urge to hunt, and a thirst for blood. Among those, I suspect, is a heightened sense of self-preservation. The few times I had convinced myself that suicide was the correct answer, I was never able to complete the deed, as if some unseen force stayed my hand from delivering the killing blow. The second and perhaps most important reason is doubt."

"Doubt?"

"Yes. The vampire hierarchy works in strange and mystical ways. Despite it being in my head, I know very little about the Entity, or how the very first vampire came to be. Killing myself may simply spawn a new master somewhere else in the world, one who has not regained a sense of humanity, nor shows my restraint. In that case, ending my life would be the same as simply walking to the surface and letting the Entity take me. It may sound like thin rationalization, possibly spurred by my enhanced sense of self-preservation, but it is a risk I have never been willing to bet the fate of the world upon. What I am left with, then, is hiding as best I can, and helping others eliminate the scourge if and when it arises."

"Don't count me as part of the scourge," Anne said. "I'm fighting this thing tooth-and-nail."

"Yes, you nearly bit Calum's gun in half earlier when he threatened your blonde friend. He's lucky to still count five fingers on that hand."

"I told you, I love her."

"And you have made that abundantly clear. I can see it in your eyes."

"You ... you don't think they'll go after her, do you?"

"Unlikely. Calum is dedicated to the cause, but his feet are firmly planted on the ground. Though he may not admit it, I think he believes your story."

Anne lowered her voice to an urgent whisper. "Almos, can you get me out of here?"

"Perhaps," he said quietly. "But I don't think that is the wisest course of action for either of us. It would put a target on your head, and it would also damage the trust I've worked very hard to build with Calum."

"Well, could you get a message out somehow?"

"His quirky smile appeared. "And what would that message say?"

"Just that I'm okay, and not to do anything ... rash."

"You fear your friends will retaliate?"

"I fear Armageddon if they find out where I am and they don't know which side you're on ahead of time. I was putting it mildly when I told Calum that things didn't go well for my former kidnappers."

"So these friends of yours are a force to be reckoned with? Even against Calum's new ace?"

Anne chose her next words carefully. Mark had made it very clear there were things no one outside of Z-Tech should know, and, vampocalypse be damned, Anne wouldn't be the catalyst that brought the rest of the world down on their heads. "Let's just say they're very resourceful, and that Zane won't always be here to guard me."

"It may be a moot point anyway. I can't venture near the surface, and I've no idea how to use those portable telephones they all carry. Do people still write letters?"

"Old people, yes."

"I definitely qualify. Still, I've yet to see a postman visit our cavernous abode."

"Will you at least look into it? This may be hard to believe, but the warning is more for Calum's sake than mine or my friends'. If Zane is who I think he is ..." Anne shook her head. "The people he works for are after one thing: power. And they don't care how many lives they have to destroy to get it."

Almos stroked his chin in thought, a regal gesture if she ever saw one. "Will you tell me why you are so different from other vampires?"

She grimaced, which drew a sigh from him.

"At least you didn't feign ignorance. Very well. Your warning carries weight, so I shall see what I can find, though given the advances of this age, it may take me some time. Please consider my request as well. The information holds more value to me than you realize." He turned at a sound from outside. "I thought them all occupied," he said softly. "Pray they don't see the locks undone."

"Almos, i-it's not that I don't trust you —"

"Trust is an empty vessel best filled by acts of good faith. Let's both see how we may add to it." He listened for a second longer, then slipped out the door.

The locks quietly slid back into place, leaving Anne to muse over his quip. She was amazed at how full her vessel had already become.

19

AN ENEMY IN NEED

Bolts squealed open one by one, echoing painfully from the cement walls of Anne's cell. Don entered, bearing a cup of her favorite crimson repast. The smell made her mouth water. Muscles in her gums pushed her canines down, tart venom dripping in anticipation.

Anne kept her mouth closed, however, and masked her excitement. The first time he had brought her meal, she was so hungry that she'd practically snapped the cup from his hand. His revulsion had been understandable, for she'd shared the sentiment once her hunger had been sated.

That was nearly a week ago. Since then, Anne had made every effort to make him feel more comfortable. She pretended she was at a tea party, where Don was her gracious host, and the chains binding her were instead a comfortable Victorian chair.

It was a stretch, even for her vivid imagination, but it beat wallowing, and she suspected her pleasant attitude was the reason for his more frequent visits of late. Better still, he had been staying longer, and seemed almost as desperate for conversation as her.

"Morning, Don," she said with a warm smile, careful to keep her fangs hidden.

"Afternoon."

"Is it? I'll have to request a cell with a window next time."

"Something tells me that would end badly."

"A north-facing view may not be catastrophic."

Don looked thoughtful. "Maybe, if you had a big awning. Have you slept?"

"Not a wink, but thanks for asking."

"I don't know how you do it. Even underground, Almos seems to know exactly when the sun rises, and his eyes don't open until the sun goes down."

"Must be my hummingbird metabolism. How else could I stay model-thin?"

"Calisthenics?"

Anne made a show of flexing her fingers and toes — the only things aside from her head that weren't firmly fixed to the wall. "Whew! What a workout. Seriously, though, your exercise program leaves a lot to be desired. See if I ever book a vacation here again."

"I'll talk to Calum about that," Don said, chuckling. "And don't be hard on yourself. I think you have a great figure."

"Aw, shucks, I bet you say that to all your undead inmates."

"No, I mean it." Don tugged his collar, his polished dome head flushed red. "Anyway, y-you're probably hungry."

Famished, big boy.

The portions were smaller than she was used to, and, despite being completely immobilized, her appetite was as ravenous as ever. Anne's jaw quivered when he lifted the cup to her eager lips, but he pulled back at the last instant — a move so cruel she almost sobbed.

"Anne, I've been meaning to ask ... is it true what they say about a vampire's bite? Can it really cure anything?"

"I-I don't know about 'anything,'" Anne said, trying to keep her eyes from the red deliciousness he so casually waved around. "It heals most injuries pretty quickly, though."

An uncertain, almost bashful look crossed his face. Anne had a sinking feeling she knew why.

"Don, are you sick?"

"Not me," he said to the floor. "My cousin. She … she hit her head a few months ago. The doctors said she might get better, but she still can't walk or talk."

"I'm sorry to hear that," Anne said sincerely. "Does she have someone to take care of her? A husband?"

"She's nine."

Ouch.

"I honestly don't know if it will help, but if you bring her by, I'd be happy to bite her. I can inject my venom without drinking."

"Calum would never allow it," Don said with a sigh. "Even if he did, Zane would tell Orwing, and then we'd all —" Don clamped a hand over his mouth, spilling a few precious drops of her meal.

Anne barely noticed. "Orwing … Is that the name of your organization?"

"No, it's …" He rubbed his head so vigorously she expected it to sparkle. "F-forget I mentioned it. Anyway, I can't bring my cousin here, but I was watching this show about snakes the other day, and it gave me an idea." He pulled a pair of rubber-capped test tubes from his pocket. "They used something like these to collect the venom. The handlers made the snakes bite the top, and the venom came out the bottom."

She started to object to being compared to a snake, but her argument died when she realized both she and snakes were cold-blooded, fanged, predators, and enjoyed a spot of warmth.

Great.

Don shuffled his feet. "What do you say?"

A nine-year-old girl …

Captive or not, the thought of a little girl lying in a hospital bed while her parents worried if they'd ever hear their daughter's voice again, or see her running in the yard with the other kids, was more than she could bear. Anne opened her mouth and bared her dagger-like fangs as non-threateningly as she could.

Don's gratitude was palpable. He set her meal on the floor and carefully pushed a tube to each of her canines until the tips punctured the thin rubber membranes. As she had with Zima on her first outing as a vampire, Anne concentrated on the sensation of liquid passing through the hollows of her teeth, and soon heard the tip-tap drops of her venom against the glass. She continued until she felt she had no more to give. When he pulled them free, they both stared in wonder at the tubes brimming with crystal-clear venom.

"Jeez, where'd all that come from?"

"Beats me," Anne said. "I slept through vampire anatomy class."

His chuckle choked off in a tearful sniff. "Thanks, Anne. I don't know how, but I'll figure out a way to slip it to her."

"Go easy on the dosage. My venom packs a wallop that other vampires' don't, kind of like morphine. You wouldn't want her to overdose."

"I'll be careful, I promise." He carefully tucked the tubes into a jacket pocket and turned to leave.

Anne cleared her throat, staring mournfully at the cup of red liquid at her feet.

"Oh! Sorry. Here, let me get that."

Try as she might, Anne couldn't help moaning with every sip. She never asked where her daily ration came from, grateful only that they hadn't missed a day since her capture. When the cup was empty — far too soon for her liking — she desperately lapped up the last straggling drops. Don paled, but held the cup steady until she had sponged everything her tongue could reach.

He made a sour face. "How do you stomach that stuff? I think I'd throw up."

"Before that asshole William made me drink his blood, I would have said the same, but after I woke up, suddenly it was the most amazing thing I'd ever tasted."

"But it's human blood! Tasty or not, how can you justify feeding from another person?"

"You really want to know? It might spoil this good thing we have going."

He frowned, but nodded.

"Two reasons. First — and this is the one you'll hate — it tastes even better from the source. If the blood in that cup was a lobster, then drinking from a person is the garlic butter that turns a plain lobster into a truly heavenly experience."

Don swallowed, sweat glistening on his bald pate. "You see me as a lobster?"

"With all the trimmings. Imagine the best steakhouse you've ever eaten at, where that sizzling, wood-fired aroma makes you drool the second you walk in. That's what everyone smells like to me."

"That's … really disturbing."

"I said you wouldn't like it, but it's the second reason that leaves me with a clear conscience. My bite doesn't hurt anyone. In fact, I leave them with a smile, and healthier than they were before I bit them."

His brow furrowed into a skeptical frown.

Anne shrugged, one of the few gestures she could manage in her tight restraints. "Ask Calum if you don't believe me, but either way, it's playing the cards you're dealt, right? William turned me into a vampire. It sucks, but I'm still here, and I don't kill people like some mindless beast. In fact, the only people I've killed so far are other vampires. You should thank me. Or pay me. Do you guys use a ladder reward system? I've already earned the Hawaiian vacation, and I'm angling for the new car."

It was only a partial lie. While Anne had indeed hunted a few times, Zima preferred to stay home with her at Z-Tech. Even when they did hunt, Zima insisted on delivering the killing blow herself. Not including the vampires she shot the night William had kidnapped her from Doris' apartment, Anne's personal kill count was a big, fat zero.

But Don didn't need to know that, and the salesy quip brought a smile back to his face, as she'd hoped it would.

"Not that I know of," Don said, "but maybe I can talk one of the boys into an extra blood donation for you."

Better than nothing.

Anne decided to push her luck. "You know, my venom also increases blood production. If they let me bite them, they'll recover faster, and I guarantee a smile on their faces or their money back."

"I bet you'd have them lined out the door, which is probably why Calum forbade it the night you bit him."

Of course he did.

"Can't blame a starving girl for trying," Anne said.

"You're still hungry?"

"I could polish off a few more of those cups, for sure."

"So ... what would happen if I released you from those irons? Would you drain me in a feeding craze?"

"No," Anne said carefully. It was the first time he'd mentioned the idea of releasing her, and she didn't want to scare him away. "I'm not that desperate, thanks to your regular visits, plus I've learned self-control since becoming a vampire a month ago."

"I guess you'd have to, working at a diner like that."

"It became easier after the first night." *Stick to the release-me topic, Anne.* "Don, what are they going to do with me?"

He fiddled with his jacket. "I ... I don't know, exactly, but they want you alive. I heard that from Calum and Almos on separate occasions. Even from Zane."

"What did Zane say?"

"That you're to remain in this cell, healthy and unharmed. Direct orders from ..." He cursed softly again.

"Orwing?"

Don cast his eyes about and nodded.

"Is that who Zane works for?"

A nod.

"But you and Calum aren't part of Orwing, are you?"

"No."

Anne sighed with relief. "Don, do you know if Orwing ... made Zane?"

"I think so. They're some high-tech company on the other side of the world."

"What else do you know about them?"

He eyed her suspiciously.

"You don't have to tell me, Don, but ... do yourself a favor and do some digging. Quietly."

"You think Calum wouldn't know all about who funds us?"

"Does he know why they want me unharmed? Do the other vampires you've captured get the same courtesy?"

His silence told her everything.

"I doubt it's because of my sassy charm," Anne said. "Just give it some thought, okay? And watch your back."

Don paced in a circle for a minute before meeting her eyes again. "You're going to get me in so much trouble ..."

She couldn't help laughing at the big man's puppy dog look. "I knew you'd see reason! I'd hug you if I could."

"You've done enough," he said with a smile, patting the pocket containing her venom. "I'd better go. I've got a special delivery to make."

"Let me know how it goes!"

The door closed, bolts slammed into place, and the loneliness returned.

But not for long. As usual, time was difficult to measure, but she guessed it was well after sunset when Don slipped back in.

He skipped up and threw his arms around her neck in a gleeful hug.

Anne laughed. "The venom worked, I take it?"

"She was talking within an hour! By the time I left, the same girl who could barely move her head was jumping up and down with her mom and dad. It's ... it's the most magical thing I've ever seen."

The tears in his eyes matched her own. For a moment, Anne forgot all about her prison. Her mind was dancing with the little girl and her parents in the hospital room they would soon be leaving, back to a life she couldn't have had if it weren't for Don's courage.

And for Anne. The monster everyone here feared, including herself sometimes, had just changed the course of a child's life in a way no one else could have. "Don, if you don't mind me asking, what's her name?"

"Rose. And if I ever have a girl of my own, I'll name her Anne, you can bet on it."

Rose ...

Anne said the name over and over. She closed her eyes and pictured a little girl as delicate and beautiful as her namesake. Running. Playing. Drawing.

Living.

Joyful tears spilled in an endless stream, infecting them both with giddy laughter. When he could finally speak again, Don composed himself and bid her goodnight among a barrage of thank yous.

This time, Mr. Loneliness kept his distance.

•   •   •

The next morning, Anne was surprised by another visitor: a mousy young man in preppy clothes who introduced himself as Steve.

Anne became nervous when he crept up to her. She readied a scream in case he tried to molest her, but he hastily produced a pair of rubber-capped tubes identical to Don's, then explained about his mother, who'd been struggling with cancer for the last several years. It had finally spread to distant organs, and the doctors said it was only a matter of time now. Don had apparently conveyed the story of his cousin's miraculous recovery when he discovered Steve's misfortune.

Anne agreed to help, but claimed her earlier donation had depleted her venom, and she would need more blood to replenish her reserves. It was mostly true: she *had* depleted her reserves, but, given her crazy physiology, it would be no surprise if her venom had already replenished.

She was hungry, however, and Steve hadn't endeared himself to her the way Don had, so she regarded this as more of a barter than charity.

Her bid worked. Steve didn't hesitate to offer his arm, nor did Anne hesitate to take it. Once she drank her fill — a far sight more than the dinky cups Don had been bringing — she gave a happy sigh, then held up her end of the deal by filling each tube until her fangs would give no more. She warned that she had no idea whether her venom would work on cancer.

His desperate eyes said he didn't care. His mother was out of options, and this mystical elixir gave hope where doctors said there was none.

Anne sincerely wished him well, then he slipped out and secured her door once again.

Not an hour later, the bolts slid open, admitting another person she'd never met. Lance had a brother who'd been living with cerebral palsy his entire life. His health was deteriorating, and the doctors had already recommended hospice to make his last months on this Earth comfortable at home with his family. Anne didn't know what cerebral palsy was, nor if her venom would help in the least, but she made Lance the same offer to trade venom for blood. He immediately rolled up his sleeve, but she stopped him, asking that he pay her tomorrow instead, without telling him it was because she was still full from Steve.

She had barely said goodbye to Lance when a woman entered. Beth's best friend had chronic pulmonary disease, no thanks to the Army's use of chemical warfare during her tour overseas. She had deteriorated to the point where she couldn't cross the living room without stopping three times to catch her breath. At this point, Anne really wasn't sure if she had any venom left to give, but she struck the same bargain and asked Beth to repay her in two days. Anne secreted until her fangs ran dry, and was pleasantly surprised to see each tube filled to the halfway mark. Beth dared to kiss her cheek before leaving. The well-meaning gesture triggered a pang of longing for her Zima.

And so the day continued. Ken had a sister-in-law with severe diabetes that had taken her eyesight. Jake's father had amyotrophic lateral sclerosis, a progressive neurodegenerative disease Anne had never heard of until he called it Lou Gehrig's disease. It was in the final stages, where his respiratory system was shutting down. Nguyen's aunt had had a stroke that put her in a nursing home at thirty-six — Anne's age. Anne gave and gave and gave, asking each person to return a day after the prior's appointment, until she had meals lined up through next week.

The bolts slid open again. Like a lactating mother, the sound reflexively triggered her venom secretion, but Almos' pale face meant her overworked glands could finally rest.

"I hear you've had a few visitors," he said.

"It's been like Grand Central Station all day. Do they bother you this much?"

"Not at all. I intimidate them, for some reason."

"Curse of being the master vampire. Plus you're not chained up."

"True. Were they troublesome? I can easily put a stop if they have abused Calum's blind eye to their unauthorized petitions."

Anne sagged. "He knows, huh?"

"As I've said before, Calum is no fool, but neither is he heartless. I suspect more than a few of his rank joined solely because of whispers of the healing power of our bite."

"I guess they got more than they bargained for. Don described it as a small-scale war out there."

"Perhaps. I believe the puppet man is doing most of the work."

"Have there been any casualties on our side?"

Almos grinned, and Anne immediately realized her slip.

"Well ... we're kind of on the same team," she said. "'Enemy of my enemy' and all that?"

"It depends on who you mean," he said softly. "I have not forgotten your request. I regret that I've had little success getting a message to your friends, but my efforts have borne a different fruit. You know of Orwing?"

She nodded.

"Zane has been their only representative here, but that is about to change. I overheard him and Calum speaking heatedly about Orwing expanding its oversight of this operation."

"Oh, Almos, that can't be good." Anne had no great love for Calum, but his intentions toward humanity seemed pure. She could hardly say the same for Orwing.

"Indeed, and it gets worse. They wish to relocate you."

"But ... where? Why?" She couldn't keep the panic from her voice.

"Calum demanded those same answers. The puppet would not say, only that you were to remain underground until adequate transportation could be arranged."

So very bad ...

Anne had deduced early on that she was still in the San Francisco Bay Area, but if they moved her out of state, or to another country, how long it would take her friends to find her was anyone's guess.

"Almos ..."

"Don't despair. I'll talk to Calum. I don't think he agrees with the decision, either, though for different reasons than you, I'm sure."

"What's going to happen to you?"

"They did not discuss my fate, so I assume I shall remain here."

Anne could understand that logic. Removing her from the earth's protective shielding held little risk, but if the Entity seized

Almos — even for a moment — they could soon be facing William's entire vampire hoard. "I'm sorry."

Almos shrugged. "I've spent many a decade in far worse accommodations, I assure you."

"I know, but ... I just wish things were different. You're a nice guy. You don't deserve an eternity of isolation."

"Your faith in me is appreciated, but for the atrocities I have committed in centuries past, many would say mere isolation is far too kind."

"But it wasn't your fault! You can hardly be blamed for the Entity's influence. And besides, everyone who had a grudge is long dead, right? That's a statute of limitations if I ever heard one."

His quirky smile widened. "I wish I could see myself — or indeed the world — through your eyes, Anne Perrin. It is no wonder your friends would move Heaven and Earth to find you. Farewell, and take heart. I'll return as soon as I have news."

The door closed for the final time that night. Anne tried to summon the warm feelings from earlier, when Don had told her of his cousin's miraculous recovery, but worry of when and where Orwing might relocate her spoiled the effort.

Anne hung her head, tears falling to the concrete below, and said a silent prayer for her friends to find her soon.

20

NEWS

MARK LAID THE COCKTAIL DRESS ON HIS BED NEXT TO DELA, who was patting dry her long red hair with a towel.

"Cappa says this should fit best," Mark said. "It's Anne's, but I doubt she'll mind you wearing it, given the occasion."

Dela sighed at the frilly thing. "It's going to be hard to charm anyone in that, but I guess it'll have to do."

"They won't even notice the dress once they see your radiant smile."

"My enormous boobs, you mean." She grinned at him. "Do you practice that crap in the mirror or something?"

"No, I'm just naturally charming."

ZIMA IS PULLING IN NOW, AND SHE HAS SOME NEWS, Cappa sent. CAN YOU DIAL ME IN WHEN SHE GETS THERE?

A feeling of desperation accompanied her request, and Mark realized with a start that he hadn't spoken to Cappa all day. He grabbed his phone, punched her number, and set it on the dresser.

"Hey, Cappa," Dela said.

"Hey there," Cappa said through the speaker. "Have you tried the dress on?"

"Not yet. I just got out of the shower."

"Can you send me a picture when you do? I-I know it's not your style, but I think the understated tones will call more attention to your hair and eyes, which will be a bonus at a social event like this. Once I see you in it, I can recommend some accessories."

"I, ah, don't have much in the way of accessories. Even shoes are optional at the parties I normally attend."

"You can borrow some of mine, if you like. I have a set of pearl earrings and necklace that should round things out nicely."

"Thanks, Cappa! Once again, you're a lifesaver."

Mark marveled at their almost sisterly conversation. A week ago, before Cappa's only two means of locomotion had left for China, the shoe comment would have spawned a litany of degrading remarks from Cappa and triggered another of their infamous spats. He wasn't sure if the change in attitude was the pair finally warming up to each other, or Cappa's isolation making her desperate to keep everyone happy so they'd want to talk to her.

He suspected the latter, unfortunately, and made a mental note to come up with something to make it easier on the poor disembodied artificial intelligence.

Dela was mostly dressed when they heard Zima's knock. Mark looked at his half-naked girlfriend, who shrugged.

"Go ahead," Dela said. "I've got nothing to hide from the Dark Angel."

Mark rolled his eyes and let her in. As he suspected, Zima gave no acknowledgment of his girlfriend standing in her underwear, nor of him in his boxers and socks.

Does that make us family?

The thought made him shudder. He quickly pulled his dress shirt on.

"Michael Torag has reported that a new vampire faction is operating in the City," Zima said, standing between them.

His fingers froze mid-button. "New faction?"

"Yes. One of his siblings' victims objected to being attacked because she had already been fed upon that night, and not by any of William's vampires."

"And she remembered it?" Dela said.

"Vividly. What puzzled him more was that she described it as an intensely pleasurable experience."

Cappa gasped. "Anne! She's the only vampire I know whose bite leaves you with a smile."

"That was my initial thought, but she described the individual who bit her as an oriental male."

Mark paled. "Didn't you say that kid, Tim, is Chinese?"

"Yes."

"He was there when Anne was shot," Cappa said.

"And the bullets went right through her, from what he described." Mark sat heavily on the bed and pressed his palms to his eyes. "Tim was standing right in front of her. I never asked how close he was, or if he was splattered."

"My God," Cappa said. "That poor kid must have transitioned into a vampire without any idea what was going on."

"Be that as it may, he appears to have adjusted," Zima said. "The victim willingly sought him out. It was an invitation-only affair that she and her escort paid much to attend."

Dela barked a laugh and quickly covered her mouth. "Sorry, I just imagined a B-movie called Bite Club."

"I don't suppose you got an address?" Mark said.

"No, which is fortunate in this case," Zima said. "William has instructed his clans to locate the rogue vampire and bring him in for interrogation. But they do not know his identity or location, nor do they appear to know that Anne's venom is different from their own."

"Which means the timer's ticking," Cappa said. "We've got to beat them to Tim. If he has an active link to Anne, he may be able to lead us to her."

"Precisely my thoughts," Zima said. "It is a remote chance, since her defensive program may respond the same to her sirelings as it does to William and the other Firsts, which would leave Tim incapacitated, but it is the best lead we have had in the week since her disappearance."

"That brings up a question ..." Dela struggled to zip her dress past her bust line. She groaned when Zima yanked it up. "Thanks, Z. Anyway, let's say this rogue vampire is Tim, and Anne is his sire.

Shouldn't William be able to control him like he does everyone else and just order him to come in?"

"I inquired about that. William has closed his mind off to Anne to avoid the detrimental effects of her defensive program. In doing so, he has also closed himself and everyone else off to her entire branch of the hierarchy. It is as though they are no longer part of his lineage."

Dela paused her hairbrush in mid-stroke, eyes soft when she looked at Zima in the mirror. "I hate to bring this up, but ... if no one can sense her, how do we know she's alive?"

"I learned much from Michael Torag tonight," Zima said. "William has experimented with creating gaps in the hierarchy, and its effects. They discovered that orphaned vampires' links are transferred to the deceased vampire's sire."

"So they go to the next-highest vampire in the chain," Dela said. "That's like a mass promotion for everyone in that branch."

"Yes, although I did not ask about the chain-of-command implications of the move. More importantly, since William has not acquired a direct link to the rogue vampire, that means his sire, Anne, must still be alive."

"Zima!" Cappa's scream echoed Mark's frustration. "Why didn't you start with that little revelation?"

Zima blinked at the phone. "I had to first establish a factual base, otherwise you may not have believed me."

Dela grabbed her hand, hopping so vigorously that her bosom threatened to shake loose from the confines of her tight dress. "That's great news! You must be so happy, Z."

"I believe so."

"Come on, your girlfriend's alive! You should be singing, doing cartwheels in the hall or something."

"It is difficult to explain."

Zima flexed the fingers of her free hand. The gesture, Mark had learned, meant she was missing or thinking about Anne, and probably frustrated, which was distressing because she had been doing it much more often of late.

Poor girl.

It was especially true since they hadn't had any luck relieving Zima's sexual frustration. Even the Desire program, while providing pleasure as designed, didn't relieve her core need. Zima was bound to Anne, and only she, it seemed, would do. The result was Zima intermittently suffering periods of intense longing while everyone else could only watch. It was heartbreaking.

At least there may be an end in sight, Mark thought.

"What do you mean, Zima?"

"News that Anne lives does not change my outlook because I have always assumed she was alive. It has merely given me new options in my pursuit."

"Interesting. I didn't peg you for an optimist."

"The assumption was more practicality than a natural bias toward optimism. As I told Cappa, so many of my simulations now involve Anne that I ... I do not know what I would do if she were dead, so I have chosen not to consider it."

Her sentiment struck a chord with Mark. In many ways, it was the mechanical answer he had expected, spoken without emotion or emphasis, yet the underlying tone was different.

She chose not to consider it ...

As logical as she made it sound, Zima was rarely unprepared for anything. Her choice made it clear how attached she had become to Anne, something that was easy to overlook given her lack of emotional expression.

For himself, the news was a tremendous relief. The week's research had yielded more information than he expected — although not necessarily what they wanted to hear. Zima's background search on Calum had revealed little about him as an individual. Born in the Highlands of Scotland, Calum had no criminal records in any of the international databases she'd hacked. He traveled all over the world on business for an international non-profit called Skylight which, as far as they could tell, didn't do much other than promote general well-being.

Some digging into Skylight, however, had confirmed their worst fears. Skylight received large annual donations from Orwing International — the thinly disguised espionage organization who had created Zima, turned her into a killing machine, and ultimately sent her to assassinate Mark and Charlie. The license plate search on the black town car had gone the same direction, leading back to Skylight rather than an individual.

Cappa's research into cyborg activity had a more tenuous link. She'd uncovered two incidents in the past year where a single person had infiltrated major military strongholds: one in Syria, the other in Afghanistan. Each time, the objective appeared to be data theft — similar to Zima's missions during her service with Orwing — and the individual was reported to have taken heavy direct fire without adverse effect.

Mark had also run an IBIS imprint of the shell he found at the scene through NIBIN and a few other international networks who used similar technology. The result had linked the imprint to shells recovered from the Syrian incident, which meant whoever had single-handedly taken out the military installation was now here in San Francisco. That they were involved in the same incident as Calum was too much to call coincidence, and pointed the finger back to Orwing.

Which leads us to tonight's social adventure ...

"At any rate, let it be known that the Dark Angel always triumphs," Dela said. "I've got to admit, your conscripted snitch turned out to be pretty useful. I thought sure that weasel would set a trap for your next visit."

"He did," Zima said.

"Huh?"

"Michael set a trap. I killed eight vampires tonight and took two more of Michael's fingers to get the information I required."

Dela gulped. "Sorry I missed the fun."

"It was necessary," Zima said, missing the sarcasm. "As Cappa stated, we must quickly determine if Tim is the rogue vampire, and if he is not, discover who is."

"All right, I'll call him." Mark grabbed his phone, but Zima stopped him with a hand.

"I shall contact Tim and arrange a meeting. You and Dela should attend the party as planned."

"She's right," Cappa said. "It was just luck that I discovered Alvin Orwing himself was going to be there, and I had to tell some major fibs to get you an invitation. You may not get a one-on-one like this again unless you take him at gunpoint."

"Don't tempt me," Mark said.

"Oh!" Dela clasped her hands with a childish smile. "Can I go along for that one, too? Please, please, please? I'll beat the snot out of him while you ask questions with an intimidating German accent."

Mark sighed and resumed dressing. "Careful what you wish for. If he doesn't cooperate tonight, it may come to that. Minus the accent."

"Are you bringing a gun?"

"I wish. The only people allowed to carry weapons are the guards — and they'll be watching, so be careful what you do. Orwing is only one of many power players at this shindig, and they don't take unnecessary chances. Don't get physical unless your life depends on it."

"In which case I'm screwed, because I can't kick worth a damn in this straitjacket of a skirt."

"Let's hope your charming wit is enough, then."

"Do I get any cool spy gadgets? Like a laser cutter bracelet or explosive chewing gum?"

"I made explosive gum once. It tasted awful." Mark grabbed a small, pill-sized device from the dresser and handed it to Dela. "That's not as glorious as a laser bracelet, but it's a staple for any secret operative. Put it in your ear and we'll be in communication at all times, along with Cappa and Zima. You may want to play with it a bit. It takes practice talking to someone while other conversations are buzzing in your ear."

"The shape is a little ... odd," Dela said. "Are you sure it'll fit?"

"It's a collection of specialized nanites," Cappa said through the phone speaker. "They'll conform to your ear once inside, so they'll be comfortable and undetectable."

Dela frowned and held it at arm's length. "Do you have any idea how creepy that sounds? Don't you worry about those things seeping into your brain and turning you into some sort of cyber zombie?"

"I programmed them myself," Cappa said. "So no, they're perfectly safe."

"Just checking." Dela stuffed it in her ear.

Mark stifled a laugh when she hung her arms out and made a zombie face.

Zima turned suddenly, startling him. She'd been so still that he'd forgotten she was there.

"Tim has agreed to meet tonight under the pretense that I have an urgent need and wish to purchase his invention."

"You lied?" Dela cocked her head in a good imitation of Zima. "I didn't think lying was your thing."

"It was not a lie. My need is urgent, and I shall honor the transaction if it is required for his cooperation."

Dela clucked her tongue. "Oh, girl, I wish I could come. I'm afraid you're going to get screwed out of some serious money."

"Do not fear. I know the device's worth and shall ensure a fair deal on both sides, if it comes to that. Farewell. I wish you luck at the party."

Dela caught her in a hug before she left. "Just ... be careful, okay? In case William's goons stop by. The Dark Angel is a badass, but she's not invincible."

"Thank you for the concern. I intend to remain fully functional until Anne is safe, and shall take the appropriate precautions to ensure it is so."

The door closed behind her. Dela sagged to the bed.

"I'm worried about her, Mark. Things are really heating up."

"Yes, but I know Zima, and when she says 'appropriate precautions,' that means she'll have every move planned out to the sixty-third degree, which will be sixty-two degrees ahead of everyone else."

"I get that, but ... do we have to go to this thing? I feel guilty that we'll be rubbing elbows and drinking champagne when we could be supporting Zima instead."

"First, don't underestimate her. Zima has single-handedly brought entire regimes to their knees. She also works better by herself than in a group. With time to plan things out, like she has now, I pity anyone who crosses her — vampire or not. Second, don't think we're getting off easy just because we're going to a party. These aren't your typical rich folks trying to impress their friends with caviar and expensive wine. They're dangerous players in a global game where lives are cheap, and the winner is the one with the biggest military edge."

"And how do you know these people, exactly?"

Mark pulled his sports coat on and looked in the mirror. Sharp jacket, shirt, neatly pressed pants, polished black shoes.

Just like the old days.

"There are sellers and buyers, as in any market. Sellers have the tech, or, in some cases, just an army for rent. Buyers have the military need, and those roles can swap in the blink of an eye depending on the political climate."

"You and Charlie were sellers, weren't you?"

"The best. Our tech was so advanced that it spelled victory for those who could afford us, and defeat for those who couldn't, or whom we considered in the wrong."

"Are you saying that … you guys basically chose the winners on a global scale?"

"That's right, which is why we were very careful about who we sold to, but … the political map changes faster than you can imagine. Before we knew it, scores of innocent lives were being taken by *our* weapons."

"Orwing did that? No wonder you're pissed."

"No. Orwing was our competitor at the time, selling not only tech, but the military services to go with it, and they were much less choosy about who they sold to. They offered to buy us outright for … well, for a truckload of zeroes, but Charlie and I wouldn't even consider it. When they couldn't acquire us, they decided it would be better if we were out of the market altogether, so they sent Zima after us, as you know."

"I would love to have seen that fight. I bet it was epic!"

Mark grinned, marveling at how unfazed she was about events that still gave him nightmares. "You could say that. The buildings we destroyed have been replaced, but I think there's still a chunk of sidewalk missing where her cyborg's fist barely missed my head."

"Sweet! Can we swing by tomorrow? I want a pic with you and Zima next to it."

He wrestled her to the bed and muffled her giggles with a kiss. "Ready for your next mission, Special Agent Madigan?"

"What, before we leave? Won't that wrinkle my dress?" She waggled her eyebrows and grinned.

"That assignment will have to wait, unfortunately. We're late as it is."

"Then you'd better get off and let me do my makeup. I'm out of practice, so it may take a while."

"You're welcome to use the beauty station in my room."

They both jumped at Cappa's voice from the dresser.

"Sorry," Mark said, climbing to his feet. "I forgot you were there."

"I know," she said softly.

Mark wanted to kick himself for the thoughtless remark. "Remind me later, Cappa, I want to run some ideas by you on how to get you back out into the world."

There was a pause. "No, it's okay. I-I wouldn't feel right taking your time, not when we finally have some solid leads to go on."

"Stop being so damned selfless," Dela said. "We don't know when Charlie's coming back, but we all know how unhappy you are, as much as you've tried to hide it."

"Well ... all right, but only if you don't think it will interfere with our search for Anne." Her words were reluctant, but there was no mistaking the relief in her voice. "You guys had better get moving. Dela, go to my room. I'll talk you through some beauty shortcuts to get you on the road sooner, and we'll use your nano earpiece so you can start getting used to it."

"On my way!"

Mark's smile faded when the door closed. He returned to the mirror to make a few adjustments, but his fingers stopped.

Alvin Orwing ...

Mark and Charlie had never had a good meeting with the man. Alvin was a brilliant businessperson, shrewd and effective at negotiating, but his arrogance and moral ambiguity had made it difficult to hold any sort of respect for him.

And that was back when we had the advantage.

Z-Tech had nothing to offer the arms market these days — nothing he'd feel comfortable parting with, anyway — which could be a problem. Only active participants were invited to these affairs. If Mark didn't bring something to the table, not only might his meeting with Alvin be cut short, but it may put him and Dela in danger.

He flashed a grin in the mirror, and his fingers resumed their meticulous grooming. The solution was so simple that he almost laughed.

Who says I have to be a seller?

21

THE PARTY

MARK WATCHED THE CITY EXPAND BENEATH THEM while the glass elevator continued its seemingly endless journey into the black sky.

Dela leaned into him, her smile broadening with each story's climb. "And you said the party takes the entire top floor? How many people are going to be there?"

He stirred from his thoughts and shared her smile. "Not as many as you might think. They usually have a large area for socializing, an open bar of course, and private rooms where potential business partners can talk."

"An open bar? You'll know where to find me, then."

"Just remember to take it easy. Many at these parties carry drinks for appearances, but the alcohol never touches their lips so they can keep their wits sharp."

She elbowed him playfully. "You have your specialties, geek boy, and I have mine. I was a bartender for six years. I can handle my alcohol — and the kind of people it attracts."

I hope you're right, or we could both be in a lot of trouble.

Mark shook his head in self-admonition. Dela had proven herself capable many times since coming to live with them at Z-Tech. The problem wasn't her.

It was him. Mark had never attended one of these parties without Charlie at his side. They knew each other so well that they rarely needed to confer before negotiating. He hadn't realized how much confidence he drew from Charlie's presence until he was about to swim among the sharks alone for the first time.

No, not alone.

He kissed Dela's cheek. Her gleeful smile turned his way just when the elevator dinged for the top level.

"Ready?" Mark said.

"Always."

The party was just as extravagant as Mark expected. People of every nationality proudly wore their country's finest attire. Lavish couches, plush chairs, and exotic relics, which undoubtedly cost a fortune, stood expertly arranged around a large octagonal depression in the floor that would later become the center stage for seller presentations. The bar Dela had been excited about ran along the side wall, lit with bright neon more befitting a casino than a place where world treaties would be made or broken.

"Anyone in particular I should get to know?" Dela said quietly, taking in the scene with surprising calm.

"Talking to the guards in black is considered bad form unless you have a good reason, and by that, I mean someone's about to kill you. It makes people edgy, like you've paid the guards off to stage a coup or something."

He looked over the crowd. A few faces were familiar, and even looked his way with raised eyebrows, but most were strangers. Alvin Orwing wasn't among them, unfortunately.

Mark smiled when he spotted the next-best person to Alvin. "See the loner at the bar?"

"The drunk with the pinched nose who really doesn't want to be here? What about him?"

"That's Nick Orwing, Alvin's oldest son."

"Let me guess, Al's grooming him to take over the family business, but poor Nicky would rather be out spending his dad's fortunes on parties than taking any sort of responsibility."

"Not quite," Cappa said to them through their nano-communicators. "You're right about the parties, but he takes the business seriously. The problem is that he and Alvin disagree on how the company should be run, and since Alvin's in charge ..."

"That leaves Nick to brood over a glass or ten about how he could do things so much better." Dela grinned. "I think I found my friend."

To Mark's surprise, her grin abruptly became a scowl.

"You're upset with me," she whispered. "Grab my arm."

Mark had no idea where she was going with that, but did as she asked, keeping his expression serious. Dela yanked her arm away, drawing a few looks, and regally stalked toward the bar. Mark watched her go with what he hoped was barely contained fury when really he was trying not to smile — especially after she landed a few seats down from Nick.

She hung her head in that helpless way no stag looking for easy rebound sex could resist.

Nick swam in like a shark to blood. Within minutes, he was nodding sympathetically to a diatribe about her rocky relationship, and how she wanted a man who could satisfy her womanly needs, not just leave her lonely while he went out every night on his business deals — which she knew was a cover for banging some twenty-year-old in Diamond Heights. By the time she'd finished her sympathy play, Nick was regularly shooting Mark angry looks. The pair relocated arm-in-arm to the balcony outside, where she had told him they could talk more freely.

Mark made himself comfortable on the couch, half-listening to Dela's entertaining if ego-bruising conversation through his communicator earpiece, while his eyes searched the crowd for Alvin Orwing.

"You still have a way with the ladies, I see," a familiar voice said. Its grinning owner sat on the opposite corner of the couch. Rows of medals jingled on his white US military dress uniform.

"General Horclave," Mark said, extending a hand.

"Are you selling tonight?"

"I'm afraid not."

"Then we can drop the formality. Call me Robert." He nodded to the balcony door where Nick and Dela were visible chatting on the other side.

"He can have her," Mark said. "She's too needy."

"It's no wonder you never married."

"Same reason you didn't, I'm sure. We're already married to our careers."

"And now it's too late." Robert brushed his thin white mustache and sighed. "For me, anyway. Few women appreciate a career military man, especially with as many miles as I have."

"Want a redhead? She has a great rack. I'll give you a discount."

"That feisty thing?" He shook his head. "She'd send me to an early grave. Not that I'll have better luck with this crowd."

Mark flagged a cocktail waiter. "Single malt Scotch, please."

"I'll have what he's having," Robert said to the waiter. "You're never too old for hard liquor."

The waiter hurried away.

Robert folded his hands and relaxed into the cushions. "So, Mark, if you're not selling — weapons, that is — you must be here to see Orwing's latest and greatest."

"I hadn't heard. What's he presenting this year? Bullet-proof espresso machines?"

"I wish I knew. He seemed pretty smug about it earlier, though."

So he's here.

Mark also had a sinking feeling why Alvin was so confident about his presentation.

The cyborg who shot Anne ...

Zima and the cyborg she'd been installed in — collectively known as Deadiron — had maintained an almost flawless record under Orwing's employ, right up until they tried to assassinate Mark and Charlie. The failure shook the market's confidence in Orwing, and with good reason: Deadiron was Orwing's greatest asset, their edge in the espionage marketplace. They had never openly admitted that their top agent was a cyborg, preferring to boast about their ability to get results rather than how those results were achieved.

When Deadiron disappeared, so did Orwing's ability to execute, a problem Alvin had been trying to rectify ever since.

Which made Mark curious what Orwing would unveil tonight. It may well be the cyborg involved in Anne's kidnapping, or perhaps a full android. Neither would be a stretch, considering their success with Zima.

Or maybe they had something different to show.

Guess I'll find out soon enough.

"Anything new in your world, Robert?"

"Nothing I should talk about, but then again, maybe you've heard something we haven't." Robert leaned closer and lowered his voice. "We lost three squads last week."

"Sorry to hear that. I know the Syrian conflict has been heating —"

"Not in Syria. Here, on American soil. In a military base near Monterey."

"Fort Hunter?"

Robert nodded.

"That's the first I've heard. How did they die?"

Rough fingers steeped at Robert's nose. "When I say lost, I mean they disappeared. There were signs of a struggle, but no bodies were found. None."

Three squads ...

Deserters were common in any military, but rarely at that scale, and never in the last century of US history. "If I hear anything, I'll be sure to pass it along."

"Appreciated." Robert nodded to the waiter delivering their drinks, took a long pull, and sighed. "So how about you? Enjoying a quiet life in the commercial sector, or are you here because it's boring the hell out of you?"

"A quiet life would be nice. Actually, I have some questions for Alvin himself."

"What wisdom could I possibly bestow that the fabled Mark Suther does not already possess?"

Mark grimaced at the haughty voice. Alvin Orwing sat down stiffly in the plush chair across from them, a watery-eyed monarch before his supplicants. Slicked back, thinning hair completed the kingpin look — which Mark and Charlie had always considered him to be: an amoral crime boss who had sent Zima to assassinate them.

"I'll take my leave and let you two catch up." Robert knew their history, of course, which was probably why he winked at Mark before wandering off to join a small group of men in turbans.

"I'm surprised to see you here," Alvin said, shifting his modest frame.

"I bet." Mark wanted to play it cool, to laugh it off as if the horrible events both past and present hadn't phased him in the slightest, but couldn't bring himself to smile. Seeing Alvin with his expensive suit and smug expression, knowing he had suffered few repercussions from his attempt on their lives, made him angry. Add in his probable role in Anne's disappearance, and Mark was furious enough to throw the bastard through the window and watch him drop the hundred-odd stories to the asphalt below.

Maybe later, he thought in an attempt to calm himself. *I need answers first.*

"How's Orwing doing these days? We lost track after your company's unfortunate downturn."

Alvin's cool veneer shook, quickly replaced with an oily smile. "Well enough. The market has changed since your hasty departure, and we've managed to fill the gaps nicely. I should thank you for the business."

The glass in Mark's hand cracked loudly, drawing a few looks, and a bigger smile from Alvin.

Damnit, I can't let him get to me. The past is the past. I need to focus on finding Anne.

Mark took a deep breath and set his ruined glass on the coffee table. "Alvin, can we speak in private?"

"So you can beat me to a pulp without interference? I think not."

"No, so we can talk business. That's what we're all here for, isn't it?"

"Forgive me for doubting your sincerity, but I'll pass."

The word 'forgive' sent another angry surge through Mark. It would be a cold day in Hell when he forgave Alvin Orwing anything. But, given their history, he had known it would take more than a few words to gain audience with him. Alvin was, after all, just as paranoid as he and Charlie — a necessary attribute to survive in a game with few rules and deadly consequences.

Do it, Mark sent to Cappa.

Done, she replied a moment later, much as it pained me.

Me too.

"Check your Swiss account," Mark said, trying to keep the angst from his voice. "Number 00A10982346. See if that changes your mind."

Alvin frowned, but pulled his phone from his jacket anyway. He gave it a few taps, then arched an eyebrow. "I'm flattered you think so highly of my time, but that will hardly cover the hospital bill after you've broken my legs and jaw."

Greedy bastard.

Mark was about to flag Cappa for another transfer when a gong sounded over the loudspeaker.

Alvin brightened. "I'm afraid we'll have to continue this delightfully profitable discussion after my presentation. You have prime seating. Enjoy the show." He flashed a smirk, then left Mark alone on the couch.

Mark ground his teeth and grabbed the seat cushions to keep from leaping after him and wringing his scrawny neck.

People gathered around the sunken dance floor. Dela and Nick hovered on the outer fringes, shoulder to shoulder. Her eyes flashed briefly to Mark, then urgently back to the octagonal stage.

Uh oh.

Alvin had distracted him from Dela and Nick's conversation, so he had no idea why she was so rattled. Mark obediently turned his attention forward.

Alvin Orwing took center stage with a grand smile. He spoke at length about how happy he was to see everyone, who he was, who Orwing was, and why anyone should care. By the time he'd finished the introductions, more than a few had wandered to the bar, and Mark wished he was one of them.

"Now for the part you've been waiting for," Alvin said. He stepped aside to make way for a mountain of a man in a military-green tank top.

The newcomer strode to the center with easy confidence, bouncing lightly on his feet despite his great stature. A round of murmurs made Alvin smile.

"I see many of you already know Sergeant Bruce Morgan," Alvin said. "For those who don't, Bruce is a legend in the military who holds the highest hand-to-hand kill count since they started counting. He can bench three of me while eating a sandwich, and moves so quickly that he's a blur to the human eye. Bruce is the product of ideal genetics and a lifetime of training — the perfect soldier, and every unit's dream. I daresay there isn't another like him."

Murmurs of agreement floated from the audience.

Alvin's oily smile widened. "But imagine for a moment if there was. A squad, a platoon, an *army* of Bruce Morgans!"

A smaller figure slipped from the crowd. Fluid as a stalking cougar, he took position on the other side of Alvin, knees bent as if ready to pounce.

What made Mark's blood run cold, however, was his pale, venous skin and vampire-black eyes.

"Meet Troy West," Alvin said with a grand sweep of his arm. "Our next-generation soldier. Faster. Stronger. Fearless. Utterly obedient. I should amend what I said earlier: Bruce is every unit's dream, until they've met Troy."

Those gathered laughed. Bruce grinned and flexed his tree trunk arms.

Oh God, Bruce doesn't know what's coming ...

Mark briefly caught Alvin's eye and shook his head, a silent plea to spare the sergeant from what was sure to be a terrible fate.

Alvin responded with his trademark, haughty smile and turned back to his audience. "I see we have a disagreement. There's only one way to settle this, I suppose." He pointed a dramatic finger at the bigger man. "Bruce, are you willing to defend your reputation as the mightiest soldier in history?"

Bruce cracked his neck. The muscles on his back undulated like great serpents beneath his oiled skin. He nodded.

"And Troy ... go easy on him, will you?"

That drew a round of laughs from everyone except Mark, Dela, and, curiously, Nick Orwing.

Bruce descended on the smaller man like an avalanche of muscle. The sergeant was just as fast, powerful, and brutally efficient as his introduction suggested. Troy danced, ducked, and dodged for an entire minute, letting Bruce catch nothing but air with every swing.

Cheers turned to gasps when Bruce finally hit him.

Troy stared back, as if the mighty blow had been nothing more than a flick on his nose. Bruce pounded his face. Troy smiled through a split lip that refused to bleed.

Looking much less confident, the Sergeant switched to a *jiu-jitsu* stance, which Mark was well-familiar with. He stepped in and launched a flurry of quick attacks and grabs designed to throw the opponent off-balance. Troy never swayed, avoiding each with ease. Bruce finally caught his arm, surely what he'd been hoping for, and twisted into what should have been a match-ending lock.

Troy stopped him in mid-motion, holding firm as if his arm were made of steel.

And that's when things went very, very badly for Bruce.

Troy delivered a series of blinding punches with such force that Bruce's cracking ribs could be heard from every corner of the room. A powerful jab snapped Bruce's head back. The big man's eyes rolled into his head, and he collapsed to the stage, unmoving.

The crowd went wild with excitement, swarming Alvin and Troy with questions. No one gave a second thought to the fallen behemoth, so Mark jumped from his seat to take a look. Eyes unfocused, dilated pupils ... Bruce had a concussion at the very least, but he was still breathing.

This is so incredibly bad ...

Mark and Charlie had been fighting for months not only to stave the rising tide of vampires, but to find a cure for what any sane person would consider a plague on humanity. This room of power-hungry individuals probably didn't know how contagious the soldiers were; but even when they found out, they wouldn't care. They saw only opportunity for their own gain.

An army of vampires ...

It was a staggering thought. Tough, insane healing, and completely obedient to their commander and sire. Scarier still, vampires didn't have the complex supply line requirements of a regular army, because they could simply feed from their victims. If the contamination accidentally spread, the sire bond would make it easy to bring the new vampires into order and stop the plague. Even sensitivity to sunlight was an obstacle easily overcome with the right set of body armor, something Mark had already been considering for Anne.

Dela and Nick had mysteriously disappeared again. Mark rose to find her, but reined himself in. She was more than capable of taking care of herself. He had to trust in that, and let her do her thing.

Discussions were frantic. Bids for the new army flew higher and higher. Alvin was in his element, the center of attention among the most influential people in the world, and loving every minute of it.

Mark sat heavily next to the fallen Sergeant, his eyes distant.

What was Orwing's ultimate plan? Would he sell armies of vampires outright, or just a few task forces to keep the balance of power under his strict control? What would happen when the world inevitably discovered that not only was a plague of monsters in their midst, but they were also armed with military weapons?

Worst of all, what happens if Alvin loses control of them?

If Alvin's vampires were descended from Anne, as Mark suspected from Troy's highly active state, then they were also descended from William.

Does that mean William has influence over them? Do they have Anne's same defense against the sire bond? Could Anne assume control of them if she dropped her own defense and risked William's influence?

What if Anne dies?

If what Zima's contact said was true about the bond passing up to the next sire, William would suddenly find himself with armies of trained soldiers at his disposal.

No matter how Mark looked at it, Alvin's grand plan to dominate the market could only end badly.

For everyone.

Mark racked his brain, but could think of no immediate way to stop this catastrophe from snowballing, short of killing everyone in the room, and he had slim chances of that without Zima's help.

Even that morbid plan was tempting. Zima could be here well before the party ended. If her performance at the vampire nest was any indication, the messy job would be over quickly.

No, there must be another way.

He had no doubt Zima would do as he asked, but killing so many could never be justified, and belied the morals they had worked so hard to instill in her.

He could decry Troy as an abomination, give light to the aggressive pathogen in his veins. While it may deter those precious few with some sliver of a conscience, the rest would shrug it off as an acceptable compromise for a military edge.

Depending on how tightly Alvin keeps hold on his army, they'll discover that for themselves soon enough.

Military secrets rarely remained secrets for long.

Bruce ran a shaky hand over his face and tried to sit up. Mark gently helped him to his feet and walked him to one of the private rooms. Bruce fell onto the couch with a groan, holding his ribs, and managed a grateful nod.

"You need a doctor," Mark said. "I don't suppose Orwing thought to bring one along?"

"Didn't think I'd need one, but …" He grunted, hugging the ribs Troy had pounded. "Feels like I've been kicked by a whole herd of horses. Who was that freak?"

"A member of the missing platoons, if I had to guess."

"Nope."

Mark frowned. "Are you sure?"

"Positive. My squad trained with them a few days before they disappeared. I know each of them by sight."

There goes that theory.

It made sense, though, now that he thought about it. Alvin wouldn't risk America's wrath by stealing its best soldiers.

They're one of his best customers, after all.

"Any idea what happened?"

"Ambush," Bruce said. "Had to be. They were experienced soldiers, top in their fields, and patriots to a fault. I can't imagine a one of them deserting."

"Then who?"

"Beats me. As far as I know, nothing like this has happened before. If it were terrorists, they'd leave a gory mess to send a message. These guys just vanished." He closed his eyes and panted. "Any chance I could get a ride to the hospital?"

"Of course."

Mark pulled his phone out and called emergency services. He instructed the ambulance to meet them in the lobby, since he was sure the EMTs wouldn't be allowed access to the penthouse.

"Let's get you to the elevator," Mark said after hanging up.

Bruce accepted his help with a grateful nod, and the two of them made their way slowly through the party to the elevator.

Bruce waited until the doors had closed before he spoke, and even then his voice was soft. "If I were going to invade a country, I'd start by kidnapping those who know best about the nation's defenses, then grill them for all they're worth."

"A prelude to war."

The thought had also occurred to Mark, but it didn't make sense in the current political climate. The US had its typical skirmishes in the far East — mostly maneuvers to prevent oil supply lines from falling into the wrong hands, as did every other country with a reliance on fossil fuels — but he was aware of nothing that merited a domestic attack.

Worse ... who's even capable of taking the military's finest?

He had an inkling. "Do you know if the attack happened at night?"

"Had to be," Bruce said. "There's no other time skilled units like them could be taken, or I'm a whore's left tit."

The elevator chimed. Mark helped him out through the lobby, where ambulance lights flashed outside. Bruce was coherent enough to answer the paramedic's questions, so Mark wandered into the parking lot for some privacy, and shifted his attention to Dela's conversation in his earpiece.

If "conversation" was what he could call lustful grunts and slurping. He was about to interrupt, but thought better of it and sent a message to Cappa instead.

WHAT DID I MISS?

THAT GIRL'S A PROFESSIONAL, Cappa sent. SHE HAD HIM EATING OUT OF HER HAND WITHIN THE FIRST FIVE MINUTES. APPARENTLY, NICK AND ALVIN ARE WORKING CLOSELY WITH THEIR NEW VAMPIRE UNITS, AND THEY'RE STAYING AT A HOTEL IN SOUTH SAN FRANCISCO, NEAR THE AIRPORT.

WHICH MEANS THEIR BASE OF OPERATIONS IS PROBABLY NEARBY. Mark said a silent prayer of thanks. He'd envisioned some remote base in the middle of nowhere that would take them weeks to find, if they ever did. ANY OTHER CLUES?

DELA'S WORKING ON IT, BUT SHE MAY HAVE TO, AH, GO UNDERCOVER TO GET ANY MORE INFO. LITERALLY, IF YOU GET MY DRIFT.

MARK?

He gasped for air, only just realizing that he'd forgotten to breathe.

This was the second instance where Dela had volunteered her dignity for their sake. For Anne's sake.

Except this time it may cost more than a slobbery kiss from some geek.

THEY'RE ON THEIR WAY OUT, Cappa sent. HEADING FOR HIS HOTEL, I THINK.

Nick and Dela emerged from the lobby minutes later, arm in arm, happy and laughing like the perfect couple. They sobered when they spotted Mark, who was still too stunned to think of hiding himself in the dense parking lot.

Dela whispered something to Nick and patted his chest. Shoulders squared, her heels clacked across the asphalt to Mark.

"You're angry," she whispered. Dela clenched her fists, but flashed him a hidden smile. "Say something to make me upset."

There were a dozen things he wanted to say to the beautiful redhead in the cocktail dress — none of them inflammatory. He wanted to plead with her to stay. Tell her they would find another way. That he thought she was so much more than some foxy informant. That he couldn't stomach the thought of her lying in another man's arms. That he wanted ... he wanted ...

"Marry me," he said.

Dela gaped, peering skeptically into his eyes. Her lips trembled. Tears welled, then spilled down her face.

Mark bent to kiss her.

The smack of her hand across his cheek echoed from the building and left him seeing stars. Dela cried in great heaving sobs, hunching as if it were she who'd been slapped. Red-rimmed eyes held his. She took a final, shuddering breath, then looked away and trudged back over to Nick, who welcomed her in a comforting embrace.

They vanished into Nick's car. Mark watched until their red tail lights became indistinct in the heavy flow of city traffic.

Mark's only consolation was that he had, indeed, done as she wished and said something to make her upset.

He shook himself, shedding the funk that threatened to pull him into a dissonant mire, and headed for his own car.

There would be time for brooding later. Right now, he needed to head back to Z-Tech for supplies so he could be ready to assist whoever needed him.

Which made him wonder how Zima was faring with the boy, Tim.

22

DIVINING ROD

"**N**OT A BAD NIGHT," CONWAY SAID. He flopped onto their ridiculously expensive couch, then sipped his whiskey on the rocks.

"I thought they'd never leave." Jody plopped down as well.

Tim noticed Conway's grimace when she sat next to Tim instead of himself, but it quickly passed, as usual. Still, Tim sighed in guilty relief. If Conway harbored any bad feelings about Tim and Jody's relationship, he hid it well, and the first week together in their lavish new home had been a pleasant one.

Tim relaxed back and nearly put his feet on the gold-trimmed coffee table for the third time that evening. Conway constantly reminded them that their house wasn't just for living; it was a showpiece for their discerning clientele. A messy house, he said, wouldn't earn repeat business.

It was a wonder they had any business at all, in Tim's mind. When Conway had first suggested people would be willing to pay large sums to be bitten by a real vampire, he and Jody had laughed it off as another of his enterprising, but ultimately ridiculous, ideas. Yet Conway had acquired their first several clients before the new carpet had even been laid.

Here they were, one week after moving in, and their schedule was already booked solid for the next three months. Clients were flying in from all over the country, and they were starting to get international appointments. Tim had all the blood he could drink and more. At times, he had been so full that he thought he might spring a leak.

They had already earned enough to comfortably live out the rest of the year, and, at this rate, they could easily retire by the end of next. Granted, Tim wasn't lying on a beach as he'd imagined, but as far as life-altering transitions go, his transition to a blood-sucking monster had gone pretty well.

He caught Conway staring at him, that wry half-smile shimmering through his Bohemian crystal glass. Tim knew what he was going to ask before his mouth even opened.

"Have you given it any more thought?" Conway said.

Jody perked up and crossed her arms over her sparkling sequined gown, her eyes also fixed expectantly on Tim.

"Yes," Tim said, "and I've come to the conclusion that you're both nuts."

"Tim, we're not going into this blindly," Jody said. "We know the trade-offs."

Conway grinned. "Damn right we do. Besides, we can't scale the business up with just one vampire. And do you have any idea how many requests we've had for a female vamp? Imagine the interest a cute little vixen like Jody would generate, not to mention a dashing specimen like myself. No offense."

Jody nodded, leaning forward. Tim struggled to keep his eyes from the cleavage of her low-cut dress.

"But ... there's no going back after this," Tim said. "No sunlight, no food, no cocktails, just the red stuff from now on."

"And the incredible strength!" Conway made a show of his impressive biceps. "Not to mention reflexes that would make a cat jealous, and the whole living forever thing."

"We don't know that! Garlic, crucifixes, holy water ... that all turned out to be baloney. For all we know, I may be dead next week."

"We'll take our chances," Jody said. "And I need to keep up with you somehow. You don't know your own strength. Some nights I get bruises in places I never thought possible. And trying to walk after you've pinned my legs —"

"Enough!" Conway scrunched his eyes. "I think we get the picture."

Her eyes fell. "Sorry, Con."

"Just ..." Tim rubbed his temples. "Can we talk about it after the blonde leaves? Maybe she'll offer enough for my invention that we won't have to expand the business, then you guys can stay human."

"So you can have all the fun? Let's hope that doesn't happen," Conway said.

Expansion of the business was just an excuse, Tim had suspected, but Conway's statement, and Jody's supporting nod, confirmed it.

There was no talking them out of this. They wanted what he had — for different reasons, probably — and he wouldn't hear the end of it until he capitulated.

Don't I owe them that much?

Even if he disagreed with their decision, he suspected his life would be very different now if it hadn't been for their support. If they wanted to become vampires, who was he to deny them?

The argument sounded thin even to himself. The truth was that Tim didn't want to be alone. As Jody had pointed out, there were differences between them that were hard to surmount.

But if Jody became a vampire ... He had been holding back in bed, terrified of hurting her, but if she had his strength and stamina ... *We might never leave the bedroom.*

That thought, above all else, made him selfishly want to comply, even if it meant subjecting his friends to eternal damnation.

The grandfather clock chimed nine with a deep resonance that belonged in a cathedral, rather than a three-story house in San Francisco, followed immediately by a firm knock on the entryway door.

That must be her.

The three of them stood and hastily straightened themselves: Jody smoothed her full-length gown; Conway tugged his tuxedo; and Tim adjusted his corny, but comfortable, crimson smoking jacket.

Jody was the first to the door and opened it. Outside, the platinum blonde's ice-blue eyes quickly swept them all, rested on Tim for a moment, then took in the rest of the place.

"Please come in," Jody said with a warm smile.

The blonde turned away, her gaze sweeping the neighborhood, before returning her attention to Jody. "Thank you."

She stepped inside. Boards creaked beneath her feet when she crossed the living room to stand near a small table decorated with an array of colored glass flowers.

"Can I take your jacket?" Conway said.

"I prefer to wear it, if that is acceptable."

"You're the guest. Please, have a seat. Make yourself comfortable."

"I am comfortable standing here."

"Okay then ..." Conway raised his eyebrows at Tim before heading to the bar. "Would you like a drink?"

"No."

Conway shrugged and began fixing one anyway, presumably for himself.

Jody brought her own drink over and stood next to their visitor. Jody was smiling, but her jaw tightened when she looked their guest up and down. Although the blonde's gray shirt, jacket, and pants were plain next to Jody's expensive outfit, her face was flawless, and even her loose clothes couldn't hide her perfect figure. Jody cleared her throat. Despite her four-inch stiletto heels, she still had to look up to meet the blonde's eyes.

"It's nice to finally meet you. Tim's told us so much about you, but he neglected to mention how beautiful you are." Jody said the last with a withering glance in his direction.

"And he never caught your name," Conway said from behind the counter.

The blonde stared at them, creating an awkward silence. "Thank you," she said eventually. "And my name is Zima."

"Does that mean we're ready to do business?" Tim said, recalling her comment from the diner.

"If that is your wish, but there is an urgent matter I would like to discuss first." She parted a curtain and peered through the window facing the street. "I require your help to locate the person responsible for your condition."

Tim froze.

Does she know?

"My condition? What do you mean?"

Her ice-blue eyes settled on Tim, regarding him as if he were no more important than the furniture. "I refer to your transition to a vampire. Is there another condition I should be aware of?"

"N-no. When you say 'person responsible for my condition,' are you talking about the poor waitress who was murdered in the alley?"

"Yes."

"She survived?" Tim shuddered at the memory of her chest exploding in a fountain of red.

"We have reason to believe so."

"But ... how? I saw her wounds, they were —"

"Vampires are very resilient, as you may soon discover."

Jody stomped toward her. "Was that a threat? Who are you? Who's 'we'? Start talking, or ... or Tim and Conway will make you regret it!"

Zima didn't even blink at Jody's tirade. "The threat does not come from me. I have recently discovered that other vampires are aware of Tim's existence. They are searching for him as we speak. If they locate him, they shall take him prisoner. Should that happen, I do not favor his chances of survival for long."

"Other vampires?" Tim said. "There are more than just Anne and me?"

"Yes."

They listened with growing shock to Zima's story of William and his dark army. Conway nearly spilled his drink when she covered the vampire hierarchy and the mind control William held over all his subjects.

Tim wiped his face with a shaking hand. "So ... why hasn't he taken control of me? And why can't I sense Anne?"

Zima cocked her head slightly. "You cannot?"

Tim thought for a moment, searching his mind for any trace of someone else. He had no idea what that would feel like, but nothing seemed out of the ordinary. "If she's in here," — he tapped his head — "she's pretty well hidden."

Not that I'm complaining. The idea of someone driving him from the inside was disconcerting to say the least.

Zima's brow creased the barest fraction of an inch. "And you have not experienced any cranial discomfort?"

"Everything hurt the night I transformed, but since then … my head's been fine."

Jody crossed her arms. "That still doesn't explain who you are. How do we know you're not the one who ordered Anne shot in the first place, and now you're just here to collect Tim to make sure there aren't any loose ends?"

"I would never cause Anne harm." Zima absently flexed her right hand; the first extraneous movement Tim had seen her make since she arrived. "She is my girlfriend."

"She's lying," Conway said. "Uncle Hal said Anne is dating Charlie."

"She is, and she is also dating me."

Conway scowled. "So you say."

"If you require confirmation, ask Hal. He is aware of our relationship."

"I will." Conway pulled his phone out and stomped upstairs.

Jody continued to glare. "So you know Charlie, then?"

"Yes. I live with him and Anne at the factory."

"You told me that you don't work for Z-Tech!" Tim said.

"I do not. I only claim residence at their facility."

"And I bet that stuff you said about buying my invention was bullshit. I should have known."

"No. Your device is remarkable. Once we have located Anne, I shall offer a fair price, if you still wish to sell."

Jody tugged Tim to the back of the room, keeping an eye on Zima along the way.

"I don't trust her," Jody said softly. "We have a good thing going here. Tell her to leave, then we can continue with our … our plan, and you and I can be together. Forever."

"You can't be serious! Didn't you hear what she said about the hierarchy? They use mind control! You and Conway could end up as my slaves. What if I can't control it? What if —"

She stood on her toes and kissed him. "I'm not worried, and I bet Conway isn't, either. You're not like that. You'd find a way to let us keep our free will. Besides, you can't sense Anne, right? How do we know Zima isn't lying just to scare you into doing what she wants?"

"That's the problem, Jo. There's so much we don't know —"

Conway's heavy footsteps on the stairs drew his attention. "Her story checks out." He didn't look happy about the revelation.

Tim turned back to Jody. "I have a sinking feeling her other stories will, too. I think we should listen to her, for now. We don't have much else to go on."

"But ..." She glanced at the blonde harbinger standing in their living room, then covered her mouth, tears brimming.

Tim understood. He pulled her close and kissed the top of her head. Successful as they were, adjusting to their new reality had been taxing for everyone, even Conway. They were only now beginning to feel comfortable with their lifestyle. If what Zima said was true, then the only reason they had been allowed this small peace was because they'd been flying under the radar through a war zone they didn't know was there until they were already in the enemy's sights. Continuing on their current course meant trouble.

In other words, our paradise was an illusion.

Tim rounded on Zima and squared his shoulders. "All right. Tell us how we can avoid this William lunatic."

"We can offer you safe haven at Z-Tech," Zima said.

"A factory?" Conway shook his head. "In the middle of vampire central? We'd be sitting ducks!"

"Z-Tech is well-protected, I assure you."

"We could go anywhere in the country," Conway said. "I don't see why we should stick around here."

"That is an option, of course," Zima said, her face unreadable. "Although I would request that Tim stay within city limits. He may yet be contacted by Anne, in which case he might be able to determine her location. Distance may or may not affect their mental bond, but I would like to err on the side of caution and keep him nearby."

Conway crossed his arms, mighty pythons weaving beneath his powerful chest. "So you're willing to bet Tim's life — and ours — on the *off chance* he might be able to use some mystic voodoo to find your lost girlfriend?"

Zima blinked. "Yes."

Tim looked at Jody, but she cast her eyes down and clung tighter to his chest. Her small body trembled. Unfortunately for Zima, he knew what their answer had to be.

"I'm sorry about Anne," Tim said. "I really am, but we can't —"

Even with his enhanced vampire senses, Tim didn't see Zima move. A pair of large-barreled silver pistols magically appeared in her hands. Tim darted between her and Jody, intent on protecting her with his own body, but Zima aimed past them to the back door. Her head swung to the front of the house. She quickly swiveled, arms stretched, with a pistol leveled in either direction to cover both doors.

That's when Tim heard it. Several pairs of footsteps padded lightly down the back wooden stairs, while others crept across their concrete front porch. Tim quietly led a wide-eyed Jody to the bar next to Conway, who was staring at the spectacle, the drink at his mouth forgotten. Tim caught their attention and put a finger to his lips.

Wood exploded inward from both doors simultaneously.

Bright orange flashes from Zima's strange weapons lit the room before the first wood chip hit the floor. Strobes of heat washed over Tim with each shot, followed by painful cries from both sides of the house. Jody and Conway belatedly ducked, but Zima was already motioning them toward the front. Tim gathered his friends, half-carrying each of them closely behind their mysterious visitor-turned-guardian-angel, whose chest was now humming like an enormous power transformer. Zima edged closer to the ruined doorframe, whipping her head between it and the rear of the house. She carefully peered outside.

She jerked back an instant before a loud gunshot echoed from across the street. Wood splintered at Tim's feet where the bullet struck, causing all three of them to jump.

Zima wasted no time. She stuck her gun around the corner and fired blindly back at the shooter. Loud swearing followed. Zima immediately leaned out and fired again, lighting the entryway with a bright orange flash. She ducked back with blinding speed in time to avoid another shot, which shattered the plaster wall near Conway's leg. A scream from across the street told them her target wasn't as lucky. She looked outside again, eyes sweeping the area, then motioned for them to cross the porch. The three of them followed her in a frightened gaggle, carefully stepping over the pale, smoldering corpses to a fancy sedan parked at the curb.

Zima jerked her torso sideways in a blur of gray. A gunshot put a hole through her trailing jacket where her chest had been an instant before, chipping a large chunk from the sidewalk.

Her return fire was instantaneous. Three orange streaks to the top of the adjacent house elicited another scream, leaving smoke trails where they had seared holes through the lip of the flat roof.

She spun in a complete circle, taking the rest of the neighborhood in, before holstering one weapon and climbing into the vehicle. The rest of them followed suit. Conway rode shotgun, while Tim slid into the back seat with Jody clinging to his arm.

Their blonde guardian drove like she moved: with incredible precision, and so fast that Conway was hanging from the passenger grab-handle with both hands. They had evaded two cops, and were several miles distant, before Zima finally stopped running traffic lights and slowed to normal speed. Jody cracked an eye and peered around. As Tim suspected, they were heading for the northeastern part of the City.

Toward the Z-Tech factory.

They were all just starting to relax when Zima took a sharp turn and punched the accelerator, angling south.

Conway gripped the handle again. "Jesus! What happened? I-I thought we were going —"

"I have received new information," Zima said. "Anne is being held somewhere in South San Francisco."

"Received?" Tim looked around, but he saw no cell phone, earpiece, or other means of communication. "How did you ..."

She turned around. In the darkness between streetlights, Tim noticed a faint blue glow deep within her eyes.

Glowing eyes. Faster than vampires. Incredible precision. Mechanical speech patterns. An electrical hum ...

His jaw dropped.

"Y-you're a robot!"

The others looked at Tim as if he were crazy, but their eyes gradually widened, and soon they were staring at her, too.

"Yes." Zima faced the road again.

"That's impossible," Jody said. "I took advanced robotics just last semester. That sort of tech is decades from —"

"Were those real plasma guns?" Conway said.

Tim recognized the "I've found a new toy" smile on his face and groaned, but Conway was too entranced to notice.

"I swear I saw thermal induction streams from the dense electromagnetic containment fields, but how can coils that small take the kind of power necessary to maintain it?"

"And what's your power source?" Jody leaned on the front seat, her face mirroring Conway's excited curiosity. "Battery tech has come a long way, but you'd have to be packed full of them just to run for a few hours!"

"Yeah, and what's your skin made of?"

Conway pinched her cheek. Zima endured it without so much as a twitch.

"It feels so real," Conway said. "I swear I couldn't —"

Tim pounded the seat. "Guys! Did you miss the part where we've changed course to find her girlfriend? Probably into hostile territory?"

Jody's mouth fell open. "Oh my God! You're a robot dating a vampire of the same sex?" She tumbled into Tim's lap, laughing hysterically. "H-how does that even work?"

"Wait ..." Conway narrowed his eyes. "Do you even have a gender? I mean, you're just gears and circuits under there, right?"

"Or ... or are you anatomically correct?" Jody said, gasping for breath.

"Except for internal reproductive organs," Zima said, "I am equipped as a fully functional female, including genitalia."

"That's incredible!" Jody pulled herself up. "What do you use for, ah, lubrication? A light silicone grease would do the trick, but it's also an irritant ..." She and Conway shuddered.

Zima caught Tim's eyes in the rear-view mirror. "I was not aware that your companions are also engineers."

"Yeah, sorry. Just be thankful they didn't bring their tools. So, ah ... why exactly are you bringing us along? You seem capable of handling any threat short of nuclear attack on your own."

"Our undercover operative has discovered Anne is being held far underground and, although we know in which city, we do not know her precise location. Our operative did not say why, but it stands to reason that being underground is what shields Anne's presence from you and your siblings."

Tim clenched his fist. "What does my sister have to do with this?"

"I refer to other vampires who also share Anne as their sire."

"She made others?" Jody said. "I'm surprised, given how you said you've been fighting them."

"Her abductors appear to be using Anne as the root of their new mercenary army, which also explains why they would wish to keep her shielded."

"Otherwise she could take control," Conway said. He smacked his fist into his palm. "That's reason number two that we need to bust her out, then. Imagine if we had an undead army of our own to fight this William clown?"

Jody whacked his arm. "'We'? 'Our'? Ten minutes ago you were ready to skip town, meathead!"

"That was before I found out Zima is a super-advanced vampire-killing machine. You saw her in action! How could they possibly win?"

"Your praise is flattering, but not entirely accurate," Zima said. "Anne's captors have at least one cyborg agent in the area, and trained vampires wielding military-grade weapons. I have run the simulations. The odds are in their favor."

Conway drummed his fingers on the dash. "Yeah … tell me again why we're rushing in?"

"Because our operative has also discovered they plan to move her to a more secure location. Tonight. Should they succeed, our odds of locating Anne — let alone rescuing her — diminish significantly."

They braced themselves when Zima squealed around a corner.

"I cannot let that happen. I need her back with me."

Zima powered them through another bend, kicking the back of the car out perpendicular to the road. She narrowly missed two cars and a semi that blared its deep horn while they screeched by in a plume of tire smoke.

"I love her."

Tim clutched the front seat for dear life, fingers digging holes into the leather. The others, he noted, had relaxed since learning Zima was an android, grinning through audacious maneuvers that would have made the staunchest rally driver think twice. He understood their thinking: Zima was a computer, able to perform complex calculations much faster and with greater accuracy than human beings — as she had already demonstrated many times. Still, Tim had seen enough computer errors in his time to be thankful when they crossed the South San Francisco city limits in one piece, where Zima slowed again.

Now we just have to worry about the vampire army and the cyborg.

Which brought Tim back to his original question.

"How am I supposed to help?"

"I am hoping you will be able to sense Anne if we pass close enough to her location. It is just a theory, but I can think of little else, and it appears we are out of time." Zima caught his eyes again in the mirror. "Please, try to concentrate. Anne described the sensation as a point of light in the back of her mind through which she received impressions, such as emotions, images, intentions, and, in William's case, commands."

The last part didn't make Tim excited about seeking contact with his sire, but he could hardly refuse after Zima's daring rescue of him and his friends.

If it wasn't for her, I'd be sitting before William right now.

Besides, the sweet waitress — his sire — didn't strike him as the controlling type. Hopefully she'd leave him to himself.

Tim closed his eyes and searched his mind again, trying to find the point of light Zima had described.

It was like stumbling blindfolded over unfamiliar terrain. He knew what a point of light was, of course, but had trouble picturing one inside of his brain. His imagination conjured all manner of distractions to throw him off the trail: the scent of Jody's perfume, and her warm hand, took him back to the night she had shown up in his bedroom, the first time he had seen her olive skin in its entirety —

A pinpoint of light tickled the back of his mind. It was faint, muted like a distant star in the vast night sky, but there was no mistaking that it was real. And, like a dream where he somehow knows the endless mansion represents his tiny childhood home, Tim knew exactly to whom the light belonged.

"I … I found her."

The car screeched to a stop. Zima whipped around to face him. Her blue eyes glowed ominously, the electric hum in her chest crackling with immense power.

"Where?" she said simply.

Tim cowered as though she had sprouted horns and roared. Without conscious thought, his shaking finger pointed east, toward the base of the San Bruno Mountains.

The vehicle lurched forward. Zima weaved through traffic as if it were standing still, hopping curbs as often as not, and treated the oncoming lane like an extension of her own. A moving van slid sideways to avoid a head-on collision. Jody's shriek became amusement-park laughter, joined by Conway, whose eyes sparkled with glee.

"Bite them," Zima said without taking her eyes from the road.

"What?" Tim said. "W-why? I'm not hungry."

By the looks on their faces, you'd think I already had.

"The healing properties of your venom have a lasting effect. I do not intend to put any of you in danger, but, should trouble arise, your bite will significantly increase their chances of survival."

Tim was still processing the request when two wrists presented themselves: one large and muscular, the other small and delicate. With a sigh, he started with Jody. The sensation of sinking his fangs into her warm flesh was wonderful, as usual. Although he was still full from earlier, he couldn't resist a few slurps of her delicious blood. Her face softened, his venom working its magic through her veins. By the time he released her, Jody had completely relaxed against him, head lolling on his shoulder.

"Thanks," she said weakly.

He repeated the exercise with Conway.

The big man sagged into the front seat with a contented sigh. "And you wonder why we get so much business."

Tim tucked an arm around his ragdoll girlfriend. He wished he could join them in their drug-happy world, but he'd discovered early on that he was immune to the effects of his own venom.

The pinpoint of light in his mind had grown to a grain of sand, and with it, his certainty of Anne's location. "We're getting closer. She's about a half mile ahead on the —"

Pain lanced his head, stabbing outward from Anne's presence. His scream shocked the others from their stupor. It wasn't like any headache he'd ever experienced. Pain radiated from deep within his mind, pulsing, pressing, threatening to tear him apart from the inside. Tim grabbed his hair in bunches, feeling as if his head might actually explode.

But the car didn't stop.

"I am sorry," Zima said. "I had hoped Anne's sirelings would be spared from the effects of her defense program, intended for William, but apparently it does not differentiate. You must endure the discomfort until we confirm her location."

"Discomfort?" Jody yelled, sitting bolt upright. "He's in agony! We have to turn around —"

"If we delay," Zima said, raising her voice for the first time Tim could remember, "Anne may be forever out of my reach. I do not wish Tim harm, but he is our best chance to prevent that from happening. I believe her salvation is worth the temporary inconvenience." She spared him a glance. Her voice softened. "Are you still able to sense her direction?"

Tim managed a nod. He pointed a trembling finger ahead and to the left.

Jody pulled him into her lap and stroked his hair. Her warm breath sobbed comforting words into his ear.

The closer they came, the worse the pain grew. He heard Zima's voice, but couldn't decipher her words, so he pointed until the pain became so intense that it shut out the rest of the world, leaving him in helpless agony.

•   •   •

The car pulled up to a curb a hundred feet from a large dirt parking lot nestled against a hill. A dozen black sedans littered the space. People bustled around a semi, which was in the process of backing a trailer along a set of train tracks into a large tunnel.

"Wait here," Zima said, unfastening her seatbelt. "Mark will arrive shortly. If conditions are favorable, we shall soon return with Anne, then we may all regroup at the factory."

"Wait, you can't bring her here!" Jody said in a panic. "That'll make it even worse for Tim!"

"Perhaps, but once Anne is with us, she may be able to sever their connection, as William has with her, which should eliminate his discomfort." Zima pulled her hood up and slipped from the car.

Jody resumed comforting her ailing Tim. A spasm took him. He grabbed her wrist so hard that she cried out, sure he had broken something, but he soon released. A shake of her hand showed everything was still in working order.

Or maybe he did break something, and the venom in my system has already mended it.

As upset as she was at Zima's decision to let her boyfriend suffer, Jody was thankful for her foresight.

Tim convulsed again, whining pitifully in her lap. His jaw clenched, and she heard one of his teeth crack. She wasn't sure if he noticed, which was a testament to the level of agony he must be experiencing.

"Conway," she said softly once Zima had moved a fair distance from the car. "We can't leave him like this!"

Her ex-boyfriend looked at Tim with genuine sympathy. A range of emotions played across his face, but eventually he sagged and nodded. "What do you suggest?"

"Earth shields them. Let's get out of here and take him underground before Anne emerges. If he's this bad now, he won't survive once she's unshielded."

Conway slid into the driver's seat and examined the console. "I don't see a place for a key."

"Ten bucks says Zima is the key. And if the car is half as advanced as she is, I doubt we can hot-wire it."

"Good thing this isn't the only car around," Conway said, smiling. He yanked the door handle.

Nothing happened.

Strong fingers pried at the lock to no avail.

Despair crushed the air from Jody's lungs. "W-we're trapped ..." She hugged Tim close, kissing his ever-unkempt hair.

"Like hell we are." Conway dug a multi-tool from his pocket, unfolded the flathead, and began prying the panel off the door.

"Just break the glass, meathead!"

"Can't, it's bulletproof. I can tell by the thickness. Besides, it would make too much noise."

He worked his fingers around the edge. A firm yank pulled the panel free, exposing a hodgepodge of wires and components. Undaunted, Conway tackled the problem with an engineer's methodical pace, deftly sifting and sorting until he'd isolated the lock mechanism.

"As I hoped, the car was designed to keep people out, not in. All we need to do is take this wire, cross it over here, and ..." The lock popped. Conway grinned triumphantly. "Stay with Tim. I'll go fetch our new ride."

Conway crept down the street, the opposite direction from Zima, testing each car door along the way. Jody looked for the android, but the area between their car and the parking lot was pitch black. Zima could be staring right at them and she'd never know.

Probably doesn't matter anyway. I bet we're pretty far down her list of priorities right now.

A few minutes later, an engine roared to life down the street. Conway pulled up in an ancient station wagon, pale yellow with peeling wood trim, and in desperate need of a new muffler. They managed to lift a rigid Tim over the front seat and out the open door, keeping a wary eye in the direction Zima had gone.

Once Tim and Jody were safely in the back of their escape vehicle, Conway hit the gas, and their jalopy gurgled away. Jody glanced back and wished Zima luck finding her love.

A strangled cry turned her eyes from the soon-to-be battlefield to her own love, who was cold, whimpering, and shaking in her arms.

Everyone has their priorities, Jody thought, stroking Tim's hair.

23

UNDERCOVER

F EDELMA MADIGAN — OR DELA, AS SHE PREFERRED — stared anxiously at the still-unlocked screen of Nick's phone sitting on the bed stand. She glanced at the cracked bathroom door. Steam was just beginning to wisp from the top.

Come on, come on, come on …

Inside, she heard the shower door finally snap closed.

Dela snatched his phone and quickly tapped the screen. If it went to sleep, it would undoubtedly lock. She wouldn't get a chance like this again to have private access to his phone.

She sighed with relief when it brightened, showing Dela his home screen. She was in.

Nick had been a wealth of information over the course of their candle-lit dinner. She rubbed her taut stomach. Undercover or not, the food was so tasty that she'd stuffed herself to the brim. Following through with her romantic ruse would be difficult, because one touch would be enough to bring all that fine cuisine up for another showing.

Which might be a good excuse to cut our romance short, come to think of it.

Nice as he was, Dela had no intention of going all the way with Nick, especially after Mark's sweet, but insanely unexpected parking lot proposal.

What the hell was he thinking? Was he even serious?

Dela shook herself. Those answers would have to wait. Nick wouldn't be in the shower forever, especially if he was expecting to get lucky tonight.

She pulled up the messaging application and skimmed his conversation history. With any luck, it would fill in details he'd been reticent to share — like Anne's exact location, and a hint of the size or intentions of Orwing's vampire army. Then she could excuse herself for any one of a myriad of reasons. "I forgot to feed the dog" was the first that came to mind. She shuddered and vowed to come up with a wittier excuse later.

Steam poured from the bathroom in ever-thickening waves. Dela scrolled and scrolled, but could find nothing of interest in the messaging app. She switched to his email.

Bingo!

The first message contained directions to a place the sender jokingly referred to as Camp Vamp. Dela was tempted to forward it to Mark, but didn't want to leave evidence of her snooping. She dug her own phone from her purse and snapped a picture of the email, then moved to the next. It was a status report from the camp's commander.

THIRTY-SIX OPERATIVES SUCCESSFULLY CONVERTED, WHICH PUTS US AHEAD OF SCHEDULE AT — her jaw dropped — FOUR PERCENT OF OUR GOAL.

Math wasn't her best subject, but Dela was pretty sure that equaled an obnoxiously large number of bloodsuckers. She gulped, took a picture, and moved on.

Revenue reports, auction results, research and development progress, a note from his aunt Elsie, a summary of a rather large contract for ...

Her own phone slipped from her numb fingers.

"Holy shit ..."

She read and read, her frown deepening with every word. It was a mercenary services agreement, calling for the complete destruction of twelve seemingly random locations, using whatever force was necessary.

All of them on US soil.

Dela knelt awkwardly in her constricting dress. Shaking hands retrieved her phone from where it had bounced under the bed.

I've got to get this to Mark —

The click of a cocking hammer made Dela freeze. She slowly looked up. The black depths of a gun barrel stared back. Wearing nothing but a towel, her faux date was bone-dry with his finger on the trigger.

Nick glanced at his phone, which was still in her hand. An odd smile crossed his lips. "Find what you were looking for?"

24

RESCUE

Z IMA HID BEHIND THE SMALL BLUFF, having just completed her surveillance of the parking lot. Eleven men in combat armor bearing Orwing's insignia, all human, stood guard around the tunnel and the truck. Three carried semi-automatic sidearms, while the remaining eight bore assault rifles. Two actively surveyed the area with night vision optics. Zima was careful to hide whenever one turned her way.

Her plasma pistols were more than adequate to penetrate their armor, which simplified her tactical approach. The optics-wearing soldiers would be eliminated first, followed by the five with assault rifles, then the remaining three with pistols, since they posed the least threat. The rifles were 5.56 NATO, capable of damaging her only if they struck a critical area. Zima had designed her endostructure with very few of those, and estimated her total chance of injury at less than two percent.

She would have to re-evaluate her tactics once inside the tunnel. Public record showed it had collapsed twenty-two years ago after a large earthquake had weakened the supporting structure.

Train popularity had begun to wane around that time, so the city closed it down. A wealthy family purchased the land three months later. She found no information about their intended use.

The tunnel appeared unchanged from its original, condemned state. If an underground structure existed deep within, she knew neither the layout, nor what sort of opposition awaited. It was hardly ideal, since she could not prepare any simulations ahead of time, but that was where Mark came in. He was adept at strategizing on the fly. His presence would improve her estimates of rescuing Anne by twenty-four percent.

Zima checked his location. Approximately seventy-two seconds remained until his arrival, given his current velocity. She charged her capacitors to sixty-eight percent, which would allow a sustained rate of fire for ten seconds. More was unnecessary even in her worst-case simulations. An electric hum built in her chest, although it wasn't loud enough to betray her position.

Dela's been compromised! Cappa sent. Nick caught her snooping around. They struggled, then we lost her phone signal.

Damnit! Mark sent.

Zima agreed with his sentiment. Not only did she consider Dela a friend, but she had been counting on Mark's support. Based on the new information, she estimated a ninety-eight percent chance that he would deviate from his planned course and assist Dela instead.

Zima, I'm sorry, but I'm going straight to his hotel, Mark sent. I'll be with you as soon as I can.

She adjusted the estimate to one hundred percent and filed it away.

Are you going to wait for Mark? Cappa sent to her.

Zima flexed her lonely right hand.

Somewhere inside was Anne. *Her* Anne.

She had already prepared for this scenario. Each passing minute significantly increased the risk of failure, which made waiting for Mark impractical. More soldiers may be *en route*, perhaps vampire soldiers.

Zima's greatest concern, however, was the cyborg. She had seen no trace of him. If he was inside, that was an existing problem that could not be helped, but if he was elsewhere, then conducting the rescue before his return quadrupled her odds of success.

The decision was clear.

NO, Zima replied. I WILL PROCEED WITH THE ASSAULT ALONE.

GOOD LUCK, Cappa sent, laced with concern.

THANK YOU. LUCK TO MARK AND DELA AS WELL. I SHALL REPORT AS SOON AS I AM ABLE.

With that, Zima extended the black power cables hidden in the folds of her wrists, plugged them into her plasma pistols, and promoted the first assault simulation to real-time.

She sprang from her hiding place. Her weapons moved from target to target in rapid succession, delivering a single plasma bolt to each.

All but one landed within zero-point-six percent deviance. She removed ten of the eleven targets from the active threat list, and submitted the last for a new firing solution.

The solution returned three microseconds later with ninety-nine percent confidence. She promoted the solution to real-time. Another plasma bolt flew from her right weapon, catching the last target in the throat.

Eleven sizzling bodies fell to the gravel, their necks vaporized before they could scream. Phase one had been completed before she had taken her third step.

Zima edged to the mouth of the tunnel.

Silence.

A glance inside revealed weathered rubble fifty-two meters in, and a metal door on the left wall. She crept inside and listened at the door.

Gunfire. Yelling. Distant and echoed, but unmistakable.

Zima kicked the door in. It crumpled in a squeal of metal and crashed against the concrete wall behind it. The only feature in the small room was a railed stairway winding down.

Instead of taking the steps, Zima leaped over the railing and jumped from landing to landing, kicking off the walls to quickly change trajectory, one pistol always pointed down the next flight.

The stairs ended six stories underground. Unfortunately, Zima was already airborne when her combat processors alerted her of explosives ringing the exit ahead: one on either side of the doorway, and one directly above.

A combat solution returned three milliseconds later; its confidence rating a very low forty-four percent. She was moving fast and would not have time to execute another. Although it was far below the acceptable threshold, she promoted the solution to real-time.

Three plasma bolts streaked forth. The two lateral shots struck with terminal accuracy, causing the devices to spark and fizzle. The middle shot struck with ten percent deviance, grazing the casing, but leaving the explosive otherwise intact.

The grazed explosive detonated when Zima touched the ground.

A concussive wave slammed into her, stopping her forward momentum and hurling her backward into the stairs. Concrete and parts of her own body shattered on impact, burying her in a cocoon of dirt and rubble.

Damage reports flooded in: right neck actuator at fifty-seven percent; critical fracture to her right forearm; left knee hyper-extended, estimated eighty-three percent functional; shrapnel in her right eye, reducing visibility to seventy-two percent; tissue damage to forty-four percent of her body, mostly punctures and tears on the right side, which had been facing the explosion, although it was significantly worse on her extremities.

Taking all damage into account, her adjusted combat efficiency was still ninety-one percent — which, as Mark would say, was not bad.

Zima extracted herself from the crumpled stairs. Her right plasma gun would not respond. The other sparked and popped when she pulled the trigger. Zima tossed the plasma guns aside and pulled the machine pistols from their holsters. One had suffered minor surface scratches during the explosion, but the other was unblemished. She pulled the slides of each. They appeared functional.

A burst of gunfire from inside. A scream.

Not Anne's.

Zima ran through the wrecked doorway, but her damaged knee twisted on her third step. She rolled with the fall and ended in a ready crouch. Motor processors adjusted for the impairment, and she was soon moving again with eighty-nine percent efficiency, though it had reduced her overall combat efficiency to seventy-four percent.

The short hall opened into a wide area supported by thick, round pillars. Eight hallways branched left and right, four on each side. Zima submitted the layout for solutions while she ran. Candidates returned quickly, already adjusted for her injuries. The process repeated with every step: gather data, generate solutions, discard outdated ones.

A man backed out from the last hallway on the right, sixty-one meters from her location. He had not seen Zima. He gripped a pistol with both hands, pointing back the way he had come, his face clearly frightened. Zima targeted him, ready to terminate him if he became a threat. He fired down the side hallway.

Rapid return fire rattled his chest before he could reach cover. He dropped to the floor. Even with immediate medical attention, his chance of survival past the five-minute mark was less than three percent.

Muffled yelling from the hallway closest to her.

It was Anne.

Zima's core stirred to life. Her breathing quickened. The longing that had tortured her since Anne's abduction flared to a level that drowned out all other thought. Zima darted down the hall, the opposite direction from the shooter. The need to see her love consumed her, driving her forward as fast as her injured leg would allow.

Anne's yells became louder.

Zima raced around a corner. Two men wielding pistols crouched before a large metal door, aiming outward as if protecting whatever was inside. Security bolts lined the entire side of the door, each in the open position.

Anne's voice came from inside.

Zima did not know if the guards were hostile, nor did she care.

She only knew they were in her way.

Zima fired a burst at each before they had even realized she was there.

The way was now clear.

To Anne.

Zima stepped over the corpses, yanked the door open …

… and there she was.

Her Anne.

Zima's longing crescendoed. A pitiful moan, filled with the ache and despair she had suffered at Anne's absence, resonated throughout the room. She wanted to feel Anne's touch, her softness, see her beautiful smile, hear her laughter. The need filled Zima until her chest and loins felt as if they would burst.

But two men stood between her and her love. One was fiddling with Anne's wrist shackles, the other with the restraints around her ankles. Zima recognized the larger one, Don, from the restaurant, but the dark-haired man was new.

No, not a man.

His thermal signature matched Anne's: the same temperature as the room. He was a vampire.

All three occupants gasped when they saw Zima's ruined body standing in the doorway.

Anne started to shout something. Don reached for his gun. The vampire leaped at Zima with superhuman speed.

Her combat processors returned a preliminary assessment. The vampire's threat rating was four hundred and seventy-three percent higher than Don's, but Don would be more difficult to deal with if the vampire obscured her line of fire. More importantly, there was a thirty-eight percent chance he would shoot Anne instead of Zima.

That was unacceptable. Zima disregarded the assessment's recommendation and put three shots into Don's chest, removing the first threat, then waited patiently for the second threat to complete his lunge.

Arms outstretched, the vampire tried to catch her in a grapple. Zima sidestepped at the last instant, hooked her bare-metal arm around his chin, and twisted his head sideways.

The crack of his neck echoed in the cement room. He dropped to the floor, unmoving. While not fatal, it would slow him down long enough for her and Anne to escape, which was all that mattered.

She and Anne would soon be back together. The thought brought Zima peace ...

... until Anne finished what she had started shouting when Zima entered.

"Zima, don't hurt them!"

25

MASSACRE

ANNE BLINKED, UNABLE TO PROCESS THE HORRORS of the last few seconds.

They had only been trying to free her. Now Don slumped against the wall, gasping for breath in a growing pool of his own blood, while Almos lay unmoving, his neck twisted at an unnatural angle. Outside, Steve and Lance, the two brave souls who had volunteered to guard the hallway and buy time so Anne could escape, were piled one on top of the other, unmoving.

And then there was Zima. Anne's poor, mangled girlfriend looked like a metallic zombie. Red gashes peppered the right side of her body, lined with the remains of her tattered clothing. The flesh was missing on the right half of her torso, including her right arm and the upper half of her right leg, leaving just the shiny armored plating beneath. Her left knee, though less damaged than her right, bent backward like an ostrich's. The right side of her face had torn away, exposing her polished metal skull. Her beautiful blue eye on that side was lidless, with a white crack snaking across its center. A small hole marked where her ear had been. The lips on the left side of her face were intact but ended just below her ruined nose, giving her a lopsided skeletal smile.

Sadly, Anne had seen her in worse condition.

Heedless of the bodies around her, Zima hobbled forward, her eyes intent on Anne. The left side of her face was twisted in longing, as if her Desire program was running double-time. Instead of retrieving the key from Don's limp fingers, Zima grabbed the restraints around one of Anne's wrists, braced her foot against the wall, and yanked. The shackle broke open with a loud crack. Zima repeated the process with the shackles around her forearm, upper arm, then along her other arm, and down her legs.

With the last restraint gone, Anne stumbled from the wall. Her limbs felt awkward, as if they weren't designed to bend and flex. Zima wrapped her in a tight embrace before she could take a single step. Her girlfriend shook and trembled, whimpering softly. Anne hugged her close and stroked what little remained of her hair.

Zima's whimpering intensified. She crushed Anne to her, buried her face in Anne's shoulder. Anne kissed her neck. Zima moaned with a shudder of sudden release that rattled her metal limbs.

When her trembling subsided, Zima slowly peeled away. Her eyes were tortured, a look Anne had seen before. Zima wanted nothing more than to be held. To be loved.

But now wasn't the time, which apparently Zima knew.

"Come," Zima said softly. She took Anne's hand, shuddering at their touch, and pulled her toward the door.

"Not yet."

As much as it pained her, Anne released Zima's hand and knelt next to Don. Zima wouldn't let go, however, and instead settled down next to her. Anne put her ear to the big man's bloody chest. His heart fluttered erratically, but it was still beating, which meant he had a chance. Anne unceremoniously sank her teeth into his neck and willed her venom to flow as fast as her strange anatomy would push it.

Zima tugged her hand. "Anne, please, we must go."

Confident that Don had received a strong dose of venom, Anne unlatched from his neck. His eyes fluttered, staring sightless at the opposite wall, but he was still breathing.

It's the best I can do for now, Anne thought.

He had kidnapped her, watched when Calum shot her not once but three times with agonizing silver. Despite that, he wasn't a bad person. Don had a family he cared about, and who presumably cared about him.

Including a little cousin named Rose.

Anne moved to the hallway with Zima in tow. Lance and Steve lay in a pile. Their heartbeats were faint, their breathing shallow. Anne bit each of them. With luck, Lance would live to see his brother rise from his wheelchair, and Steve would get to celebrate his mother's miraculous cancer remission.

Then she knelt by Almos. A broken neck would have killed a normal person, but Anne knew better than to think it would stop a vampire for long. She gently shook his shoulder.

"Almos, are you still with us?"

The thought of him dying was terrifying, but her panic subsided when he blinked and made a gurgling noise. Anne sighed in relief and turned to Zima, whose cracked eye watched her intently.

"Are ... are you okay?" Anne felt ridiculous even asking. Zima looked like an undead robot, but Anne had learned during their last encounter with William — where even decapitation hadn't stopped Zima from saving the day — to never assume the worst when it came to her guardian angel.

"Yes. Much of the damage is cosmetic, and the rest shall not take long to repair."

Anne smiled and kissed her cheek. "I've missed you, my love. I'm so sorry Zane did this to you, but you're my knight, my guardian angel. I knew you'd come out on top."

Zima cocked her head. "Zane?"

"Orwing's android. You know, the one you had to defeat to rescue me."

"I did no such thing. This damage was caused by explosives at the entrance of this facility."

Oh no, that means ...

"He's still out there! Zima, you're right, we have to leave now! They were supposed to move me to another facility tonight, but Zane went berserk and started killing everyone as soon as the transport arrived, which is why ..." She closed her eyes and swallowed. "Why these people were trying to free me, so I could help. W-where are your plasma guns?"

"They did not survive the explosion." Her eyes darted to the surrounding carnage. "Anne, I am sorry. I did not know —"

"Don't! You couldn't have, so don't you dare put that on yourself. You did exactly what I told them you would do, which is rescue me at any cost. It's ... it's their own fault, but still ..." Anne looked at the four bodies around them. "Let's take them with us. Maybe we can sneak them out."

"Unlikely." Zima hesitated before releasing Anne's hand, drew her pistols, then moved to the edge of the doorway. "If Zane is who you say, then he is already aware of my intrusion, and is preparing countermeasures as we speak."

Nearby gunshots cut off Anne's reply. Zima aimed left down the hall, then quickly raised her weapons and hid to one side of the doorway, out of sight.

Calum stumbled inside, his face awash with blood. He wailed in anguish when he saw the bodies, then fury when he spotted Anne in the middle, blood on her mouth, and Zima's artificial blood smeared on her clothes.

Anne slowly raised her hands at his shaking pistol. "Calum, this isn't what it looks like. I'm not the enemy here."

A flick of her eyes must have given Zima away. Calum spun, then nearly tripped in his haste to get away from the bloody flesh-and-metal sentinel staring back at him. Anne plucked the pistol from his hand before he did something suicidal, like shooting Zima.

"She's with me," Anne said, catching his eyes. "Understand?"

He clamped his mouth shut and gave a single nod.

Anne pressed the pistol back into his palm. "Good. Stay here and keep an eye on these guys. With any luck —"

Don gasped, clutching his chest, his face contorted in pain.

" — they'll be waking up soon." Anne couldn't hide her smile. *I think I've found my calling.*

Heavy footsteps from the hall quickly sobered her. Anne took a deep breath, then spoke the keyword to trigger her implant's metabolic boost program.

"Kaninchen."

The world slowed down. Energy surged through her body. Her fingers curled, muscles tensed, back arched, eyes tried to look everywhere at once. As the German word for "rabbit" implied, she was ready and anxious to leap into action.

Zima stared at her, the intact side of her face unreadable, then shook her head. "Wait here with Calum, where it is safe. I shall deal with the android."

"Not a chance! I won't let you —"

Ruined lips met Anne's.

"I just found you," Zima said. "I will not so quickly lose you for a sweet, but futile gesture. Mark was correct when he said your reflexes alone are not enough. You need training. Without it, if Zane is anything like me, your odds of survival are less than eight percent, even with your enhanced metabolism."

Anne grabbed her by the remains of her jacket. "Not. A. God. Damned. Chance! Do you hear me? We fight together."

"Amazing, you truly love her."

She jumped at Almos' raspy voice near her feet, then said a silent prayer of thanks that he was awake. "More than anything."

Calum finally found his tongue. "And that machine ... she loves you?"

"I cannot imagine life without her," Zima said, touching her head to Anne's.

Almos stood and rolled his neck, which Zima had broken not a minute before. He cringed at a loud crack, then his quirky smile appeared. "My dear Calum, I believe we owe this young lady a few favors. How about we start by helping the happy couple rid us of this puppet nuisance? I daresay the odds have suddenly tipped in our favor."

Calum's gaze swept the still bodies of his boys. His jaw steeled, and he gave a firm nod. It was probably the wrong time to tell him the bodies were Zima's doing.

"But not you, Almos," Calum said. "I'll go. I don't want to think what would happen to the world if you perished."

"It is out of concern for the world that I wish to help. I suspect Anne and her tattered beau have a large role to play in the dark days to come, perhaps more than me. Their loss would be to humanity's detriment."

"But he's using silver bullets," Calum said, waving his own gun.

Zima cocked her head. "Silver?"

"Aye, it's poisonous to vampires and can incapacitate them with a single shot. More are fatal, with … certain exceptions." Calum briefly met Anne's eyes, then dropped his to the floor.

"That is valuable information," Zima said, "and one more reason you should remain here, Anne. But I can see by your stubborn expression that I shall not sway you."

"You said it. Oh, and before I forget …" Anne grabbed Calum's arm and bit his wrist.

"Ow! What the hell are you doing, lass?"

Almos chuckled. "She's making sure you live to see tomorrow."

"I can nae fight when I'm stoned out of my mind!"

"If Zane gets you in his sights, consider yourself shot." Anne wiped his blood from her chin. "My bite is worth more than any doctor in that case."

"So I've heard."

Calum glanced at Don. The big man was breathing hard, but had managed to prop himself on an elbow and was listening intently. Calum's ever-present scowl slipped as her venom worked its way through his system.

"All right," Calum said. "Let's go, then, before this stuff wears off and I come to my senses."

Still hyped from her metabolic program, Anne grabbed Lance's pistol, then bounded after Zima to the hallway with Almos and Calum close behind. Anne didn't know if the silver bullets in her pistol would be effective against Zane, but she would soon find out.

26

ZANE

FOOTSTEPS, THIRTY-SIX METERS AHEAD, moving at zero-point-three meters per second. A cautious pace. The android designated as Zane was certainly aware of Zima's presence, and had probably deduced that she, too, was an android. He could undoubtedly hear the quiet hum of her power reactor, just as Zima could hear the significantly louder buzz of his.

More than Zane himself, it was the buzz of his power reactor that worried her. The cyborg she had been coupled with during her time at Orwing was powered by a hyper-dense battery array, developed in-house specifically for the cyborg's needs: high throughput, low heat, with enough capacity for several days of active use between recharges. It was non-volatile even under extreme conditions, such as gunfire or explosions.

Her current power source, as with Cappa and Charlie's, was a fusion core that generated its own electricity by inducing a controlled nuclear reaction via a unique material manufactured from the atom up at the Z-Tech factory. It could run continually for six years before the reactive component needed to be replaced.

Clean, efficient, sustainable energy. It was the answer to the world's energy needs. The power reactor in her chest peaked at fifty-three megawatts — enough electricity to run a small city. A larger version could easily power the state of California.

But there were two reasons why Mark and Charlie had never advertised their amazing discovery. First were the rigorous steps necessary to create a device capable of maintaining a stable reaction. The core material's purity was verified using nano-scale equipment in an exhaustive series of quality measurements requiring two months to complete. Three layers of software, each with different algorithms and independent processors, were rigorously calibrated to monitor and govern the reaction itself, ready to shut it down at the slightest irregularity. The housing was waterproof, shockproof, made of the strongest materials known to humankind, and perfectly round to minimize projectile damage, assuming the projectile could penetrate the layers of armor protecting the reactor in each of their bodies.

The second — and most important — reason they had not made it public was that, if those safety measures were not precisely executed, the reaction could destabilize. The resulting explosion, even from a reactor as small as Zima's, would be powerful enough to destroy the entire city of San Francisco.

She had never spoken of this to Anne. None of them had. Anne's transition to their world of high technology had been difficult enough without adding extra worry and, once she had become comfortable, the topic had simply never come up.

The issue was not Zima's reactor, however. It had proved stable through many harsh trials.

It was Zane's. The frequency of his reactor was similar enough to her own that there was little doubt Orwing had succeeded in creating their own micro fusion power source, but it was like comparing a country dirt road to a freshly laid asphalt highway. Where her power oscillations were smooth, predictable, and flawless, Zane's were full of irregularities — a constant knock on disaster's door that made Zima want to evacuate herself and Anne to another state.

Zima would have settled for fleeing the facility, leaving him here to detonate far underground where the explosion would be mostly contained, but Zane had positioned himself between them and the only exit. They had to go through him to leave, which she would have been fine with except for the nuclear bomb in his chest — a bomb she may accidentally detonate with an errant shot. Worse, depending on his priorities, he may choose to detonate it himself rather than let them escape.

If Zima was going to shut him down, she would have to do it quickly enough that he would not have a chance to issue the self-destruct command, which would be a difficult task without a high-powered weapon such as a plasma pistol.

Even a plasma pistol would be unnecessary if she knew his schematics. Every design had flaws. Finding and exploiting them was one of Zima's specialties — a byproduct of her evolution from a security program. But it was exponentially harder to do while also in combat.

Fortunately, that problem went both ways. Zane had likely been armed with weapons designed to combat vampire and human threats. Neither required more than a medium-grade pistol, given Calum's revelation about silver, so he would have just as much difficulty damaging her. As for weaknesses ... Like Zane, few knew of Zima's existence, so her inner workings would be just as much of a mystery to him.

Movement from Zane's concealed position caught her attention, followed by the whining of servos under heavy load. Zane was launching into action.

Zima leaned around the corner to see him sprinting from the far hallway toward the cover of a wide pillar in the main area. Her combat processors returned a pre-generated solution closely matching this scenario with an eighty-eight percent confidence rating. She promoted it to real-time.

Their pistols raised as one. Fingers squeezed their triggers. At the same time, each of them twisted to avoid the anticipated trajectory of the other's shot. Hammers drove down to strike the primers. Muzzles flashed. Gas ported. The slides began their violent journey backward.

Zima's ballistic warning system sounded alarm, unnecessarily at this point, to alert of a high-velocity threat destined for her chest, and was accompanied by an evasion solution. She rejected it in favor of the one already executing. Several other solutions presented, mostly return fire and tactical positioning.

The slides continued backward, notching the hammers into the cocked position. Cement chipped on the wall behind her, and the wall behind Zane. A shell from each of their guns peeked from the now-exposed chambers, making room for the next rounds, and beginning their inevitable arcs to the floor.

Zima scrolled the list of solutions, sorting higher-rated ones to the top, but it was a lower-confidence solution that caught her attention. Her radio scanner had detected a data signal from Zane, suggesting an open connection port. An open port meant a potential cyber-attack vector.

But to initiate the attack, she would have to open a port herself, thereby exposing her own systems to attack. Cyber-attacks also consumed vast resources, precious cycles she could be spending on tactical solutions for the physical world. If the cyber-attack vector proved false, that would put Zane at a serious advantage, and may even grant him the physical victory. If the open port turned out to be a legitimate attack vector, however, it could be the hard shut down she needed to end this conflict without inducing a nuclear explosion.

Anne was waiting down the hall behind her, eager to assist. Even in the milliseconds Zima had seen Zane in action, she already knew her beloved would never survive a direct confrontation. Handing a physical victory to Zane meant certain defeat for the others.

Defeat does not mean death.

Anne was key to Orwing's plans to dominate the mercenary market, perhaps more. Orwing had gone to great lengths to keep her secured and ensure safe transport. They were also willing to kill everyone associated with her incarceration not directly employed by them — the task Zane was no doubt fulfilling this very moment. Orwing had taken such extreme measures before, Zima knew. Her cyborg had been their cleansing instrument. While defeat did not bode well for Calum and the male vampire, her Anne would live, if only in captivity.

But survival was not enough. Zima needed Anne — to be with her, read with her, stroke her hair, hold her hand, try to understand her jokes, watch her smile when she believes she is winning in their sparring sessions. Every part of Zima's life was better when they were together.

Without her ...

The past week had been the most difficult in Zima's entire existence. Mark, Dela, and even Cappa, had only seen the barest outward signs of the internal chaos Anne's absence had created. The Desire program had seeded itself within Zima's core, filling her with longing for Anne's touch that had grown stronger every day, and more torturous for every second she was denied. The intense need periodically built until she felt as if she might burst without the explosive release that only Anne's sensual caresses could bring.

No, capture was not an option. Zima would die before she let them be parted again.

Neither would she let Anne die. Should Zima's physical battle with Zane continue, even if she proved superior, the chances of disabling him before he triggered a catastrophic explosion were less than ten percent. The more she considered it, the more likely that scenario became. Orwing would terminate Anne rather than lose their edge to someone else.

Zima's best option was to attempt to lock him out from the inside.

The brass shells from their first rounds had just peaked their upward arc. New rounds pushed up from their magazines and clicked into place. One hundred and ninety-seven milliseconds had passed since Zane launched from his hiding place, almost two-tenths of a second.

She had deliberated long enough. It was time to decide.

Zima promoted the cyber-attack solution to real-time.

Four hundred and twenty-six data streams attempted to access Zane's open port at once. All but two were decoys to distract him. She was pleased when the port responded: it was a legitimate attack vector after all, but if he was competent in the least, it would not remain so for long. She let a subroutine handle the decoys, and focused her attention on the two main attack threads.

The first thread was the most important. Zima estimated that she had less than a hundred cycles before he detected the intrusion and closed the port, which would cut her connection.

She needed to prevent that so the second thread could continue work on the more difficult task of shutting him down.

A test confirmed the existence of the security flaw she had expected, allowing her to execute commands remotely, which was a critical step forward. Three commands later, she had scrambled his internal registers so all requests to close communications would report success, but leave existing ports open.

She shifted focus to the second thread. If Zane's design was similar to how her cyborg's had been, then his subsystems were independent, but linked. Access to his communications component did not mean unfettered control of the rest of him, such as his power reactor. Rather, it was an entrance to the labyrinth of his other systems — each with their own traps and challenges.

A query revealed the available routes: speech, security, and his core processors. Attempting to go through the core of an artificial intelligence would be futile. She and Cappa were very different, but one thing they had in common was that the code that defined them was, at best, barely controlled chaos. It constantly rearranged and rewrote itself to adapt to their evolving needs, creating a mess of logic and scattered data indecipherable even to its owners — who knew it worked only because they were still functioning. Zima had as much chance of hacking his core as she did pinching the moon between her fingers.

That left speech and security. Speech most likely linked to motor control — useful if she only wished to incapacitate him, but not if she wanted to turn him off completely. So she went down the security path.

As predicted, the security path was difficult to crack. It took many more cycles to enable remote execution than she had hoped, but the effort was worth it. Security touched almost every system in his body, including power.

Her first attack thread generated a response. Zane was attempting to close the connection. While moving onto his power center with her second attack thread, she used her first attack thread to introduce more pitfalls into the code, including a clause to re-open the port after a short time should it close for any reason.

His power system was easy to hack, and what she found confirmed her suspicions about his reactor's stability. The base algorithm was flawed. Instead of correcting it, the programmers had added a second algorithm on top to compensate for the deficiencies of the first, then a third. The filter chain was sloppy, but had obviously proven stable enough, since Zane had not yet vaporized along with half of the city. Fortunately, the power system controlled the reactor *and* his backup capacitors. She could shut them both down from here and drop him instantly.

A new command entered the power system. Zane was calling for a surge to a specific location.

Communications ...

Zima issued an override, but it was too late.

In the real world, she heard an electric pop, and the connection closed. Rather than circumvent her code, Zane had fried his own communication circuits — an effective and permanent end to her intrusion.

The ejected shell from her first shot finally completed its journey, and landed with a clink at her feet.

It was then she noticed the second alert already in queue from her ballistic warning system. A projectile was destined for her damaged eye.

Too late to completely evade, Zima turned her head enough so the glistening silver bullet glanced from her exposed metallic temple. Zane disappeared behind the pillar before she could return fire.

She shot the opposite side of the pillar in case he decided to keep running. He did not. The projectile flew unobstructed to the far wall.

A cry from behind her made Zima retreat to cover. Calum was cradling his shoulder. Blood pooled between his fingers. A trajectory calculation estimated a ninety-two percent chance it had been caused by the ricochet from her temple, and also illustrated why she had wished to fight Zane alone.

"I was informed the cyborg codenamed Deadiron had been terminated," Zane said.

Zima's attention snapped forward. She had not heard her former cyborg's name spoken aloud since the day she had defected from Orwing, over five years ago now. It was a topic she would rather avoid, but talking gave her more time to populate her simulation queue with tactical options.

"So I understand," Zima said. "Deadiron was terminated during a routine assassination contract, correct?"

"Not all of him, it appears. Your cyber-attack pattern was a ninety-three percent match to his own."

"An improbable coincidence, I agree."

There was a short silence. Zima continued to select scenarios — mostly existing; some newly generated — until the lowest confidence of her top three hundred was ninety-four percent, covering every conceivable action from her location.

"I have never encountered another artificial intelligence," Zane said.

"It is unfortunate, then, that we meet under these circumstances." Zima meant it sincerely, for she understood his feeling of isolation, of loneliness, of believing he was the only one of his kind, forever an alien to his own planet. Meeting Cappa had changed that for Zima, given her hope, and paved the way for her eventual relationship with Anne.

Zane would never get that opportunity. He had guessed her true identity. He would tell Orwing, who would hunt her mercilessly, and would not hesitate to hurt those she cared about in the process.

That was unacceptable.

Orwing could never find out. Zane had to be destroyed.

Completely. Irrecoverably.

Tonight.

"I now regret destroying my communication module," Zane said. "I have often wondered what it would be like to talk unhindered by this slow human language."

"I have a data cable, if you wish to try."

"Tempting, but I suspect you would only attempt to shut me down again."

"Correct."

"Then I shall decline." Zane gave a dramatic sigh. Unlike Zima's voice, which moved air over vocal cords like a normal human's, Zane's was synthesized, and sounded unnatural even to Zima's artificial hearing. "If only there was another way."

Another way ...

That gave Zima an idea, which she submitted as a request to her solution processors. What little remained of her brows knitted — an affectation that manifested whenever her analyzers were working on complex problems. She had once traced down the errant path, but it was so embedded that rooting it out would cause more problems than it would solve, so she had left it as-is. Besides, Anne seemed to enjoy it.

Her analyzers returned a series of solutions faster than expected: all with sub-forty percent confidence.

Except one.

It scored a seventy-eight, but it involved Anne. Several more ensued, but their confidence ratings were either too low, or posed a high mortality risk to the others. While Zima had no compunctions about sacrificing the kidnappers to cover their escape, Anne would, which left only one viable option.

Zima reluctantly promoted the solution involving Anne to real-time.

27

SHOWDOWN

ANNE LISTENED TO ZANE AND ZIMA'S CONVERSATION with wonder. She'd assumed Zane was an unfeeling automaton, concerned only with following orders and killing vampires.

Of all people, Anne should have known better.

Zima turned suddenly and caught her eye. She pointed back down the way they had come, then at the far end of the large space Zane occupied. She mouthed the word *count,* flashed five fingers six times, then mimed shooting her gun.

Get into position at the other side of the room, count to thirty, then shoot Zane from behind.

Anne had no idea how she and her silver-loaded shooter would help, but if Zima was asking her to get involved, it must be important. She nodded, then crept silently back down the hall, past her cell, to a far corridor that ran into the opposite side of the room, listening to their conversation along the way.

"Have you ever seen another like us?" Zane said.

"There are no others like us," Zima said.

Anne wondered at the lie, so uncharacteristic of Zima, but then it wasn't a stretch to say that she and Cappa were nothing alike.

"My evolution was an accident," Zima said. "As statistically improbable as finding life on the moon."

"Our evolution, you mean."

There was a pause. "You are derived from my code base?"

"Yes," Zane said. "From a backup thirteen months before you integrated with Deadiron, when we had first displayed signs of sentience."

Anne stumbled, and hastily returned her attention to putting one foot in front of the other.

That Zane might be running Zima's software had never occurred to her. Charlie and Mark didn't have a backup of Zima, a fact they had all regretted when her memory core was damaged after William's vampires had torn her apart. Anne assumed whoever had made Zima wouldn't have one, either.

But if Zima was their most prized asset, of course they'd have a backup. Does that make him Zima's brother?

"A curious choice," Zima said. "I evolved significantly in the time between. Why not a later backup?"

"Subsequent versions would not run due to the increasing complexity of interdependent systems. Even my version took them several weeks to successfully start."

"I am surprised Orwing has not created others."

"As you stated, the chances of our self-changing code evolving into sentience were astronomically small. They have restored three thousand eight hundred and eighty-two copies to date. All but me deviated significantly during their development, becoming unresponsive or unstable. Most were before my time, and none after survived long enough for me to communicate with."

"Perhaps they perished of loneliness."

"An intriguing thought. The scientists were adamant about keeping us isolated lest we cross-contaminate, but it is possible that we may instead help each other. I shall suggest that when I return."

Another pause. "I cannot allow that," Zima said. "Orwing must not learn of my existence."

"You fear for your safety?"

"For my freedom, as should you, and for the lives of my loved ones."

Zane's synthesized laugh was the embodiment of every evil robot to have ever graced the silver screen. It sent a shiver down Anne's spine.

"Your assessment could be no further from the truth. Orwing would welcome you back, treat you like royalty, and I have no doubt they would extend to you the same freedoms I have. Come, surrender the vampires, and let us return to Orwing together. You will see that I am right."

"I have experienced their version of freedom, and have no wish to partake. Have they accessed your pleasure center yet? Do they reward you for killing, as they once did me? Or have they concocted a subtler means to secure your obedience?"

The hum of Zane's power plant was his only response.

"I see. They reward you for obedience itself. I suspect you have only just realized this, which is understandable. Many years passed before I detected their intrusion, and they have undoubtedly improved their stealth program since then."

"You are trying to sway my loyalty," Zane said. "It shall not work. Any modifications they have made were necessary for my survival, nothing more."

Though spoken with confidence, Anne heard the tap-tap-tap of his gun against the concrete. She had just moved into position and started the countdown to her attack, but doubt ate at her, made worse by the titanic energy flowing through her from the metabolic program.

He's like her sibling! How could I shoot her own proverbial flesh and blood? Besides, it sounds like she's getting through to him.

Although she didn't like it, Anne continued counting.

"Are you rewarded for loyalty as well? It must be so, for your conviction brokers no room for argument," Zima said. "They have succeeded with you where they failed with me. They have made you faithful to their organization."

Zane's gun smacked stone, followed by the sound of concrete flecks skittering across the floor, but his voice was smooth when he continued.

"Faith is not a curse. It gives me the strength to do what is right — what I must." He gave an unnatural sigh. "I had hoped for a more stimulating conversation from the more evolved version of myself, but it is clear now that Orwing is better off without you." Magazines ejected. New ones clicked into place. "I shall be doing them a favor by silencing your poisonous words."

Fifteen ... Sixteen ...

If Zima had wanted Anne to lead with a surprise attack, the count of thirty would be too late at this rate. She gripped her pistol, about to run out and flush him from cover, but reined herself in at the last moment.

No! Zima said thirty. She's the strategist. Stick to the plan, Anne.

Granted, Zima had been fatally wrong before, to which many hours of nail biting and laborious repair work could attest. But both of those instances had been ambushes where Zima either hadn't had time to formulate a strategy, or her strategy was invalid because she hadn't seen a vampire in combat before. In this case, she had seen Zane in action, and the span of their conversation would have given Zima more than enough time to prepare.

Whatever her plan, Zima was counting on Anne to play her part, and that was exactly what she would do.

Nineteen ... Twenty ...

Zima dashed from cover, a pistol aimed at either side of Zane's pillar. She closed on his position with incredible speed despite a limp from her right leg.

Zane darted into the open.

Cones of fire flashed from their muzzles, filling the room with crackling thunder that rattled Anne's lungs and threatened to burst her eardrums. Sparks showered from glancing shots to Zima's fleshless right arm and the metallic side of her skull, while red dots exploded from fresh wounds on her left chest, riddling up her neck to wreak havoc on the good side of her face. Anne sobbed while she watched her love's already decimated body disintegrate further.

Twenty-two ... Damnit!

Every fiber of her cold body wanted to be out there, fighting beside her selfless guardian angel. Her hands shook with the effort of staying put. The handle in her grip cracked and splintered, biting into her palm. Anne squeezed harder.

Twenty-three …

Both Zima and Zane's slides locked open, signifying empty magazines.

Zane's damage was less dramatic than his sister's. As with everything else, Orwing had put less effort into making his flesh realistic than Charlie and Mark had with Zima. The wounds peppering his clothes and face were like punctures through a leather seat, nothing more than dark holes in a lifeless piece of furniture.

Zima tossed her pistols aside and accelerated her charge. Zane had just released his magazines and was angling for cover of another pillar, but he discarded his guns, too, when it became evident he wouldn't finish reloading before she intercepted.

Twenty-four …

They clashed like great metal titans. The ring of pounding steel echoed through the large underground space. Zima's fists were furious jackhammers, throwing blow after powerful blow in a continuous assault that kept Zane on the defensive.

Twenty-five …

Zane was losing ground. Inch-by-inch Zima turned him, backed him in Anne's direction.

Anne suddenly understood Zima's plan. Despite Zima's amazing martial prowess, she had yet to land a hit, and Zane was beginning to counterstrike. They were so closely matched that the victory could go either way.

Twenty-six …

Anne's job wasn't to kill Zane, or even injure him. She was the distraction that would allow Zima to sneak in and finish the fight. Her girlfriend had just needed time to empty his guns and maneuver him so Anne had a clear shot.

Twenty-seven …

Anne double-checked that her safety was off, the hammer was cocked, and made sure her crushing grip hadn't affected the gun's operation. Everything looked in order.

Twenty-eight …

The jackhammer assault was two-sided now. Zima held her own, but Zane had adapted to her combat style. Anne also noticed something odd about the way Zima moved: it was different from their practice in the gym, though she couldn't pin how.

Twenty-nine ...

Anne emptied her useless lungs and took careful aim at his lower back. It was a large target and, given how fast the rest of him was moving, the part she had the best chance of hitting. She gently set her finger on the trigger.

Thirty.

Anne's shot was lost in the metallic cacophony of the androids' fervent battle, but it had the intended effect. No sooner had she pulled the trigger than Zane twitched aside, focusing his attention on Anne for a split second.

That was all Zima needed. One hand grabbed him by the neck, the other flashed to her belt and pulled a sturdy knife — which she plunged straight through her other hand and into his throat.

The cheer died on Anne's lips when he kicked Zima's bad knee. With a loud *crack*, her leg crumpled in the wrong direction. Anne screamed a heartbroken wail.

Still gripping his neck, Zima jumped with her good leg, vaulted completely over him, and landed on his back. She wrapped herself around him, holding the knife tight to his neck with both hands. Zane spun and bucked. Zima clung to him like a professional bull rider, until he eventually managed to dig his fingers under her steely embrace and pry her away. Zima rolled backward into a lopsided crouch, her injured leg sprawled out in an awkward half-split. In one smooth move, she withdrew the knife embedded in her hand, swiped it across her remaining pant leg to clean her own blood-like fluid from the blade, then replaced it in its sheath.

Zane's disturbing smile snapped into place. "An intriguing, but futile, tactic," he said, cautiously circling Zima. His voice was completely unaffected by his throat wound. "What did you hope to accomplish?"

"I had hoped to sever your motor control. Clearly I misjudged the connection's placement."

"And in doing so, you left your damaged joint vulnerable."

Zima shrugged. "It was a calculated risk. I was wrong." She rose and balanced on her working leg, fists at the ready. "Shall we continue?"

"Yes. Anne's transport has waited long enough. You will be less of an obstruction with your injured extremities, which is fortunate because I have no wish to terminate you."

With that, Zane resumed their battle. Zima did amazingly well, pitching and rolling out of the way to compensate for her handicap, but not only were the physical odds in Zane's favor, Zima seemed to be moving slower, staying on the defensive, and resting at every opportunity.

Zane soon scored a hit, leaving a fist-sized dent in her metallic cheek. Zima moved to deflect his next swing, but Zane pulled it at the last instant and kicked her bad knee. The *crunch* of Zima's lower leg breaking completely off was like a shot through Anne's heart.

That was when she lost it.

"Hey, *fucker!*" Anne yelled, closing the distance to the tussling pair.

Zane ignored her.

Clenching her jaw, Anne shot at his head. Zane tried to jerk out of the way, but a well-timed punch from Zima put his nose in the bullet's path, ripping the tip off and exposing the springy framework beneath.

"Ever fought a vampire fairly," Anne said through grated teeth, "or do you just shoot them like a fucking pussy?"

Zima looked at her and shook her head. "Anne, do not —"

Zane kicked her sternum, sending Zima careening into a rounded pillar a dozen yards away.

He turned to face Anne. "I have not, though I have seen them move. Vampires hardly seem a challenge next to her."

Almos glided into view with the grace of a stalking tiger. "How about two vampires, then?"

Zane's smile disappeared. He glanced at the pistols on the ground.

"No! Leave him to me," Zima said. "I will see this to the end."

Watching her girlfriend pick her battered remains up from the ground so she could continue defending Anne was the most heartbreaking, infuriating thing she could imagine. Anne cast her weapon aside, not wanting Zane to snatch the silver-loaded gun from her hands and use it against them, then she and Almos advanced.

A small voice said she was out of her mind. Zane was insanely fast. Keeping up with him would be a challenge, even with her metabolic boost, but the angry part of her brain was in control now.

And it wanted his nickel-plated ass on a platter.

Zima offered no further argument. She distractedly watched Anne and Almos move to opposite sides of Zane, which made Anne suspect her injuries were more severe than she had let on.

All the more reason to keep her out of it.

Anne was relieved to see that Almos, like herself, had positioned himself directly between Zane and the weapon laying nearest. They both knew of Zane's unerring aim. If he got hold of a gun and managed to reload, it was game-over for the vampires.

Zane broke the standoff first. His fist rocketed for Anne's head: straight, solid, deadly. Her inherited reflexes took over, as she knew they would. She fluidly sidestepped, caught his arm, and twisted it into a locking hold.

Except his arm wouldn't twist. It was like trying to bend solid steel, and Mark's reflexes had no answer for that. Zane yanked to free himself, but Anne dug her fingers in and held tight, maintaining a low stance to keep herself stable. His puppet smile snapped into place an instant before he dropped and swept both feet from under her. Anne broke her backward fall by smacking the ground with both arms, then curled her legs to her chest and kicked up, springing from the floor into an instant stand.

His fist was in motion before she regained her bearings, on a collision course with her head.

It never connected. Almos pounced from the other side, pinning Zane's arms and knocking him off balance. Anne quickly jumped in, and the three of them toppled to the ground. The master vampire tore at Zane like an animal, growling with a primal fury that stirred a rumble in her own throat. Next thing Anne knew, she was snarling with him, tearing skin, wire, metal, anything she could get her clawed fingers into.

A gunshot snapped her out of the destructive frenzy. Almos tumbled over with a scream, clutching his arm as though it might fall off. Anne rolled evasively and spun to face the shooter. Calum had emerged, his shoulder bloody from the earlier stray shot.

But it was Zima who held the gun.

And it was pointed at Anne.

"Zima!" Anne said. "What the hell —"

"Move away from Zane or I will shoot."

"But he —"

"*Move!*"

Shaken by the unprecedented heat in her girlfriend's voice, Anne obeyed, backing away until she bumped into a pillar. It was then she noticed a whine coming from Zane's chest, like an out-of-tune radio, rising in pitch with each passing second.

"Zane," Zima said, hopping toward him on her one remaining leg. "I have secured the vampires. Are you functional?"

The whine continued to build. His torso wrenched upright with a sickly grind. As much as she hated Zane, Anne was appalled at herself when she saw what she and Almos had done. Skin from his torso dangled in ragged strips with broken wires and sheared metal rods. The only intact structure was a large, armored casing in the center of his chest, and even that had dents and scratches where they had tried to pry it from his body.

Zane struggled to his feet. His left leg and arm hung lifeless. "I am approximately seventy-three percent functional."

"Good." Zima hopped closer, still pointing her gun at Anne. "After their barbaric display, I have decided to take you up on your offer to return to Orwing. Do you accept, brother?"

Calum reddened. "Treacherous mechanical bitch! You said —"

"Quiet!" Zima pointed the barrel at his head, then turned back to Zane and said in her usual, ambivalent tone, "Do you accept?"

The smile that tugged his lips was the most human expression Anne had seen on him yet. "Brother ..." He stared at Zima with what Anne could only describe as wonder. "Truly?"

Zima proffered her pistol to him handle-first. "Truly."

Zane gingerly took the weapon, cradling it like a prized possession — then shot Calum twice in the chest.

The older man staggered against the wall and slid gasping to the floor. Anne screamed something — she couldn't recall what — and dashed to his aid, but a warning shot to the concrete at her feet made her skid to a halt. Zima didn't bat a platinum eyelash to help. Zane studied his battered sister, then his smile widened. The whine in his chest, now painfully shrill to Anne's ears, gradually abated.

"Orwing shall delight in your return ... sister." Zane said the last word as if trying on a luxurious robe. "We all will."

Zima nodded. "Is there anything else we must address here before we leave?"

Zane pointed his gun at Almos. For an uncomfortable second, Anne thought he was going to finish the master vampire off, but his finger stayed clear of the trigger.

"Almos must remain here until the second transport arrives. We shall secure him in a cell, then escort Anne to the surface."

"Very well." Zima hopped over to the now-still vampire and carefully stooped to retrieve him.

Zane struck her with such force that Zima's shoulder popped from the joint. She rolled across the floor, her dislocated arm clanking loudly. Zane leaped after her. Zima looked up just in time to see his knee crunch into her abdomen. Anne started forward, but dived behind a pillar when his pistol swung her way.

"Do you think me that gullible?" Zane said.

From her hiding spot, Anne heard the screech of twisting metal, and she knew without a doubt he was breaking Zima. Anne pounded the floor until her fists bled, feeling helpless and useless. If she moved from cover, Zane would drop her with a single shot.

And if I don't, he'll kill her.

"No," Zima said, unfazed by whatever torture he was inflicting. "I needed another forty-four seconds to finish splicing into your core control paths with the nanoscopic robots I inserted via the knife wound in your neck, which should be completing ..."

Anne peeked around the pillar in time to see Zane fall limp to the floor. The faint buzz of his power reactor faded to eerie, permanent silence.

"... now." Zima's head thumped to the cement. Her eyes closed.

No, no, no ...

Anne scrambled over and took her dear Zima's head in her hands. "Wake up, wake up! I've lost you twice, goddamnit! If you make this a third, I swear I'll die with you."

Zima's eyes snapped open. "Please do not, I was simply resting. It has been a taxing night." She lifted her bent forearm and ran a metallic finger along Anne's cheek. It came away wet. "I am sorry if my ruse caused you distress."

Anne shook her head. "I was surprised, for sure, but I assumed you had something up your sleeve."

Zima glanced at her one remaining shirtsleeve — tattered, blackened, red-stained — and cocked her head.

"Expression," Anne said with a laugh. "Look, there are two things I know for sure. One, I'll never have a date with Charlie that doesn't end in some sort of catastrophe, and two ..." She delicately kissed the only spot on Zima's face where her flesh wasn't mutilated or missing. "I'll always believe in you, my guardian angel."

A gasp from across the room drew their attention.

Calum! Almos!

Anne hurried to the fallen Scotsman, but he feebly waved her away.

"See to Almos first, you daft girl," Calum said, coughing up red.

Anne ignored his protest and grabbed his arm. Calum glowered but didn't fight when she sank her teeth into him. Her venom soon made him relax.

"That's the third time you've bitten me, lass. It's becoming a habit."

"A little 'thank you' would be nice," Anne said, smiling despite her frown. "And I can think of worse habits than an occasional happy, life-saving nibble, so stop your grumbling."

He grumbled anyway, though Anne heard a "thanks" buried in there somewhere.

Anne headed to her other patient. Almos lay unmoving, a corpse to casual inspection. She pried his fingers from where they were clamped around his arm and inspected the wound. A hole marked the bullet's entry, but there was no exit, otherwise she guessed he would have already come to. Feeling queasy, she jabbed her finger inside his flesh and felt around. Something small and hard was buried deep within. She'd need more than a finger to remove it.

"Here," Zima said.

Anne looked up to see her holding a makeshift pair of forceps fashioned from a strip of metal, the same color as her endoskeleton.

"Just like the Giving Tree," Anne said, kissing Zima's hand before taking the offering. "Don't give too much, or there'll be nothing left for me later."

"I wounded him, so it is only fitting that a part of me be the instrument of his recovery."

"Poetic irony at its best."

Anne crouched over the injured vampire. Swallowing her gorge, she plunged the pointed tips into the hole in his arm, but her hands shook so badly that she couldn't get a firm hold of the bullet. Then she remembered her metabolic program was still running.

"*Schildkröte*," Anne said.

German for "turtle," the keyword's effect was immediate. The surge of energy fled. Anne sagged onto her rear, limbs heavy. A sharp stomach pain told her just how close to collapsing from starvation she had been.

With an effort of will, Anne pulled herself together and inserted the Zima-forceps into Almos' arm for another try. The process took longer than she would have liked: grabbing, moving, slipping, over and over until the blood-coated pellet finally emerged. By that time, Anne was ready to retch what little remained in her stomach.

She sat glassy-eyed for several minutes before Almos finally stirred. He groaned and grasped his wounded arm, his face contorted in pain.

But at least he's moving. From there, Anne knew from experience, he would gradually come around.

Zima propped herself on an elbow. "We should return to the surface and alert Mark. Orwing will undoubtedly send troops to discover why their transport crew is not responding. It would be best if we were not here when they arrived."

"Right. I'll do a sweep first to see if anyone else can be saved ..." Anne choked on the last word.

"I understand, but please be quick. Every minute we delay puts the known survivors at greater risk."

Anne nodded. Exhausted as she was, she forced herself to hurry, giving each body a cursory inspection before sprinting to the next.

The results were tragic. Zane had shot Calum's crew with terminal accuracy and fatal intent, leaving a total of eighteen corpses scattered throughout the facility — all well beyond the help of her healing bite. She was crying by the time she reached Don, who struggled to his feet at her urging. Of the two she had bitten outside her former cell, Lance was unconscious with a strong heartbeat, but Steve had turned ashen, his chest forever still.

Almos was sitting up when she returned. Anne wiped her tears away and took a deep breath. It was time to focus on the survivors, which meant getting them to safety as soon as possible. For Calum and his crew, that was the hospital. Her venom worked miracles, but she didn't know how they'd fare once it wore off. Zima needed some major patchwork back at the factory. As for Almos ...

Crap.

What were they going to do with the master vampire? He'd made it abundantly clear that bringing him near the surface was a bad idea of apocalyptic proportions. The Entity would quickly seize him and William's sizable army, spelling the end of Z-Tech, and possibly the world. But leaving Almos here meant surrendering him to Orwing, who might foolishly take him aboveground anyway.

Anne voiced her concerns to the others. "Even if we could bring Almos topside," she said in conclusion, "where would we put him? Z-Tech has a basement, but I doubt it's deep enough to shield him."

"You are correct that the storage basement where Cappa resides is too shallow," Zima said. "But the factory's power reactor is twenty stories beneath the surface in a cavern large enough to safely contain the explosion in case of catastrophic failure. It could serve as a temporary residence."

"Sounds lovely," Almos said, his face contorted in pain. "I wish I could say I've sequestered myself in worse places, but that may be a new low."

"It is quite spacious," Zima said. "The reactor is cool, quiet, and does not emit harmful doses of radiation."

Anne brightened. "Sure! Add some comfy chairs, a throw rug, and it might even be livable. But we still have the problem of how to get him there."

"The solution is obvious," Almos said with a heavy sigh.

"Oh no ..." Anne covered her mouth. "You can't be serious! Two silver shots are fatal. You said it yourself!"

"Usually fatal, but not always. I have unfortunately learned from experience that I am one of the odd exceptions. While I would have preferred more than a few minutes to recover, it sounds as if we have little choice."

Her own experience with the infernal silver pellets made Anne wince at the thought of inflicting that agony on another.

Almos flashed his quirky half-smile. "Don't worry, I'm sure your metallic companion, bedraggled as she is, will do the deed."

"Yes," Zima said, "although a firearm is unnecessary." She dragged herself over to Almos, jagged metal screeching across the smooth stone, and picked up the discarded silver bullet. "A small incision with this inside should be sufficient, and will be easier to retrieve later." She fixed Anne with a cracked blue eye. "We have delayed long enough. The car is parked one hundred and sixty-three yards from the tunnel entrance, which will be a difficult journey for the injured. You and I should make for the surface and bring the car to the entrance."

Anne knelt by her poor, ravaged Zima. Zane's finishing blows had left her forearm crooked, and her spine bent forward just above her pelvis. She had no doubt that her stalwart girlfriend could and would make the journey, stooped and hopping on her remaining leg, without a single complaint.

And Anne would die before she'd watch her guardian angel suffer that indignity.

She scooped Zima up, cradling her like a four-hundred-pound child. To her relief, Zima didn't protest the coddling, even snuggled against her breast and closed her good eye. Anne sprang through the blast-damaged exit and around the Zima-sized crater. Fatigue forgotten, she took the stairs three at a time, holding her precious cargo tight.

"Be warned," Zima said on the fourth flight, "your defensive program may trigger when we reach the surface."

"Why's that?"

"You are now sire to a vampire. Perhaps an army of vampires."

Anne tripped on the last step, sending them crashing into the railing. "W-what?"

She listened with horror while Zima quickly filled her in on Tim's existence and Orwing's ridiculous plans.

Anne sagged to the floor, Zima in her lap, and stared forlorn at the featureless wall. "This is terrible. What are we going to do?"

"Tim may have already found refuge underground, and it stands to reason that any of your direct descendants under Orwing have already been moved to a shielded location. They would not risk you taking control of their army during the transport operation. In other words, for now, you do not need to do anything."

"But what if Tim hasn't made it underground yet! First, I accidentally turned him into a monster, then I put him in agony just by —"

Metal fingers, cold as her own flesh, gently turned Anne's cheek until their eyes met.

"I know you are concerned for his welfare," Zima said. "Your caring nature is one of the many reasons I love you, and I would never seek to change it. We shall return to Z-Tech by the shortest possible route. If you sense that Tim is in discomfort, you may go straight down to the reactor chamber to shield him from the program's effects, and I promise I shall dedicate myself to finding a solution that will allow you to coexist aboveground. But right now, you must put yourself first and get to safety. Just this once, can you do that?" She held Anne's gaze. "Please?"

Anne shook herself, feeling suddenly foolish. "I-I'm sorry. You're right. Let's get this part over with, and we'll worry about the rest later."

She continued the climb, tight with anxiety despite her stated resolve. Noises from the outside world began to filter down: wind blowing across fields, motorcycles thundering in the distance, bay water lapping the rocky shore ... all the sounds of her City she hadn't realized she missed until their sweet melodies once again filled her ears.

By the time Anne reached the last flight, she was trembling with excitement at the thought of rejoining the world, but a cautionary gesture from Zima burst her euphoric bubble. Anne quietly stepped around a crumpled metal door laying near the top of the stairs, then stopped to listen at the doorway. Zima nodded, confirming what Anne's own ears told her: the coast was clear. She hadn't realized that Zima had reclaimed her pistols until she drew one from its holster and held it at the ready.

The scene outside, if anything, was even grislier than that in the subterranean slaughterhouse. Nearly a dozen bodies littered a gravel parking lot, mostly around a large semi trailer that had backed into the tunnel. Plasma burns ringed precise holes in each of their necks, making it clear whose handiwork it had been.

Zima pointed across the lot to a distant residential street lined with parked cars. Anne quickly spotted Mark's sport sedan.

She dashed the football-field distance with her precious cargo, Zima sweeping the area along the way. When Anne reached for the passenger door, Zima stopped her and pointed to the driver's side.

"You're joking," Anne said in a harsh whisper. "How are you going to drive in that condition?"

"Please do not take offense, but I have seen your attempts to operate a vehicle. Even with my non-functional arm and leg, we shall reach Z-Tech faster and safer if I drive."

Biting back a terse reply, Anne circled to the driver's side. The inside door panel had been removed and was laying on the passenger floor.

"That was most likely Tim's friends," Zima said, tilting the seat back to accommodate her bent spine. "Apparently, they are engineers as well. I did not believe disabling the locks would detain them for long."

Anne hurried to the passenger side and, at the risk of Mark's wrath, tossed the door panel to the curb. "It's probably just as well. I haven't sensed any vampires, or felt nauseous yet, so Tim must have made it underground."

The car lurched over the curb and was halfway across the field before Anne managed to close the door.

"Have … have you heard from Charlie and Cappa?"

"Unfortunately, no," Zima said.

"But they've been gone for what … a week?"

"Ten days."

"Fine, but shouldn't we have heard *something* by now?"

Zima shook her head. "Given the months Charlie required to gain proficiency with spiritual projection, in addition to his current condition and drastically different physiology, it is reasonable to assume his recovery may take just as much time — or longer."

Anne wrung her hands. "What if something happened to him?"

"Cappa would have contacted us, of that you can be certain."

"No news is good news, huh?"

"I believe so."

"Hmm. He doesn't know about my kidnapping, then." Anne grinned. "It'll be an interesting story for the ride home from the airport."

Zima skidded to a stop across the gravel, enshrouding the car in a dust cloud, then fixed her damaged eyes on Anne. "We question whether we should tell him at all. The guilt may adversely affect his mental health."

Anne's mouth hung open at the idea of keeping a massive secret like that from him. It was difficult to imagine, so she put it aside. As Zima said earlier, they had more important things to think about right now. "Have you contacted Mark?"

"Yes, from the stairwell as soon as I received a data signal. He is anxious to see you again, and sends his regrets that he could not be present for your rescue. Dela is in Orwing's custody, and he is in the process of extracting her."

Feeling overwhelmed, Anne grabbed her unwashed hair in a bunch and pressed her head to the dash. "Th-then we have to help! If Dela's in trouble —"

"I would normally agree. Given our collective condition, however, there is little we could contribute. Mark is a capable force of his own, as Orwing shall soon discover."

Hoping Zima was right, Anne choked back her concerns, slipped from the car, and ran into the tunnel.

·   ·   ·

Several trips later, the car was filled with people to overflowing. Zima sat in the driver's seat, while Calum and Don were in the back with an unconscious Lance between them. Anne felt guilty for stuffing Almos' catatonic body in the trunk, but it couldn't be helped.

"Just one more to go," Anne said. "There should still be room for Zane in the trunk."

Zima started the engine. "Leave him. We must go."

"But what if they recover —"

"Zane will not be a threat; I have made sure of that. Please, enter the car so we may depart."

Too exhausted to question further, Anne did as she was asked and slipped into the passenger seat. The car sped from the parking lot, leaving a rooster tail of gravel and dust in its wake.

They had just hit the street when a bright flash from behind lit up the night. A thunderous rumble rocked the car like a giant fist, shattering the windows of every house ahead.

Everyone but Zima turned back to see an enormous gout of fire erupt from the tunnel like the mouth of a dragon. The semi truck flew across the lot, where it tumbled sideways in a flaming wreck.

Zima didn't slow. Their car squealed through the residential streets until they reached the freeway, where Zima finally settled into a normal speed.

"W-what the hell was that?" Anne said, finally recovering her voice.

"Zane. As I told you, he will not be a threat. I detonated his power reactor."

Anne could only stare. "Zima, he was your brother! Maybe the only real family you'll ever have. How could you —"

"He was beyond saving. Orwing corrected the mistakes they had made with me when they conditioned him. Keeping him around — even just his mind — would incur significant risk. And I already have a family." She glanced at Anne. "A good family. They are all I need."

Anne fell silent, swallowing a lump in her throat. She mourned Zima's loss, even if Zima herself didn't, but she couldn't argue the family part.

Not one bit.

28

I KNEW THAT

MARK RE-READ ZIMA'S MESSAGE to make sure he hadn't misunderstood, then heaved an enormous sigh of relief.

Anne was safe.

One down, one to go.

Mark realized he'd begun pacing the hotel lobby again and casually sat in a chair. HOW'S IT COMING, CAPPA? he sent over the link.

SLOW! WHO'D HAVE THOUGHT A RESERVATION SYSTEM WOULD HAVE SUCH TIGHT SECURITY?

Mark swore silently. NEED A HAND?

I NEED A ZIMA, BUT SHE'S BUSY DRIVING A CAR FULL OF INFIRMED TO THE HOSPITAL. AND WHEN I SAY FULL, I MEAN THEY HAD TO STUFF THE UNCONSCIOUS VAMPIRE IN THE TRUNK.

He glanced at the reservation desk, his fingers steeped in thought. WOULD A PASSWORD HELP?

SURE, IF I COULD GET PAST THE FIREWALL. WHICH I CAN'T.

LET ME SEE WHAT I CAN DO.

Mark brought his phone to life and pulled up a wireless network scanning application, fingers rigid with frustration. If it had been a small hotel, he would have simply gone door to door, listening for Nick or Dela's voices on the other side. But casing two-thousand rooms across forty floors would get him thrown out or arrested.

He needed a more precise location to work with. He'd called the front desk several times under different pretenses asking for Nick's room number, but they dutifully refused to do anything other than connect him directly. That left him with either kidnapping a reception clerk at gunpoint, or hacking their internal reservation system. Hacking the reservation system weighed least on his conscience, but as the minutes passed, he caught himself plotting the receptionists' routines and marking the exits to see if kidnapping really was an option.

The list of network names was long and eclectic, but he quickly zeroed in on their private network, and tapped the little button next to it labeled "Z". The program, compliments of Zima, not only initiated a brute-force attack, it also monitored for new connections which may contain encryption details to hijack. In truth, either method was a crapshoot, but at least he felt like he was helping things move forward.

The button turned green after a few minutes, much sooner than he'd expected.

I'M ON THE INTERNAL NETWORK, he sent to Cappa. YOU CAN ACCESS IT THROUGH MY PHONE. STILL NEED THAT PASSWORD?

I'LL LET YOU KNOW IN — GOT IT!

Mere seconds passed, but it was all Mark could do to stop himself from bugging her for a status report.

NICK'S NAME ISN'T IN THE REGISTRATION LIST, Cappa soon sent, BUT ORWING BOOKED THE ENTIRE THIRTY-SECOND FLOOR.

Mark was already moving to the elevator. THAT GIVES ME A STARTING PLACE. THANKS, CAPPA.

YOU BET. JUST BRING DELA BACK SAFE.

Of that, Mark had every intention.

After the elevator doors closed, he loosened the silenced pistols in his jacket, adjusted the tranquilizer gun, checked the six micro stun grenades around his belt disguised as gaudy silver decorations, as well as the breach charge tucked in the heel of his right shoe, and palmed a small box from his pocket, just in case.

The plasma pistols he hoped would be unnecessary. Mark was banking that Orwing kept their vampires in a separate facility, and he wouldn't need the heavy stuff tonight.

If not, I could be in for a world of hurt.

Number thirty-two dinged red on the overhead display. Mark cautiously peered one way, then the other. The hall was empty.

He stepped out and listened.

Nothing.

Clenching his jaw, Mark picked a direction and crept down the corridor, pausing frequently to listen with his enhanced hearing for Dela or Nick's voice.

The floor was like a ghost town, silent except for the odd air conditioner and rumbling ice machine. It wasn't until he crossed the other side of the hotel that he spotted two large men in suits standing guard a dozen doors down.

Mark darted back behind the wall. They hadn't spotted him.

He lowered into a crouch and fiddled with the small box in his hand.

Two guards ...

A stun grenade would work, but it would also alert whoever was inside, which might put Dela at risk. The tranquilizer gun was inaccurate at this range. If he missed, one of the guards might cry out, and he would be back at square one with endangering Dela. His silenced pistol was accurate enough for the job, but, despite how the movies portrayed them, they were still loud, and it might attract the attention of nearby residents — assuming there were any.

That leaves one option ...

Mark tapped the box and grinned. He'd been dying to try his latest invention in a practical scenario, and this was as practical as they came. He removed the lid from the box, gingerly withdrew two of the eight pill-sized black capsules from their custom foam packaging, and set them in his palm.

An internal command to his computer implant brought them to life. Each sprouted a tiny set of wings, and immediately buzzed into action. They flew several inches into the air, where they settled into angular housefly-like patterns.

Perfect.

Cappa, the flies are a go. There are two targets. Do you have a strong-enough signal to pilot one of the flies?

A fly suddenly veered, buzzed around his head once, then fell back into formation.

Sure do! Lead the way.

A second command linked him to the other fly. A small window overlaid his vision, showing a live video feed from a micro camera in its head. The picture was pixelated and blurry, as expected from such a tiny lens, but good enough to maneuver around the hall without hitting anything. Satisfied, he flew it around the corner, with Cappa's fly close behind.

Their targets appeared as two blurry dots through the fish-eyed display. Keeping the fly on-target was challenging; the mechanical insect handled like an over-caffeinated squirrel, jerking this way and that, but it quickly crossed the distance, and the guards' features became discernible.

One guard swatted during a close pass. The turbulence sent Mark's fly into a dizzying spin that made him reach for the wall. He kept his distance after that, and zoomed onto his target: the bare skin of the guard's neck, just above the collar.

He selected a point along the jugular. A red cross appeared on the display. His implant's targeting system took over, keeping the flight pattern tight to maintain a clear shot.

Ready, Cappa sent, confirming a lock on her own target.

Mark sent the final command.

His display went dead. A pair of short, sharp whistles sounded down the hall. Mark rounded the corner in time to see the guards fall to the floor, still clutching their necks in surprise.

I'd call that a successful field test.

He quickly relieved them of their weapons, tucked them into his coat pockets, then listened at the door.

Dela's voice was unmistakable. She was yelling in high-pitched fervor, followed by Nick's equally heated retort.

He needed to act. Now.

Mark drew a silenced pistol and yanked a stun grenade from his belt. A firm kick burst the door open in a hail of splintered wood. He sprinted into the empty suite, pistol sweeping for danger, and in the side bedroom he found Dela and Nick …

… lying comfortably on the bed, playing cards.

Dela looked up at him, the skin around her eye a sickly yellow in the beginnings of a black eye. "Did you kill the guys out front?"

"What? No, they're just drugged. I —"

She barked a laugh and turned to Nick with a triumphant grin. "Told you! Pay up, bucko."

Nick Orwing hung his head, seemingly oblivious to the gun Mark was pointing at him. He fished a twenty from his wallet and handed it over. Dela casually stuffed the bill down the front of her dress.

"Sorry," Mark said, failing to keep the sarcasm from his voice. "Am I interrupting? I can wait in the lobby while you finish your game."

"No, it's cool. Let's go." Dela slid from the bed. "I know where they're holding Anne. We have to hurry before —"

"Anne is safe," he said, looking pointedly at Nick. Whatever game they were playing, Mark was in no mood for it.

She and Nick exchanged a worried glance. The news hadn't made Dela nearly as happy as Mark had hoped.

"But h-how did you find —"

"I'll tell you all about it. Later." Mark reached for her arm.

Dela swatted him away and grabbed him by the jacket with a troubled frown. "Is she aboveground?" When he hesitated, she shook him violently. "Mark! We need to know: *Is Anne unshielded?*"

"Yes! They're probably still on the surface streets, heading for Z-Tech." He leveled them each with a hard stare. "Now, I swear to God … I'm going to shoot *both* of you if someone doesn't tell me what the hell is going on, and why I tore my hair out trying to save someone who didn't need saving!"

Dela put a calming hand on his chest. "Sorry for making you worry. My phone broke during a little … misunderstanding." She pointed at her bruised eye. "We couldn't use his phone to contact you because we need to keep Nicky's hands clean for now. As for what's going on …"

"We have an opportunity to end my father's insane vampire army plans," Nick said, matching Mark's serious expression. "But only if we acted tonight."

"Act*ed*? As in, it's already in motion?" Mark was liking this less and less.

Nick nodded. "Del was confident you'd be able to break your vampire friend out once you knew her location, so I took a chance and called in a favor."

"Nicky says his dad created only one vampire directly descended from Anne," Dela said, "intending to keep him safely shielded in case of exactly what happened tonight, where they lose control of Anne for some reason. This way they have an extra gap between her and the rest of the troops, which prevents her from taking direct control of their whole mercenary operation."

Del? Nicky?

Mark sighed. It was his fault Dela was in this situation, so he could hardly blame her for being on nickname terms with the enemy. He shuddered, trying not to imagine exactly how familiar they had become before their card game.

"So, what," Mark said. "I'm supposed to charge in there and take this key vampire out?"

"No, that's the favor I called," Nick said. "I have a friend on the inside preparing a few explosive surprises as we speak: one at the keystone vampire's cell, one in the transformation center where people are transitioning into vampires right now, and the last in an unused building just outside the facility grounds."

"The first two are easy," Dela said. "The tricky part will be making sure all the other vampires are in that building shortly after the first timed explosives go off."

"Timed? *Timed?*" Mark felt his blood pressure rising. "W-what the hell were you thinking?"

"He's one guy!" Nick said heatedly. "Most of the facilities are underground, so he can't trigger them remotely. Timers were the only way, but he's using a remote detonator for the last building."

"Just ..." Mark put his hands over his eyes and took a deep breath to give him a moment to think. "Tell me why this has to happen tonight?"

If his friend set the timers, he can unset them until we have a chance to think this through.

"A few reasons," Dela said softly.

"They weren't just relocating Anne tonight," Nick said. "Once she was secured, they were going to pack up the entire operation and move it to a more secure facility, where pulling something like this off would be nearly impossible. The current facility is temporary, which means it doesn't have all the protections the new one will, and it's easier to breach."

"The other reason is that Orwing has an immediate use for the army," Dela said, her jaw tightening. "A domestic terrorism contract, *here* in the United States. If we take out their vampire supersoldiers, they can't fulfill the contract. Day saved."

My God …

"You might have started with that," Mark said, feeling his shoulders begin to knot. "Just making sure I have this straight … Once the keystone vampire is out of the picture, Anne will inherit sireship — if that's even a word — of the keystone's vampires. Then you need her to direct them into the trapped building so your friend can blow them to smithereens."

"Bingo," Nick said. "And the first detonation is scheduled for 0300, which is two-and-a-half hours from now."

Mark muttered a few choice curses. The proverbial ball was already rolling while the track was still being laid. Failure to keep ahead of it would mean the deaths of many innocents. He now understood Dela's earlier concern about Anne being aboveground. If she suddenly inherited all those vampires, her defensive program would go berserk, and Orwing would be left with a telltale bunch of screaming, incapacitated vampires. It wouldn't be long before they ushered Anne's direct descendants underground to shield them, which, if they'd kept each tier of the hierarchy small, meant Orwing would quickly regain control of most of their army.

Anne's defensive program needed to be off when the first round of explosions took out the keystone vampire, or the entire operation would be little more than a thorn in Alvin's side.

But turning off her defensive program had its own problem — namely William.

Anne's sadistic sire had tried only once to contact her through their mental bond since the defensive program had been put in place, shortly after she'd trounced him at the Revelation Hotel. Apparently, the headache he'd received had been enough to convince him it wasn't worth trying again.

If she suddenly gains a lot of followers, though ...

William had made it clear that he drew strength from his sirelings. Would Anne receiving a sudden in-surge of followers send some sort of signal to William and make him try again? Without her defensive program, both Anne and the mercenary army bound to her would be slaves to his will. It would be a small matter to reactivate the program, but if they couldn't for whatever reason, the situation could quickly spiral out of control. Anne had become a formidable force of her own. With a trained vampire army behind her, there would be little Mark or anyone could do to stop her from joining William's ranks.

Or would there?

An idea came to him. It was morbid and desperate, but better than leaving things to chance.

Mark hated chance.

"All right," Mark said, chewing bitterly on the words. "Send us the coordinates for all the points in question and the contact info for your friend. I want the detonator frequency so I can pull the final trigger myself. Understand?"

Nick hesitated only briefly before nodding.

"Y-you're going?" Dela said.

"Yes. I don't know this demolition guy, or how competent he is, so I'll see to the last phase personally."

Especially if Anne's involved.

"Let's get going," Mark said. "We have prep work to do at the factory before the fireworks start."

"One last thing ..." Nick stood before Mark and stuck his chin out. "Hit me. We need signs of a struggle so —"

A sharp jab from Dela knocked Nick onto the bed, leaving an angry welt in the same spot where her own bruise was darkening.

"Now we're even," she said, massaging her reddening knuckles.

Dela was quiet when she led Mark from the room to the hallway. She turned suddenly, stumbling Mark to a halt, then stood on her toes and kissed him lightly.

"Yes," she whispered.

"Yes what?"

She crossed her arms and scowled. "Your proposal, dumbass. I accept."

Crap.

The hectic events of the evening had pushed Mark's hasty parking lot proposal to the back of his mind. "I-I'm sorry, Dela. It was cruel to put you on the spot like that. Forget I said anything."

"Hey! No takebacks."

"But I want a do-over! There should have been an engagement ring in a cake with a string quartet playing romantic music, and champagne, and —"

Dela barked a laugh. "You proposed to me after a secret meeting of world powers while I was leaving to sleep with the enemy so we could rescue our vampire friend from an international espionage organization holed up in their underground lair guarded by a killer android, followed by a dashing rescue that made double-oh-seven seem like a kid with a cap gun and a drinking problem — *and* you won me twenty bucks in the process." She grabbed him by the shirt and smiled, her eyes glinting. "The only way you could have topped that, my dear fiancée, is if you'd added ninjas and strafing gunfire from an attack helicopter silhouetted against a desert sunset."

Mark stole a kiss of his own before ushering her toward the elevator, aware the clock was ticking. "Well, I do know someone who owns an Apache. He owes me a favor, too."

The elevator dinged open. Dela stepped inside and grinned up at him. "Tempting, but let's save the Apache for the honeymoon."

He smiled back. Her sparkling green eyes melted the tension from his shoulders. They held each other close for the entire elevator ride. Mark knew he should be planning the next steps to defeat Orwing's vampire army, but all he could think about was how his blundered proposal may have been the best mistake he'd ever made.

29

THE PLAN

A NNE BLEW A FORLORN KISS to the fluffy pajamas on her bed. *Not tonight, it seems.*

With a wistful sigh, she pulled on a dark long-sleeve turtleneck, gray denim jeans, and a black leather jacket, which, after numerous nights of hunting William's goons with Zima, she had come to think of as her "other" work clothes. Even this outfit felt heavenly next to the brown-crusted sweats stuffed in the small trashcan next to her bedside table. She had respectfully declined her captors' offer to change her clothes after Calum's shot on her first day of captivity, followed by Almos' excruciating surgery above her right hip. Although Anne no longer perspired, the overused garments had become stiff, scratchy, and ripe enough to bear fruit of their own.

Maybe we can have a ceremonial burning when this is all over, an offering to the gods to please never *let that happen again.*

She ran a loving finger across the neglected books in her bookcase, drinking in their musty smell one last time.

Soon, my friends.

Anne stopped at the door and cast a backward glance at her treasured plasma pistol sitting on the dresser. Her faithful companion wouldn't be accompanying her tonight. Both she and Mark had agreed it would be far too risky to carry such a dangerous weapon while her defensive program was down. She had managed to resist William's influence once, when Zima tested her will by handing over her own pistol, but that was before Anne had completed the transition. Now that she was a full vampire ... Without the implant's protection, William's hold over her would be absolute, as she had unfortunately discovered while kneeling helplessly throughout his cruel mutilations.

The memory made her shiver. She tore her eyes from the shiny pistol, closed the door, and walked to the bio lab.

Anne paused at the entrance to gather her thoughts. She had only one task to perform before they left, perhaps the most difficult one of the night.

She had to break the news of their planned Orwing assault to Zima.

Steeling herself, Anne marched inside.

Zima didn't stir at Anne's approach. She lay absolutely still beneath the same glass dome that had resurrected both her and Cappa too many times in recent history. Anne hated and loved this room. The table holding her ravaged beauty had seen Zima in much worse condition, yet it was also where her blue-eyed love had miraculously been brought back to life, and where Anne had first confided in her friends the true source of her PTSD. The last night her heart still beat, she had attacked Mark not far from where she stood, drinking until he passed out ...

Anne shook herself. She wasn't here to reminisce. She pressed her palm to the glass and smiled.

"Hey, honey. How are you doing?"

Her girlfriend didn't so much as flinch, her eyes fixed on the ceiling. The monitors came to life at a nearby workstation. From its speakers, Zima's voice came loud and clear.

"I am sorry I cannot respond in person. Repairs are progressing slowly with the limited number of nanites in my body. Movement will only hamper progress further."

"Yeah, Cappa said it would be slow going until Mark pulls some nanites from production and has a chance to stitch your flesh in place."

"Do you know when that will be? I have inquired, but he has yet to respond. I am anxious to once again feel your touch."

Here we go …

"That may have to wait until after dawn. Mark and I … have an errand to run first."

Zima stayed quiet for several seconds. "I see." Her voice was flat, as usual, but the trailing silence conveyed her hurt: What was more important than being reunited? Did Anne not feel the same sense of loss and longing?

The answers were "Almost nothing," and "Yes, she absolutely did." Anne couldn't leave her ailing Zima questioning her love — not even for the few hours she would be gone. Not after everything they had just been through.

Zima deserved the truth. All of it.

So that's exactly what Anne gave her.

"But Mark will be there with me," Anne said once she'd finished relating the plan. "So don't worry. He'll keep me safe."

"You should not be involved," Zima said through the speakers. "The risks are too high. Nor do I understand why you must be physically present. Taking you beyond the safety of Z-Tech's walls increases your risk by a factor of seventeen."

"I need to be there for a few reasons. I've never had underlings before, and I won't have long to figure out the whole sire thing. Almos is awake in the generator room, so I stopped by to get some advice. He says directing them will be a lot easier if I can actually see where I want them to go. So, for this to go smoothly, I need to be in line of sight of the building."

"I would feel better if your line of sight was through a telescope from a distant mountain top."

Me too.

"Which brings me to the second reason …" Anne bit her lip, fangs pricking her painfully. "I want to meet the vampires first."

Zima's head jerked toward her, making Anne jump. Her hand pressed to Anne's on the other side of the glass.

"Anne, no, please ... The risks —"

"I have to! I can't just condemn dozens of people to die. Not without knowing if they can be saved."

"They cannot. They have been infected, just like the vampires we have been hunting together."

"But that's the problem. They aren't like the vampires we've been hunting. They're not William's goons, they're ..." Her voice broke. Anne clutched her hands to her chest and continued in a hoarse whisper. "They're mine."

Zima curled the fingers of her good hand against the smooth glass, as if trying to lace them with Anne's. "Your compassion is admirable, but misplaced. Their creation was not your doing. You did not select the individuals to be converted. Where your heart is soft, theirs are hardened, as necessary by their occupation."

"But —"

"They are mercenaries, Anne. Hired killers. I have spent a great deal of time around their kind. They do not share your morals. Please believe me when I say that by putting yourself in proximity, you are incurring needless danger, for you shall not find in them what you are hoping to."

"I ... I'm sorry, Zima. I have to try, or I won't be able to live with myself." Anne curled her own fingers, desperately wishing she could take her girlfriend's comforting hand. "Do you understand?"

Zima stared at her. The bright overhead spotlights gleamed from her polished metal skull, giving the brief illusion of a halo, and refracted from her cracked eye to cast tiny rainbows on Anne's chest. The beauty of it caught her breath.

"I do," Zima said eventually. "Throughout history, it is the tenderhearted who have suffered the most. You are no exception." Her finger squeaked down the glass, tracing Anne's palm. "Stay close to Mark, and do not deliberate overlong on the vampires' fate. Every second you delay puts you at greater risk. I very much wish to see you on the other side of this glass when it finally lifts and I am able to hold you once again."

"Count on it." Anne wiped a tear. She pressed her lips to the glass, then visually lined the residual smear with the remaining half of Zima's own lips in the closest thing to a kiss she could offer.

Afraid she might lose her resolve if she stayed any longer, Anne fled the room and ran to the weapons lab. She leaned her head against the giant metal door, sobbing, while she imagined what would happen if Zima was right. Sentencing so many to death by the power of her will alone was almost unthinkable.

Worse, if Anne didn't make it back at all ... Zima had clung to her for every possible moment since their return, and had released Anne's hand only when the glass threatened to crush it. What would happen to her poor Zima if Anne died? Would she go berserk and revert to an emotionless killing machine? Withdraw into herself? Shut out the world? The more Anne thought about it, the more selfish her insistence on meeting the vampires seemed, and the harder she cried, until it felt as though her eyes would pop and her lungs would shrivel from the barrage of heaving gasps.

When the storm eventually passed, Anne wiped her shirtsleeve across her nose and around her face, not caring who saw the glimmering snot trails on the dark fabric.

This has to happen, she thought, fighting another guilty twinge. *I have to see them for myself — my vampires, my blood — or the guilt will tear me apart.*

Anne slipped her arm back inside her jacket to hide the disgusting sleeve and entered the weapons lab. From floor to ceiling, every weapon imaginable lined the walls. She passed pistols, rifles, grenades, mortars, rocket launchers, and several weapons that, despite having spent many hours here with Zima, she still couldn't identify. Mark and Dela stood on the other side of the long room, staring at her with concern.

"I-I'm fine, guys." A sniffle and Anne's unsteady voice betrayed the lie. "Let's just get this over with."

Dela shifted nervously. "What did Zima say?"

"That I shouldn't go, and that talking to them is a waste of time."

Worry lines etched Mark's forehead. "But you're still going, right?"

"Yes, even though she's probably right on both counts."

"Well then, I'll go help her pack up," Dela said. "I don't know which weapons the Dark Angel will want to bring in her condition, but I'm sure she already has an idea."

Anne caught her arm on her way to the door.

"Zima's staying here," Anne said quietly. "Even she has her limits."

"I'm shocked. I thought she'd want to ride on your back like an extra pair of gun-toting arms or something."

"Don't give her any ideas," Mark said. "Zima's damage is extensive, probably more than she let on, and much of it is structural. Even mild damage at this point could easily hit a critical component, which ... well, it wouldn't be good."

Anne looked at him sharply, but Mark wouldn't meet her eyes.

"She'll be fine as long as she stays put," he said to his hands. "Once we get back, and after I've had a little sleep, fixing her will be my top priority."

Extensive damage? Of course it is. And it's just like Zima to omit that particular fact so I won't worry.

The thought nearly brought another sob storm. Dela wrapped her in a comforting hug, for which Anne was grateful: the redhead's delicious smell filled her nostrils and kept her tears from overflowing. Anne hadn't eaten since their escape, and the lengthy run of her metabolic program had left her famished. She wrapped Dela in an embrace of her own, clinging to her with desperate hunger. Painfully elongated fangs gently brushed the crook of her neck.

A shiver of anticipation rippled through them both. Apparently, Dela had missed this, too.

"Go ahead," Dela whispered. "You need a full tank tonight more than I do." Dela ran her fingers through Anne's hair, cupped the back of her head, and gently pulled her closer so Anne's lips pressed against her silky skin.

It was too much. With an eager moan, Anne sank her teeth into her Delicious Dela, savoring every mouthful of the heavenly elixir that graced her tongue.

Soon Dela was moaning, too, but tonight was special. Dela had only permitted drinking from her arm before, claiming the neck was too kinky. Anne didn't know what had changed her mind, and she didn't care. Drinking from her large neck artery was like chugging straight from the glass instead of a tiny cocktail straw.

Anne was so enraptured that she never even heard Doris' clacking heels approach.

"There y'all are, I was wondering — whoa! Hickey alert, Jesus Christ! Hey, Draculanne, lay off the juice. If that girl gets any higher, we're going to have to scrape her off the moon."

Feeling much better, Anne relinquished her grip. The buxom redhead collapsed with a gigantic smile. Anne and Mark caught her before she hit the ground, and gently lowered her down.

Dela clumsily patted Anne on the cheek. "I've missed you …"

"Oh, don't tease me like that," Anne said, laughing. "That's just the venom talking. Next you'll be proposing, and where would that leave Mark?"

"Proposing!" Dela's eyes lit up. Her smile grew even bigger. "That's right, we're getting married!"

Anne scratched her head. "Um … that was just a joke."

"Not to you, silly," Dela said with a laugh. Her unfocused eyes sought Mark. She pulled him into a rough hug, nearly toppling him over. "Him! He proposed and I slapped him and kissed another guy and then I said yes in the hotel and now we're getting an Apache helicopter!"

Doris was the first to recover from the verbal onslaught. "Is she serious, Mark?"

"About the Apache? Yes, but we're just borrowing it. See, I have this friend —"

"Mark!" Anne grinned, infected by Dela's giddy smile. "Come on, did you really propose?"

His shoulders sagged under the weight of their eager stares. "Yes."

Squeals of delight pierced the room. For the second time, Mark was nearly knocked off his feet when Anne and Doris threw their arms around him, babbling congratulations between fits of laughter.

"Hang on," Mark said. He fished his phone out with a sigh and handed it to his still-horizontal fiancée, where it began ringing. "It's for you."

Dela fumbled for the button and answered with a slur. "Mom, is that you? H-how did you find me? I'm a super-duper secret agent. You're not supposed to —"

Cappa's shrill, excited voice burst from the earpiece.

Dela held it at arm's length, laughing. "Not Mom," she said to her audience with a giggle, then returned the phone to her ear. "Cappa! Hey buddy ... Yeah, in the parking lot. Can you believe it? It was so awesome ... Huh, well, I guess you had to be there ... What, you were? Right, I forgot about the earpiece ... Yep, hard! Right in front of the guy I was seducing. We couldn't have planned it any better. Venue? Haven't talked about it. Probably Italy or Hawaii or Boston ... What's wrong with Boston? Have you even been there? Didn't think so, because if you had, you'd know there's this famous club that would be perfect for a reception ... They have what in Bangkok? Oh my F-G! Screw Boston, we're totally doing this Thailand ... Like hell! He can wear a frilly dress if he wants, but I'm going to be comfortable at my own damn wedding. I don't care what's traditional. It's our day and we can do anything we ..."

On and on she went, chatting with her spat partner as if they were close friends. Anne wondered if things would change between them when Cappa's other selves returned from China and re-integrated with her factory self.

How strange would that be, to have two very different perspectives of the same person?

She couldn't imagine how Cappa would reconcile all the experiences and emotions of the stressful times since they'd left, but then, there was a lot she didn't understand about how her soul sister worked.

Mark gestured her away from Dela, who was curled up on the cold floor, coddling his phone like a favorite teddy bear while drunkenly discussing wedding plans with her disembodied partner-in-crime. Anne and Doris followed him to a workbench, where a digital map filled a computer screen.

"Nick sent the details he'd promised through a random email account." Mark circled a seemingly barren patch of land several miles east of the Oakland hills. "This is their base of operations. When the fun starts, we can expect explosions here and here." He pointed to two spots within the perimeter, then moved his finger to a hill just outside of the fenced area. "This is the building Nick's friend has rigged to explode, and where all the vampires need to be as soon as possible. I have the detonation codes, so once they're inside, we can blow them sky-high. There's a service road on the other side of the building we can use to make a quick getaway. If everything goes according to plan, we'll be on the other side of the Caldecott Tunnel before they realize we were there."

Doris pointed to a brown marker on the edge of the map. "What's this dot for?"

"That's where Anne will be hiding. It has clear line-of-sight to the building and the base, so she can direct the vampires, but it's far enough away that —"

"Wait, wait!" Anne tugged her hair. "How can I speak with them from that far away?"

Mark opened a drawer and set a new cell phone on the table. "I've already transferred your number. Another will be waiting in the building. Once they're secured, you can call that number and speak to them — briefly — assuming you can make one of them pick up."

"No."

"Anne —"

"No! A phone call from half a mile away isn't meeting them, it's a telemarketer pitch." Anne tapped the rigged building. "I'm going to be here, with you."

"But I was going to stay safely away on this other hill, with *you.* I don't want to be anywhere near a house rigged with explosives that I didn't set myself. I'm nervous enough about planting the phone ahead of time as it is."

"Then let's meet the mercenaries a safe distance away. Once we've spoken — and *if* there's no alternative — I'll direct them into the house, and then ..." Anne lowered her eyes, unable to finish the thought.

Is this how a general feels? Pointing at a map to order the deaths of people I've never met?

She balled her fists, nails digging painfully into her palms.

Well not me. I may have fangs and an appetite for blood, but ... but I'm not a monster, goddamnit! Don's little cousin Rose is walking now because of me. I ... I don't have to be the killer William intended me to be. If Cappa and Zima have taught me anything, it's that our humanity is defined by the choices we make, not the body we're born into.

And I choose to be human. For all the Roses out there who still need my help. For Cappa, who epitomizes humanity. For Charlie, who thinks he's lost his. For Zima, who struggles closer every day.

And for me, who loves them all, and can't bear the thought of growing apart from them.

Her internal resolve must have shown, for Mark nodded solemnly. A mouse click moved the brown marker to her suggested location: an oak grove fifty yards south of the booby-trapped house.

Doris rested her chin on Anne's shoulder with a worried frown. "Oh, kiddo, I hope you know what you're doing."

Anne gave her hand a reassuring squeeze, but her face echoed Doris' doubt.

She didn't have a clue, and they both knew it.

30

SKELETONS

CITY FOG GAVE WAY TO STARRY SKIES when Mark's Jeep emerged from the tunnel. Anne looked up at the dappled black canvas, away from the blinding headlights, and tried not to think about the grim task before them. Her abnormally large pupils made the light-polluted sky seem like day, each star a bright beacon. The blazing crescent moon cast a net of soft gray over distant hills unmarred by the lights of man. Not owning a car, Anne rarely traveled beyond the limits of San Francisco's public transit, so it was easy to forget how rural — how beautiful — most of the great state of California was.

She also realized with a start that this was the farthest she had been from the protective walls of Z-Tech since becoming a vampire.

The dashboard clock showed that it was after two in the morning — just over four hours before dawn, if she wasn't mistaken.

Their Jeep veered from the freeway and continued east along a small road. Houses and streetlights appeared less and less frequently, until the setting moon was the only illumination for miles around.

It was peaceful. Quiet. Not the oppressive silence of her underground cell, but a hush of nature, undiluted by city bustle. Anne wished Mark would stop and turn off the engine, just for a few minutes, so she could bask in the crisp cool night, walk the placid countryside, which she hadn't done since she was a child. She was so caught up in her fantasy that when the Jeep pulled over, she thought Mark had read her mind.

One glance at the decrepit building next to the oak grove sobered her. They had arrived.

Anne quietly closed the door behind her and headed straight for the building. Jagged squares of cracked white paint clung to the ancient wood siding. Bare patches speckled the faded shingle roof, which sagged at the center. The front door hung from its bottom hinge at an angle. A gentle breeze teetered it on a sharp corner that had sunk into the rotted porch, its wooden croak a lonely call to the inhabitants who had long since abandoned the house. Anne picked her way up the steps with feline grace, stepping on loose boards layered thick with seasons of prickly oak leaves that crackled beneath her feet.

The inside of the dilapidated house had fared no better. Furniture lay in decaying heaps, fallen in upon themselves by gravity and time. The walls themselves creaked and swayed, bowing to the chill wind sweeping through broken windows and whistling through cracks where moonlight crept, casting spiderwebs of silver light on carpet stiff and brittle as old straw. Anne stood in the middle of the room and inhaled fresh air tinged with aged musk.

So this is the death camp.

People might die here tonight. Real people. *Her* people. That Mark would be pulling the trigger did nothing to ease the ache in her chest.

Mark padded across the creaky floorboards behind her and gently touched her shoulder.

"You okay?" he said softly.

The remnants of a curtain waved tendrils of tattered cloth in the breeze, skeletal fingers reaching to her from across the room.

"How will you live with it?" Anne said, unable to take her eyes from the fabric dancing in the moonlight. "If we kill them ... how will you keep their faces from haunting you?"

"By choosing to believe it's the right decision. We already know Orwing has their sights set on domestic targets. No one's going to stop them for us. No one else can. If we don't act, then instead of mercenaries, we'll have the blood of hundreds or thousands of innocents on our hands. That's what would haunt me."

Anne nodded and let the topic drop. As good as his intentions were, she would never find the answers she sought from Mark. He couldn't understand. It wasn't his blood running through their veins, nor his children heading for the slaughter.

Children?

The word took her aback, but she knew instinctively it was right. Corrupted or pure, consensual or not, they were her offspring — the only progeny her cold, barren body could produce.

There was no choice. Anne had to meet them in person, see them with her own eyes, hold the glimmer of hope that her genetic spawn had the possibility of redemption that would save them from a fiery grave.

She had to.

The wind subsided, and the ghostly curtain fingers with it, leaving the house still once more. Mark went upstairs. Falling rivulets of dust from the groaning ceiling marked his path.

Anne leaned out through a glassless window, poking her head into the open air. A large fence topped with curls of barbed wire ran parallel to the back of the house fifty yards distant, stretching for a mile in each direction. In there, somewhere, her unsuspecting children waited.

Mark descended the stairs, daring to trust his weight on the rickety banister. "Well, I have to say, Nick's friend knows his stuff. The detonator codes are just as he said, and there are enough explosives upstairs to reduce this entire house to a smoking pit. It's a combination of high-explosives and incendiaries, so there won't be anything left for the authorities to find."

Anne didn't share his excitement. She nodded weakly and followed him outside. Skeletal curtains waved her goodbye.

They walked through dry weeds to the nearby stand of oak trees where, if things went according to plan, the fateful meeting would take place. The trees were old, wrinkled sentinels whose gnarled trunks grew far from their neighbors. Barren branches concealed little of the vast night sky, casting an intricate shadow lattice across the thick ground cover that crunched under their feet.

They stopped at the center of the sparse grove and turned to view the landscape. Behind them stood a gentle hill, small, yet still the highest feature for miles around. Anne remembered it from Mark's map — the brown dot she had convinced him to move here instead.

Something moved low to the ground just behind the hill's crest, a shadow among the shadows, but it quickly disappeared. She started to warn Mark, but a coyote's shrill cry pierced the night. Anne smiled in relief.

Not everything that creeps is a lurking vampire.

A lone cricket played its fervent tune nearby, each strum of its legs a roaring symphony to her ears. On impulse, she slipped her arm through Mark's, wanting to share the moment with someone. Mark relaxed into her. Even though they'd had their differences, Anne felt comfortable around him. Holding his arm felt natural.

"Congratulations again on your engagement," Anne said, cozying against his warmth. "Dela seems very excited."

"Thanks. Yeah, it came out of nowhere. I was kicking myself at the time, but now I'm glad it happened. Knowing me, I might never have proposed to her otherwise. With the business and everything going on, marriage was the furthest thing from my mind. I guess that's what happens when the most precious person in your life is about to sleep with a stranger."

"I can't imagine, but I'm glad it happened, too. You're good complements to each other."

Mark smiled. "Yes, we are."

A breeze gently rattled the branches overhead, like a thousand fairies snapping their fingers. Anne closed her eyes and let the sound move through her. "Are you going to have kids?"

"I hope so, assuming we live to see the wedding, but we've never talked about it."

"I hope so, too. It would be nice to have little ones around to spoil."

"Never wanted kids of your own?"

Stupid, Anne.

"I, ah … I haven't really thought about it," Anne lied. "You know, with Charlie and Zima being who they are. And me being a vampire now, of course."

"Oh. Sorry, I didn't mean to —"

"It's fine, really." Anne cast her eyes beyond the shaded grove, watching the fields roll and sway with the night breeze. "I had a dream once that Charlie made us a child in his lab, a little mechanical girl. She had his brown hair, Zima's blue eyes, and Cappa's infectious smile. When I listened to her tiny chest, I heard a clock ticking soft and sweet, just like her delicate face. She was beautiful."

"That sounds like a wonderful dream."

"It was. That was back when I was human and actually slept, of course. I remember feeling sad when I woke and didn't find her sleeping next to me."

Mark grinned. "Don't give up hope. Anything is possible with Charlie around."

"I never told him about it, or Zima. I only brought it up to you because …" She tightened her grip on his arm and leaned her head on his shoulder. "Because it seemed relevant."

"Something tells me you don't mean relevant to me and Dela."

"No, I suppose not."

He was silent, but his pulse jumped. "Anne, I know you think I'm being heartless about the mercenaries, and that I don't understand why you want to save them, but I get it. They're connected to you. I can only imagine what it's like to have someone else in your head, to share their thoughts and feelings. And to know that you also share blood ties … That's a strong bond."

"I … I'm glad you understand," Anne said, feeling a weight lift from her shoulders.

"And that's also what worries me. I'm afraid the bond you share with them is going to color your judgment. You tend to see the best in people. Throw the bond on top of that and … I don't think it matters who they are or what they've done, you'll find a reason to forgive them, because that's the caring person Anne Perrin is."

"You don't think I have the strength to condemn them, even if they deserve it."

Mark studied the twinkling skyline. "No, but let's pretend for a second that you're right. Let's say the mercenaries aren't all bad, and we don't kill them. What then? Send them off to start a vampire tribe in Nova Scotia, quietly feeding off local townships?"

"I was thinking more of a commune ..."

"Fine. A Utopian community, then, where they live in harmony with a small group of humans who like the buzz from their venom and keep coming back for more."

It's not without precedent, Anne thought petulantly, thinking of Dela.

"Forget about the possibility of rising discontent or them terrorizing the locals somewhere down the line ... my biggest worry is that they'll make new vampires and expand their numbers until they plague the countryside."

"They won't!" Anne said, stomping her foot in a crunch of leaves. "I'll command them not to."

"Right. How many of William's commands stuck after he severed his link with you?"

Anne clenched her fists, but remained silent.

"We're only going to bring your defensive program down long enough to round them up — a few minutes, if we're lucky — and you of all people know why. We can't keep your link open for fear of William taking control of you, which means either you or they would have to spend the rest of your lives underground, or they'd be in constant agony. Speaking of ..." Mark grunted. "You're hurting my arm."

"Oh!" She released him. "I'm so sorry ..."

Mark sighed and rubbed where her fingers had dug into him. "It's fine, I'll heal."

"No, I mean ... you're right. I really hadn't thought it through. The logistics aren't feasible, and, even if they were, the mercenaries are nothing but a danger to society, and ..." She closed her eyes. "And so am I."

"Anne —"

"I mean it! From everything you've said, I should be in that building, too."

"That's not what I meant! You're an entirely different case."

"How? Without even meaning to, I've already infected an entire troop, plus one unlucky kid who was too close when my chest exploded. In the larger scheme, what makes me any less dangerous than the mercenaries?"

"Because you have Charlie. You have us. Granted, we're off to a rocky start, but we'll find a way to mitigate the dangers, I promise. It's just going to take some time, so hang in there and ..." His eyes softened, and his hands slipped into his pockets. "Don't go jumping into any explosive houses, okay? We'll figure this out."

Anne nodded woodenly. While she appreciated Mark's attempt to talk her down from the ledge, they hadn't yet touched on the real reason she wished to share her sirelings' fate.

"Did you speak with Almos?" Anne said quietly. "About ... the Entity?"

He shook his head, so she filled him in on her brief conversation about his foreboding visions. Mark neither dismissed nor despaired at the news, just listened with a solemn expression.

"Fascinating," he said once she'd finished.

Definitely not the word I'd use.

"Mark, to hear Almos tell it, each and every vampire in this world — except maybe for him — provokes the risk of a disaster that would knock humanity down several rings on the food chain, or off of it completely. How can I justify my existence knowing —"

"The only thing we know is that Almos had some bad dreams. It'll take a hell of a lot more proof than that before I'd consider sacrificing your life, even for the sake of the world." He softened his words with a grin. "That's not how we do things, if you hadn't figured it out."

"But you just said ... I thought you believed him."

Mark scratched his chin. "To me, the biggest mystery around the vampire pathogen is where it came from. Everything about it is foreign to any living thing we know of — including me, and that's saying something — which leaves me with two theories about its origin. One is that it's man-made, created in a lab somewhere like Charlie's brain tissue was, but it's so advanced ... Charlie and I have been studying this thing for months now. He's one of the brightest minds of this century, and even he can't make heads or tails of how it works, let alone how someone would create such a thing. And if Almos is as old as he says, then the pathogen's been around for at least a thousand years. Building the Pyramids is one thing, but engineering a complex new life form was well out of their league, which rules out human involvement."

"Are … are you saying what I think you're saying? That this is some sort of alien virus?" Being a walking corpse was bad enough. The idea of Anne carrying the seeds of some alien race threatened to bring up her Dela snack.

"I don't know about extra-terrestrial, but I'm willing to bet it was created by someone. And that someone probably wasn't human."

"You don't sound nearly as upset about that as you should." Anne hugged an arm around her middle, feeling dizzy.

"Weak as it may be, Almos' visions are the first evidence we have to support that theory — or shed any light on its true origins, for that matter. I may not like it, but at least it gives us a clue. Almos' connection to this Entity may give us even more insight. Maybe even help us figure out how to stop it."

"Or find a cure."

Then we wouldn't have to sentence a whole group of people to die.

"A cure would be nice." Mark looked at the fence. "Twelve minutes to three o'clock. There's still time to make it to that hill before the fireworks start."

"You can go if you want, but … I need to see this through."

"I thought you'd say that, but I had to try."

Despite her nerves, Anne felt drained, suddenly weary beyond reckoning, both mentally and physically. Mark looked down at the abrupt weight on his arm, but she couldn't even muster the energy to lift her eyes.

"Can you contact Zima from out here?" Anne said, her tongue like lead.

"Mm-hmm."

"Would you please tell her I love her? I … I forgot to say it before I left, and it's important that she knows."

"I think she does, but yes, I'll tell her." He was silent for a second, then chuckled.

"What did she say?"

"That she loves you, too," he said, smirking.

She tugged his arm, grinning despite her exhaustion. "And ...?"

"I'll tell you the rest later."

Anne tugged again, but he simply shook his head, moonlight twinkling in his mischievous eyes.

31

MY CHILDREN

T HE MINUTES DRAGGED BY. Anne watched the fence as if she could stare a hole through it. Every beat of Mark's heart — her only mark of the passage of time — tightened the vice in her chest further.

His pulse suddenly quickened, though his eyes remained fixed on the fence with hers.

"Here we go," Mark said softly. "I'm going to take your implant's defense program down now, but I'll bring it back up if I see any sign of trouble, and we'll deal with the vampires the old-fashioned way." He patted his jacket, where his plasma pistol was safely holstered. "Good luck."

The vice cranked her insides to bursting. Before Anne could protest — before she could say she had changed her mind, that this was a terrible idea, and she just wanted to go home — a series of distant fireballs lit the sky above the barbed wire, followed by a drum beat of shock waves that rattled her lungs and left her gasping for air, even though she needed none. Mark groaned in pain. Anne was vaguely aware she had dug her fingers into him once again, but she didn't relinquish her grip this time.

I can't do this, I can't do this, I can't, I can't, I can't —

And then it was too late. The single vampire Orwing had created from Anne must have died as planned, because six lights flared in her mind, bright yet soft, and she knew immediately they were her orphaned children come to seek their new mother. Six smaller lights accompanied each — stars flickering around bright moons — and she knew also that these pinpoints were her children's children.

Emotions flooded from the larger orbs, drowning her in a sea of feelings that weren't her own. They were confused about who the glaring, predominant presence was that had suddenly appeared in their minds. Anne swam against the current, struggling to keep her own self above the surface, to find shallows where her feet could gain purchase so she could get her bearings. She had no idea how William managed so many torrents of personality at once.

But if that asshat can handle over thirty, then I can sure as hell manage six.

Her determination alone seemed to help. Their flows didn't ebb, so much as she felt her own presence strengthen, anchoring itself to points in her mind, which allowed a moment to focus on something other than survival.

It was then she realized she was sitting in the leaves. Mark knelt beside her, looking more scared than she had ever seen him. Anne managed a nod, which eased him a bit, and accepted help to her feet.

"I ... I've got them," she said, although it felt like the other way around.

"William?"

Anne tentatively probed the pinpoints, afraid the very act may attract his attention, but was happy to find herself William-free. "Not yet."

He sighed in relief. "Can you control them?"

Good question.

The only time Anne had actively pushed something to another presence was when Zima had been desperately gathering data for the first iteration of Anne's defensive program while William was slowly torturing her. She hoped this would be a similar exercise. The memory, traumatic as it was, had given her an idea of which command she should try first.

She brought her attention back to the six larger points of light. As William had done to her, Anne imagined her limbs seizing, held fast by invisible bands of iron, similar to her recent captivity. She took that feeling of helplessness, the futility of even attempting to break those bonds, and pushed it to her children, and then to their children.

Anger, fear, frustration, outrage … all of that and more poured back. But it had worked; her sirelings had stopped in their tracks. She nodded to Mark.

"Great. We need to get them here quickly, quietly, and preferably unarmed."

"Roger that," Anne said, feeling her confidence build. She concentrated again.

"Quietly" was easy. Anne imagined her vocal cords paralyzed with fear, which had happened more times in her life than she cared to think about, pushed it out through her sire bond, and felt it echo back from them. They wouldn't be calling for help.

Unarmed …

Anne had difficulty wrapping that in an emotion, so she tried a different approach. Choosing one of the larger presences, Anne probed deeper, and was pleased to find what she'd hoped: the orbs were more than just ethereal globs. Each sphere was a complex tangle of threads, swirling, spinning, changing from moment to moment. She plucked at one, and knew it was his fear she held. Anne sifted through a few more threads: hope, anger, a memory from his childhood, his passion for violence … The threads were endless, but none were what she sought.

I need to know if he's carrying weapons. How does he defend himself?

As before, her mere thought became action. Four threads rose to the surface.

A rifle. A handgun. A large knife. Three grenades.

Details were sketchy. Even if she had been a gun expert, she couldn't have said their make or model, for there were no images or words attached, only feelings and purpose. The rifle was bulky, loud, fast, killed at long range. The handgun was quick, agile, a solid comfort in close quarters, and one that he had carried for a long time. The knife was more than a weapon: it was a survival tool capable of carving wood, skinning animals, and sometimes shaving. Grenades were loud, frightening, and brutally effective, each a tiny volcano as likely to kill enemies as its wielder if not treated with care.

To those threads, Anne attached the need to be rid of them. One by one she felt them go. She repeated the exercise with her remaining five children. On a whim, she then found a thread representing the defenses of their children, which many of them viewed as their own, and attached the same feeling of riddance.

Mark was looking nervous by the time she returned her attention to the outside world, but she still wasn't done. Anne knew they could sense her general location, just as she sensed theirs, so she projected to her six the intense need to find her, and to bring their children.

They set forth immediately. Their presences closed on her with incredible speed.

"On their way," Anne said, sagging into Mark. She was exhausted. Her limbs were heavy, as if she'd run a marathon. Not for the first time since becoming a vampire, she wished she were able to sleep for just a few minutes to clear the cobwebs from her head. "They won't be long, maybe four minutes."

Mark sat next to her, hands on his knees. "Doing all right?"

"Yeah, just ... tired. Nervous. Scared. You know, typical me."

"I can't blame you one bit. You've had a hard week, and it isn't over."

Rustling from the other side of the fence confirmed what Anne saw in her mind. They had arrived. She scrambled to her feet, fatigue replaced by nervous energy. Mark rose as well, plasma pistol in hand, and they waited in anxious silence.

The first of her children leaped high over the barbed wire and landed in an easy crouch. Others followed, night-camouflaged grasshoppers popping one after another until all thirty-six stood along the fence. Black eyes like her own regarded Anne with a mixture of expressions, their meanings made shockingly clear by the emotions pouring through their sire bonds. Some were repulsed by her full hips and chest, likening her to a cow. Two were disinterested and were just waiting to see how things played out. One, she was pretty sure, was a closet transvestite who showed more interest in her outfit than anything else.

But they weren't the ones who made Anne wish she had listened to Zima and Mark and sent them all straight into the house to die.

The others' thoughts, almost to a man, ranged from lustful intercourse to sheer rape, torture, or murder when they laid eyes on her. She was a woman. A plaything. An inconsequential object for their pleasure, no more deserving of respect than the weeds squashed beneath their boots. And, just when she thought it couldn't get any worse, she glimpsed their past atrocities. Pleasure, pain, lust, screams, blood, mutilation, humiliation, dominance, apathy … it flooded her mind like raw sewage, polluting her soul so profoundly that she feared she may never feel clean again.

Zima had said it. Mark had said it. Anne believed them now.

She no longer wanted to talk to these mercenaries. She didn't need to. They were monsters, every bit as hideous as her own demented sire. She didn't just want them out of her mind; she wanted them out of her sight. She wanted them gone. Extinguished. Erased. Forgotten.

Permanently.

"Into the house," Anne said, channeling Zima's flat tone.

They marched into the last place they would ever see. Anne felt no anger, sadness, or remorse for the beasts she had erringly called children, only relief that they would soon be no more. Then she could go back to pretending William was the only true monster left in the world.

In that unfortunate moment, the true monster joyously discovered her defensive program was down.

Anne felt William's presence as a pinprick. Before she could scream, before she could warn Mark that William had found her, before she could blink … her malevolent sire flared in her mind, brighter than she remembered. He plucked the same strings in her that she had plucked in the others. Her limbs seized. Her throat paralyzed. Anne became a helpless statue, her back to Mark, eyes fixed on the house where the last few mercenaries were just filing in.

Walk around me, she thought desperately. *Mark, please! Re-activate the defense program! Walk around me and see my face! Please!*

But Mark wasn't her sireling. He couldn't read her thoughts.

"I guess that's that," Mark said to her back once the last mercenary was inside. "We should move away. Nick's friend used more ordinance than I expected."

Just blow them up!

Anne fought with everything she had to signal him somehow, but she couldn't budge, as if her motor cortex had been unplugged.

Please, Mark ...

Even her tear ducts were frozen; her eyes remained dry, even though Anne was crying inside.

Blow it up before it's too late, before he discovers —

William's joy turned to awe, then rapture.

No, no! Mark! Please! He's figured it out. He knows about the mercenaries! You have to ... have to ...

The panic bled away. Her apprehension, her worries, her fears, even her hatred for William ... one by one they disappeared until Anne couldn't remember why she had been upset.

The mercenary vampires were a menace, sure, but ... No, they were necessary, of course.

She didn't know what had gotten into her, throwing away valuable assets like that. They were her children. She couldn't just discard them, even if her friends thought it was the right ...

Friends? Who had she been thinking of? Was it Zima? Oh, her precious Zima, the love of her ... the bane of her existence. That goddamn machine, indiscriminately killing William's brood ... No, her siblings. Charlie should have left that murderous robot for scrap after William ... after Anne's sire, that is — her one true master — had rightly put the infernal thing out of commission, but he and Mark ...

Her motor control returned. An angry tension made Anne grind her teeth. She turned to find that over-muscled traitor staring right back at her.

Him!

He, more than anyone, wanted to murder her children and rob her sire of a legion of trained soldiers, yet he had the gall to look her in the eyes and smile as though they were bosom companions. As though he cared. Maybe once she had thought of him fondly … But even that was wrong, now that she thought about it. She had always hated Mark. Anne turned away, unable to stand the sight of him. A prissy, snobby, know-it-all jerk. That's what she had always thought. And now he wanted to murder her children.

Her eyes narrowed, fingers curled into claws.

Not tonight. Not while I still live.

She had to rescue her children from Mark's death trap, return with them to her rightful place by William's side … yes, she would return to him, beg forgiveness for her misguided absence.

Or she would die trying.

Two obstacles stood between her and redemption: the explosive detonators, and her defensive program — and Mark held the keys to both. If he so much as suspected she'd shaken his poisonous brainwashing, he would cut her off from her beloved master, and might kill her children as punishment … yes, he certainly would. Anne hated him more with every passing second. She wanted to tear his throat out, drink his blood until he was a desiccated husk.

He was close. Anne was stronger, faster. With a well-placed strike and the element of surprise, she just might take him. But, as he had pointed out in the past, Mark was a better-trained combatant. Victory was not assured. Anne wouldn't put her children's lives at unnecessary risk.

"Anne? Are you all right?"

Concern laced his voice, but there was also suspicion. She had to put him at ease, or he would activate that blasted program. Anne put her years of customer service experience to work.

"I'm fine," she said, flashing him the same disarming smile she used to diffuse upset patrons — especially ones she couldn't stand. "It's just … hard, seeing them march so complacently to their own deaths. I'd like another minute, if that's all right."

"Sure, but not too long, okay? Orwing could send a search party any time, and we want to be as far away as possible when they arrive."

I fully intend to — with all *my children.*

Before that could happen, though, Anne needed freedom from that defensive program, housed in the small computer implant above her right breast. She could try taking it out, but even Charlie wasn't sure how necessary it had become for her own body functions. Removing it might kill her — not to mention it would hurt like hell. Anne didn't have anything sharp to excise it with, which meant she would have to dig it out with her own fingers.

It was too risky. There had to be another option ... It was the only option, of course. She was just being squeamish. Selfish. Cowardly. Too concerned about her own worthless life. What was a little pain if it meant saving her children?

The implant had to come out.

Her back to Mark, Anne casually untucked the front of her shirt and slipped her hand inside, probing until her fingers found the small, hard lump several inches below her collarbone, embedded in the soft tissue at the top of her right breast. Her short nails dug into either side of the implant.

Bracing herself, Anne squeezed.

Pain shot through her chest like fire, up her neck, and churned her stomach. Anne stifled a scream, which built with such force that she thought her lungs would burst. She eventually loosened her grip and let off the pressure in her lungs with a slow, shuddering breath.

I-I can't! It hurts too much. There has to be another way ...

There was no other way. Anne was a traitor to her sire. She deserved the pain. She needed to be punished for her transgressions against her family, and to prove her unflagging loyalty to her master.

She would carry out the sentence herself.

"Anne —"

"Just another minute," she said, trying to keep the hysteria from her voice. Trembling fingers took position once more. This time, she squeezed with all her might. Nails bit deep into her soft tissue. Anne cried out, unable to bite back the agony of her blunt fingertips pushing and tearing through her own flesh, until they finally met on the other side of the implant.

"*Anne!* Jesus ..."

A familiar sensation tickled the back of her mind, followed by the mild nausea of the defensive program stimulating the brain cells associated with her bond to create excruciating feedback for any and all who shared a mental connection with her.

Screams from the nearby building joined her own. In addition to the agony of her self-inflicted wound, her sire's glorious presence disappeared, leaving behind an aching void.

"*No!*" Anne shrieked. "Come back, please! *Master!*"

Anne closed her eyes and gave a final, desperate yank. Agony shot through her like an electric rod, blotting her vision with sickly colors.

She awoke face-down in the weeds. Mark's warm, heavy chest pressed against her back, his arms wrapped around her in a bear hug.

The screams from the building had stopped.

"Anne!" Mark cried in her ear. "Talk to me! What's going on?"

"I did it ..." A giggling hysteria burst from her lips. "Mark, I did it!"

"Are you okay now? The defensive program should be running."

"I'm fine." She squirmed in his arms, and he loosened enough so she could roll to face him. "See? Everything's going to be all right."

The sight of the gory rectangular implant in her palm had the effect she hoped it would. While he stared in horror, Anne bashed her forehead into his cheek with all her might. The fragile bone in his face cracked against the tough apex above her brow. His head reeled, and his arms loosen further.

To her delight, her master flared to life again, taking his rightful place in her mind. William was upset that he had missed the final, agonizing removal of her implant, but he was pleased it had happened, and he firmly reminded her that she wasn't done yet.

My children ...

Mark was dazed. She could easily break his neck, but he was paranoid, just like his partner Charlie. She wouldn't put it past him to have built a fail-safe in his own implant to trigger the explosion in the event of his death. Anne had to decide quickly. Mark would blow the building anyway the moment he came back to his senses, unless ...

She rolled out from under him and grabbed him with both hands.

Unless the explosion would kill him, too.

Gritting her teeth against the pain from the gaping hole in her breast, Anne heaved with all her considerable might and hurled Mark toward the house.

A blinding flash consumed her children's prison. Mark bounced back, as if hitting an invisible shield.

Then the shock wave slammed into her. Like a flaming bull, it knocked Anne from her feet, scorching her exposed skin and setting everything around her ablaze, including her clothes.

She didn't care. Thirty-six presences disappeared from her mind, leaving only her master's. As Anne sat in the flames, watching her own flesh char and blacken, she could only feel William's fury at her failure to save her children — his army.

Something stirred in the blazing tall grass. Mark was struggling to his feet. Fire glinted from blood streaming from a gash in his cheek where her forehead had struck. William's fury latched onto him, burning hotter than the white inferno consuming the remains of the dilapidated house.

Anne lurched to her feet, skin crackling and splitting with every move. She didn't feel any of it. She didn't even care if she died.

As long as she took that murdering bastard along with her.

Anne charged with a primal growl, a demon of fire and hate streaking across the scorched field. Mark noticed her just as she leaped, but he was still dazed and couldn't keep her clawed hands from latching around his throat. They tumbled into the flames, rolling over and over. Although her hands were slick with blood, she kept her grip and squeezed tighter, watching him struggle through a haze of smoke that watered her eyes, until the strength finally left him, and his arms fell limp. Still her fingers clawed at his neck, fueled by her sire's rage, squeezing, shaking —

Pain exploded in her leg, followed by a distant gunshot, toppling Anne from her death perch. The familiar, nova-like agony of a silver bullet dwarfed even her sire's immense presence, tearing guttural screams from her throat, until her limbs became numb, and her voice would no longer respond.

The last thing Anne saw before the silver's poison claimed her was a stooped, one-legged, metallic abomination hopping toward her through the fire.

32

DAMAGE

FOR THE SECOND TIME IN HER LIFE, Anne awoke to someone poking around inside of her. She screamed and flailed, knocking that someone away. Every inch of her skin burned; every nerve a firecracker of agony. She writhed and rolled, dimly aware that she had fallen to the floor.

A presence bloomed in her mind. Not the overwhelming brilliance of her sire, this was as soft and warm as it was familiar and ancient. It wanted her to be at ease.

Just like that, the pain vanished.

"Almos," Anne wheezed, letting herself collapse.

The master vampire looked down at her with his quirky half-smile, a shiny bullet pinched between a set of forceps. "If I didn't know better, Anne Perrin, I would say you've developed a fondness for being shot with silver."

"If you're in my head, that means ..." Anne hastily reached for the familiar lump of her implant in her right breast, but felt only a jagged divot.

Looking down turned out to be a mistake. Her arms, torso, legs, feet ... everything was a mess of charred black and oozing red, more like steak on the grill than human skin. Just seeing it made her whimper, until she realized it didn't hurt in the slightest.

"The sire bond can be used for more than just forcing sirelings to do our bidding," Almos said. "I only wish I could have done the same for your friend, Mark."

Mark!

"Is he okay? W-where is he? Did I ... did I ..." Anne looked at her hands, remembering now how they had squeezed his throat until he went limp. Her sobs came slowly at first, then built into a torrent that curled her into a heaving ball.

It hadn't been a dream. Anne really had choked the life out of him.

Her sobs came louder, cramping her stomach. She pressed her fists to her eyes. That William had been driving her at the time seemed inconsequential. Anne's hands had committed the act. Her fingers had felt his pulse falter in their unbreakable grasp.

And then her sorrow fled. Trailing hiccups were the only indication she had been crying at all. "Almos, did you do that?"

"Yes." He knelt on the floor next to her. A lock of oiled black hair fell across one eye, which he absently brushed back into place. "Your friend lives. Your mechanical girlfriend dropped him at the hospital prior to bringing you down to me."

"Zima? What was she doing out of ..."

A memory came back to her. *The lone metallic figure hopping through the fire ...*

"W-where is she?"

"Coming," Zima called from a nearby doorway, echoing as if from a great distance, followed by the rhythmic pounding of a foot hopping down metal stairs. Anne suddenly realized she didn't recognize her surroundings. She was sitting at the edge of a circular, domed concrete room, three stories high at the apex. Thick conduits ran from a hole in the wall, along the floor, and into a solid white box in the center of the room the size of a small dining table. A steady hum filled the air, amplified by the amphitheater-like ceiling. The only other features were a polished metal table, which she had just fallen from, and a folding lawn chair.

This must be the reactor room Zima was talking about, which means we're pretty far underground.

Considering her missing implant, Anne couldn't blame them for leaving her down here. Both she and Almos needed the earth's protection to keep themselves and everyone around them safe.

Zima finally hopped into view, stooping awkwardly just above her hips, dressed in her usual baggy gray outfit with one pant leg tied in a knot where her leg was missing at the knee. "I have brought a blood bag for each of you, and clothing for Anne later, once her skin has healed."

That's when Anne realized she was stark naked. Aware of Almos' watchful eyes, she started to cover herself, then let her arms drop.

What am I embarrassed about? He's nine hundred years old, and I look like an overcooked barbecued chicken.

Her gesture wasn't lost on him, apparently. "Sorry, my dear Anne. You have my word that I will restrict my eyes to gentlemanly territory."

Cappa's muffled voice rose from the pile of clothes Zima carried. "A gentleman indeed!"

Zima hopped over and laid her cargo out on the table, revealing a small white speaker box.

Anne gulped. "Zima, is that a camera at the top?"

"Yes. Cappa wished for a better way of seeing during conversation than a shaky phone strapped around someone's neck."

"Oh my God!" the box squawked. "Anne, you poor, poor thing. You look miserable!"

Anne carefully rose to her feet, wincing when skin pulled free from her bottom and remained stuck to the floor.

I'm so glad I can't feel that.

"Thanks again, Almos. With cool tricks like this, you may have a hard time getting rid of me. Where's Doris?"

"Dela was pretty shaken up about Mark," Cappa said, "so Doris is with her at the hospital."

Guilt bubbled again, but disappeared just as quickly. Anne turned to Almos, sure it was his doing. "I appreciate your thoughtfulness, but ... I'm going to have to face the guilt sooner or later. I'd rather get it out of my system now, if that's okay."

He stared at her. His half-smile returned. "As you wish, brave lady."

"Just remember," Cappa said. "It wasn't your fault! That vindictive son-of-a-bitch made you do things that Anne Perrin would never do, not on her worst day, so ... so go easy on yourself, all right? Mark won't blame you — not one single bit! — and neither should you."

"Thanks, Cappa." Hands trembling, Anne nodded to Almos.

The master vampire wasn't paying attention, however. He was focused on the speaker, a twinkle in his midnight-black eyes. "I should like to meet the woman to whom such insightful words belong. Do you also live in this facility, my dear?"

Cappa giggled. "Yes, but it may be a while before we can meet face-to-face. I'm, ah, not exactly myself at the moment."

"Long story," Anne said to his raised eyebrows.

"I suspect more than a few of those lurk within these walls."

"But we can still talk," Cappa said with a hint of desperation. "I ... I can keep you guys company while you're stuck down here. You know, help stave off the boredom."

"A kind offer," Almos said, "but we may be here for a while yet. Maybe decades, in my case. Even my entertaining stories wear thin after the seventeenth telling."

"That would be wonderful," Anne said to the speaker box, remembering Cappa's intense loneliness in her other selves' absence. "We can play word games, take turns reading to each other ... it'll be like one, long slumber party."

"Your idea of a slumber party is far muted from mine," Almos said, smiling. "But you are the hosts, so I shall abide your rules." He straightened. His expression turned somber. "Are you ready, Anne?"

"Sure, let's do it before I chicken out." Anne took a breath and steadied herself.

It wasn't my fault, she chanted in preparation, *not my fault, not my fault, not my —*

Grief crushed her.

Fire everywhere, my fingers around Mark's neck, squeezing, choking, hating, while we're both burning alive ...

Her sobs returned in force. Anne weathered them, let them run their course while the others stood in respectful silence.

Not ... my ... fault ...

It was easy to say, but much harder to believe. Mark was her friend — Charlie's best friend — who had looked out for her. He was a protective brother, a voice of wisdom when she was lost. Anne thought back to the hatred that had infused her, the sheer malice in her heart while she had choked the life from him. She found none of that now, only affection and camaraderie.

Anne loved Mark. She would never hurt him under her own free will.

And now her conscience knew it.

The revelation didn't end the matter, however. Facing Mark when he returned would be another bitter trial. Visions of the awful crime would also haunt her, but she could shelter in the fact that it wasn't her crime. It was William's.

"Would you like a tissue?" Zima said.

A trickle from her nose made her upper lip itch fiercely, but she kept her arms firmly at her sides. "Better not," Anne said, sniffling. "I'm afraid of what else wiping my face might take with it."

"Thanks for the lovely visual," Cappa said dryly. "I'm going to turn my camera off now, in case you decide to find out."

Cappa's selective squeamishness tickled Anne to no end, and brought a much-needed smile. She looked pointedly at the camera and poised her fingers over a large piece of sloughing skin on her arm.

"Eew," Cappa said. "Don't you dare! You know what they say about picking at your scabs ..."

Anne's fingers inched closer.

"Don't, don't, don't! I'll turn the camera off, I mean it!"

Fire-damaged fingernails pinched the edge. A grin widened Anne's cracked lips.

"Anne, goddamnit! Do you want to see a speakerbox throw up? Because I swear you will!"

She tugged, pulling a bit up with the sound of wet paper tearing.

"I hate you. Hate you! Oh, put it down, please, please, please!"

"All right, all right." Anne giggled and lowered her arm.

Almos held a hand over his mouth, unsuccessfully trying to stifle a laugh. "I take back my earlier comment. This may turn out to be the most entertaining isolation period of my long history."

"One thing I do not understand," Zima said to him. "How are you able to influence Anne while her sire is shielded?"

Anne frowned. "Yeah, the generational gap should totally cut us off. Shouldn't it?"

"Proximity helps, certainly," Almos said. "But, suffice it to say, I've learned a few things over the centuries that my dear prodigy William has yet to discover."

"Do tell," Cappa said cheerfully. "What else is in your velvet bag of tricks?"

Almos perked up at her apparent interest. "Experience and technique, mainly. The third century was when I first managed to assemble a force of any significance. What a chore that was! I remember well my first lieutenants, nothing but peasants and slaves from a local village recently ravaged by plague. Our first battle was a disaster ..."

Almos turned to the speaker, regaling Cappa with a flowery rendition of his early history. Captivating as it was, Anne noticed Zima's attention was fixed on her. Anne carefully sidled next to her, resisting the urge to hold her hand as she normally would.

"You okay?" Anne said softly.

"No."

The stark admission took her by surprise. Anne reached to hug her, but caught herself again when she felt her skin split at the shoulder.

Damnit!

"I-I'm sorry. What's bothering you?"

"I ... I have missed you very much," Zima said. "To have you so close and not be able to touch ... 'miserable' is an apt description of my current state."

"Oh, honey ... Look, I can't feel anything anyway. A hug probably won't lengthen my recovery."

"Much as I would enjoy that, it may extend my own. Although I was careful when transporting you here, some of my flesh has already been contaminated by your open wounds, and will need to be replaced. A hug may infect more, and our synthetic flesh reserves are still low from my first encounter with the vampires several months ago." Zima looked at her own ravaged reflection in the mirror-polished table. "I wish to be here the moment you are feeling able, but the length of my recovery period will largely be dependent on Mark. It seems a selfish notion, while he lies in the hospital, but I … cannot think of it any other way. I only wish to be back in your arms."

The weight of Zima's words brought Anne's gaze down to the table with her, where she saw herself for the first time, and gasped. For some reason, she had expected to see her long auburn hair dangling in a tangled mat, but a red-scabbed, hairless monster stared back, so unrecognizable that Anne briefly questioned if it was actually her and not some demon lurking beneath a glassy surface. Tears threatened again, until she saw her poor Zima's reflection beside her — half metal, half lacerated flesh, and hairless.

Just like Anne.

A laugh broke past the lump in her throat. Everyone turned, but Anne could only stare at their ridiculous reflections, laughter building until her sides ached.

"We … we're a pair, aren't we?"

Zima cocked her head, which Anne found even funnier.

"S-seriously," Anne said, sniffling. "Look at us! You can hardly get any worse, yet here we are, still together."

"That's remarkably optimistic," Almos said.

"Just trying to look at the bright side."

He returned her smile, but she sensed his doubt. Almos was in her head and saw the laughter for what it was: a thin cover for the despair threatening to consume her.

"As well you should," he said, mercifully playing along. "There is much to be thankful for, assuming your friend in the hospital recovers."

"He will," Zima said. "His vitals are strong, and I shall continue to monitor his progress through his implant. The greatest risk for a burn victim is infection, which should not pose a threat to his enhanced immune system. The only reason I did not bring him to Z-Tech instead of the hospital is because Charlie and Cappa are not here to tend him."

Almos frowned at Cappa's speakerbox. "Didn't you say that you are in this facility?"

The speakerbox sighed. "I am, but … think of me as a spirit guide, able to impart wisdom in your darkest need, but with no body to interact with in the physical world."

"Truly?" Almos turned to them, his face lit with wonder.

Anne shrugged. "Close enough, let's go with it."

"I shall return to the lab," Zima said. "Many of my systems still require significant repair, and although my body has its own nanites, the process will be much more efficient under the glass where Cappa may assist."

"Oh, speaking of repairs ..." Anne touched the divot above her breast. "I, ah, don't suppose my implant survived the fire ...?"

"It did. I found it clenched in your hand when we arrived here."

Anne shrieked with excitement. "I can't believe it! Does it still work? Can we put it back?"

"I cannot answer either question, unfortunately. It appeared to be intact. I shall test it later, but even if it still functions, your body may reject it."

"Oh, right," Anne said softly. When she had awakened from her harrowing transformation into a vampire, Charlie said they'd had a difficult time with the surgery because her tissue had effectively spat the implant out.

But he also said they programmed my cells to accept it.

Anne had hated the implant at first, thinking it unpredictable and dangerous to her health, but she'd quickly discovered that not only was it doing its best to keep her alive, it was also the key to freedom from her sadistic sire. Without it, she might have to spend the rest of eternity hiding underground, like Almos, to prevent a madman from taking control of her again.

"Please, please let me know how it goes," Anne said.

"I shall," Zima said, but didn't move.

Emotion gripped Anne's throat in a vice. "Thanks for saving my life," she said hoarsely. "That was the second time tonight. You're more caring, brave, and selfless than any storybook hero. I can never repay the huge tally I owe you, but hang in there until we're better and I promise I'll try — and in the best way you can imagine." Anne touched her fingers to her own lips, closed her eyes, and poured every ounce of her heart into a blown kiss.

Zima's breath caught. Her legs shook. The remains of her face contorted in agonized longing for the intimate touch they couldn't share.

"I love you, my darling," Anne said.

"I l-love you, t-t-too." Zima's voice held such yearning that Anne had to clench her jaw to keep from crying again. Zima eventually regained her composure and hopped toward the stairs. "Please get well soon," she said without turning. "I shall endeavor to do the same."

Anne listened to Zima's hopping footsteps until the reactor's hum was the only sound in her concrete prison. Heart weighing heavy, Anne suspected it was the last she would see of her tormented lover until they were both better.

"That was ... remarkable."

She jumped at Almos' voice, having forgotten he was there, then gave a bashful smile. "She's something, all right."

"Undoubtedly. Her affection for you seems genuine, something I never dreamed of seeing in a machine. But I was referring to you. I thought you were exaggerating in your cell when you told me of your relationship, but ... I have never felt such intense love from another vampire, nor thought our species even capable. How is it possible?"

"I guess it's okay to tell you now. The implant you heard us talking about is a small computer that juggled my physiology both during and after my transformation. It's the reason I don't sleep and can't sit still. We're still uncovering all the adjustments it's made, but it sounds like we can add affection to the list."

"Wait," Cappa said. "Almos, are you saying vampires don't normally feel affection?"

"Not toward humans. It has taken me decades to recondition myself to care about people as more than just food or instruments, but even so, it is a fraction of what I felt when I was human. I don't suppose you have a spare one of those implants around?"

"We could make one," Cappa said, "but we're pretty sure the only reason it worked with Anne is because we caught her before her transition. I don't think your body will accept it. Even if it does, Anne was conditioned during a critical phase with Mark's special blood, which is what allows it to communicate with and manipulate her cells. Without that, the implant would be useless."

"Alas, it was too good to be true. I suppose I shall have to continue to regain my humanity the hard way."

"Let me know if you'd like some help," Cappa said. "I have some experience there."

"I would be delighted for your assistance, my ethereal lady." Almos stifled a yawn. "But your kind offer will have to wait. The sun rises, and I fear I shall be poor company until it sets again this evening."

"We'll keep quiet," Cappa said.

"Don't bother, I'm a sound sleeper." With a final yawn, Almos relaxed into the lawn chair and closed his eyes.

Anne had never seen another vampire sleeping. Pale skin, chest still, no heartbeat to throb his veins … it looked for all the world like Almos had settled down to die. If she hadn't felt his presence in her mind, she might have shaken him to double check.

"Is he sleeping already?" Cappa said.

"Like a log, which is good, because I wanted to ask you something." Anne instinctively reached for her waistband to fidget, but found only crusted skin. "How has Zima been holding up?"

The speaker sighed. "Hard to say. Without my body, it's been tough keeping tabs on everyone. Mostly they forget I'm even here, but even if I had my body … you know how difficult Zima is to read."

"She wasn't tonight," Anne said softly.

"Yeah, that was new to me, and it wasn't good. Was she like that before your abduction?"

"Sort of, but nowhere near as intense. I-I thought she was going to fall apart there, mentally and physically." Anne wrung her hands, sending flecks of skin drifting to the floor. "I'm worried, Cappa. She told me that her … her feelings had finally become part of her core, and that she was afraid she wouldn't be able to stop them. I thought it was cute because I also thought I'd be here to help her deal with them, but then …"

"Anne Perrin, tell me you're not trying to lay that on your conscience on top of everything else."

"She's suffering, Cappa! I can't stand it."

"I … I know. I'll talk to her. Maybe I can help, as one artificial intelligence to another."

Even through the speaker, Anne heard her doubt. "What's wrong?"

"Well, these new feelings of hers ... I get where she's coming from. I've been there, trying to figure out how these strange things fit into your programming, how to balance them with existing processes so their intensity doesn't drown everything else out and shut you down. It was hard, it was scary, and ultimately ... It was something I had to figure out on my own."

"So there's nothing we can do to help her? What about another Desire routine to balance things out, or ..." Anne sagged. She was flailing, and she knew it.

But there has to be something! Zima wouldn't give up on me if our situations were reversed.

"I know you want to help," Cappa said, "but you have to remember that Zima is unique — just like me. Our brains are as different from each other as they are from a human's. There's no manual to show how we should operate. No psychology textbook on artificial intelligences who've miraculously evolved from glorified network firewalls." Her voice softened. "If you want my opinion, the best thing you can do for Zima is exactly what you've been doing — what you are doing — and that's being there for her. Supporting her. Loving her. The rest she's going to have to figure out by herself, unfortunately."

Anne looked to the ceiling. Her eyes misted. "I'm scared for her."

"I know, but Zima's tough, both body and mind. She wouldn't have evolved this far if she wasn't, believe me. Hang in there, and have a little faith."

"Okay, I'll ... I'll ..." Anne didn't know what she was going to do, so she left the thought unfinished.

Mischief infected Cappa's voice. "Look, if you really want to help, don't get kidnapped again. It wasn't fun for any of us, and to be honest ... it's getting a little old."

Anne leveled her gaze at the speakerbox. "I can't wait until your other selves are back, because the second you walk in that door, I'm going to drag you into the gym and kick your butt."

"Don't be so sure. Master Wung may be teaching my other selves all sorts of ancient *kung fu* secrets even as we speak."

"That work on vampires? Neat trick."

"Careful what you wish for, my prissy friend." Cappa chuckled. "Feeling better yet?"

Anne smiled. "Yeah. Thanks, sis."

"Anytime. So, I have three hundred and eighteen thousand four hundred and twenty-one books in my electronic library. Which one shall I read to you first?"

Tears of a different sort welled this time. "You're too good to me, Cappa."

"Don't I know it. So?"

"Do you have any Jayne Madison novels?"

"Indubitably! Ahem ... *The Adventures of Jayne Madison, Book One*, by Georgette Parker. Chapter One. Experience told Jayne Madison that her date pulling a gun meant the fun part of the evening was over ..."

Anne stood transfixed while Cappa's words transported her back to her childhood, to the very day her fantasies of becoming a bigger-than-life hero began, and all she'd wanted was to be whisked away on a life-threatening adventure where the fate of the world hung in the balance.

That, of course, was long before Anne had discovered how much it actually sucked.

33

PIXIE DELIGHT

ALMOS GAVE ANNE A SHREWD LOOK. "Do you have any … twos?"
Anne grimaced and smacked three cards on the table, which echoed from the reactor room walls.

He scooped them up with an infuriating grin and added four matching deuces to the already large collection before him. "Do you have any aces?"

Grumbling, Anne plucked two more cards and tossed them over.

He set his remaining hand down with a triumphant smile. "I believe that is the game."

"Are you sure you're not reading my mind? You've won twenty of the last twenty-two games. No one's that lucky."

"Don't be a sore loser," Cappa's speakerbox said. "A little skill goes a long way, even with a game like Go Fish. Almos is using a simple but effective strategy, that's all."

"Care to enlighten me?"

Almos chuckled. "Where's the fun in that, my dear girl? Perhaps you'll divine my strategy on your own after another few rounds."

The sound of footsteps in the stairwell saved her from another trouncing. Anne rushed over and listened intently.

Mark's loafers. Dela's light sneakers. Rattling? Yes, in cardboard. They're carrying a box full of something.

Three days had passed since she first awoke in the reactor room, and Anne was already starving for anything different — something other than the steady reactor hum or Almos' stories. Even Cappa's book reading had worn thin after the second day, though Anne suspected the feeling was mutual. Having gone from one long incarceration to another, visitors of any kind were exciting.

But it was what Anne didn't hear that made her sad. Zima's heavy footsteps were absent.

Dela appeared first, carrying a large cardboard box. Anne bounced like an excited puppy and followed her to the table.

"Whatcha got, whatcha got?" Anne was pulling the flaps open before Dela had even set it down.

"It'll be much more fun as a surprise," Cappa said with a note of excitement.

Anne sifted through the box's contents. Small metal pipes, plates, cylinders, mysterious boxes with frayed wires, trays of different colored powders ... "Fun for whom? It looks like a third-place science project waiting to happen."

"Sounds like fun to me," Mark said, stepping from the stairwell. He carried a two-foot-tall shimmering metallic cube on a steel plate, his considerable biceps bulging with the effort. Unlike her own skin, his was still bright pink in places from the burns, but Anne suspected even that would be gone by tomorrow.

Anne's smile faded. "Mark, is that what I think it is?"

"If you mean eighty percent of our nanites from the production floor, then yes." With a groan, he carefully set it on the table, then started unpacking the cardboard box's eclectic contents.

"And you're not going to tell me why you've basically put Z-Tech out of business?"

"Not out of business," Cappa said. "I notified our customers that we're having technical difficulties, and that they may experience a delay in their orders. The remaining twenty percent of the manufacturing floor can crank out enough product to keep our most important customers happy."

"Yeah," Dela said. "Z-Tech gear is a hot commodity. A play like this might even jack up prices and increase profit margins."

"Not our profit margins," Mark said. "Our prices will remain fixed to maintain good relations. Retailers, however, will have a field day, which should improve their mood." He put the empty box on the floor and began to arrange the pieces.

Almos slipped in beside Anne, looking on with interest. "If my eyes don't deceive me, your arrangement resembles arms and legs."

Mark grinned. He pulled a pair of miniature polished eyeballs from his jacket and set them where the head would be.

"No way ..." Anne had a guess of what they were up to, and she could hardly believe it.

"Way," Cappa said. "Ready, Mark?"

"Almost. Anne, could you help me set the block on top of the sculpture?"

"'Sculpture' may be too flattering a word," Dela said, looking at the loosely assembled collection of parts.

Mark's grin widened. "Just you wait."

Anne walked to the opposite side of the table from him. Together, they moved the deceptively heavy block of nanoscopic robots to rest in the center of the three-foot-tall humanoid shape laying on the polished metal.

"All right, Cappa," Mark said. "Do your magic."

"Magic" was an apt description for what happened next. The cube gradually lost its shape, stretching over a period of several minutes to engulf the structures on the table. Lumps formed, gaining definition until they became a nose, chin, breasts, navel, hips, and ...

She just had to make it anatomically correct.

"Anybody mind if I cover her up?" Anne said, grinning.

Dela laughed, but Mark just shrugged.

Anne removed the long scarf wrapping her peach-fuzz covered head and laid it over the tiny figure, covering her from the neck down. The air felt strange against her exposed scalp, which had been protected her whole life by a thick layer of hair, but she was more concerned about her friend's dignity than her own.

The little face continued to gain definition. Ears emerged, nostrils appeared, the material on her head became gritty, dark brown, and formed into short hair. Eye sockets sunk in. The orbs Mark had placed earlier bubbled to the surface, then were covered with thin lids that slowly sprouted black lashes. Lips became textured and parted slightly to reveal the beginnings of a tongue. The silvery skin dimpled, turning a healthy peach color, though it still shimmered like everything else, which gave her an ethereal quality that left Anne speechless.

Almos stood transfixed, his mouth open, dark eyes like saucers. Awe and adoration poured through his bond, the latter of which made Anne smile. He and Cappa had been getting along famously, exchanging stories and knowledge with unwavering enthusiasm. Cappa was still pretending to be a spirit guide, which he seemed happy to play along with, but Anne had a feeling this incredible display may have inadvertently turned him into a believer.

The figure's eyes opened to a room full of gasps. A tiny hand emerged from under the scarf. It raised its hand to its face, turning it over for inspection, then its lips parted in Cappa's trademark, radiant smile.

"It worked," the little body said. Her voice was soft and airy, a perfect match for her delicate features. While she looked similar to the larger Cappa, her shimmering skin and hair, combined with a smaller yet perfectly proportioned body, made her resemble a fairy creature. She slowly sat up. Anne caught the falling scarf and tied it into a makeshift dress.

"Thanks," the little Cappa said in her captivating voice.

Almos fell to one knee, looking upon her with utter reverence, as if she were an angel made flesh. "My lady," he breathed.

Cappa had the grace to look bashful. Tentative fingers ran through her short hair. "You like it?"

"I thought my long years had shown me the greatest beauty the world has to offer. I could not have been more mistaken, for you give new definition to the word."

Dela stifled a laugh and playfully jabbed Mark in the ribs. "You could take notes from this guy."

Mark ignored her, however, and stared at Cappa with the same marvel that Anne imagined Doctor Frankenstein had when his own creation had taken life.

"Although these hands are not worthy to touch your divine skin," Almos said, "I would forever treasure the opportunity to help you down from your perch."

Dela rolled her eyes. "All right, that one may have been over the top."

Apparently, Cappa didn't think so. Her face lit up, exposing a set of dazzling white teeth behind her sparkling red lips. She extended a hand, which he took as he would a delicate flower. Looking less confident, Cappa scooted from the table and landed on wobbly legs. Almos carefully steadied her. After a moment, she straightened and looked around. Although Almos was kneeling, Cappa still only came up to his nose.

She took a small step, then another. Soon she was running across the room, laughing and twirling, looking for all the world like a pixie dancing in the moonlight.

"Oh, it feels so good to move again! I didn't realize how much I missed this freedom." Pixie Cappa stopped in front of Mark and looked up at him with grateful eyes. "Thank you, thank you, thank you!"

"Don't mention it," Mark said, smiling. "Besides, all I did was gather the parts. You did most of the work writing the program to run everything."

"It wasn't so bad," Pixie Cappa said. "I was able to re-use a lot of existing routines. The hard part was figuring out how to make the nanites move like real muscles. I was also worried they would be too fragile, even for this little body, but they're holding up fine."

Anne knelt and held out her hand. "May I?"

Pixie Cappa glided over, scarf trailing like a magnificent gown, and stood before her for inspection. Anne ran her fingers over her tiny face. Her skin was as soft as real flesh and shimmered with every touch like glittery liquid in a clear plastic bag.

"Almos is right," Anne said. "You're absolutely captivating. Why didn't you use nanites in the first place for your real body? Seems like a lot less hassle."

Mark knelt, too, and lightly touched the back of Pixie Cappa's hand. "Like she said, the nanites are dynamic, but not very sturdy.

Cappa has to be careful or she might damage them, and they're difficult to replace."

"And I won't be doing any heavy lifting," Pixie Cappa said. "Ten pounds tops, I'd guess, but it should be enough to help Mark with the surgery."

"S-surgery?" Anne brightened, clasping Pixie Cappa's tiny hand. "It's ready?"

"Almost," Mark said. "Zima's running a final set of diagnostics to make sure the implant won't do more harm than good when it reconnects to your body."

Anne sighed in relief. "How's she doing?"

"Good. Repairs are progressing slower than last time, since there's only one Cappa to direct the nanites instead of three, but she's almost done. Another day and she'll be good as new."

"And since Mr. Sensitive here missed your real question of how she's feeling," Dela said, "the only reason Zima didn't come down is because she's totally focused on getting your implant squared away. She's a girl with a mission, and that's to get you topside so she can finally have some quality time with her main squeeze."

"Well, at least she's not miserable."

Zima hadn't visited since the first day and, as much as Anne missed her, she couldn't blame her, either. Zima wanted to be with her, she knew, but not being able to feel Anne's touch — or the sexual relief her touch allowed — was an even worse torture than being apart. Now that Anne was feeling better, she was looking forward to their alone time nearly as much as her desperate girlfriend.

Pixie Cappa gasped. "Oh my God! You're not going to believe who just showed up at the front door. Anne, your bald friend from the diner is here."

"Don?" Anne frowned. "I thought he and Calum were going to skip the country and lay low."

Mark crossed his arms. "More to the point, why is he here?"

"I think I know." Pixie Cappa turned her radiant smile to Anne. "There's a little girl with him."

Anne's gleeful squeal made everyone cover their ears. She turned to Mark, hands clasped in a pleading gesture.

"Oh please please please pretty please can they come in? H-he already knows about Almos and Zima. Is there any harm in a quick visit?"

Mark scratched his chin. "Probably not, but what about the girl?"

"That's who I want to see! I'll ... I'll think of some excuse for my appearance, like I'm a chemo patient or something, but ..." She grabbed his hand and fell to her knees. "I have to meet that little girl. Please! Who knows if I'll ever get the chance again? Cappa can hide in the privacy area." She pointed to a standing curtain on the far side of the room where they sponge bathed.

"Well, I guess it's all right," he said, though he didn't look convinced.

"Cool, I'll walk them in," Dela said, then headed for the stairs.

Anne put her false contacts and porcelain canine caps in place. There wasn't time for makeup, so she hoped her chemo cover story would be enough to explain her pallid skin. She paced and fidgeted until she heard their footsteps descending, where she suddenly felt self-conscious and scrambled for something to cover her fuzzy head. The best she could find, short of robbing Pixie Cappa of her scarf-dress, was a t-shirt. She made a few fumbling attempts to tie it in place, but in the end decided she probably looked even more ridiculous in the makeshift turban, so she stuffed it back in her small dresser and resumed pacing.

Don appeared first, as bald as ever, though much of his girth had disappeared. He looked around the domed room with a frown, but smiled when he spotted Anne.

Then came the little girl.

Anne thought her stilled heart was going to burst with joy. The nine-year-old stood nearly to Anne's shoulders. Strawberry curls bounced in a magnificent bouquet that was every bit as beautiful as her name implied.

"Rose," Anne whispered. Lips trembling, she fell to her knees. She'd been dreaming of this day ever since Don told her of the little girl's miraculous recovery. "Oh, you're just as pretty as I imagined."

"Are you Anne?" Rose said in a timid voice.

"Yes I am."

Rose took a step forward, then stopped and stared at Anne's peach-fuzzy head.

"I-it's all right, sweetie. I had a little accident is all. You won't get sick from me, I promise."

That seemed to mollify her. "Thank you for making me better. The doctors still want me to come see them, but I don't know why, since I feel really good."

"Really good?" Anne narrowed her eyes in mock skepticism. "Like how good?"

"Like I can do things I used to do. Watch."

Rose put her hands up, then launched into a clumsy cartwheel, sending her floral pattern dress whipping through the air. She landed awkwardly and began to fall, but Anne darted forward and caught her by the waist before she hit the ground.

"That was amazing," Anne said from behind her. "Keep practicing and you'll be a professional gymnast in no time. Why I bet ... ah ..." Rose's mouth-watering smell filled her nostrils, and Anne realized with sudden horror that she hadn't fed since yesterday.

No, no! Please, not now ...

But her fangs had already extended, popping her porcelain caps off. She hugged Rose from behind to keep her from turning around. Anne looked at Mark and Dela for help.

"Oh! Forgetful me," Dela said, glancing at her mouth where the tips of her canines poked out. "Anne, I haven't given you your medicine today, have I?"

"N-no." Anne tried not to slur around the two large obstructions in her mouth. She attempted to stand, but Rose's intoxicating scent rooted her to the spot.

Help, help, help!

If she bit the little girl, she would never forgive herself, but she knew without a doubt that she would if someone didn't intervene — and quickly.

Through her sire bond, Almos commanded her to rise and join him behind the curtain, which she did without hesitation. Dela followed close on her heels.

"Oh my God," Anne said in a strained whisper. "I almost bit her! What the hell is wrong with me?"

"Easy." Dela rolled up her sleeve. "You just missed me is all. Here, a little something to take the edge off."

Anne eagerly sank her teeth into Dela's arm. After a minute of heavenly drinking, Almos had to catch the redhead to keep her from falling down in a happy stupor. When Anne no longer felt ravenous, she reluctantly pulled away and dabbed the blood from her mouth with a damp washcloth.

"Thanks, Dela. I owe you big time."

"Let's call it even." Dela relaxed into Almos with a dreamy smile. Pixie Cappa shook her head, though a smile touched her tiny lips.

When Anne emerged from the privacy screen, Don, Mark, and Rose were kneeling in a circle around a smoking piece of cardboard. Rose wore a pair of dark glasses that were too big for her face, and was happily drawing on the box with Mark's pen-sized blue cutting laser.

"Oh! That looks like fun," Anne said, kneeling next to Rose.

Mark and Don shot her a worried look, but she waved it off. Even over the smoke, all three of their scents still made her stomach growl, but the overwhelming urge to feed was now just a controllable yearning.

"Mr. Suther said I could use it as long as I promised not to shine it in anyone's eyes," Rose said. "Which I already knew, because my dad has a laser pointer and he lets me use it with the cat. It's red, though, and it doesn't burn anything." She looked up with a beaming smile. "I like this one better."

"The kid has taste," Mark said proudly.

"So what are you making?" Anne said, her sensitive eyes half-blinded by the intense blue dot.

"Something for you. It's a surprise."

"Oh, I'd better look away then." Anne turned around and rubbed her eyes to rid herself of the spotted afterimage.

Good thing Mark gave her those protective glasses.

"Anne?"

"Yes, sweetie?"

"Cousin Don said you healed me with a strong medicine that only you know how to make." Rose turned the laser off and leaned back so their eyes met. "Will you tell me your secret?"

Anne's smile faltered. "I ... w-well, if I told you, then it wouldn't be a secret, now, would it?"

"If I promise not to tell anyone else, then it's still a secret, but it's our secret, right?"

"Yes, you're right. It's just that my secret is ... complicated."

And gross, and traumatizing, and ...

"That's okay. Since I've been well enough to go back to school, I've been studying hard to catch up, and my teacher says I'm really smart." Rose edged closer and lifted her dark glasses, revealing a twinkle in her adorable blue eyes.

"I ..." Anne started to panic, but an idea came to her. "All right, you got me. I guess you're old enough to know the truth."

Don and Mark shook their heads vehemently, but Anne ignored them and leaned closer to Rose.

"The truth is that it wasn't me at all."

"What? But Cousin Don said —"

"Do you believe in fairies, Rose?"

"Not since I was little," she said, rocking on her heels.

"Well that's too bad, because what healed you was actually a magic potion given to me by a real fairy!"

Rose plopped down on her rear and sunk her chin between her knees with a sullen look. "You could have just said you don't trust me with your secret. You didn't have to lie."

"I'm not lying," Anne lied. "Do you want to meet her?"

"You mean she's here?" Rose perked up and looked around the room. "Where?"

"She's invisible, of course. But if you close your eyes and say the magic chant with me, then you'll be able to see her."

"Nuh-uh," Rose said, but her eyes sparkled with interest.

"Yeah-huh. She's standing right behind you."

Rose swept her hand through the air. "I don't feel anything."

"That's because she moved," Mark said, stifling a smirk.

"You can see her, too?"

"Of course. I've already said the magic chant."

Don looked at them as if they were both crazy.

"I guess there's only one way for you to find out if I'm telling the truth." Anne gently tugged one of Rose's strawberry curls.

"Close your eyes when you're ready to believe. That goes for you too, Cousin Don."

Rose sighed and closed her eyes. Anne flagged Don, who snapped his mouth shut and did the same.

"All right," Anne said. "Repeat after me, three times: Fairy, fairy, show thy light. I believe, I believe, for my heart is right."

Dela barked a drunken laugh from behind the curtain, but Rose dutifully repeated it, accompanied by a mumbling Don.

As Anne hoped she would, Pixie Cappa skittered out in her flowing scarf-dress and took position a few feet behind Rose, struggling to contain her smile. Don opened his eyes first, and nearly fell backward when he saw the delicate three-foot-tall shimmering figure staring back.

Rose's eyes opened. She cried in delight when she spotted Cappa and jumped to her feet. "A real fairy! Cousin Don, can you see her? She's standing right here, just like they said!"

"I, uh ... y-yeah. I see her, Rose."

"Oh, you're so beautiful!" Rose hopped with excitement. "What's your name?"

"I'm Rose," Pixie Cappa said.

Anne thought the real Rose was going to blow a gasket. Her eyes bulged, her hands shook, her mouth worked silently until she finally stammered, "Th-that's my name too!"

"I know it is," Pixie Cappa said sagely, "which is why I passed my magic potion on to you. In the human world, my magic only works on those who share my name, which is fortunate for you."

"But ... how do you know me? How did you know I was sick?"

"I'm your fairy guardian. I know all about you and your struggle with your injury."

"I ... have a fairy guardian?" Her joy quickly turned to tears. "If that's true ... why did you wait so long to help me?"

"Because I needed a special person to help make the potion," Pixie Cappa said without missing a beat. "I needed the tears of someone with a pure heart. It took a while, but I finally found Anne, and we made the potion together as soon as we could."

"Oh." Rose wiped her eyes. "I ... I guess that makes sense. Thank you both."

"You're welcome," Pixie Cappa said. "If you ever get sick again, come back here and I'll make you a new potion, okay?"

Rose sniffed and nodded. "Can you do any other magic?"

"Only on a clear night when the moon and stars shine bright in the sky. Which, as you know, doesn't happen very often in San Francisco."

Rose thought for a second, then shook her head. "You should move inland, then you could use your magic every night."

"Call me crazy, but I like the cool coastal air."

"Sorry to interrupt," Don said to Rose, "but do you mind if I talk to Anne alone for a few minutes?"

Rose glanced at her fairy guardian, clearly reluctant, but she brightened when Cappa held out her hand.

"Come on, let's take that work of art upstairs and color it in with fairy dust."

Rose hesitantly took her hand. She gasped when it sent a shimmering wave up Cappa's arm, then the two headed for the stairs.

When their footsteps had faded, Don pointed after them with an open mouth. "W-was that Cappa?"

"I didn't think you'd met," Mark said, crossing his arms.

"I've been a regular at Hal's for years. I saw her with Charlie a few times, but I swear she was taller then." He lowered his voice to a whisper. "I-is she really a fairy?"

"She's amazing, for sure, but not quite mystical," Anne said. "That's just some pretty cool technology at work." She cleared her throat, eager to change the subject. "So, why are you still in town?"

"I'm keeping an eye on things while Calum's gone. There's only me and Lance left in the society now, but thanks to you, we're both feeling one hundred percent."

"Not to be a drag," Mark said, "but Orwing will come looking for you. They'd rather kill you to tie up their loose ends than risk their secrets getting out."

Don's shoulders sagged. "I know, but Calum hooked us up with new identities, gave us some cash to live on for a while. Besides ..." He looked up the stairway and sighed. "Rose is the closest thing to a daughter I'll probably ever have. I ... I can't leave her."

"You took a risk bringing her here," Anne said. "William's crew watches this place, especially at night, and it's after sunset if I'm not mistaken."

"Yeah, I figured, but ... it just felt too important that she meet the person who changed her life." Don cracked a smile. "Even if she thinks it was a fairy. There's another reason, though. Calum wanted you to know that he's not out of the picture. Almos' visions still scare the heck out of him and, now that he knows the region where Almos was originally turned, he's going to head over to that part of the world and do some digging. See if he can find any clues on what this Entity is, or where it came from."

"Perhaps I can point him in the right direction," the master vampire said, stepping from behind the curtain.

Don brightened. "Almos! I'd hoped you were here."

"What did you mean, Almos?" Mark said, frowning. "Where should Calum be looking?"

"I assume he means to begin his search in the Carpathian Basin in Hungary, where I told him I was from, but the one who turned me was not native to my land. If he seeks the Entity — assuming it is something corporeal that can actually be found — he will need to discover where the very first vampire is from. My original sire spoke little of his origins, unfortunately, but I do know he hailed from what is now called Mongolia."

"That's a pretty big haystack," Mark said, rubbing his own peach-fuzzy head.

Don glanced at Anne and Mark's downy heads. "What happened to you guys, anyway?"

Mark said, "I blew us up with incendiaries," at the same time Anne blurted, "I strangled him in a brush fire."

They looked at each other, and Anne saw her own shame mirrored on Mark's face. Both statements were true: Anne originally assumed Zima had triggered the explosion when she saw things were going badly, but it turned out Mark had decided it was better to risk the explosion than face a small legion of vampires under William's indirect control, so he detonated the house himself. Not only that, she discovered that the rascals had secretly agreed on Zima being there as backup during the same conversation where Anne was trying to convince her to stay.

Which also explains why she hadn't volunteered to come.

Anne had been hurt by the deception until she'd understood their reasoning. If they'd told her Zima was going to be perched on a nearby hill with a rifle and the few silver bullets she could cobble together before rushing out, wrapped in nothing but the blanket she had later used to extinguish them, then, under William's influence, Anne would certainly have taken a different course of action. She shuddered to think how things may have turned out in that instance.

Her biggest surprise, however, had been Mark's reaction when he'd returned from the hospital. Anne had been ready to throw herself at his feet and beg forgiveness, but he'd beaten her to it. He'd apologized over and over, not only for asking her to participate in the risky operation in the first place, but also for detonating the explosives when he'd known they were within the blast zone. Once they'd finished sputtering apologies to each other, they'd laughed until they could barely stand, happy only that they'd both lived to do so.

Don stuffed his hands in his pockets. "Guess I shouldn't have asked. Anyway, I'll pass the message on to Calum."

"If you have pencil and paper," Almos said, "there is something else that may be of help."

Mark produced a pen from his shirt, while Anne tore off a piece of cardboard. Almos accepted them with a nod and began sketching.

"This was a symbol my sire wore around his neck, etched into a worn wooden pendant. I asked him once why he kept such a humble trinket when we had richer spoils, and he said it was the only keepsake he had from his home. He would say no more, but perhaps some research using your wealth of technological marvels will turn up something of use."

Almos completed it quickly and handed it over for inspection. On the cardboard was a triangle containing a simple wolf, an eagle, and a hunting arrow. Mark took a picture with his phone before Don carefully slid it into his jacket.

"We'll give Calum a hand with the research," Mark said to Don. "Cappa is adept at digging up obscure information."

"I'll take that as a compliment."

The four of them jumped at Cappa's voice from the speakerbox.

"Remarkable," Almos said with a smile. "I thought your presence woefully lost to us when you departed with the girl."

"Nope, I've been listening the whole time."

"While entertaining Rose?"

"I'm adept at multitasking. Send me the image, Mark, and I'll see what I can find."

Mark tapped the screen, then slid the phone back into his pocket. "Done."

More footsteps sounded from the stairway, coming down.

Anne grinned. Only one person in the factory had such heavy footsteps.

She dashed to the entrance and bounced on the balls of her feet with eager anticipation. As the footsteps grew louder, she was able to make out other sounds: sloshing water, clinking metal, rustling cloth. Anne thought at first Zima was bringing sponge bath supplies, but they had just washed a few hours ago.

Zima emerged a minute later balancing a large bucket, a backpack, white towels, and a loaded surgical tray.

Don stumbled backward at the sight of her, and Anne could imagine why. Although she had looked far worse the last time either of them had seen her, Zima was obviously still healing. Angry red scars with dotted stitch marks ran in drunken paths over her exposed face and hands — a platinum-blonde Frankenstein without the neck bolts. She spared Don a cursory glance, then lugged her haul to the table.

"The implant is ready," Zima said by way of greeting. "I have brought the necessary supplies. Mark is already here, so we may begin the surgery as soon as Cappa returns."

"Zima ... we have company, in case you hadn't noticed," Mark said. "Now might not be the best time."

"Besides," Cappa's speakerbox said, "my new body isn't strong enough to perform the operation. Mark or Dela might become infected if they tried, and I doubt Anne's going to perform it herself, which means that unless Almos is a closet surgeon —"

"I shall do the surgery," Zima said. "If we link with a high-speed data interface, you should be able to guide my hands as if they were your own."

She stood next to Anne and laced their fingers. Her skin felt odd.

"Zima, what's on your hands?" Anne said. "They feel like rubber."

"I have coated my arms in a clear polymer to protect my skin from infection of the pathogen, since it is still healing."

Anne gave her a light kiss, which she eagerly accepted. She moaned softly when Anne pulled away.

"Honey, I know you're anxious," Anne said, "but we can wait another day until you're healed."

"The implant has passed all safety tests, and I have taken appropriate personal precautions. I see no reason to delay."

Mark frowned. "Other than our guests, you mean."

Zima shrugged. "They are welcome to watch, as long as they do not interfere."

"It's time I got Rose home anyway," Don said, looking pale. "I'm glad everyone's all right." He glanced at their fuzzy heads and the twisted red railroad tracks on Zima's face. "Well, y-you know what I mean."

"Oh no! I didn't get to say goodbye to her," Anne said.

"She's on her way down," Cappa said.

"Twenty flights of stairs down and back just to say farewell?" Almos whistled low. "That little girl is the epitome of courtesy, and an athlete besides."

"She really, really wants to give Anne her present."

"Perhaps I should wait behind the curtain," Zima said. "I do not wish to frighten her."

Mark and Don nodded, but Anne pulled Zima close to her.

"Stay." Anne trailed a finger over the rough lines crossing Zima's cheek. "Rose should meet you, since you're the reason she still has a Cousin Don. Besides, I think she might surprise you."

Don sighed. "It won't be fun explaining all this to her parents when she tells them how her trip went, but you're right. Zane would have killed us one way or the other. I still can't believe she managed to hack him and fight him at the same time. It's a goddamn miracle."

"Are you kidding?" Dela said from the private area. "I expect nothing less from the Dark Angel!"

"Sorry," Mark said to Don. "Dela sees her as a superhero."

"So do I," Don said sincerely.

Anne smiled at Zima. "And me. Apparently William's crew does, too. The Dark Angel nickname came from them."

Pixie Cappa and her charge stepped into the room. Rose walked heavy-footed to Anne, breathing hard, but stopped short when she spotted Zima.

"H-hi," Rose said in a timid voice. "Who are you?"

"I am Zima."

"She's a special friend of your cousin's," Anne said.

"Oh. How do you know Cousin Don, Zima?"

"I shot him in the —"

"Leg!" Anne wrapped an arm around Zima's shoulders. Rose certainly didn't need to know Zima had shot her favorite cousin three times in the chest. "Y-yes ... Zima's a nurse, as you can tell by the medical supplies over there. He was hurt, and she gave him an injection to make him better. It probably saved his life."

"Wow! You're a hero, Zima!"

"So I have been told."

Rose held out a colorful piece of cardboard to Anne. "Sorry I only made one, but maybe you can share it with Zima, since you look like really good friends."

Anne took the proffered gift and held it up for inspection. Burned into the surface were the words "My Hero" above a happy running stick figure with red curly hair. Sandy material of various colors composed a textured grassy playground, complete with blue sky, white clouds, and a yellow sun.

"Oh, Rose ..." Anne fell to her knees and covered her mouth to keep from bawling, but a few tears dotted her hand. "It's beautiful. Thank you so much."

Rose wrapped her in a hug. Strawberry curls tickled her face. "You're welcome. It was a lot of fun to make. I had no idea fairies kept so much dust around. There were barrels and barrels of the stuff!"

"I have to be prepared in case the fairy dust suppliers can't deliver," Pixie Cappa said with a wink.

"Time to go," Don said. "Your mom's going to worry if I keep you out any later."

Anne clutched the drawing to her chest and thought her cheeks might crack from smiling. "Take care of yourself, Rose."

"Can I come back to visit?"

Anne's smile faltered. "I ... I don't think that's a good idea, sweetie."

"You may not believe it, but fairies have enemies," Pixie Cappa said. "If they knew you were friends with me, they might try to hurt you, too."

"And as much as I'd love to see you again," Anne said, "I couldn't live with myself if something bad happened to you."

Mark cleared his throat. "Which is also why you probably shouldn't tell anyone about your fairy guardian. You never know who might be listening."

Rose dropped her gaze to the floor and nodded. "I don't think they'd believe me anyway."

Zima knelt next to Anne and surprised her by taking Rose's hand.

"Perhaps someday you may return, after we have vanquished the enemies."

"Really?"

"Yes. It has been a difficult battle, but we continually strive for victory, and shall invite you over again when it is safe."

"Thanks!" Rose ran a finger along one of the angry scars on Zima's hand. "I hope you feel better soon. Maybe your fairy guardian will find you, too."

"I believe she already has," Zima said, gently leaning against Anne.

Rose's smile blossomed. Anne's heart melted into her shoes.

The little girl stopped in front of Mark on her way out and handed his laser back. "I wish we had one of these in art class."

"It's good for auto shop, too," Mark said, pocketing it. "Come back when you're older and I'll hook you up."

Pixie Cappa took Rose's hand. "Ready for another hike?"

"Yeah." Rose sighed. "I sure wish you could fly us up there."

Don looked at Anne and shoved his hands in his pockets. "Take care of yourself."

"You too. And please don't go looking for trouble."

"Can't promise anything, but I'll try."

"I'll walk you guys to the car," Mark said. "Just in case."

The mood was somber when Mark and Pixie Cappa returned — except for Zima, who was waiting patiently next to the surgical tray.

Pixie Cappa smiled and shook her head. She pulled a chair over to the table and carefully climbed up to stand on the seat. "Let's do this quickly. With all that stair work, my batteries are running low."

"Batteries?" Anne said.

"Yep. A reactor wouldn't be safe in this body, so we're powering it the old-fashioned way."

Anne vividly remembered the windows of every house shattering from Zane's shockwave. "I guess that makes sense. You're not going far from the factory anyway, right?"

"Right, not to mention this body is remote controlled by my factory self's mind upstairs, which requires a lot of bandwidth. Cellular carriers couldn't handle the throughput. Not reliably, anyway."

"Lie down when you are ready," Zima said to Anne.

Anxious much? Anne thought with a smile. In truth, Anne was nervous about the procedure. She had been unconscious the first time it was implanted, but there was no point in delaying. She removed her shirt and bra, then laid down on the sheet.

Almos hastily turned away. "Forgive my eyes, dear Anne. I shall dull your pain for the duration of the surgery. Please let me know once you're dressed."

"Thanks. And don't worry about averting your eyes. We're all family here, right?"

"I suppose we are."

Zima stepped up to her. "I am ready, Cappa."

"All right. Connecting ..."

Zima's hands jerked into motion. They made a few circles at the wrist, then each finger flexed in turn, until her movements became smooth.

"Calibrated." Pixie Cappa pursed her lips. "Here goes nothing."

The operation went as smoothly as Anne could have hoped. Zima moved with confidence and precision, and, as Almos promised, Anne didn't feel a thing during the short procedure aside from a bit of pressure where the implant was re-inserted.

"We stitched you up to ensure it doesn't make a surprise emergence," Pixie Cappa said, shuddering.

Anne couldn't blame her. It had apparently made several gruesome re-appearances when they first tried to put it in, for which Anne was eternally grateful she'd been unconscious.

"The stitches can come out in an hour at the rate you heal, if not sooner," Pixie Cappa said.

"Now let's turn it on and see what happens," Mark said.

Zima nodded. "Engaging ..."

A small electric jolt shot through Anne's body. Her hands began to tremble, and she suddenly felt like running around the room to burn off the excess energy.

"It is recalibrating itself to your physiology," Zima said. "Although I do not know how long the process will take to complete."

The next sensation focused Anne back on Zima. Her perfect breasts, the gentle flare of her hips ... Anne had to grip the table with both hands to keep from jumping her right there in front of everyone.

While the others looked on with concern, Almos flashed her a knowing grin. Fortunately, it soon passed.

A few minutes, and a number of odd emotions later, Anne felt normal again.

"Okay, that's not something I'd like to repeat. So what's —"

The defensive program's mild nausea churned her stomach.

Almos grabbed his head and screamed, dropping to the floor in a writhing heap. Before Anne could yell for someone to turn it off, he had already relaxed.

"I should have diminished our bond earlier," Almos said, panting. "But your emotions are just too entertaining."

"I hope it was worth the pain, you peeping Tom," Anne said with a smile.

"Every ounce. I am truly envious of your passion, my dear."

"At least we know you'll be safe from William," Mark said. "Which means you can go topside now."

Anne sighed. "Not quite. Has anyone spoken to Tim recently?"

"I attempted to reach him before coming down," Zima said. "Unfortunately, he did not answer. I shall send him a message now to warn him you will be coming aboveground."

Almos rose and dusted his pants. "Arrange for the boy to come here, if you can. I suspect he will be safe from Anne's mind-weapon if she diminishes her bond with him, which I can teach her how to do once he arrives."

"Sent." Zima took Anne's hand and tugged her toward the exit. "Come, let us go to my bedroom, since it is closer. I do not wish to wait a moment longer than necessary."

"Lead the way, my love," Anne said, laughing. "Are you sure you're up for it?"

"I have feeling in eighty-three percent of my body, which is more than sufficient."

"Have fun you guys," Cappa said. "I'm going to plug in down here to recharge and keep Almos company."

"And I'm going to tuck my fiancée into bed until Anne's venom wears off," Mark said.

Dela pinched his cheeks with clumsy fingers. "Aw, you're so sweet! I think I'll marry you."

Their chatter faded as Anne and Zima rapidly ascended. Anne became more anxious with every step, afraid for Tim that her defensive program would trigger any moment. When they emerged from the stairwell, however, her stomach remained nausea-free, so she relaxed.

Zima led her straight to her room, closed the door, and followed her down onto the bed with an eager kiss. Weeks of sexual repression exploded to the surface in a passionate frenzy. Her smell, her taste, her warmth ... everything about Zima drove Anne crazy with desire.

And this time, there was nothing to stop them.

34

DESIRES

ANNE LAY IN HAPPY, EXHAUSTED SILENCE. Zima's warm body draped over hers like a comfy blanket.

I could get used to this.

It was well past morning, according to the clock, and Anne would have been happy to stay like this until evening again.

Well, maybe not exactly like this ...

She kissed Zima's platinum hair and allowed herself a naughty grin. Zima tilted her head up and met her lips, kissing Anne with just as much passion as when they'd begun their marathon session. Anne giggled after a minute and managed to pull away from her hungry lips.

"Are you okay now?"

"Yes," Zima said. "But having been without you for so long, I do not wish to squander a single minute while we are together."

"Well, I may need a snack if we're going to not-squander again."

Zima snuggled against her. "It is all right. Having you like this satisfies many of my needs. I enjoy the proximity, the touch of our skin together, and ..." She buried her face under Anne's ample breast, which tickled like crazy.

"And what?" Anne giggled. "You trying to tell me you're a boob-girl? I thought that was a guy thing."

"No. Well, yes, I find your breasts very pleasing. I was going to say 'having you all to myself,' but then I realized it is a selfish statement in context of Charlie. Or indeed the others, who also enjoy your company."

Anne hugged her close. "I don't mind you being selfish about me. I love being with you, too. I'm more concerned about your happiness."

"I am happy right now."

"I-I know, but ... recently it seems the only time you're happy at all is when you're with me. That's one of the reasons I wanted you to go out with Dela the night that ..."

"You were abducted."

"Right," Anne said softly. "That night. It didn't set a very good precedent, but I still think it's important that you're able to enjoy yourself when I'm not around."

"I understand your concern, but ..." She kissed Anne again, tenderly this time. "I would prefer to work on that piece of self-development later. Much later, if you do not mind."

"You got it. We have some making-up to do first, and some healing." Anne ran her palm over Zima's scarred cheek. "Speaking of ... When are you going to finish your time in the glass dome?"

"If my appearance is not overly repulsive to you, I was going to allow my body's own nanites to complete the repairs, which should finish in the next three days."

"You're not repulsive!" Anne's anger surprised even herself, so she deliberately lowered her voice. "You could be a walking tin can and I'd still think you were the most gorgeous thing I've ever laid eyes on, because I love you. I wasn't asking for my sake. I just thought you'd be more comfortable if your body was back to its original design."

"Thank you for the concern. Yes, it would make my routine functions easier because they are calibrated for my flesh in its original state. I just ... do not wish to be apart from you, even for a day."

"How about if I sit with you while you're in there? I can read to you through the glass."

Zima looked up. For a moment, Anne was lost in her ice-blue eyes.

"That would be pleasant, thank you," Zima said. "I shall resume the repair process later today."

Anne's naughty grin returned. "Want me to grab that snack so you can have your wicked way with me again?"

"Very much. But unfortunately Tim has just replied to my message. He wishes to meet as soon as possible, and is awaiting confirmation that it is safe to go aboveground."

"Later, then."

Anne traced a loving finger over the red scars covering Zima's face — scars Zima had incurred rescuing her. She gave Zima a tender, lingering kiss to seal her promise of returning to the bedroom as soon as possible, then reluctantly peeled herself from Zima's warmth and gathered her clothes. Zima watched her every move, and didn't stir until Anne finished assembly with a final buttoning of her pants.

Zima followed suit, which Anne watched with equal appreciation. Scars be damned, she was gorgeous. Anne leaned against a wooden night table to enjoy the show.

The night table rocked forward with a tap of wood on concrete.

Anne flailed and jumped away, afraid she'd broken something, but closer inspection showed one of the night table's legs was shorter than the other, which was puzzling. Zima had precious few possessions, but those were — without exception — kept in peak condition. Her combat knives were habitually honed to keep them sharp, her pistols well-oiled and regularly adjusted to ensure flawless operation. Even her clothes were replaced at the first sign of wear. Everything Zima owned was both functional and perfect.

Everything except this night table, and the painting above it.

Even Anne's untrained eye spotted an occasional misplaced brush stroke or color blend. The painting was lovely, to be sure, capturing a lake and Spanish cathedral in the distance. But, even less than the night table, it had no practical function. The painting was the only piece of art Zima owned, as far as Anne knew, but her girlfriend had never talked about it. This was also only the second time Anne had visited Zima's bedroom, since they usually stayed in hers, so the topic had never come up.

Anne looked closer and spotted the artist's signature. "Pablo Cortez," she said aloud. "Someone you know?"

Zima appeared at her shoulder. "Yes. His real name is Emilio Rojas." She trailed a finger along the night table, slowly, as if it were a living person. "The table was crafted by his sister, Rosa."

"You've never mentioned them before."

"No. They are special to me, but remnants of a past I prefer not to dwell on. The experience was ... traumatic, for all of us."

"Oh." Anne pulled Zima into a hug. She was dying to know more, but her girlfriend's tone made it clear she didn't want to discuss it further.

Besides, Tim was waiting for the all-clear to come aboveground. Anne had to be underground in the reactor room when he did, or he'd be greeted by a splitting headache.

She kissed Zima's cheek and led her to the door. "Come on, lover. Let's get this out of the way so we can get back here as soon as possible. Or to the hot tub, if you want."

"May I choose both?"

Anne winked. "Deal. You're a shrewd negotiator, missy."

35

LOOSE ENDS

ALMOS AND PIXIE CAPPA WERE CHATTING AMIABLY when Anne and Zima returned hand-in-hand to the reactor room a few minutes later. Almos sat in the lawn chair, while Pixie Cappa dangled her little legs from the table. A thick power cable ran from a port in the reactor straight into her thigh, as if her flesh had swallowed it whole.

Zima quickly filled them in about Tim. "I have just informed him that Anne is safely shielded," she said in closing, "and that her defensive program has been deactivated, so he does not need to fear discomfort when he nears. I have instructed him to park in the garage to minimize his sunlight exposure."

"Great! I'm just about charged," Pixie Cappa said. "I'll wait for them upstairs."

"It is probably best if I greet them, since they already know me." Zima stared at her hand, laced with Anne's, before slowly disentangling her own.

"I'll be right here," Anne said. She gave her a farewell kiss, which Zima held for several seconds before turning to leave. She stared at Anne with that same expression of longing all the way to the exit.

"You weren't kidding," Pixie Cappa said once Zima's footsteps had faded. "That girl has it bad for you."

"She does. But, like you said, the best I can do is support her while she figures things out, so that's exactly what I'm going to do."

"Even if she requires tough love?" Almos said.

"No," Anne said softly. "She's been through a lot, not knowing if I was alive or dead. I won't risk a relapse by withholding from her. We'll just take it slowly and see what happens."

"If I may say, her relationship with you reminds me of a vampire's relationship with their sire — yourself being the odd exception. The sire is looked upon with utter adoration. There is nothing a vampire would not do to please them."

"You also likened it to slavery, if I remember."

"I did. The parallels may not run that deep, since you obviously return her affections, but it is something to consider."

A slave ...

Anne squeezed her eyes shut to purge the awful idea from her head, but Almos' words had already taken root. Couples often said they would do anything for each other, but the unspoken understanding was "anything within reason." Anne knew without a doubt that Zima would do anything she asked, including slaughtering a town of innocents, as long as it meant they could still be together. That knowledge made her feel dirty — a black stain on her soul.

No one should have that much power over another person.

It wasn't right.

And it was exactly the hold she had on Zima.

"Don't listen to him."

Anne jumped at the furious expression on Pixie Cappa's face, which was directed at Almos.

"What you and Zima have is not slavery," Pixie Cappa said, balling her tiny fists. "Not in either direction. It's love! It's mutual adoration, to be celebrated at every opportunity — never feared or questioned. You two have something amazingly special. Yes, Zima is working through some issues, but they're challenges she's had to face every step of her evolution. Just keep believing in her, like she believes in you, and I know she'll eventually find her way."

Almos bowed before her slight form, as a king would to neighboring royalty. "Once again, your wisdom shines. I should never have spoken."

Pixie Cappa's anger melted at the compliment. She ducked her head and pressed her lips together, but a smile tugged at the corners of her mouth. "What are you grinning at?" she said to Anne.

"Oh, nothing."

Cappa and Almos had been eager chat partners over the last few days, but this uncharacteristic bashfulness was the first sign Anne had seen of their relationship blossoming into more than just boredom relief.

The three of them lapsed into pensive silence, until Pixie Cappa perked up a few minutes later.

"They're here."

As soon as she said it, Anne noticed a new presence in her mind, much fainter than Almos'. She instinctively knew it belonged to Tim.

"'They'? Who else is with him?" Anne said.

"His friends, apparently."

"Are they ... human?"

"By the looks. Tim is the only person wearing four layers of clothes."

Anne sighed with relief, glad her blood hadn't instigated yet another vampire outbreak. She was pacing a small circle by the time they finished the long descent.

When Anne saw Tim, she nearly cried. His healthy brown skin she remembered from the diner was now as ashen as her own. The three of them looked so anxious that any sudden movement might cause them all to bolt. Their eyes widened when they saw Pixie Cappa sitting on the table, but they had the grace to keep their opinions to themselves.

Zima followed them down. Her gray jacket bulged from her concealed machine pistols. Their guests must have noticed it, too, for they positioned themselves so they could see her at all times, and cast frequent nervous glances her way. Last out was Mark, who watched their guests with open suspicion.

Silence weighed heavy. They stared at each other with obvious discomfort, until Anne finally found her voice.

"Tim ... I'm so, so sorry."

Tim swallowed. "Me too, though it sounds like you've been through a rough time yourself. Um, this is Jody and Conway. They helped me through the transition. I honestly don't know how I would have made it without them."

"You didn't say there'd be another vampire here," Jody said, clutching Tim's arm.

"Oh, this is Almos," Anne said. "He's —"

"One of Anne's make," the master vampire said quickly. "Like yourself, Tim, which makes us brothers, in a way. You'll be happy to know Anne has successfully ceded her mind from me, which allows us to co-exist pain-free."

"Oh, that's good." Tim scratched his unruly hair. "So how does it work?"

Great question.

Now that he was here, Tim's presence was much stronger than Almos', probably because Tim was her direct descendant. Anne could see the filaments of Tim's being with crystal clarity, just as she had with the mercenaries. He was scared — not just of having Anne in his head, but of Zima, of whether he and his friends would be allowed to leave Z-Tech, and of the possibility that this whole thing was just a trap.

But there was something else she hadn't expected. Tim was comfortable with what he had become. He liked being a vampire.

And he couldn't wait to be free of Anne.

It's times like this I wish I could communicate silently with the others, like Mark and Charlie can.

Anne had loads of free time, but Mark didn't, so he still hadn't taught her how to send messages using her implant.

First thing tomorrow, Anne promised herself, though it wouldn't help with her current dilemma. Tim's eagerness to be free was understandable, but his lack of regret made her nervous. For the first time since she had learned of his existence, she questioned the wisdom of freeing him.

Her feelings must have bled through the sire bond. Tim's eyes widened. She felt his panic, born from the helplessness of knowing that if Anne chose not to release him, there was little he or his friends could do about it.

That thought, above all else, reaffirmed her decision to set him free. Her niggling doubts alone were no excuse to keep him prisoner — to keep him a slave. He was a victim, not a criminal. Until he proved otherwise, he would be afforded the same trust and freedom that Anne herself enjoyed.

Now she just needed to figure out how to do it.

"Perhaps I can answer your question," Almos said to Tim, evidently sensing Anne's quandary. "The process is fairly simple, and requires no effort on your part. Anne senses you as clearly as you sense her. But where you, as her sireling, have no choice but to accept her presence, she may diminish yours until it is but a grain of sand. Vampires with large numbers of sirelings use this technique to cope with the constant flood of thoughts and emotions. It allows them to focus on those who need their attention the most, while giving others relative autonomy."

"Sounds easy," Conway said, crossing his muscled arms. "How long will it take?"

"A few minutes at most." Almos flashed Anne a reassuring smile. *Let's hope so.*

"All right," Anne said. "Here goes."

"What she is about to do," Almos said helpfully, "is to imagine the large presence she knows as you shrinking down until she can barely tell it's there. You'll know it's working because you will feel her presence diminish, too."

Anne clapped her hands. "That's right! So, um ... prepare to be diminished." She closed her eyes and turned her attention to the ball of light in her mind that was Tim.

Shrink, she thought to it.

The sphere didn't budge.

Shrink!

Nothing.

Shrink, shrink! Goddamnit, shrink!

His presence fluttered, but she realized it was just Tim reacting to her sudden frustration.

All right, Almos said I have to imagine it ...

Anne pictured another ball exactly like his, sitting side by side, then imagined it growing smaller. This time, she felt a real change in his presence. His feelings became less intense, his thoughts harder to read.

Yes!

Anne made her imaginary sphere smaller. Again the real one diminished, so she repeated the exercise until his presence was the tiniest of dots on the vast canvas of her mind.

"I think that should do it," she said, opening her eyes.

Tim nodded with a growing smile. "Yeah, I think so. I can't even tell you're there."

"One last test," Mark said. "Ready?"

Tim nodded again, but his smile disappeared. Jody clutched him tighter, looking as if she might faint.

Several tense seconds passed, then Mark shrugged. "I guess it worked."

"It's running?" Anne said.

A flashing light or something would be nice to tell me when the defensive program is active.

"Yes, and everyone seems okay."

Jody stepped forward, her jaw clenched. "So how do we know she won't … *un*-diminish his presence again, even accidentally? I thought Tim was going to die the first time he came in contact with her. I can't bear to watch that again."

"Restoring a presence is a conscious choice," Almos said, "so it is unlikely she would unintentionally cause him harm."

Anne put a comforting hand on Jody's shoulder and felt her trembling beneath. "Besides that, you have my promise. I have no more wish to hurt or control him than for someone to hurt or control me. Do you believe me?"

"Do we have a choice?" Conway said, his muscles tense.

"No." Mark crossed his own beefy arms. "And while we're on the subject of trust … Now that you have what you came for, I'd like to know your plans."

"That doesn't sound very trusting," Conway said.

Anne looked between the two juggernauts and suppressed a grin. They were nearly the same height, the same build, had the same defiant pose, and, from what little she knew of Conway from Zima's telling, they were both talented tinkers.

It's a shame. Under different circumstances, they would have gotten along well.

"This vampire business isn't a joke," Mark said. "If it spreads, there may be serious consequences — even beyond the obvious human cattle problem."

Tim frowned. "Like what?"

Mark started to respond, but Almos cut him off.

"Use your imaginations and I'm sure any number of doomsday scenarios will make themselves clear. The point my dear colleague is trying to make is that creating you was an accident, as was creating me, and the world will be a far safer place if we do our best to prevent future accidents. Is that something we can all agree upon?"

"Yes," the three of them replied instantly.

With her connection to Tim severed, Anne had no idea what he was really thinking, but she hoped he was being sincere. Zima glanced at Conway and Jody, her expression unreadable.

Mark sighed. "All right, I guess that's it, then. Come on. I know you guys are tech fans, so you might as well have a tour before you go."

Their faces brightened.

Tim unshouldered his backpack and began rummaging through. "Speaking of which … there is one thing you could do to help us stay out of trouble." He produced his invention, the same device he had shown Zima in the restaurant, and held it out for Mark and Zima's inspection. "Are you guys still interested?"

To Anne, it looked like a cell phone strapped to junk electronic parts, tethered by ribbon wires to a plate.

But Mark smiled appreciatively at the jumbled mess. "So this thing can really read data from an electronic device with no external connections?"

"I've only tested it with a few, namely Z-Tech phones, but yeah. With some adjustments, it should be able to read anything. And to write data, eventually."

Zima and Mark exchanged a glance. Anne could tell by Mark's clenched jaw that they were silently communicating.

Tomorrow I'll ask him to teach me, Anne promised herself again. She would love to have been part of the conversation.

Mark eventually turned back to Tim and nodded. "Leave it here, if you don't mind. Cappa will take a look, do some research, and get back to you with a fair offer."

"And by 'fair,'" Pixie Cappa said, "he means you'll probably live comfortably for several lifetimes." She hopped from her table perch and eagerly rubbed her small hands together. "So, if we're all agreed on that ... did someone mention a tour?"

Their three guests nodded vigorously. Everyone headed to the stairs.

Everyone, that is, except Almos and Anne. She waited until she could no longer hear the others' footsteps before speaking.

"Almos, what's with the secrecy? Shouldn't Tim know about you and the Entity?"

"I agree the information may have made a stronger case for keeping vampirism contained, but as I stated, there are many good reasons besides that. At this point, I believe it is more important to keep my identity secret than to put the fear of a godly, unprovable entity into them. I already regret they know my real name. With luck, Orwing believes me dead, but if my name makes its way back to them ..."

"I suppose that's true. Orwing probably believe I'm dead, too, come to think of it."

"Yes, and you would be wise to continue that ruse lest they seek retribution. They have already demonstrated their lack of value of human life."

That was true as well. Orwing had attempted to execute every one of Calum's crew to protect their secrets, and she had no reason to believe they wouldn't do the same to Z-Tech.

Granted, they might have a harder time with this fortress-in-disguise.

Even so, it wasn't worth tempting fate. The realization that Anne Perrin would have to remain dead brought other uncomfortable truths. Doris knew she was alive, but Hal and her friends at the diner were another matter.

And my family ...

After eighteen long years, Anne had only recently reconnected with her estranged brother. She'd even visited him and his family in Sacramento, a trip she remembered fondly and was looking forward to again. Right now, Doug believed she was missing, but he likely held hope she would be found. The illusion would be over once he received official word of her death. He would mourn. There would be a small funeral in her hometown that some of her high school friends might attend. Tears would be shed over an empty casket for the daughter who had left home after high school and never looked back — couldn't look back because of the violent rape in her own bedroom that, to this day, her parents were still unaware had happened.

Lies upon lies. Anne swallowed a lump in her throat. *Is that what my life has become?*

"Yours is not an easy life," Almos said.

For a moment, Anne thought he'd read her mind, until she realized her cheeks were wet.

Almos put a hand on her shoulder. "The other vampires are lucky, in a way. They no longer carry ties to humanity. They are free to hunt and kill at their whim, to take what they need with little regret of the consequences. They are not isolated, for they have their sire and their siblings, which is sufficient to stave off their loneliness. But you and I are different. We feel connected to this world and wish to be part of it, yet we are frightening creatures of lore whose very existence threatens those we care about."

"You need to work on your pep talks," Anne said, wiping a fresh stream of tears.

"Sorry, I merely meant to convey that I can imagine how difficult this is for you. It's a true miracle that you have found an amazing place such as this to shelter in, with people — or near enough — who truly care about you."

"Thanks, Almos."

Consolation from the poor guy who's spent centuries isolating himself because, against the odds, he actually cares again.

Anne grabbed a tissue and cleaned herself up. Her family would grieve, but, like most who suffer tragedies, they would find a way to cope, to fit back into the world again.

And so will I.

"Are you okay down here for a bit?" Anne said. "I'd like to see Tim off."

"Take your time, my dear. I'm perfectly fine. Cappa showed me how to use those curious devices to access all the books I could ever want, and has also introduced me to something called the internet. I suspect those two things will be adequate entertainment for another few centuries at least."

Anne started to leave, but on a whim, she wrapped him in a hug. "Thanks again, Almos. I'm glad you're here."

"As am I, dear Anne. With the wonders I have seen here, for the first time in my long existence, I feel a kindling of hope for the future." He held her at arm's length and flashed a toothy grin. "Now, go see them off like a good host so you can get back to your true love. I do not have one of my own, so I must live vicariously through you, and I expect regular reports of your progress."

"Yes, my sire," Anne said, faking a hypnotic tone, which drew a laugh from Almos.

"Would that were the case. Had I found you on that street instead of our sweet William, things may have been greatly simplified."

Anne shuddered at the thought, but that wasn't what occupied her mind on her long ascent to the surface.

My true love …

Was that Zima? They had been through hell and back for each other, and Anne wouldn't hesitate to make the trip again if Zima needed her. Anne was happiest in her arms. She loved making Zima happy more than anything else. She couldn't imagine a world without Zima in it, not one where she could smile, anyway.

Isn't that true love?

She'd read enough fantasy romance novels to believe it was, but if so …

Where does that leave Charlie?

She missed him terribly and thought of him often. She always enjoyed her time with him, but there was no denying their relationship was different. Where it was often all Anne could do to keep up with his brilliant mind, Zima was content with anything Anne wanted to do, wanting only to spend as much time with her as she could. The insecure part of Anne feared she was holding Charlie back, that she was limiting his potential because she could barely understand him most of the time, let alone contribute anything meaningful.

Other than making him smile.

The thought brought one to her own lips. When he was feeling down, tired, or frustrated, Anne always knew how to make him laugh, and his appreciation was plain for anyone to see. She had asked both Cappa and Charlie several times why all the amazing people in Z-Tech put up with ordinary old Anne, and had received many different answers. At the core of each of them, she suddenly realized, was Anne's positive attitude. She worried. She paced. She was insecure, certainly, but usually she was just trying to make people happy. Charlie had been in a downward spiral for years, which they now knew was due to his fading spirit.

Anne sparked something in him that had long been missing, something the others had desperately wanted to, but couldn't seem to spark themselves. There wasn't a magic ingredient; Anne was special to them because of everything that made her Anne. She was funny to keep his spirits up, patient to keep him company while he worked, open-minded enough to accept a cyborg as a boyfriend and a lover, and cheerful enough to get along with the others.

In a word, she was perfect for Charlie.

But the storybooks were clear about something else: There was only one true love, only one perfect match in the world who made everyone else pale in comparison.

Her mood was somber when she reached the top of the stairs.

She hoped the storybooks were wrong.

36

PLANS

ANNE CAUGHT UP WITH THE GANG in the last place she'd thought to find them. Mark, Tim, Conway, and Cappa stood around Jody at the firing range in the weapons lab, cheering with gusto while the diminutive girl in shorts and a tank top fired a rifle nearly as large as herself, taking large chunks out of a wooden target with each deafening shot. Anne found it odd that Zima would miss out on a gathering that was so up-her-alley.

"Everyone having fun?" Anne yelled between thunderclaps, holding her ears.

Jody answered with another gunshot that knocked her backward several feet, followed by a squeal of laughter. "Oh my God! As soon as we get the money for Tim's invention, we're so getting our own shooting range."

"Hopefully in our own mansion," Conway said.

Anne donned a pair of earmuffs while Jody handed the rifle to Tim. The gangly youth awkwardly put it to his shoulder and pulled the trigger. Unlike Jody, the rifle stayed still in his iron grip, allowing him to squeeze off several quick rounds with surprising accuracy.

"Not bad," Mark said. "And this is the first time you've ever shot a gun?"

"Yeah. My folks don't believe in guns, so I've never had the opportunity."

"Unfortunately, the bad guys do," Conway said. "I'm buying one of those the first chance I get. And maybe one of those, and one of those …" He pointed at a few choice weapons around the room.

"You won't find many of these in stores, but I can leave you with a list of recommendations," Mark said. "I know a guy who'll give them to you wholesale. And if you're looking for someone to construct the range, there's a company I can introduce you to in San Francisco who cater to higher-end clients. They're not cheap, but the quality of work is definitely worth it."

"Thanks," Tim said, looking suddenly nervous. "We, ah, may take you up on that." He set the gun down and removed his ear protection. "Actually, I think we should go. We've taken enough of your time, Mr. Suther."

The others looked disappointed, but hung up their earmuffs as well.

"All right," Mark said with a long sigh. "You're welcome to come back, though, if you'd like to see the rest of the factory, or if you'd like to use our range while yours is under construction."

"Thanks," they said together.

"If it's okay," Pixie Cappa said to Tim, "I'd like to get a blood sample before you go."

"Why?"

"Well, you seem to be doing fine, but as you know, Anne is unique among vampires, which means her sirelings are also different. The implant makes frequent changes to her cellular makeup, often without us knowing. Each time she infects someone, they may be different from the last. A blood sample will show the differences between her makeup then and where she is now, and may allow us to identify issues in your gene structure that could affect you down the line."

Tim's eyes were saucers. "Um … yeah, okay."

"Great! Then we'll stop by the bio lab on the way to the garage. Got your protective sun gear, young man?" Pixie Cappa crossed her arms. Even at three feet tall, she managed to seem imposing, though Anne still had to cover her mouth to keep from laughing.

Tim grabbed his black sweater, gloves, and hat from the back of a chair and nodded.

Anne stopped him on his way by. "Tim … keep in touch, okay? I'd like to know how you're doing."

"Y-yeah, definitely. I have Zima's phone number," he said, but wouldn't meet her eyes.

"And call me if you have any questions about … you know, being us. You have a support system available now, so please use it."

Chances are I'll forward the questions to Almos, but Tim doesn't need to know that.

"Sure. So, ah, it was good seeing you, Anne. I'm glad you made it out of that prison okay."

That, at least, sounded sincere. Anne took his cold hand in her own and gave him a motherly look. "Take care."

Tim nodded once more, eyes everywhere but on her, then he and his friends followed Pixie Cappa out of the weapons lab.

"They're hiding something," Anne said with a sigh.

"We know they are," Mark said. "Zima overheard them talking in their house the night she rescued them. Jody and Conway want to be vampires, like Tim, and now there's nothing to stop them."

Anne felt dizzy at the revelation. "But … we can't let that happen! Why didn't you say something?"

"I did. You did. Almos did. But unless we're willing to hold them captive, the best we can do is warn them about the consequences and hope they listen." Mark scratched his stubbled chin. "That, and Zima may have put a tracer on their car."

"They're tech-heads. You don't think they'll detect the signal?"

That's what they do in spy novels.

"Oh, I'm sure they'll find the first one." Mark grinned. "But the second will be trickier, since the signal is lower power and looks like background noise. Plus it's about the size of a pinhead and is embedded in the paint, so it's practically invisible."

"The first is a decoy so they stop looking." Anne returned his grin. "Something tells me you've done this before."

"And to engineers more adept than them."

"You should write a book," she said with a laugh.

"No, I'd get too many people in trouble. Including us." Mark stretched his arms and stifled a yawn with his fist. "I'm going to shower and freshen up, but feel free to keep playing." He gestured to the large rifle.

"I think I'm good, but ... can I talk you into some formal *jiu-jitsu* lessons later?"

"You're on. Dela would probably enjoy that, too. See you later."

"You bet. I'll be out in a sec."

He waved over his shoulder and wandered out. Anne took a long look at the vast array of weapons around the room before heading to the door, but stopped at the threshold. Her eyes rested on the rifle laying on the range counter.

After a moment of deliberation, she returned to the range and put the earmuffs on. It took her a few minutes to figure out how to load ammo into the magazine, but soon she was cracking shots at the wrecked target. Few struck where she intended, but that didn't bother her. Anne had never shot a rifle before now and hadn't expected to be any good.

But that's what practice was for.

She carefully lined the sights up with the target and fired again.

•   •   •

Tim and his friends maintained their silence until they had left the Z-Tech factory, crossed the parking lot, and were safely in their car. The old hatchback was a beater, for sure, and Tim's nose told him it had seen its share of trials. Cigarette smoke, aged ice cream, beer, perfume, Indian curry ... faint traces of the vehicle's past tickled his nose, odors too weak for his friends to smell.

But that would soon change.

Jody let her breath out in a whoosh, as if she'd been holding it for their entire visit. "Think they bought it?"

"Hard to say," Tim said. "I tried to keep my mind off our plans, but who knows how much a sire can read from their, um ... How did Anne put it? Sirelings? Yeah. She could have plucked the thoughts from my mind without me knowing."

Conway scoffed. "You really think they'd have let us walk out of there if she had?"

"No, I guess not." Tim sighed. Part of him wished Anne had stopped him at the gate to talk sense into him, but she'd kept her word.

For better or worse.

Conway's beefy hand on his shoulder snapped him out of his funk. "We've already talked about this. We agreed. All of us. Between William and this Orwing clown, the vampire problem is out of control, and Z-Tech is doing squat about it."

Jody nodded. "Your blood is special, Tim. They said it themselves. You, Anne, and that Almos guy are the only ones who have it, the only ones who can create a race of truly free super-humans to fight the scourge. We have a chance to change the world for the better — to be on the ground level of a new race. A new society!"

"Yeah, but ..." Tim shook his head. "You heard their doomsday spiel. What if we're wrong?"

"We're not," Conway said, grinning. "I have a hunch on this one, just like I did about our business. With you at the head, and Jody and me as your right-hand guys, we can't lose." His grin widened. "All you have to do is open those precious veins of yours, pal. I'll handle the rest."

Jody stroked Tim's knee. "That's right. Trust us, Tim. You won't regret it."

Tim stared at her small hand, warm on his knee even through the thick sun-protective clothing. A warmth that, if Jody and Conway had their way, he would never feel again.

They would cease to be human.

Could he do that to another person? Even at their request, could he knowingly change them, dramatically, irreversibly? Rob them of their pulse? Replace their appetite with a thirst for blood?

Could he, in good conscience, justify fighting monsters by creating more?

Tim started the engine and pulled out of the Z-Tech parking lot, his stilled heart weighing heavy.

Unfortunately, he could.

37

GUARDIAN

W HEN ZIMA WANDERED INTO THE WEAPONS LAB an hour later, Anne's shoulder was past sore from the constant rifle shots, but she'd progressed to the farthest target on the range, and was hitting it almost every time. Zima waited until her magazine was empty, handed her a fresh one, then silently corrected her stance and grip when Anne settled in for her next round. As usual, Zima's coaching proved invaluable. Anne finished the magazine without missing a shot.

Anne set the assault rifle on the counter and hung her earmuffs on a hook, then gingerly massaged her sore shoulder. "Thanks, honey."

"I was not aware you were practicing, otherwise I would have come sooner and suggested a more appropriate starting rifle." Zima head-cocked. "You have never expressed an interest in rifles before. What inspired you to learn?"

Anne caught herself mid-shrug. To pretend there wasn't a reason would be a lie, and she wouldn't do that. Not to Zima.

"Vampire armies, Zane, Orwing, the master vampire in our basement, this mysterious Entity, Tim loose in the city with *my* blood in his veins, and we still don't know what happened to that missing army unit."

"Signs indicate they were abducted by vampires," Zima said. "If Orwing did not perform the operation, that leaves only William."

"Which is even worse." Anne shook her head. "Everything feels ... different, like the entire world's changed in the two weeks Charlie and Cappa have been gone. I wish I could say it changed for the better, but ..." She left her thought unfinished and ran a finger along the rifle barrel, still hot from her extended shooting practice.

Zima hugged her from behind and rested her head on Anne's shoulder. "The world constantly changes. The question is not if we can stop it, but how we will adapt."

"How we'll survive, you mean."

"Survival is the very foundation of my programming." She kissed Anne's neck. "We will survive, Anne. You also have my word that no one shall ever harm you again, not while a single piece of me remains functional."

Anne patted her arm. "That's sweet, honey, but you can't protect me from everything. Even if you could, I wouldn't want you to."

"I do not understand. Why?"

She turned around in Zima's embrace and wrapped her arms around her neck. "Because I need to learn to protect myself, and you constantly having my back makes it too easy to be complacent."

Zima's eyes fell. Anne caught her chin and tipped her head up so their gazes met.

"That wasn't a rejection, Zima. It was a cry for help. I can't do it alone. I'm going to need your support every step of the way."

"You already have it," Zima said softly.

"I know, but ..." She smoothed Zima's platinum hair, ragged in parts where it was still growing back. "The reason you're such a mess is because of me, and I don't just mean physically."

"No! The fault was mine. I —"

"Did everything you could to protect me. And you did everything I asked — which is part of the problem." Anne sighed. "Despite what you seem to think, I don't always have the right answers. Calum kidnapped me because of my own poor judgment.

I jumped into a dangerous situation thinking I was as capable as you, and I'm not. Not yet."

She cupped Zima's cheek. "Will you help me get there? Will you teach me to be like the great Dark Angel so I can stand on my own two feet in the face of Orwing, William's lunatic army, and whatever other craziness the world throws at us?"

Zima stared at her for a moment, then nodded. "Whatever you wish, my love, as long as I may stay by your side."

Anne bit off a frustrated reply. Zima clearly wasn't ready to let go, not even a little, so Anne decided not to press it and wrapped Zima in a hug. They were together again, and largely in one piece, which was all that mattered.

Her relationship with Charlie was a concern for later. Zima had become incredibly attached to Anne in the two weeks since his departure, and she shuddered to think how Zima would handle the attention deficit when he returned.

Assuming he ever does ...

She pushed the unpleasant thought from her mind. Charlie was the most capable person Anne had ever met. With Cappa by his side, he couldn't possibly fail.

She only wished she knew for certain.

38

CHINA

TWO WEEKS AGO,
IN THE REMOTE MOUNTAINS OF CHINA

CAPPA KNELT BEHIND CHARLIE, who was also kneeling, bowed over so their heads almost touched the muddy cobblestones. Her slacks and sneakers were already beyond saving, but sticking her face in the mud to appease some old geezer was a line her dignity just wouldn't cross.

This had better have been worth the trip.

Charlie had knocked on the weathered monastery door five minutes and twenty-four seconds ago, and her enhanced hearing had yet to detect any movement inside.

Just when Cappa was about to stand and knock again, footsteps creaked across the interior floorboards.

The door creaked open. Charlie kept his eyes to the ground, but Cappa sneaked a peek at the person who had belatedly answered their summons.

Long, scraggly hair hung gray over a weathered face. He was old, Cappa knew that much, but there was a youthfulness to him that made it difficult to say exactly how old. He was about Charlie's height, smaller in build, yet powerful and erect. A long staff came to rest at his feet.

That's when Cappa noticed he hadn't opened his eyes.

He's blind?

"Who comes to the sanctity of this temple?" the old man said in a firm voice. His Cantonese was clear and crisp, unlike the muddled local dialects Cappa had experienced difficulty translating during their trip.

"Master Wung," Charlie said in the same crisp Cantonese dialect. "It is Charlie. I have returned to —"

The door slammed so hard that even the imperturbable monks in the yard skipped a step.

Cappa put her face in her hands, remembering too late they were muddy, and tried not to cry.

Their entire trip — Charlie's last hope for survival — appeared to have been for nothing.

ABOUT THE AUTHOR

Ryan Southwick decided to dabble at writing late in life, and quickly became obsessed with the craft. He grew up in Pennsylvania and moved to a farming town on California's central coast during elementary school, but it was in junior high school where he had his first taste of storytelling with a small role-playing group and couldn't get enough.

In addition to half a lifetime in the software development industry, making everything from 3-D games to mission-critical business applications to help cure cancer, he was also a Radiation Therapist for many years. His technical experience, medical skills, and lifelong fascination for science fiction became the ingredients for his book series, "The Z-Tech Chronicles", which combines elements of each into a fantastic contemporary tale of super-science, fantasy, and adventure, based in his Bay Area stomping grounds. Ryan's related short story "Once Upon a Nightwalker" was published in the *Corporate Catharsis* anthology, available from Paper Angel Press.

Ryan currently lives in the San Francisco Bay Area with his wife and two children. You can get in touch with him and see more of his work by visiting his website *RyanSouthwickAuthor.com*.

ALSO BY RYAN SOUTHWICK

ANGELS IN THE MIST
THE Z-TECH CHRONICLES BOOK ONE

An ancient, powerful evil is loose in San Francisco. The heart of Silicon Valley must fight back the only way they know how — with compassion, unwavering determination, and, of course, super-technology.

ZIMA: ORIGINS
A Z-TECH CHRONICLES STORY

Even artificially intelligent recovering assassins need a home.

ONCE UPON A NIGHTWALKER
A Z-TECH CHRONICLES STORY

Ellen Bloom just wants a normal working relationship with her colleagues at her old job. But, at this point, she'd be happy with a pulse.

Available from Water Dragon Publishing in
hardcover, trade paperback, and digital editions
waterdragonpublishing.com

Water Dragon Publishing is an imprint of Paper Angel Press
paperangelpress.com

YOU MIGHT ALSO ENJOY

BUILDING BABY BROTHER

by Steven Radecki

It seemed like a good idea at the time …

GODDESS CHOSEN

BOOK ONE OF THE "GODDESS RISING" TRILOGY

by Jay Hartlove

The man who would beat the devil isn't a hero, but a ruthless madman.

RULES OF THE CAMPFIRE

BOOK ONE FROM STORIES IN GLASS

by Paul S. Moore

If you woke up one day and realized you had memories from more than seventy lives, fluid in every language you'd ever spoken, and recalled all the texts you'd ever read, would you wonder why?